Let The Music Cry

Drifters, Book Seven

SUSAN RODGERS

For my amazing film school class, VFS FP119
and especially for Marco
who I know fought valiantly
and who taught me
that sometimes
believing in others is everything.
Miss you, buddy.

Contents

Chapter One

"Momma?"

A tiny hand floated into Jessie's field of vision, which was foggy like the clouds around her mountain-hugged city of Vancouver on days when they wanted to let out the rain but couldn't quite muster the energy. The hand was accompanied shortly by a small set of fretful pale blue eyes and a gentle shake of Jessie's arm as it lay unmoving on a scratchy beige comforter. The eyes were damp and worried.

As Jessie blinked her way to consciousness, she became aware of a baby crying somewhere nearby; its yowling was vaguely familiar, as were the little blue eyes peering fearfully at her now through the misty cloud. She forced herself up on one elbow and tottered there, weaving and fighting the urge to vomit.

"Oh, shit," she moaned, clenching her jaw tightly to combat the piercing headache accompanying the nausea. "This can't be good."

She forced her eyes into slits, wide enough so they could at least see the little girl standing by the side of…where was she? Looking around, Jessie turned her head slowly to keep the nausea and knife-slices at bay. A bed… she was on a bed, a double, one of those old ones from the forties with a wide hollow russet metal-tubed headboard. Relieved to find herself fully clothed, Jessie swung one leg carefully over the edge of the mattress, following it slowly with the other for fear quicker movements would result in the need to empty her topsy-turvy belly.

"Emily-Grace," she managed, reaching for her three-year-old daughter, who was wringing her small hands anxiously around her favorite toy, a soft

1

foot-long Anne of Green Gables raven-haired Diana doll she called, fittingly, Diana-dowwy.

As Emily-Grace stood by the side of the bed, shuffling her weight from one foot to the other, the child absently twisted the small doll's legs up over her body.

"C'mere, baby girl." Holding her aloft for a moment, Jessie scrutinized her daughter quickly, eyes darting over the small body as she ran a hand over the anxious arms and legs looking for scrapes or bruises. "You okay, beautiful girl? Are you hurt?" Heart racing, she was relieved to see no obvious marks on her daughter.

"Momma, pee," was Emily-Grace's urgent response.

"Okay. Okay, sweetheart, let's…" Scanning the area, Jessie tensed upon sighting a sparsely outfitted kitchen across from her in the dimly lit open space. A retro gray Formica and chrome table with matching vinyl-padded chairs sat stoically alongside dull plywood cupboards, which were punctuated by a mustard yellow stove and matching refrigerator. Covering the cement floor were thin tan patchwork rugs in bland geometric patterns. At the far end, a set of cement stairs beckoned hopefully—they led upwards out of what Jessie thought appeared to be a basement apartment, judging by the few smallish rectangular windows fringing the low ceiling on the wall against which the bed was placed.

Standing cautiously in the hopes she could manage without either fainting or puking, Jessie positioned her squirming daughter on one hip. She tiptoed to her son's stroller, which was set up a few feet away with him, thankfully, in it, healthy and angry, according to his flailing fists and vociferous cries.

Jessie reached a hand down to him. Since David appeared okay at first glance, she prioritized and glanced around for a bathroom. "One minute, baby boy, Momma's got to find a bathroom for your sister. Back in a sec. You just hang on."

The space was small, maybe 600 square feet at most. As she started towards the back end, where she spied a hollow old brown plywood door she prayed opened up to a washroom, Jessie stopped suddenly. A large mirror was positioned in an odd place on the kitchen side of the wall, above the

Formica table. Heart sinking, she took note of its odd placement in the room and deduced it was some kind of one-way viewing window. Although she could see herself and her child reflected in the four-by-six foot mirror, she had the uncanny feeling someone was watching her from the likely darkened other side.

Sickened, Jessie pushed the disturbing thought aside for the moment, since Emily-Grace was wiggling and whining in her arms. Making her way to the mysterious door, she pushed it open.

"Oh, thank God," she breathed, while at the same time Jessie's scratchy voice caught in her throat at the simple towels and new packages of toiletries stacked in the space, on the square vanity and lining the top of the toilet tank. Sucking in air, then emitting a low whistle through gritted teeth, Jessie whipped her head around to the kitchen counter. A closer study than her previous scan revealed more of the same. Newly purchased products greeted her—rows of packaged dried goods and cans, and neatly piled dishtowels and tableware that, it seemed, someone hastily left in the space.

Seemed someone was expecting Jessie and her children to stay for a while. Shaking her head, which resulted in a dizzying reach for the stability of the doorframe, she eyed the steps leading to the outside door. Jessie's pale eyes wilted at its apparent sturdiness, yet she pulled a hopeful optimism up from somewhere deep inside her soul and whispered a silent prayer that it would open.

First things first. Small mercies. She was relieved to see the toilet was clean. It was old, the same age as the decaying yellow stove and fridge, she thought, but despite a little brown hard water staining, it was fine, as were the accompanying sink and bathtub. As she knelt before her daughter, helping her undo the snap on the small jeans and nudging them down so she could pee, Jessie let her gaze drift over to the tub.

Oh, fuck, she muttered inwardly. More wrapped packages of soap and neatly stacked facecloths greeted her, price tags diabolically glaring their newness in some weird, sick welcome.

When Emily-Grace was done, Jessie helped the little girl pull up her pants and wash her hands, then she handed back the plush doll, took her daughter by the hand, and led her outside the washroom. She let go long enough to vault up the half-dozen stairs. Staring at the door, Jessie hesitated before grabbing the large round metal doorknob. Both knees melted underneath her when she turned, pulled, and yanked, to no avail. The door wasn't budging. It was locked from the outside.

There was one more door in the space, a similar thick metal one that beckoned her from across the room. It was exactly opposite, about seven feet beyond the stark double bed. Fearing she would face the same nefarious result, Jessie headed for it anyway. Accompanied by her baby son's increasing wails, she gave it a good tug. It remained locked tight—from the other side.

Wheeling slowly, Jessie turned back to the bed. Emily-Grace, silent, always an observer, was watching her for cues.

"Come here, honey," gestured Jessie with one arm as she tried to still the panic rising in her chest, sucking out her breath. "Just sit quietly for a moment, sweetheart, while Momma feeds your baby brother, okay? Then he'll stop crying."

Maybe, she added to herself, not sure she could relax enough to feed him, and wondering at the same time what nauseating drug was in her system and whether it would hurt her baby when she brought him to her breast. Memories of a syringe held high at the end of a raised arm of one of her balaclava clad abductors shot into Jessie's addled brain. *Oh God,* she moaned, weighing her options. *Do I feed David or not?*

Lifting her howling six-month-old son up out of the stroller, she brushed her lips against a frantic red cheek. "It's okay, baby. Momma's here. You're okay." Inspecting him closely, she looked for marks the same way she'd done with Emily-Grace earlier. Once she was relatively convinced he wasn't overtly damaged, Jessie closed her eyes, said a silent prayer, and brought the baby to her breast.

The immediate result was a modicum of silence, apart from the gurgling sounds of her infant, for which Jessie's aching head and Emily-Grace's nerves were grateful.

Jessie dropped down onto the edge of the sketchy bed, nestled close to her daughter, and took a closer look at her situation. The more she thought about it, the more rapidly a steady fear escalated up her arms and down her legs via sizzling goose bumps that left trails of doom as they passed. Simply being here, held against her will in this dingy apartment with her two children, was beyond frightening.

As David fed, Jessie snuck one hand out to grasp her daughter's small fingers. "It's okay, baby girl," she whispered, with more confidence than she felt. She aimed her gaze at the weird mirror and narrowed her eyebrows. "You and me are fighters. And there are people out there who love us. We'll be just fine. This is just a little holiday. That's all."

But the sick sense of dread was working its way not just up, but *into* her body now, filling every interior crevice with a loathsome sludge. By the time it got to her chest, her breaths were quick rasps. It felt like her airway was closing over.

Then Jessie's thoughts slid to her husband. She closed her eyes.

Oh sweet Jesus, she whispered silently.

Josh.

~ ~

He was standing, feet a hip's width apart, at the safe house, when Matt showed up. It was five a.m.

Josh rubbed the back of one trembling hand over his face as he watched Matt stride up the walk, head down and knuckles clenched in the eerie mask of streetlight-lit yellow semi-darkness. Licking his dry lips, Josh inhaled quickly and deeply, tasting blood from the lip he'd bitten all night as he waited for news.

Matt faced him silently.

"What?" Josh demanded, fear creeping over him like some ghoulish caul. "What the fuck is happening, Matt? Where're Jessie and my kids?"

Matt didn't answer right away. He studied Josh and wondered how to tell him they were now living in a nightmare. For how long, was anybody's guess. Already Josh was losing it. Ulysses had left Big Dan with him for the night, with orders not to let the actor leave the residence. And reports from Dan were of almost coming to blows with Josh in order to keep him under cover. For, at this point, the threat to the small Sawyer family wasn't clear. Was Josh a target as well? Part of Matt wondered if that would almost be best. For now, he had no choice but to destroy this young husband and father by telling him his family was not only officially missing, but presumed kidnapped.

"Matt, if you don't fucking—"

Angry dark eyes snapped at the Keatings' ex-security chief. Fists curled and uncurled. But the hardest for Matt to bear was the terror in Josh's bearing, in the way he stood tense and tight as if he would literally snap if Matt reached out a finger and touched him.

Matt waded in, softening the blow as best he could by trying to keep a steady tone. "The police found the BMW. The driver's side window was smashed. Jessie and the kids…they weren't there."

"How…where…?"

"A back alley near Cambie and Main. Ulysses talked to Chris from ROAM. The barista. He said…" Matt's lips twitched. He knew Josh wouldn't like this next bit. Sucking his lip, he paused before continuing. "He said Jessie was talking to Jacob on her cell when the young kid with the note showed up. Chris thought Jacob might know something. He did. He said she was going to GPS the new café where she thought she was supposed to meet you, that it was near Cambie and Main. The police found the SUV almost immediately."

"And no one told me because…" In his weird hyper-tense anxious state, Josh pictured a self-righteous Charles Keating demanding he not be told, that he be kept out of the loop.

"You weren't told because the police didn't need you showing up and breathing down their backs. Partly for your own safety."

Frantic for information, Josh cut in. "What else, Matt? What fucking else?"

Matt gulped. His voice cracked. "No cell phone, and no note to study for fingerprints. No tire tracks behind the SUV. In case you didn't notice, an almighty rain poured down half the night. Any possible traces were washed away. And no sign of struggle on the ground between Jessie's door and where the van she mentioned on the phone might have been parked."

Josh waited, the nerve on his cheek twitching in overdrive, his eyes wide, threatened, scared.

"Emily-Grace's car seat was intact. It's presumed they simply lifted her out. David's carrier was gone, which makes sense. Other than a sippy cup, the van was, for the most part, empty."

Swallowing down the bile in his throat, Josh gasped, "The stroller?"

"No. No stroller."

Another thought struck Josh. "Emily-Grace's doll? The Diana one we got at the airport in Charlottetown last summer?"

"There was no doll, Josh."

"That's…that's good." Josh deflated, visibly relieved at this small grace. "She'll want that Diana doll. It goes everywhere with her." A choking sob escaped from his chest as his daughter's little blonde ringlets and hopeful, happy pale eyes accosted him.

"The Gibson? Jessie for sure had it with her, she was playing kids' songs at Emily-Grace's play date before she was supposed to meet me."

Matt shook his head.

"Matt? What about blood, Matt? Was there any blood?"

"No, not that anyone's found yet, anyway. Look, Josh." Stepping forward, Matt touched Josh's elbow, and indicated he should sit on the nearby couch. Once they were seated, he leaned forward, elbows on his knees, and continued. "There's only one reason some diabolical screwball wants Jessie and your kids, and that's to hold them for money. They won't hurt them if they want to get paid. So we sit tight and wait for the call, okay?"

Lifting a hand to scratch his head, Matt carefully studied Josh, who sucked in a breath and nodded.

Hands clasped in front of him as he leaned over and tried to breathe, Josh offered, "Jessie's the strongest person I know. She can handle this, Matt. She'll take care of our kids."

This time it was Matt's turn to struggle to maintain his quickly cracking composure. He'd been to the crime scene; he eyeballed the smashed glass, the crookedly parked SUV, Emily-Grace's vacant car seat…

The emptiness, the fear, the unknown actions that transpired in the dead end alley chilled and sickened him. The visual reminder would haunt him forevermore. He was glad they kept Josh from the area …the heartbreaking image would undo him entirely.

Matt couldn't respond to Josh other than by placing a trembling hand on his shoulder and nodding uselessly. He buried his face in his other hand, so Josh wouldn't see his tears.

Chapter Two

"Nadia, stay put for now. As long as you're in Toronto, you're under their radar if and when they start nosing around me. And they will, you know they will, because they'll investigate everyone in Jessie's circle."

A pouty silence met Morgan's insistent demand. Then Nadia threw in her two cents, her voice liquid honey despite the scowl permeating the sensuous red lips . "Fine. But stay away from her. Don't cave, Morgan. Just watch her and the kids, and make sure she doesn't do something stupid like freak out and drown them or something. Otherwise..." She drifted off.

"God, Nadia. Seriously?" Morgan's stomach clenched at what his wife didn't say. She was desperate to put herself in Josh's bed. She *needed* his kids. Beyond that, he wondered if she was capable of caring about the little ones at all.

He did. Morgan cared. He knew the kids, and despite the stark reality that they would likely never really give a shit about him, he loved them.

Now, watching them from the dark side of the one-way mirror while he stood talking with Nadia on the landline, Morgan absently tapped a finger on a crossed arm. It took some getting used to, watching Jessie and her kids this way, through this one-sided viewing portal. Morgan had slowly worked his way to a center position behind it, tentatively studying Jessie's reactions the whole time to ensure she couldn't see him. He figured she clued in instantly as to the large mirror's purpose, judging by the way she furrowed her eyebrows and looked through it. But she never acknowledged ever catching his eye, no, there would have been shock and surprise in the icy blues if she knew he was her kidnapper. Instead, Morgan figured, to her it likely seemed her unseen watcher was a ghost. When she looked at the mirror, her eyes darted from one side to the other, or looked right through him.

He was on the outside looking in, a nameless, figureless presence, which suited Morgan since life felt that way anyways these days, and had since the day a beady-eyed doctor stoically delivered his and Nadia's son's terminal diagnosis.

Now, Morgan watched as Emily-Grace, at the kitchen table, swiped a yellow crayon over a picture of a duck. She was swinging her legs and singing a nonsensical tune, happy enough, he thought, considering she likely had no understanding of her nefarious circumstances. Little David was on his back on the bed, sucking on a teething ring retrieved from his stroller. Lips pressed tightly into a straight line, Jessie was mutely changing her baby's diaper, getting at the business of living this new life the best way she could, while, Morgan reckoned, also trying to sort out the whys and whats and hows in her mind.

Jessie and the kids had been his 'guests,' as he called them, for five days now. Nadia was desperate to fly back to Vancouver so she could sneak peeks at the singer and her famous children—whose safety the whole world was deeply shocked and worried for—but Morgan knew now was not the time. His wife needed to keep a low profile and not be moving back and forth across the country until the hype surrounding the disappearance of their superstar guests settled.

Morgan watched Jessie fasten David's diaper and then glance up to the mirror. He knew she'd figured out when he was in the house, based on the sound of his truck pulling to a stop outside as well as on his heavy footsteps above her, and on the stairs leading to his half of the basement. He'd swapped out the silver van for a nondescript pickup truck, a generic 2012 Ford F-150, which crunched over the gravel and gave his comings and goings away every time.

Sometimes Morgan thought she stared at the mirror just to get a rise out of him, maybe to soften him up, or to wordlessly glare at him in a voiceless curse that clearly said *fuck off*. But he wouldn't cave. He was getting used to the routine now, to the idea of having Jessie completely dependent on his ability to bring her food, for one, and so his stomach was settling a bit and he was able to eat and sleep again, although his nights were filled with despicable dreams about wars and battles and sitting in the back seats of cars while Nadia drove in slow motion.

Each day was the same—go get a few groceries, always at different stores. There was no shortage of those, between neighboring Surrey, Metro Vancouver, Coquitlam, Burnaby, and of course Langley itself. Take the groceries home and place them in a basket just outside the basement door, then unlock the door so Jessie can bring the kids outside for some fresh air. Later in the day, sneak around and retrieve the basket Jessie would leave outside for him that she'd filled with garbage, diapers, sometimes nasty notes or simple requests—there were always two baskets in play each day.

Morgan always wore the balaclava in case Jessie got to the door before he could run back around to the side of the house and make his exit through the twelve foot high wooden gate he hired a local carpenter to build—he'd told the guy he was planning to install a pool and didn't need any stray animals falling into it. There were no neighbors around for miles, so animals were the only concern. The guy bought the story, of course, and the high fence was too smooth and high to climb over, so even if Jessie decided to make a break for it by leaving her kids behind, no way could she get over it. She'd tried, Morgan knew—the very first day he'd watched her muscled dancer's body scratch and scrape at the new boards until her fingertips were raw. She'd finally collapsed on the cold ground in frustration.

The backyard was well treed, but only outside the fence. That was one reason the Langley house worked so well. It was isolated, so even if Jessie screamed for help (and she did, until her voice was hoarse that first day), no one could hear the desperate cries.

Each night, while Morgan settled for sleep in the small one-and-a-half story cedar-shingled home, he often thought of his captive guests down there in the basement and, in particular, Jessie, curled into dreams under that cheap nondescript comforter. Morgan was still cowed by the woman—her fame, the pretty ice-blue eyes, her surreal presence on stage and screen. No way could he even meet her eyes most times when he was working for her, which was easy to get away with since the main part of his job was spent scouring Jessie's immediate vicinity anyway, for…well, for creeps like suddenly he turned out to be, and for star-struck fans like his wife who decided to play a vicious little game with this famous family. So he refrained from touching Jessie. But sometimes, especially alone in bed at night, Morgan couldn't help but wonder what it would be like to be with her in the way Nadia wanted to be with Jessie's husband. Those nights were long, sleepless.

But Morgan was a good man, in his heart.

And so, apart from his disturbing staring, he left his captive alone.

In the grungy basement apartment, Jessie was feeling the presence of someone behind the mirror. She was staring viciously at it, blue eyes darting daggers towards the invisible shape. In her mind, she called who she assumed was a guy—judging by the periodic stomping of heavy boots above her head and down what appeared to be wooden steps to the basement—a lot of nasty names. Apart from screaming outside on the first day, Jessie didn't feel she could say anything vicious out loud for fear of scaring her small daughter, although sometimes she caught Emily-Grace fearfully watching her anyways, a forgotten crayon suspended over her coloring.

Who are you, you fucking bastard, Jessie whispered angrily to herself now as she dared her captor to reveal himself. *Coward. Fucking coward. Are you someone I know?* That thought chilled her. She shivered.

Emily-Grace distracted her with a question. The little girl wandered over to the bed and, with both hands resting on the mattress' edge, she leaned towards her mother. "Momma, I wanna go outside."

Exhaling slowly, Jessie extended a hand and let a palm rest against her daughter's soft cheek. "I'm sorry, baby. We can't go outside right now."

She was grateful for their time outdoors in the mornings, and had figured out she could soak up fresh air in the tiny yard for as long as she liked. Each day, Jessie looked forward to the harsh telltale unlocking of the hateful deadbolt, which usually happened daily around mid-morning.

However, inevitably their brief blue-sky respites from this hole in the ground got cold—it was November—and so sometimes all they got of exercise and indigo sky (or grey sky, many days) was a mere hour or even less. The three of them only had the outerwear they'd had on when they were snatched, and these were okay, but they weren't necessarily meant for rainy weather or extended periods outdoors in late fall. Sometimes Jessie found clothes in the basket that was left outside the basement door on a daily basis. She hoped a few kids' snowsuits would show up someday—if they didn't get out of here soon—but so far, no such luck.

When she allowed her mind to go to Josh, Jessie tried to send him strength. It was a hard thing to do during the day because she didn't want to lose control of her emotions in front of her daughter, who was old enough to sense her mother's angst and frustration, but who wouldn't understand seeing her mother cry. But at night when the children were asleep—David in his stroller and Emily-Grace in the bed beside her momma—Jessie couldn't keep the worries at bay. As she lay on the hard mattress each night trying to settle her frazzled mind, she prayed to God for help and strength, and then she drifted on to meditating in a desperate attempt to connect with Josh, to converse somehow with him.

She and Josh had always felt intuitively tuned into each other. Maybe somehow he would get her message and sense she and their small children were okay.

Always, those silent pleadings ended in body-shaking sobs for the impossible situation in which Jessie found herself—for her children, for whose lives she feared, and for her husband, who she knew must be losing his mind with worry.

Baby, she begged the murky darkness each night, *be strong. You can get through this. Be strong, for us. We need your strength.*

This would change him. This loss would kill her husband.

Little did Jessie know, she could have cried during the day instead of just at night. Emily-Grace often heard the panic released to the darkness anyway, and it scared her to watch her mother's back shake. Jessie's gut-wrenching sobs stayed with Emily-Grace all night, manifesting themselves in nightmares. The fear the crying unleashed also eventually started to appear in her drawings. Yet, each night, the little girl lay in silence, scared and unable to understand her mother's sadness. And slowly she withdrew into herself, into an imaginary world of stories and songs, because, at least in her fantasy worlds, there was light.

That was the other thing—there was no natural light in the basement space. There were the two half windows, but they were closed over from the outside, presumably with boards. Too tiny for Jessie to even consider climbing through, they remained dark all day long.

So, as each day ticked interminably on, Jessie's nighttime panics escalated. Her patience with the kids was admirable, given the unremitting worry over their situation, but she spent more and more time, when indoors, staring at the mirror and willing it to speak. She refused to put any of the supplies away or even rip off their tags, except when she was using them, because, to Jessie, that would seem like capitulation, and no way was she bowing down to this coward and his apparently absent partner.

Day-to-day needs kept her sane. Dirty diapers had to be tended to; Jessie left them outdoors with other refuse, in the basket she dropped by the door when she took her babies outside. She bathed herself and her children, force-singing Emily-Grace's favorite bath time tunes and playing with the little ones to try to maintain a kind of schedule the kids were accustomed to. The Gibson was her savior. Making up silly songs with her daughter was an exercise in hope-instilling creativity. Where there was music, there was courage, in Jessie's experience.

Eventually, as the days ticked inexorably on, the angry words she tried to hold inside started to creep out. Confused, Emily-Grace watched as her momma tossed them at the mirror, spitting the nasty thoughts out through clenched teeth. And then, one day, Jessie felt something inside herself give entirely. When she and the children were outside one morning—Emily-Grace running around in circles, dangling her Diana doll from one hand while singing to herself in babbles; David in Jessie's arms talking in his baby voice to the birds that landed on the top of the old wooden picnic table she was sitting on, which she had been disheartened to find chained to the ground and therefore unable to aid any type of escape over the fence—Jessie's weary mind decided she'd had enough.

When they went back inside, she dropped David rather roughly into his stroller and banged her fists against the mirror. Jessie screamed, she begged, and she cried.

Then, she looked down. Something was clutching her leg—no, someone. Emily-Grace. The child was standing there with both arms wrapped tightly around Jessie's thigh, staring in terror up at her momma, tears streaming down both pink cheeks. She was sobbing, too.

Jessie gasped, turned her back to the mirror, and slid to the floor, which was one place she knew her captor couldn't see her. She pulled her daughter into her lap. Together they ushered their grief unto the world.

"I'm sorry, baby girl. I'm so, so sorry," Jessie sobbed into her child's blonde ringlets. "It's okay to have a sad day once in a while. It's okay. Everything's going to be okay."

After a few moments, when both Jessie and her daughter were hiccupping away the last of their tears, Emily-Grace sat back and touched her momma's trembling lips. With the backs of her little three-year-old hands she wiped away the last of her own tears. Jessie watched the child minister to herself, aching with all her heart to take away her sorrow. She was witness to Emily-Grace's increasing disappearances into little fantasy worlds, and the gaps from reality frightened her.

"I'm sorry," she whispered again. "Momma will try to do better, Emily-Grace. I promise. I'm sorry for frightening you."

"Momma," the little girl wept now in solemn response, melting in her own personal three-year-old agony, "I miss Daddy." A new round of tears left salty trails on the small cheeks.

"So do I, baby," was Jessie's honest and equally agonized response. "So do I."

She rocked her daughter there, on the floor, beneath the eyes of their abductor, in a safe place where they could lay their pain bare. Shortly, Jessie rallied. She had to. David was still a baby and, in some ways at least, he was getting a modicum of stability, at least in terms of place, which was more than Emily-Grace had gotten for much of her three years. But he was too little to feel and experience the level of ache Jessie knew her daughter was now exposed to. She resolved to be stronger, to try harder to stay cool in this tempestuous and unbelievable situation.

"You know something?" she said to her daughter, trying to pull up a modicum of strength and light from someplace deep within.

"What, Momma?" asked Emily-Grace, wiping a stray hair out of her eyes.

"When Momma feels bad, she does stuff to make her feel better." Jessie peered down at the little blonde child who was completely dependent on her for survival…and for hope.

"Like what, Momma?" The pint-sized hands were folded in Emily-Grace's lap now, patient, waiting.

"Like…hmmm," Jessie thought. *What can I do to get us through these days? Until…until help comes. Until they find us.* "You know something? I think you're old enough to do Yoga with Momma. Let's you and me do some Yoga. Okay?"

"Okay, Momma. Woga."

Puffing up her cheeks and blowing out a cleansing breath, Jessie hoisted her daughter to a standing position, then maneuvered her own tired soul up as well. Standing alongside her child, she grasped a warm hand.

"Let's just see that David's okay first, honey." They tiptoed to the stroller and peeked in at him. Jessie smiled and, through her son's leather slippers, tickled the tiny toes. "See, Emily-Grace? He's happy. We're okay, all of us. See? He's playing with his toes. He's laughing."

Glancing down at Emily-Grace, though, Jessie saw only a deep sadness. There were no smiles lighting the piqued face. The child knew something was desperately wrong in her formerly idyllic world, but she was too young to understand the truths now haunting the Sawyer family.

Jessie bent before her.

"I promise you, baby, everything's going to be okay. You have to believe Momma, okay? We'll see Daddy soon. And you know what he'll do when he sees you?"

"No."

Jessie's voice was crackly. Sticks juggled for dominance in her throat. "He'll grab you and swing you up high and then he'll give you one of those raspberry things in your belly that always tickles you and makes you laugh. That's what he'll do. So when you miss Daddy, you think about that. You picture him doing that, and you see his smile, and you will feel better, okay?"

"Okay, Momma."

"Do that now, okay honey? Think about Daddy like that right now." Crooking her neck, she watched her daughter. There was still no smile forthcoming, only a heavy sigh. Jessie frowned. "Are you doing it? Can you see Daddy laughing with you?"

A little curve appeared at Emily-Grace's lips, barely discernible, and the attempt at a smile didn't reach her eyes, which remained chilled, devoid of light.

Jessie moved David's stroller closer to an area in front of the bed. She fought back more tears. *I've got to get out of here,* she thought desperately, feeling like she was back in P.E.I. during her childhood as a huge Nor'Easter blizzard blew through, keeping her trapped inside, sometimes for more than a day. *I've got to get the fuck out of here.*

She gestured to her daughter. "C'mere honey. Yoga cures a lot of ills. Let me show you how to do a downward dog."

"No, Momma, real Woga. Not a game Woga."

A hearty laugh escaped from between Jessie's lips, surprising her. It snuck out in the midst of despair. "Emily-Grace! There is something called a downward dog in real Yoga. I swear! Come here so Momma can show you."

They passed the time with a few small smiles for the next half hour. Jessie found herself actually laughing more than once as she grabbed her daughter by the waist and pulled the small bum up in the air for a downward dog pose, which required both hands be placed flat on the ground, legs be positioned a hip distance apart, and bum be aimed high in the air, so the body forms a triangle. Even Emily-Grace giggled a few times as she practiced this fun new hobby alongside her momma. Soon, Jessie moved David onto the area rug with them. His sister soon had the baby giggling loudly as she tickled him and played with him.

Then it was time to make dinner, and to do some laundry in the machines Jessie found at the base of the stairs the first time they ventured up the back stairs and outside.

Emily-Grace went back to coloring. When Jessie leaned over to see her picture, which was really just a lot of dark, angry scrawls, and which was half obscured by Diana-dowwy's raven locks, the little girl was babbling again. Jessie bent closer to hear what she was saying.

"Daddy Daddy Daddy Daddy Daddy Daddy..."

A lightning pain almost sliced her in two. Wheeling around, forcing new tears to remain at bay, Jessie went back to her meal prep, which pissed her off as much as anything else about their seclusion since her food choices were pretty much dictated by her captor. Today, Jessie and Emily-Grace were having hotdogs and Kraft Dinner, both of which Jessie abhorred for their lack of nutritional value, and which she did not want to feed to her daughter.

But at least the activity kept her hands and mind busy, and Jessie was able to turn her back away from Emily-Grace as her shoulders shook and new tears silently fell.

Chapter Three

Matt left La Casa resolving to never again enter the doorway of the lovely butter yellow home with its graceful archways and mahogany trim. He stormed into his Audi sedan, slammed the door, and hammered the steering wheel with a fist.

He wasn't angry. He and Charles had come to some kind of tentative peace over this latest Jessie-related drama. But the heartbreak in the producer's eyes was too much to bear. Charles was stooped, his eyes black-shadowed underneath, and he hardly spoke. As for Dee? Matt didn't even get to see her. She was in bed under a doctor's care.

They were two weeks into the disappearance of Jessie and her children. The fourteen days were filled with only a desperate silence—they were frighteningly mute, absent of leads. Not a word from the kidnappers made its way to Josh, to the Keatings, or to the police. There was no ransom note, there were no calls, there was nothing. The debilitating absence of light left the days darker than sin. The souls of those who ached for Josh were watching him slowly die; they themselves were wilting away into a blank nothingness.

Matt couldn't stand the useless torpor. This was why he had left the Keatings' employ. This was why he wanted to be with his brother. Kelly was a dramatic high-maintenance princess at times, but Matt much preferred her little hissy fits over this eternal excruciating ache for Jessie, the sad woman he never seemed to be able to save. And now the two Sawyer children...

Oh Jesus, Matt cried to his steering wheel. He forced himself to get a grip. One more difficult stop remained today.

Firing up the Audi, he pointed it towards the Lion's Gate Bridge.

At Josh's place, Matt found Steve and his good friend sitting in bitter, hopeless silence. Both were pensive, aching, and seemingly lost in personal agony. Hunched down in a part of the house Matt knew the Sawyers rarely used—Josh and Jessie's more formal living area—the guys didn't even look up when he stepped in.

Josh was unshaven, greasy hair carelessly framing his face like in the ragged way the *Drifters* art director insisted he wear it back when Josh played an ex-Civil War soldier. He hardly blinked when Matt entered through the sliding door.

Steve did, though. He blinked. And when he straightened, the subtle movement jarred Josh, who grimaced, grunted, and forced himself to meet Matt's damp eyes.

Then both faces resorted to a masked indifference. The men were afraid to ask for news.

Matt saved them. Raising a palm, he held it outwards. "Nothing new," he immediately proclaimed, his voice edgy. Inwardly he hoped neither of the guys would notice his red-rimmed eyes and sallow complexion. He, like the rest of them, was not eating or sleeping.

"What's the latest?" Steve managed.

"The police are still interviewing people. Some for the third and fourth time. Jacob's with them again now."

"Any tidbits at all?"

Steve was doing all the asking. Josh remained, for the most part, quiet. He chewed on an already wrecked fingernail while staring at Matt and uneasily trying to read the man's expression. Something was amiss...

Matt shrugged and accepted a beer from Steve. He focused on the label for a moment before suddenly looking up at Josh. Knuckles white, Jessie's husband was gripping a beer tightly in one hand. Shaking any worry about Josh's history of addictions away, Matt silently chided himself.

Give the man a fucking beer, he demanded the universe. *Give him a goddamn 2-4 if he wants it.*

"What's new..." he muttered, twisting the cap off the Granville Island Brewery's pale ale under his fingers. "There's nothing in the Deuce McCall

19

camp. There are no red flags, at least in the immediate family. They're looking at cousins now, second and third cousins." He nodded once at Josh. "Ulysses is putting Morgan on you for a bit. The kid's heartsick. Ulysses thinks he needs to be around, to…to just be around, I guess. Three days. Then Susanne will be in the city for the weekend."

Josh just turned his head and stared out at the pool. Security for himself was not high on his list of priorities at the present time. He wished the asshole that ripped his family right out from under him would come get him too, and torture or beat him, whatever. Physical pain would be better than the unbelievable white heat swelling his brain and stomach, threatening an imminent explosion as if his body was mutating into red-hot glass that could shatter at any moment.

Josh just wanted to be with Jessie and their children. Swallowing past a venomous lump in his barren throat, he fought against the incessant barrage of tears constantly draining him dry.

Outside, the gate clanged and weighted footsteps started down the flagstone steps. Momentarily, Jacob appeared at the sliding door. He stood outside, unsure, hesitating, and then he caught Josh's eye. Sliding open the door, he shoved both hands in his pockets and carefully made his way inside, holding Josh's heated gaze as he entered.

Steve handed him a beer, so Jacob dropped down next to him, across from Josh, kitty corner to Matt.

All of them were silent, watchful. They drew on their beers with reckless abandon, trying to drench a deepening desperation.

Jacob had just come from his third interrogation with the police. He, too, was fatigued from lack of ability to sleep, but there was a fresh fury and pain surrounding him, like some raging black halo. Through his previous meetings with the police he had yet to face Jessie's husband. Now he slugged back a hefty drink and tipped the nose of his bottle towards Josh.

"I don't know how you stand it. I can't fucking stand it, Sawyer." Choking on a sob, he sucked back hard again on the beer.

Josh was non-responsive. He went back to staring idly out of the window towards a bank of grey clouds hovering ominously over the Pacific Ocean.

Matt cautiously eyed Josh before turning to Jacob. "What'd you tell them,

Jacob? What did they want to know today that was different from the last two times you talked to them?"

Jacob gulped. "It sucked. They were all over me. They wanted to know everything Jessie and I talked about that last day at ROAM. When she got that fucking fucked up note."

Steve was watching him. Jacob threw back a good third of his beer the next time he tipped his bottle back. "What *did* you two talk about that day?" Steve asked.

"Stupid shit. I don't know. David was fussy so it was kind of a distracted conversation, for the most part."

Now Josh fixed his eyes on Jacob. Really, as much as there was a dual jealousy between he and Jessie's co-star, he recognized that Jacob was the last to speak with his wife. Jacob was the last of their group to hear the voices of Jessie, Emily-Grace and David.

"What did you talk about?" he insisted, his mostly unused monotone voice emerging like an old horse trail, bumpy and rough.

Guffawing, pressing a thumb and forefinger to the outsides of both eyes, Jacob spoke candidly. "You don't fucking want to know, Sawyer."

"Don't I?" Josh held his breath, gripped his bottle tighter, and eased a very satisfying long drink down his throat and into his gullet. "So, like, are you now officially a suspect, or what?" He spoke coolly, in a detached sort of way, which echoed the way he felt he related to the world these days.

Matt and Steve straightened. Over the last few years the guys had done okay managing their feelings towards Jessie when in each other's company. But this was not a normal day. The world was off its axis, the stars were not aligned, and emotions were raw.

Jacob sat forward. He spat at Josh. "I told her I loved her. And I reminded her of a night when your daughter was a baby when I knew she wanted me." He wiped a hand across his face. He, too, was unshaven. The hand came back feeling as raw as his soul.

No one spoke. Then Josh set his beer bottle on the arm of the large chair he was half-buried in. He looked blankly outside, then swallowed and turned back to Jacob. "She never cheated on me. Least of all with you, you lying bastard."

"She wanted to that night. She was lonely, she was tired, and we were connecting like we always do, only that night it was surreal. We were lying on her bed talking about serious family shit. She was upset over her sister's son Ren seeing those nude pictures on the Internet…I was telling her stuff about my dad, and then we were touching, Sawyer. Her leg was over mine and her hand was here." He shoved a hand just inside the waistband of his jeans, a place where Josh knew only too well Jessie liked to position her hand in the beginning stages of sweet lust. "And I could feel her breath on my neck."

"Jacob," came a warning voice from his left, but Jacob was too riled up to notice, or to even attempt to hear. Leaning forward, he rested both elbows on his thighs and waved the bottle at Josh as hot tears escaped unfettered and slid on salty tracks down his rough cheeks.

"She moved her hips against me, Josh. Her face was buried in my neck and she was moaning. She wanted me. She fucking wanted me, and I—" He didn't get to finish the sentence that was tearing Josh even further in two.

Like a raging bronco, Josh pitched forward. Grabbing Jacob's shirt at the chest, he yanked him upright so fast that Jacob dropped his beer bottle, which smashed against a coffee table.

"You fucking bastard," he growled. "Did you sleep with her? You and her get something going in Miami? Huh? You been fucking her all along, rat-faced Ryan?"

Steve and Matt were up as quick as Josh. Steve leapt over the coffee table and grabbed Josh from behind, almost knocking him over. He wrapped strong fingers around his good friend's biceps and forced them behind his back.

Matt threw Jacob backwards, hard against the wall. The singer was weeping openly now.

"No!" he hollered at Josh. "No, I fucking didn't, you goddamned panty-wipe asshole! But that's the sting of it now, you see, because I fucking should have! I should have taken her that night when it was pretty fucking clear which man she wanted, and I bet we would have started something that I'd still have today. But what do I have, Josh? Huh? Nothing! That's what I god-damned have! Nada! I know it sucks for you, man, but you had her a helluva lot longer than I did. And I'll tell you one thing." Shoving Matt in the chest,

22

he marched forward. "When she and the kids come home, if I ever get the chance again, I'm fucking taking it. So watch your back, Sawyer. That's twice I could have had her." He held up two trembling fingers. "Twice. That time in Miami, the night you were responsible for her fucking photo hitting the world, and then that night when she was grinding against me on the bed. And what is it they say? Three time's the charm, Sawyer. That's what they say."

Shaking wholeheartedly now, Jacob drew back his shoulders and raised his chin defiantly.

As he struggled against Steve, Josh fired the next bullet. "You got her stashed away someplace, Ryan? Huh? You just admitted it. You still want her. You've always wanted her, you still want her, and for all I fucking know you have her!"

Incredulous, Jacob's tears dried up a little at that. He sniffed, and wiped a hand under his nose. "You're off your fucking rocker, Josh. I wish I god-damned had her stashed away somewhere, that's what. I wish I had her." Backing away slowly, he shoved Matt aside as he went by. He held his arms out to the sides. "You think I'd be here if I had her? Huh? No." Leaning forward, he spat at Josh. "I'd be by her side fucking her, that's what!"

The horror of that remark sank in to all of them the instant it escaped Jacob's pale lips.

The room fell deadly quiet with the exception of Jacob's intermittent sniffs. Josh, completely immobile in Steve's vice-like grip, heard his breaths coming and going and he felt his chest move, but the sounds were elevated, staccato'ed, wheezy. The clock ticking on the kitchen wall assaulted his ears in a way he'd never noticed before. The crackling of the refrigerator was deafening.

"Get—the—fuck—out—of—my—house," he demanded of his unwanted late afternoon guest. "Get the fuck out, Ryan! Go!"

And, with a new terror unleashed aloud by someone who Josh tolerated for years but now couldn't stand to lay eyes upon, Jacob backed all the way out of the room. At the sliding door, he paused with one hand trembling on the doorframe, and he fixed panicked wide eyes on Matt, and then on Steve.

"I'm sorry," he told them in a disembodied high-pitched voice. "I didn't… I mean…"

"Get the fuck out, Jacob." Steve spoke for all of them, partly because he knew Josh would tear Jacob apart if he loosed himself from Steve's grip, and partly because hearing the dark fear voiced—of someone else being with Jessie sexually—destroyed what little semblance of sanity the men were managing to hang on to.

After Jacob finally got the strength to move on without gripping something tangible, the air in the room was stifling. It was a cold, dreary November day outside, and it wasn't much warmer in the room, but it seemed like every minute molecule had the power to choke the men.

Matt broke the silence. "Josh."

Josh looked up, chest heaving and eyes tortured. "What is it, Matt?" he demanded brusquely. "Just fucking say it. I know you came here to say something, just like Ryan did. Just fucking spit it out."

Hesitating, because he knew what he had to say was going to facilitate a whole new ending, Matt spoke. "I'm pulling out of Vancouver. I'm leaving."

Both Steve and Josh stared at him. Steve voiced what Josh was thinking. "You did that ages ago, Matt. That's not news."

But Josh got the gist then of what it was Matt was really trying to say. "You're moving. Selling your house. Taking Julie and Katy."

"And I'm never coming back," Matt managed. "I can't do this. I can't be here and…and…"

"What, wonder every damn second of every damn day where she is? Again? Wonder where my kids are? Okay, so I get it. You get a free ride." He pointed a finger at Matt. "You get to walk away. You get to go on with your life while I…"

He couldn't finish. Josh sucked on his bottom lip so hard it bled. "Thanks for nothing, Matt. Go play with your princess and your rock star brother. Leave us the fuck alone."

"That's not fair, Josh." Steve's tone was harsh, gravel on a dirt road, but he was attempting to understand what Matt was really saying. When his muzzy brain cleared, the truth hit him like a ton of bricks. Staring at Matt, he sucked in a breath.

Josh's hard gaze drifted over to him. Then the truth hit him too. "Matt," he begged. "No. Don't. Don't do this. Don't…give up."

24

A single tear made its way unbidden down Matt's ashen cheek. "There's nothing to go on, Josh. The police are doing what they can, but I just feel… fucking useless. That's what I feel. And I can't stand…" He swallowed past the grit in his throat. "I can't stand the useless part of me. I'm pulling out. I'm getting my wife and daughter out of this fucked up city. Away from… away from shit I have no control over."

"Charles and Dee," Josh whispered. "They're losing it. They need their old friend here, where they can believe you're working towards something, Matt…anything."

"They gave me up a long time ago, Josh. They've got Ulysses now. And Carlotta."

Josh chortled crazily. "Like she's any help. She's as fucked up as the rest of us right now."

But Matt just shrugged. "I'm done, Josh. I'll stay in touch with Ulysses. And if there's ever anything I can help with, I promise I'll do what I can. But I need to get out of Vancouver. I can't handle it. My wife can't handle it. My marriage can't handle it."

"And you want to be sure your daughter's not a target too," Josh said in a small wounded voice.

Matt didn't respond at first. Shoving both hands in the pockets of his knee-length overcoat, he flipped up the collar and stood.

Then he said, "It was always a possibility, Josh, that your family would be a target. In the past I've worried about mine by association, but only in a very slim way. So no, that's not what's destroying me. What's destroying me is my inability to ever help you when you need it. To help Jessie. To be present for Julie and Katy in a way that makes me worthy of them. And I can't do that here, even part-time, where around every corner is a goddamned memory of my failures."

"Jessie loves you, Matt. She's always loved you. She wouldn't like hearing you talk this way, blaming yourself for stupid choices she made in the past. And this time…what happened this time had nothing to do with you. If she were here now," Josh gulped, and lowered his voice as Steve watched him, "if she were here now, she would look you straight in the eye and tell you that we couldn't live our lives with constant security. She would say

25

SUSAN RODGERS

she wanted the kids raised as normally as possible despite our fucked up careers. She wouldn't change that, Matt. She wouldn't."

"Wherever she is, Josh, she might be rethinking that scenario."

"No. If anything, she's rethinking our careers. She's wanting a small house in Prince Edward Island, on some old red dirt back road." He swallowed painfully.

Matt sighed. He adjusted his collar again, the motion a nervous gesture that only served to soften Josh's heart towards the man they all loved. "Call me, Josh. Anytime. If I hear anything I'll be in touch."

With that, he shook Josh's hand and nodded a goodbye to Steve before wheeling around and walking out of the door. Steve and Josh watched him disappear. It killed both of them to see him go, to see that last glimpse of the hunched over shoulders and spiked hair Jessie constantly teased him about.

Steve sat back down and stared at the mess of Jacob's spilled beer, which had formed little rivulets amongst shards of broken glass. He toed a piece of dark glass. It made a little scraping sound on the hardwood floor.

"'Nuther one?" he asked Josh without looking up.

"Fuck, yeah," was Josh's monotone response. He drank without meeting Steve's eyes again and later, when Sophie arrived in search of her husband, she found the men each asleep, Josh sprawled out on the big chair, and Steve on the couch opposite him. Both were dead drunk.

The pretty blonde tenderly tucked a coverlet over Josh, then laid down by her husband, pulling a homemade quilt over her and Steve as she did so. A squeaky toy made its presence known when Sophie adjusted her feet. Glancing at Josh, praying he hadn't heard it, she tucked it underneath the couch so it couldn't be seen.

Then she laid her head on her man's chest, wrapped an arm around his waist, and breathed him in.

26

Chapter Four

*J*essie knew something was seriously wrong with David when he stopped fighting an incessant cough and lay listless on the bed. He wasn't warm to the touch—he was downright hot. Sick with worry, she turned for the umpteenth time to the mirror and begged their ghostlike captor to listen.

"Do you see?" she cried. "He's not moving! Your stupid cough syrup did nothing!" To prove her point, she grabbed the offensive now empty bottle and pitched it at the mirror. It bounced off and rolled to a stop against the leg of the chair where Emily-Grace sat babbling to her soft Diana-dowwy. The little girl wrapped both ankles around the chair, tightly hugged the doll, and blankly watched her momma lose control.

"You do something!" Jessie was screaming. "You take my baby to a doctor! You hear me?" Bolting to the mirror, she hammered on it with both fists flailing, not for the first time. "He's sick! Can't you see how sick he is?! Have some goddamned mercy!"

On the other side, Morgan was retching as he watched the little tirade. He had his laptop with him today, with a Jessie Wheeler YouTube playlist on shuffle. Her beautiful voice lilted in waves over his heart as he listened in counterpoint to the hysterical screaming emanating from the small suite opposite him.

The thing is, he knew the baby was sick. David had been ill for more than two weeks now, starting with just a runny nose and a cough, but the cough had escalated over this last while. Morgan had Jessie and her kids under his thumb for five weeks now, since November 12th. It was now December 17th.

The baby's illness was definitely a glitch in the plans. Despite the fact

27

that Josh was a basket case, Morgan planned to fly Nadia out west to introduce her to him at some point over the upcoming Christmas holidays, while she was on break from her job as an accountant's receptionist. The security team—including Morgan—was no longer watching Josh, at his insistence, but Josh wasn't leaving his house, either. He was supposed to be in Toronto working on *The Wyatt Boys* by now, but Jonathon McCloud had pushed the season's production schedule to January, to give his son time to pull himself together, which Morgan doubted would happen until…

Well, the plan for Nadia was to meet Josh on some pretense that Morgan was dropping by to say a Christmas 'hey.' And then, on Christmas Eve, Morgan and Nadia planned to give the guy back his kids. Not Jessie…just the kids. So when he started work again in January, well…he would need a nanny, wouldn't he? And Morgan's drop dead gorgeous 'stepsister,' as they would introduce her, with her exotic cheekbones and captivating dark eyes… not to mention perfect silky breasts…would be the first to come to mind.

But now…Morgan gulped painfully. The baby was definitely very ill. Jessie was frantic. She was throwing up from the effort it took to scream almost incessantly at the mirror, and her little girl was now tucked up in a ball in the far corner of the room, her arms wrapped around that silly doll she never seemed to ever let go of. Morgan could only see Emily-Grace's eyes, peeking out above the doll's raven yarn-made hair.

He contemplated the still body of the baby, lying in the center of the bed on the cheap beige comforter. Morgan could see the little chest moving up and down in sporadic bursts, as if it was working hard to pull air up from tiny, inflamed lungs. He recalled when Josh was hospitalized with pneumonia a few years ago, just after Morgan started working on Jessie's security team. The actor's breaths had sounded rattly and raspy, wet; like the breaths Morgan was now hearing from the miniscule hole he'd installed in the side of the mirror frame so Jessie wouldn't notice it.

Pulling the laptop towards him, he clicked on *file*, and then on *add new tab*. He opened his webmail and tapped in an email to Nadia.

Booking you a flight for today. Just come. No questions.

Jessie kept up her rant all night. By dawn, she was lying by her baby, cradling him from a fetal position, her long legs curled up around the fiery little body. Singing softly, she was running a hand over and over his damp hair. Her daughter was feathered into her mother's back, clutching her vacant staring Diana-dowwy, silent and lost in a solitary abyss of three-year-old fear.

By six, Nadia was at the house. At seven, a harsh click woke Jessie from a drifting stupor as the interior door by the mirror was unlocked. That door had not once been used the entire five weeks Jessie and her children were locked in the basement.

Jessie stirred, a mess of tears and snot, and stared at the door. Fast and hard, it was shoved open, which startled her. It was seven feet away from where she lay on the bed with her children. Instantly she tensed, and started to jump up, but then two balaclava clad faces rushed into the space. In a matter of seconds, one small feminine body had David in one arm and his stroller in the other hand, while the other person, the larger of the two, shoved Jessie down and scooped up Emily-Grace. They were out the door in seconds, Jessie on their tail screaming and clutching at her daughter. She tried to get through the door too, but the bigger of the two captors kicked her brutally in the stomach with a work-booted foot, knocking her rapidly backwards.

The last thing Emily-Grace heard as she was ruthlessly snatched from her mother's grasping fingers was her name and the demand, "You tell your daddy to be strong! Tell Daddy to be strong! Oh God! Please take them to their father, oh God please!"

When the door slammed in Jessie's face, she collapsed against it and howled. Bending over, she retched on the bare cement floor, and then she howled again and fell forward, her hair landing in her own vomit.

She didn't move for many hours; instead, she prayed endlessly. Every prayer Jessie knew by rote was spoken to a God she prayed would listen, as she lay there clutching her sore belly in the spot where the larger captor's boot had connected and knocked her down.

When she finally moved, something soft brushed against her hand. It was Emily-Grace's beloved Diana-dowwy.

"Oh, God," Jessie cried anew. She was inconsolable. "Oh sweet Jesus."

Holding the doll close to her heart, she turned on her side and moaned.

Like some wild animal, she was still locked up, only now her babies were gone. The children had been Jessie's constant companions over the last five weeks. They were her reason for living.

They were her light.

⁓ ⁓

Jennifer Evanista was running late. The African-Canadian wife of a Calgary police detective, she had been out the night before with her husband at a charity function for the Heart & Stroke Foundation, where she imbibed in one too many glasses of Merlot. Today, besides having exactly one hour to get to her book club meeting, she needed her usual evening run in order to work off some of the 1400 or so calories she figured she'd imbibed for the sake of the Heart & Stroke. Besides, dinner was too greasy tonight. She'd made lasagna, and with it came saucy Caesar salad and too much garlic bread. The calories were adding up. Jennifer needed a good run to sweat off the shit.

Initially, because of the time crunch, she hadn't been planning to run today. But Hank was at work—he was on the night shift this week. She was antsy. This was Jennifer's usual running time. And the book club would be a sedate *oh the narrative sucked* and *omigod the dialogue was dry* kinda deal, so she laced up her Nikes and headed out of the door.

She took her usual route—through a local park. Jennifer always jogged there—she liked the soft path because it made jogging easier on her knees, and there was a neat stone circular fountain there where, in summer, little kids tossed pennies over their shoulders for luck. Jogging by it always brought back sweet memories of happy children. But this time of the year, a week before Christmas, kids were at hockey or gymnastics. It was too cold to be tossing pennies in the fountain. Anyways, the pennies would just bounce off tonight—the fountain was iced over.

But there was a child there, at the fountain, when Jennifer jogged by. There was a stroller, too, one of those expensive ones with big tires that young moms could jog behind. Jennifer slowed down. She looked around her for the ubiquitous adult that always accompanied small children. She wanted to give her—or him—a piece of her mind, because the little girl was shivering to beat the band, dressed in only a light sweater and denims. Thankfully, she seemed to be wearing little work boots, though. She was wringing her hands, as if she was used to holding something that was missing.

The child was crying—well, not exactly crying, the sound she was making was more of a moan, really. It was a constant sound, not an up and down ambulance siren kind of crocodile tear sound. It was tremulous and fearful, and the child's eyes were fretfully darting from side to side.

Catching her breath, Jennifer jogged lightly over, looking from side to side for a parent as she moved. She bent down in front of the little girl, whom, she realized, was actually saying something as she moaned.

I want Momma I want Momma I want Momma—again and again.

The child wouldn't meet Jennifer's eyes, even when the gentle dark-skinned woman tried to get her attention with, "Honey, where is your mother?" Instead, the quaking youngster, who Jennifer figured for about three years old, was wide-eyed and guarded.

"I don't believe this," Jennifer said aloud. She touched the little girl's hands. They were ice. She was trembling so hard Jennifer thought she might fall right off the edge of the fountain where she was sitting.

Still grasping the little girl's cold fingers, she stood and peeked into the stroller. The child lying prone inside was covered with a couple of blankets, a crocheted green and white striped one, and some kind of colorful pastel quilt with baby animals appliqued throughout. Something about his breathing bothered Jennifer. It was raspy, forced. She touched his cheek.

"You're burning up, little guy," she said to him, incredulous that there were no parents around these two beautiful blonde children. Then she sucked in a breath. She fingered the baby quilt. It was homemade, original. And, for the last five weeks, it was all over the news.

"God in Heaven," Jennifer exclaimed. "No way."

Bending back down to the shivering child, she placed her hands on the small shoulders. "What's your name, pretty girl? Hmmm? My name is Jennifer. Tell me what your name is." She rubbed the bony shoulders to try to get some warmth moving through the little girl.

Finally, Emily-Grace met the woman's eyes. She didn't offer her name, instead she just continued to moan for her momma. But her features were highly recognizable, not just from the last spate of publicity surrounding her disappearance, but from the many public photos gracing the rag bags—pictures of her in her mother's arms, or walking beside her father, always with a big smile, all sunshine and rainbows. As were her parents, in those photos.

"Parents," stuttered Jennifer, as the shock of who these two babes were sank into her bones. Stunned, she stood, pulling Emily-Grace up with her and, as she wrapped her arms tightly around the poker-stiff, terrified child, she whipped around and looked for Jessie Wheeler. She darted around the fountain, at the same time yanking her cell out of her pocket and speed-dialing her husband. She was afraid to look in the fountain, but she did anyway, then she exhaled in relief. No body in there...Jennifer shivered.

Hank answered on the first ring. "Honey, I'm on my way into a meeting, can I call you back?"

"No, actually, no, Hank. You need to skip that meeting. Get a car to Helen James Park. And an ambulance. This second."

Hank knew his wife. He discerned the urgency in her voice. "Jen? Are you okay?"

"Yes, Hank, I'm fine, but I have two small children in my possession who are not. Call that ambulance, and then Hank? Call your friend on the force in Vancouver. I've got Josh Sawyer's baby girl in my arms. And his son is in a stroller at my fingertips."

The line was silent for a moment. "Honey, are you—"

"Damn straight I'm sure, Hank. I'm taking them to the curb on Pleasant Street. And there better damn well be an ambulance waiting for me when I get there."

As Jennifer started to walk, Emily-Grace's moan changed and became wordless. She had heard her father's name, and she sensed the panic in this kind woman's voice. Slowly, as the woman's footsteps thudded gently on the path below, Emily-Grace let her little bones sink into the safety and warmth the woman's body offered.

Jennifer paused only for a moment, just long enough to reach into the stroller and grab the crocheted coverlet. She blanketed it around her shivering bundle before resuming her hasty march to the curb, cradling Josh and Jessie Sawyer's little girl in one arm, and hauling their baby boy along with the other.

In the distance, she soon detected the wail of an ambulance.

At the police station, Hank jumped into his car.

In Jennifer's arms, Emily-Grace went silent.

Chapter Five

*A*s Dee hurriedly threw clothes into a suitcase, Charles speed-dialed Steve.

"Get Josh to the jet. We're leaving the second we get there."

Steve was on his way down the produce aisle at the local Whole Foods. Dumping his shopping basket on a pile of wet, wilted kale, he hoofed it towards the door. "What's going on, Charles?"

Five long weeks with nothing. Five long weeks of trying to function, on at least some barely navigable level, with no news. Josh barely left his house. Dee didn't, although at three weeks she was finally coerced out of bed.

Steve held the phone to his ear and waited.

"The kids," Charles managed to utter, the two simple words weighted for Steve in ways that took a few moments to sink in.

"Charles, tell me. What about the kids?"

"They're in Calgary. At the Alberta Children's Hospital. A jogger found them in a park."

"And Jessie?"

Silence. Then, "No. Just the kids. Get Josh, Steve. And come with him, please?" It was as if the esteemed producer was begging for help, for someone he felt was stronger than he and his society wife to handle the emotion this reunion was going to engender. And no way was Josh going to be that rock. Not today.

In ten minutes, Charles and Deirdre were hurrying downstairs to their car. As Ulysses slammed the passenger side door behind Dee, Steve barged into Josh's home.

"Where are you, Sawyer? Where're you hiding?"

He found his friend downstairs in the media room, asleep on the black leather couch with one of Emily-Grace's dolls cradled in his arms. Steve didn't wait for him to be fully awake. Grabbing Josh roughly by the arm, he hauled him to a standing position.

Josh blinked at him and tried to sit back down. "Lemme go," he demanded, as Steve yanked on his arm again.

"Get some shit packed. They found your kids."

Only then, as the two good friends met each other's eyes, did Steve lose it. Adrenalin had pumped him from Whole Foods to the Sawyer home—now, emotion took over. He couldn't control the sobs that escaped—five interminable weeks of waiting and wondering. The kids were at a hospital but Steve hadn't asked why the hell they were there. He'd just assumed it was a protocol thing but now, as he stared into Josh's eyes waiting for him to start asking questions, he was painfully aware of how inadequate his responses were going to be.

He was crying, backing away from Josh, and telling him to hurry. When Josh finally moved, he shoved past his friend and vaulted up the steps three at a time. He didn't ask a single question, he just bounded up the steps and into the playroom on the top level of the home. There, he grabbed one toy for each of his children, and then he went into the bedroom he shared with Jessie and pulled open the door of a jewelry box. He rooted around for the locket he'd given her for Christmas the year he proposed. Finding it, he looped it around his fingers and watched it sparkle as it moved under the overhead light.

A hand came into view and stopped it from moving. "Not Jessie," came Steve's husky voice. "Just the kids. For now," he added hopefully as Josh closed his eyes and deflated in front of him.

They got to the jet only a few minutes behind Charles and Dee, since Josh and Jessie's house was closer to the airport. The flight to Calgary was the longest any of them had ever taken, including the crazy haul from Toronto to Vancouver the night Emily-Grace was born.

In Calgary, Hank was waiting at a private gate. He escorted Charles, Dee and Ulysses into his own vehicle, a Mazda SUV, and motioned for Josh and Steve to climb into another vehicle driven by a female detective on the force. Marked cruisers were not an option for these celebrity folks on this particular hospital run.

It was eleven o'clock by the time the third floor elevator door slid open at the Alberta Children's Hospital on the Shaganappi Trail. By then, Josh had spoken exactly three words—*are they okay?*

He didn't dare ask about Jessie yet. Hearing something negative about her fate was not something he was prepared to handle. No one was offering anything, so he remained mute on that account, praying silently with every ounce of hope he had at his disposal.

No one spoke in the cars, except for Hank, who shared with Charles and Dee the little he knew. At the hospital, the elevator ride was also mostly silent with the exception of the elevator's own whooshing and clanging.

In the hall, Josh started down the wrong way, going to the right. Hank took his elbow, gently, and turned him around. His breathing coming in short rasps, Josh faced the unknown with a mixture of trepidation and silent hope. His earlier three words had brought him the unwelcome news that his son was very sick, and that his daughter was being treated for a mild case of hypothermia. Now, he was told by the doctor who met them on the third floor to approach Emily-Grace with caution.

"She's a very upset little girl, Mr. Sawyer. Physically she's fine, she needed to be warmed up, but she's okay. Emotionally, she's exhibiting signs of trauma. I suggest you approach her carefully, since she hasn't seen you in a while and…well, she's too young to tell any of us what she's been through— where she's been, or what she witnessed."

It was the chilling truth. Eyes wide, Josh looked sideways at the doctor, who was a greying man in a white lab coat, which seemed kind of old fashioned in a weird, detached way to Josh as he walked alongside him. Steve, who flanked Josh's other side, extended an arm and gripped his buddy's shoulder.

When they reached the room where Emily-Grace was being rocked by a young blonde nurse around Jessie's age, Charles took Deirdre's hand to keep her from barging in. Steve, too, stood back.

On trembling legs, Josh was the only one to move forward. He stepped quietly into the private room and bent in front of his daughter, who was half asleep on the woman's lap, a pair of pink bunny-ear onesie pajamas on, and a hypothermic warming blanket around her body.

Josh met the ponytailed nurse's eyes first. They were a pale hazel, flecked with light. She nodded, encouraging him. Her small smile telegraphed confidence that she knew for certain this child was Josh's daughter.

Of course, Josh thought, realizing what she was wordlessly telling him. *The whole world knows what my child looks like.*

Heart racing, he forced his eyes to drift downward.

"Emily-Grace?" he asked, his voice quaking as he tentatively reached his right hand out to touch his daughter.

He drew back, afraid. This whole last five weeks had been so fucking unreal, and he'd dreamed so many times…the usual golden field dream, yes, but new ones, also, ones where he was with Jessie and the children, happy happy happy, joyous, even, and then he'd awoken to find only empty arms and a house filled with sadness. Was this real? Was this truly his daughter, or had someone made a mistake? He refused to believe she was real until she was in his arms.

Finally, Josh got up the nerve to move the blonde ringlets back from the child's face. The little cheeks were pink now, warm finally, after her wait in the icy park. The pale eyes were sleepy, but they wavered, and as Emily-Grace lifted her head and met her daddy's frightened eyes, Josh found he couldn't be that strong man the doctor asked him to be. He couldn't wait for his daughter to come to him. Reaching under the small arms, he picked Emily-Grace up off the kind nurse's lap, and he held her against him.

He turned away from everyone else whose eyes were drawn to this tender reunion.

Josh carried his daughter to the far side of the room, past the crib, towards the wall where he could hide in the semi-darkness. His shoulders shook as he cradled his firstborn, and as a thousand thoughts careened around his head—where have you been, is your baby brother okay, where is your momma?—he was overtaken by heavy sobs, sobs earned from the last five weeks of watching, waiting, and wondering.

His little girl lifted her head long enough to look at him. She placed both hands on his cheeks. "My daddy," she said simply, eyelids heavy with emotion and fatigue, and with the memory of a horrific separation from her mother still fresh in her young mind.

Josh wrapped his large fingers around her small hand and kissed it. "My Emily-Grace," he echoed, his chest heavy and aching.

Then the small eyes misted over and the equally small chest heaved with great hulking cries, yet still Emily-Grace's hands remained on her daddy's cheeks, as if she couldn't believe he was real if she wasn't touching him.

"It's okay," Josh told his daughter once he got his wits back. She shook in his arms as the heavy weight of the day overtook her. "You're safe now, Emily-Grace. You're coming home." He leaned his face into hers and inhaled. She smelled of baby soap and lemon. He guessed rightly the nurses had bathed her. Josh felt a burden lift that he had carried now for much too long. His daughter was safe in his arms, finally, and his son was down the hall. As for his wife…he shook the thought away. Tonight was about his children. It had to be.

"Are you tired, sweet girl?" he murmured to his daughter. At her nod, he cradled her into the hollow of his neck and whispered, "Sleep, Emily-Grace. Grammie wants to see you but it's okay, you just sleep in Daddy's arms and Grammie can just kiss you for now. You can see her in the morning, okay?"

"Diana-dowwy. I want Diana-dowwy."

He stilled, and then dared to rasp, "Is she with Momma?"

Josh felt her body tense. No answer was forthcoming. Instead, his child lifted her arms and wrapped them around his neck. Little sobs were buried in Josh's hair.

As Emily-Grace drifted off, small arms around her daddy and pink lips against his neck, Josh whispered one last teary sentiment into the feathery ear. "I love you, baby girl. Daddy loves you."

Dee couldn't stand it. She wasn't about to wait one more moment. The nurse had quietly crept out of the room and, as she did, Deirdre made her way in. Josh felt her hand on his back, first, and her familiar floral scent wafted by on some invisible airflow. She touched Emily-Grace's head, but the little girl had already dozed off, to some happy place of sunshine and rainbows, Josh hoped.

"She's so beautiful, Josh," Dee swooned. "So beautiful."

They strode down the hall to see David, then. He was tented to increase his oxygen flow, and was on an intravenous antibiotic drip for pneumonia. Watching the painful rise and fall of his chest, Josh was acutely aware of the effort it took to breathe. His own experience with pneumonia was not that far distant a memory.

The doctor's honest assessment of David's prognosis was chilling.

"He's been a very sick baby for far too long, Mr. Sawyer. There is a lot of fluid around your baby's lungs. But we're doing our best. We're hoping for the best."

The nightmare was far from over.

In the wee hours of the morning, Josh creaked back and forth on the steady rhythm of the wooden rocking chair in his baby son's room. He had tried twice to put his daughter down on a cot an orderly brought in for him, but still she was in his arms. Both times she had mewled and clung to him. And this was one night Josh was not about to enforce some parental code about having her sleep in her own bed.

As the rocker creaked and groaned, he had a lot of time to think. At first his thoughts were scattered, uncoordinated, but then, with the regular buzz in the hallway outside, the steady cadence of Emily-Grace's heart against his chest, and the soothing rhythm of the rocker, Josh's mind steadied.

First, he pondered this strange new turn of events. His children were here, with him, after five torturous weeks of unknowns. Jessie's whereabouts were still a mystery. She had a history of running away, but this time there seemed to be clear evidence her leaving was not of her own volition. Josh knew her; even if she had set the whole thing up, she would not return her children to him at the last second, with their son at death's door.

Also worth considering was that she was not the same woman now. In the last few years she had grown confident and assured in his love for her, in her sister Sara's love for her, in the love all their friends had for her. Things had settled somewhat with Charles and Dee, Jessie was making music, she was doing film and television and, as far as he could tell, she was blissfully happy. Once in a while, she lamented Matt's departure from their lives, but Josh knew she was still in touch with him, occasionally at least, and she saw him in Miami while *Mystic Nights* was shooting, since he was in charge of Kelly and Michael's security now.

No, she wouldn't have orchestrated this.

His son moved in the crib. Aching to hold him, Josh cringed. The wet gurgles from the child's lungs contained their own bleak terror. Every rasp was a struggle. Doctors and nurses were in constantly, monitoring vitals, checking oxygen…the minutes ticked by slowly. Was David going to survive this? How did Jessie stand it, watching him get sicker, worrying and wondering? Had Jessie even been with her children?

Emily-Grace provided no clues. Maybe tomorrow, after she slept, they could glean something from her—anything. The detective, Hank, was back and forth from the park where the children were found by his wife, which he told Josh earlier may have been carefully orchestrated. Maybe someone was aware that Jennifer usually jogged at that time and on that route daily… someone who knew she was married to a detective…Jennifer wrote a blog about running. In it, she mentioned that route, that fountain. Whoever dropped off the children likely hoped Jennifer would have, over the years, picked up Hank's detective mindset, and would therefore wonder why two small children were alone in a freezing park in very little clothing.

The kids were meant to be found. Likely whoever left them was watching, even, which meant they had some level of compassion. Which boded well for Jessie, he hoped.

Even now, Hank assured Josh the Calgary police were canvassing the area, searching the park, trying to find signs of anything that would lead them to clues of her whereabouts. What was left unsaid was that they were also unearthing frozen dead leaves, warily looking for a body.

David moved again, jarring Josh's thoughts back to him. The baby let out a little cry and shifted his legs. Then he seemed to settle again, but every movement was a new terror for a father watching over a very sick child. *What was it like for you, Jessie, when you watched over me that time,* Josh wondered. *I feel your pain.*

He closed his eyes as sleep tried to overtake him. He told himself it was just for a minute, but waves of fatigue were accosting him. Fearful of dropping his daughter if he fell asleep, Josh considered lying down on the cot. But he was afraid. If David should…well, if David…the thought was unthinkable.

Soft footsteps made their way into the room. Deirdre lightly touched his shoulder.

"Let me try to take her, Josh," she offered.

He thought about saying no, because having the child back was a dream, and Josh was half afraid that if he let Emily-Grace go she would be gone forever. But he needed to take a piss, and the little movements towards the washroom might jar his body more awake. Agreeing, he handed Emily-Grace to her grandmother. She drifted over to Dee, who sat on the edge of the cot and cuddled the child, but before Josh got out of the bathroom in the private room she was half-awake, twisting around and starting to cry for her daddy.

Vaulting the last few steps, Josh avoided the hurt tears in Deirdre's eyes.

"C'mere, baby," he whispered, lifting Emily-Grace out of Dee's arms. As Charles wandered in and settled beside Dee, Josh told his daughter, "Daddy was just in the bathroom, sweetheart. Real close by."

Emily-Grace inserted a thumb in her mouth, something Josh had never before seen her do, and with her other hand she grasped his right thumb. He was holding her seated on his lap now, and she leaned back into the crook of his left arm, curled her legs up, and leaned into his heart. The small eyes remained open and lost in his until she could no longer fight the sandman.

Josh sighed. Without taking his gaze off his daughter's cherubic face, he spoke to Charles and Dee. "Whatever happened, she's traumatized." Then, he looked up at Dee. "You and Emily-Grace were a team. I had to fight the two of you to get her to come to me."

Dee laid a hand on his arm. "She just got her daddy back, Josh. We understand. We'll be here when she's ready for us."

"She's fine, otherwise," Josh admitted gratefully. "The doctor said she is a healthy little girl. A Band-Aid on her knee, that's it. Thank God," he added painfully. "She's been fed and well taken care of."

"Then she's been with her mother." Charles wrapped an arm around his wife's waist. He regarded Josh with an air of confidence Josh simply didn't feel. He intuited that Hank's police crew was somewhere out there rooting through leaves looking for Jessie's body.

41

SUSAN RODGERS

"I can't stand it," he moaned. "We thought...after the last time...I wanted to trust happiness. To think it was possible. Forever. But why...?" Josh choked up then.

Dee added her thoughts. "It is possible, Josh. You know, because you have it."

"Past tense," he bit off to her. "This is all just one big nightmare."

David moved in the crib again, and Josh jumped. Charles saw the flicker of fear zip across his sort-of son-in-law's face, and then disappear as Josh exhaled slowly and settled back in the rocking chair.

"Someone cared for your children, Josh. They made sure they were found last night. Jessie's—"

"Jessie's what, Charles? Out there somewhere? She wouldn't leave her children. She wouldn't let David get this sick. She wouldn't leave our babies, Charles." Josh implored Charles to understand what he was feeling, so he wouldn't have to bear the weight alone. "Emily-Grace won't let me put her down. Something bad happened, and she saw it. You saw her cry earlier. She's heartbroken. She wants her momma. But for all we know, she hasn't had her momma since the day they were taken!"

"We can't think that way, Josh. We need to believe Jessie's okay. That she cared for these kids, that somehow maybe it was her who orchestrated getting them to a park five miles away from the best children's hospital in Alberta. Close to her Aunt Evelyn, by the way, who's on her way in from Canmore with her husband."

Leaning closer to Josh, he clapped him on the knee. "We're halfway there. We have your kids back, Emily-Grace will rebound, and David is being pumped full of oxygen and antibiotics. Next, we see what information we can glean from Emily-Grace, and we bring Jessie home. And in the meantime," he sat back again, "we trust Jessie to do what she does best. We trust her to survive."

Chapter Six

Jacob wasn't a 'shopping' kind of guy. Kelly Reilly could attest to that; she was always bugging him to get some new clothes. It wasn't like he couldn't afford it, and these days he had access to a stylist for far more important shindigs than Starbucks runs and dark gigs in Scottish pubs, so regular shopping wasn't generally on his mind. Even more so, he simply didn't give a shit about superficial things like fashion.

According to Jessie, he always looked adorable anyway. She was always grinning at him and yanking up the collar of his plaid shirt so it wouldn't fall off his shoulder all the time. And she still seemed to love hugging the old flannel standbys. 'Cuz she hugged him a lot. She touched him a lot. There was always an arm around his, or her head on his shoulder. Sometimes she even stuck a finger in his belt loop when she was talking to him, just casual like, although to Jacob those little overtures always gave him shivers. Hell, looking into those soulful, pale blue eyes still gave him shivers.

Today, he was wandering down the aisle of a children's toy store, feeling a little lost as he shuffled between neatly stacked shelves of blocks and action figures. He stalked uncomfortably around until he found a section peopled with dolls—rag dolls, baby dolls, fashion dolls, all different sizes, shapes, and hair colors. He had flown into Vancouver that morning after doing a sleepless overnighter on a commercial flight, after leaving the *Mystic Nights* set in Miami around midnight. Thankfully, working on the hot American show was comfortable for him these days. The cast and crew were like family in this umpteenth season, although the family was broken with Jessie gone and her character written in as 'on tour in Europe.' Doubly thankfully, apart from sympathetic gazes tossed in his direction, the other travellers left his depressed star ass alone.

Jacob wanted to see Emily-Grace and David. He needed to eyeball them, to make sure they were okay, and he needed to give them his love and his healing energy. And he needed to be one degree of separation from Jessie. He and Emily-Grace were one and the same. They were inseparable when the little girl was with her momma in Miami. He and she played dolls on the floor in Jessie's suite, and Jacob could now recite the names of each and every one of the Disney princesses.

Sometimes he'd sit on the floor in Jessie's suite and play guitar for Emily-Grace while she spun around in her adorable pink tutu and pretend to be a ballerina. And sometimes she would sit on her bum in front of him, busy hands relaxing for once on her knees, as she leaned into him and sang along while he played guitar. In her own childish way, she knew all the words to most of Jacob and Jessie's songs.

Sometimes Jacob let himself believe Emily-Grace was his and Jessie's daughter. Hell, he probably spent as much time with her as her real daddy did, since her parents were always jet setting here and there for work. He knew her. And after he landed in Van he had been told by Charles on the phone that she was inconsolable without her Diana-dowwy, so inconsolable that Dee had gone so far as to order her a replacement from Prince Edward Island. But in the meantime…

Jacob stopped in front of a display of similar eight-inch high soft microfiber dolls with yarn hair. He figured someone in the universe was paying attention to their plight, to missing-found children and a still missing momma. Because here in front of him was not a Diana doll, or even a similar Anne of Green Gables doll, for that matter. No, the doll now in front of Jacob had brown-red hair and jeans and a big peaceful smile, and an acoustic guitar sewn to her hand and belly. She could have been Jessie Wheeler. She could have been Emily-Grace's momma.

Plucking the doll off the shelf, he held it with two hands. His doe eyes were reflective, sad. "I don't know if this little girl will want you," he said to the smiling eyes, "but if she doesn't, I'll keep you safe." Picturing the amused astonishment on Jessie's face if someday she came to visit and found a doll that looked like her on his pillow, Jacob would have doubled over laughing had he not been tired and physically sick with worry over Jessie's whereabouts and safety. A mere half-smile graced his lips instead.

He had his wallet out before he got to the counter.

Twenty minutes later, Jacob was tensely seated in Charlie's newest 911, one hand clutching the bag from the toy store and the other white-knuckling a knee. The guys were on their way to the airport, where the Keating jet was waiting. Morgan would meet them there. At this juncture, everyone was worried about everyone else's security. Morgan would travel with them to Calgary.

Both Jacob and Charlie were grim, so talk in the car was brief.

"News?"

"They haven't found anything," was Charlie's quiet response. "Meaning in the park, at least. But I'm hearing the cops are going through every discarded candy wrapper and faded Starbucks cup within a five mile radius."

"Mmphh," was Jacob's terse answer. He wrapped his knuckles tighter around the hemp handles of the bag with the doll in it and stared out of the window as Charlie headed up Granville Street towards the airport.

Charlie took advantage of his passenger's silence to lay down the law. "You are not to antagonize Josh, Jacob." He glanced sideways at the quiet guy next to him. "Orders from the top." Softening, he added, "Steve told me you and Josh almost put each other through his glass door last time you saw each other."

Silent, Jacob just stared at the tightly packed clapboard homes and low bricked apartment buildings as they slid by.

"Y'hear, Jacob? He just got his kids back. No one knows if Jessie's alive or dead. You see the kids and you leave the guy alone."

At that, Jacob whipped his head around to glare at Charlie. "Jesus, you asshole. Can you maybe not refer to Jessie that way?"

Hesitating, Charlie struggled for words with the power to console his passenger without setting him off. He went with a realistic apology. "I'm sorry, buddy. But it's something we have to consider."

"Hey, it wasn't so bad last time, remember?" Jacob threw the half-assed attempt at lightheartedness in carelessly, a little wildly, even. "When she disappeared? She was in Scotland fucking me. Maybe she's just off on another dreamy adventure with some other love-struck loser." Settling into his seat, he raised his left ankle, which Jacob then dropped over his right knee. "I know none of you think she's dead. Her kids aren't, so why would she be?"

"Because she didn't show up with her fucking kids, that's why. That's fucking why, Jacob." Instantly remorseful, Charlie emitted a slow *ppffftt* and avoided glancing over at Jacob to see how the guy took that rather heartless declaration. He knifed long fingers through his dark hair and tried rather unsuccessfully to settle his nerves by practicing a few deep Yoga breaths.

The rest of the drive was spent in stark silence. When the men met Morgan at the jet, they were too riled up to look at him long enough to notice the dark circles under his eyes, or his rather noticeable weight loss.

In Calgary, Steve noticed. He crinkled his eyes at Morgan, then clapped a hand on the guy's broad shoulder. "You okay, buddy? You don't look so good. You're getting too skinny for the body-builder type." He appraised him critically. "You're losing weight faster than a cow with tapeworm."

Unable to meet his eyes, Morgan just shrugged. Steve walked away thinking *geez, poor kid, he misses Jessie as much as the rest of us,* and he resolved to be more sensitive to the security team who, over the last five weeks, were all on constant alert.

During the day, Josh and Emily-Grace had been moved into a tiny suite off David's new room. To everyone's relief, the baby was responding to the antibiotics and was out of the ICU by the time Charlie and Jacob arrived at six p.m. Evelyn and Gary had been in to visit, their matching ponytails bobbing with relief, and were now someplace in the cowtown city having dinner with Charles and Dee.

After greeting Morgan and his charges, Steve joined Josh in David's room, where he stooped over, picked up the small baby, and sat quietly so he could cradle him in his arms. Jacob and Charlie's shadows darkened the room's doorway right after him.

Anxious to see how David was doing, Morgan hovered behind. He was afraid to look at Josh, who had spent the day in a rocking chair with his daughter silently snuggled up to his chest, her head ducked down behind a cascade of blonde ringlets. Now, one delicate set of fingers was absently playing with her daddy's pale yellow vintage shirt collar.

Josh looked up when the guys entered, but he glanced away when Jacob tried to meet his eyes. He, too, had been warned not to start something with Jessie's co-star and musical partner, *for the kids' sake.*

Steve broke the silence as he studied the baby he was settling in his arms. "David's better. He's coming around."

Outside, Morgan almost collapsed with relief. He tiptoed a little down the hall to text Nadia the good news.

"Thank God." Charlie touched the top of the baby's head. "He's grown," he noted vaguely, wondering, remembering his own daughter's rapid growth in the first year of her young life. He looked just behind and beside him at his travelling partner. Jacob was staring at Emily-Grace. He seemed to be struggling with five weeks of pent-up agony, judging by the way he was shifting his feet and running fingers through his longish curls.

"You okay, Jacob?" Charlie actually thought the guy might pass out. He was an interesting shade of greenish-pale.

Something jarred Emily-Grace at that simple query. Lifting her head, she stopped fidgeting with her daddy's collar. Eyes on the floor, she spotted the old brown boots she loved on the feet of a man who was like a second father to her—on the feet of a man who took the time to play with her and take her to the playground and dance with her. Who she knew loved her mother, who she also knew loved him back.

Her face remained expressionless, but she pushed herself up higher on her daddy's lap so she could look up and meet Jacob's heartbroken eyes. A tiny wail escaped her lips then as she crumbled, and she leaned forward and reached out her arms.

Surprised, Josh let her go.

Dropping the paper bag with the doll in it, Jacob lifted the little girl.

"Oh, you got big," he whispered in her neck. "You musta ate a lotta peach pie with your momma this last little while." Then he did what Josh did late the night before—he turned his back on the rather shocked faces in the room, and walked a few feet away. Jacob knew better than to take the child out of her father's sight, but he didn't need to see Josh's stare while he welcomed

Jessie's little girl back into his arms. He sure as hell felt the glower slice his back, though, like a hot searing knife. He practically tensed for the twist he felt was coming.

Emily-Grace was doing her little moaning thing again; it was a sound that seemed to come from somewhere deep within her little soul. It was a sound the four guys all recognized as coming from a place of deep pain.

Steve turned his head away from Jacob's back, towards Josh. Handing him his son, he carefully juggled the various tubes still attached to the baby.

"I missed you," they all heard Jacob's pouty voice saying to Jessie and Josh's daughter. "You're my girl, and I missed you. I had no one to play dolls with."

The soft words calmed her down. From somewhere in Jacob's curls Emily-Grace's voice was heard for the first time that day, other than to tell her daddy she needed to pee. "Missed u too, Jacob. Momma missing you."

Another shocked silence filled the room. How recently was Jessie apparently missing Jacob? Josh caught his breath.

Jacob heard Josh's quick intake of breath, but he didn't turn or look up. He knew what he would see—a confused mixture of death rays and, perhaps, hope. Instead, Jacob simply said to the little girl in his arms, "I brought you something."

She backed off a little then and looked at him. "What you bwing me?" A small hand brushed a stray wisp of hair out of Emily-Grace's right eye.

"Well," Jacob replied, turning then and moving towards the paper bag on the floor, "I heard you are missing Diana-dowwy."

Hiccupping sobs were her reply. Jacob set Jessie's daughter down on the floor beside him as he bent over the paper bag. All the while, Josh and Steve were thinking sarcastically, *good luck, Ryan*. They knew how well Dee's earlier attempts to replace Diana-dowwy had gone.

Jacob's hand disappeared inside the bag. Pulling out the soft doll with the guitar, he held her out to Emily-Grace. In a tender voice, he sang a few lines of one of his and Jessie's duets he knew she liked.

The little girl sucked in a tiny breath and placed both hands over her mouth. Then she breathed, "Momma." A new round of hiccuppy sobs started then, but she accepted the doll and pulled her towards her heart.

Josh moved for her then, but he was full of baby David and various bits of tubing, so he didn't get far. Jacob ignored the movement and, with love for this child playing across his eyes, he picked her up again. Rubbing her back, he soothed her as Emily-Grace nestled into him. "Now we can sing songs together, you and me again, Emily-Grace. You want to sing some songs?" He looked over at Josh, finally, whose nerve on his cheek was twitching intermittently. "I am guessing they have popsicles around here somewhere. At least, a hospital did when I was a kid and had my tonsils out. You mind if we go look?"

Josh's eyes darted down to his daughter. She was still hiccupping a little, but she was, to his amazement, clinging to the doll, and despite her proclamation that the doll looked like her momma, which obviously was painful for her, she wasn't letting go. She was touching its face, its guitar, its feet. And she was calming. He could see it in the small face. Having this doll to hang on to was a blessing.

"Let Jacob take her for a little walk, Josh," offered Steve congenially, his voice quiet and soothing. "You need some time with this little fellow. And he needs his daddy's arms around him."

Josh exhaled and nodded his gratitude to Jacob. "All right," he agreed, the words husky with emotion and fatigue. "But not too long, okay, Ryan? And not off this floor."

"Okay," was Jacob's relieved response. "Thanks." Then, to Emily-Grace he said, "Let's you and me sing our way to the popsicles." He moved towards the door. Outside, his voice in song drifted down the hallway. Once in a while, a little hum or sound from Emily-Grace could be heard. The guys in the room melted.

Josh shook his head at the smiling Steve. "Damn that guy. Jesus. What is it with him and the Sawyer women?"

"It's those puppy dog eyes." Charlie guffawed and took a seat on a chair he hauled over from the far wall.

"It's the music," replied Steve, chuckling. "I think you may have another singer on your hands, Josh."

"We're getting out of this fucked up business," was Josh's stark answer, which quickly brought the room to a renewed somber tone. "No more. I've had it. With stalkers, with kidnappers, with being in the spotlight. I want my girl back, and when I get her I'm moving her and the kids to fucking Timbuctoo."

Charlie harrumphed. "That'd be letting the asshole win, Josh. Your career is on fire. So's Jessie's, to no one's surprise."

"We're always a target, Charlie." Josh waved a hand to include Steve across from him. "Don't you guys get sick of it? All the tabloid bullshit? People always trying to snap photos of your kids? The complete lack of privacy? And then…this?"

"We like what we do, Josh, " Steve stated matter-of-factly. "No one has the right to take that away from us."

"No, but they can take our kids. Hurt our families. Seems to me they're taking the right, Steve." In his arms, David stirred. He opened his eyes and peered up at his daddy. The tiniest smile played across his lips before the eyes flitted shut and he dissolved back into dreamland.

"You have to get through this, Josh," Charlie told him directly. As the sort-of adopted older brother, his word was generally listened to. "You've got these two beautiful children back, so you have to be strong. You've got to go back to Vancouver and trust Jessie to also get through this, wherever the hell she is. Those two little kids need you."

"Yeah, man," agreed Steve. "Take some time with them, Josh. Then hire a nanny and get back to work. Don't give in to this creep, whoever he is."

Outside the door again, Morgan was silently gloating. Lifting his phone, he texted Nadia one more time. He had to be careful because he, like everyone else in Jessie's circle, was still being closely scrutinized, at least in terms of being interviewed. So his text was simple: *Moving forward.* Any investigator reading that might simply think it meant the kids were home and all was well. As Morgan tucked the phone away, he reflected that Nadia wouldn't get the message until she reached Toronto. She was flying now, her time out west only long enough to drive the kids to Calgary. She had slept for the night and was, at this moment, on her way back east.

A young nurse bustled in and checked David's vitals for the umpteenth time that day. "He's doing great, Mr. Sawyer," she said shyly. Josh blushed a little, and ducked his eyes away. The way women looked at him…sometimes it was overwhelming.

The nurse hustled out, eyes on the floor.

"Are Zach and Hil flying in?" asked Charlie, trying to lighten things up a little. "Kayla and Paul too?"

"Tomorrow," Josh asserted.

"Josh, you and Jessie have always had some kind of weird telepathic connection." Steve jumped in with all he had left, a plea to some higher power he didn't really understand. "Send her strength. And start rebuilding your life. We're not going to forget about her, hell, who could? Her music's all over the radio! She would want you to live your life."

Josh was subdued as he responded to his friend. "She would never leave us in the dark again, Steve. Jessie would never leave without getting in touch if she could."

Steve sat back. "I know, man. We know."

There didn't seem to be anything more to say. After a bit, Josh handed the baby over to Charlie for a snuggle. He stood, stretched catlike, and then glanced over at the doorway.

"I wonder where the hell Jacob disappeared to with my daughter," he tossed into the room, well aware of the blatant—perhaps misplaced—irony of his comment. Grumbling, Josh stepped towards the open door, hands on his hips.

Hearing Jacob's husky voice coming from someplace down the hall, he started in that direction. Morgan was leaning against the wall just outside the room, staring at his phone. The kid almost dropped it when he spied Josh watching him. Shoving the cell in his pocket, he moved away from the wall. Drawing up his shoulders, the bodyguard faced Josh square on.

"Somethin' I can get for you, Josh?" he asked, his usual deference to his boss more high-pitched and nervous than usual.

Uncertain, Josh—like Steve—attributed Morgan's disheartened countenance to stress and grief. He knew the guy worshipped Jessie. Josh and Jessie had many silly play fights in bed with Josh teasing his wife about her love struck bodyguard. But now…something about the way the guy couldn't meet his eyes…Josh shook the thought away. No way could Morgan have driven his kids to a park in Calgary. The guy was always on standby when they needed him, either in TO, or minutes away in Van.

Geez, Josh chided himself. *Everybody's a fucking suspect.*

He swallowed, and answered the guy. "No. I'm good. Just..." Still some-what off-put, he waved a hand at the voice down the hall. "I was wondering where Jacob disappeared off to with my daughter."

Morgan was speechless. He stammered when he tried to respond. Josh clapped a hand on his shoulder as he walked by.

Rotating quietly to watch his boss stride away, Morgan started to trem-ble. He put a hand over his stomach to quell any possible eruption.

"Fuucckk," he cursed under his breath. "Nadia, you better get what you want soon. Because this is fucking killing me."

Morgan pictured Jessie in the basement space of the rented Langley home. He figured she was fine—he'd left plenty of food, he thought, and he lauded himself for even adding a few extra rolls of toilet paper. Knowing she was consumed with grief at the loss of her kids, he figured she'd just sleep any-way. Morgan didn't know how long he would be on Josh-and-the-kids duty, but realistically he figured it would only be a few days before Susanne or Dan replaced him.

A vibration in his pocket got his attention. Pulling his phone out with two fingers, he saw that a message from Nadia was to blame.

I can feel it coming in the air tonite. With one of those cursed ubiquitous smiley faces.

Groaning, Morgan replaced the cell in his jeans pocket without answer-ing, and he made a mental note to remind his wife to be more cryptic with her messages, lest the cops start to wonder what the hell she meant.

Leaning back against the wall again, he stared hopelessly at his toes.

Down the hall now, Josh paused and cocked his head. Jacob had appar-ently ducked into a small waiting area just off the main drag; he was playing with Emily-Grace's new doll, by the sound of things, although the sweet open laughter Josh was accustomed to hearing from his daughter at this kind of play was not forthcoming. He listened, and couldn't help but smile at Jacob's high-pitched put-on girly voice. Was the loser imitating Jessie?

"I have five minutes 'til I need to be on stage. I must find Jacob so I can do my vocal warm-up with him. But ohhh, Emily-Grace, I need to touch up my mascara. All this laughing and playing with you got me all sweaty, and it's starting to run!"

Nah, that's Kelly, Josh grinned. He made a move to step forward, but stopped when he saw the absence of light in Emily-Grace's pale eyes. The child was sitting on Jacob's lap facing the hall, so Josh could see her, although she didn't notice him. Jacob did, though. He caught Josh's eye. The pain Josh spied there erased any hint of lightheartedness. Because, although Josh thought his daughter was doing better with Jacob, and maybe coming out of her pain somewhat, the gloomy expression on her pinched cheeks said otherwise.

But Jacob had her attention, at least, if not the smiles he was used to, so he detached himself from Josh's gaze and inhaled. Then he started to sing, as the doll. As Jessie.

A few soft lines floated in the air before Josh saw his daughter's pink lips part. Emily-Grace angled her head just slightly as she fingered the doll Jacob was holding before her.

She spoke.

"Diana-dowwy sing too. She sing songs wif Momma."

"Yeah." Jacob stopped singing and answered her. "We used to do that at the hotel in Miami, didn't we? We had concerts with Diana-dowwy. She's a good singer. Like your momma."

Emily-Grace appeared not to hear him. Her eyes crinkled thoughtfully as she lightly brushed a finger down the hair of the new doll. "Momma make her sing the wainbow song. That her favowite."

"Yeah. Mine too, I think." Jacob was watching her closely. He was leaning comfortably back in the chair, his butt almost on the edge of it, and was dangling the doll on an invisible pretend stage somewhere about halfway between him and the child on his lap.

"When we go outside we see a wainbow."

Jacob regarded her carefully. Just outside the small space, Josh heard the catch in his voice. "In Miami?"

"No. At the wittle house."

"With Momma?"

Sucking in a breath, Josh saw his daughter slowly nod. Jacob couldn't take his eyes off her. He didn't dare make eye contact with Josh, nor did he dare move. The moment was too precious, the spell surrounding the child's inadvertent clue to Jessie's whereabouts far too dear.

When next he spoke, Jacob's question was carefully worded. "What else did you see at the little house, Emily-Grace? Besides the rainbow. Buildings? Lots of buildings?"

The ringlets bounced as she moved her head from side to side. She looked at Jacob. "Twees."

"Is that where you were? With David and...and Momma? At a little house with trees around it?" He swallowed past the dry cotton balls suddenly clogging his throat.

She nodded again, wide-eyed. Then she started to sob again, and wiped her eyes with the back of one hand.

"Momma. I want Momma."

The conversation was over as quickly and definitively as it had started.

Wrapping his arms around the trembling body, Jacob finally looked up to meet Josh's gaze. Both men were quaking, too—they had their differences where Jessie was concerned. But now their feelings were exactly the same. They were undeniably united in their quest to get her back.

Jacob shuffled his butt further back on the chair, maneuvered his body upright, and moved towards Josh. "Hey, there's Daddy," he managed to say to Emily-Grace. "Let's show him where the popsicles are, okay? In case you want another one someday?"

Looking up, Emily-Grace turned from him and moved into her daddy's arms. Josh and Jacob strode down the hall together.

Idly gesturing to a kitchenette twenty feet away, Jacob told Josh, "Popsicles are in the freezer. There."

I feel like I am a popsicle, ran unbidden through Josh's addled brain as he stared foggy-eyed at the white refrigerator Jacob was pointing out to him. *I feel frozen.*

He held his daughter close to his chest so he could feel her heart beating, while up the hall Morgan's eyes rested on the newly reunited father and daughter until Ulysses approached and asked him to stay the week.

Morgan said *yes*, before his alarmed mind darted back to Jessie.

Chapter Seven

$\mathcal{L}$ying on the bed, Jessie realized two things.

One, she had been cocooning for about six days now, without going outside to get the usual basket of groceries, without changing her clothes, without showering, without eating more than a cracker or two, and without drinking more than a sip or two of water. The only thing she forced herself to do, for the sake of her baby, was express her milk by hand.

There is still hope, she told herself. *If I keep expressing my milk, it won't dry up. I can still feed David.*

Two, in all that time, she didn't recall hearing footsteps above her, or descending the stairs to likely watch her from the mirror. So she figured rightly there were no groceries, anyway. There was likely no basket. She rolled from her side to her back now, and looked over at the far end of the small suite, where the cement steps led up to the exterior door.

"Huh," she thought. With a start, Jessie realized she'd likely been abandoned. With no way out. A new wave of desolation overtook her then. Would she ever see her babies again? Josh? Jacob? Charles and Dee, her friends? But she was all cried out. She was bone dry. And she had no tears left.

But she had to pee. She slid off the bed and, unbalanced and dizzy, slunk towards the small bathroom. Her pee was not urgent, and in fact was only a dribble. As she sat on the toilet trying to muster up the energy and wherewithal to stand, her eyes landed on something on the floor. She bent and picked it up. It was one of her daughter's crayon scribbles. Emily-Grace had asked Jessie to write on it *Emily-Grace loves Momma.* It was in the bathroom because Jessie had stuck it on the mirror by sliding it into

55

one of the metal clips so she could look at it when she brushed her teeth. It must have slipped its holder.

Trembling, Jessie leaned over and laid the picture on the vanity. She decided to interpret it as a sign.

You are a fighter, Jessie Wheeler-Sawyer, she told herself. *You lost the people you loved once before, because you felt you had no choice. But this time, you are getting them back. You will be strong, you will fight, and you will hold your babies in your arms again. You will make love to your husband again. You will live again.*

Stories of other kidnap victim survivors sprang to her mind then, all at once, as if the universe was agreeing with her, and giving her reasons to continue on. Elizabeth Smart. Jaycee Dugard. Amanda Berry. These women must have given up at some point in their captivity. Yet they survived.

Jessie stood, flushed the toilet, and made her way to the kitchen. She prayed her children were still alive—she believed they were, she had to— and, as she put a pot of water on to boil so she could make Kraft Dinner, she focused on the bright, hopeful day when she would see them again.

~ ~

Morgan's shift ended up being two weeks. The other folks on the Keating security team had families, or at the very least extended families, to celebrate Christmas with them. He had a wife he rarely saw, so he agreed to stay on…he remained at the hospital with Josh and the children until David was released. On that blissful day, the Keating jet flew him and the small reunited family back to Vancouver.

Over and over Morgan considered what he would find back at the house in Langley. Did Jessie have enough food? Did it get cold enough for the pipes to freeze so she'd be out of water? *Nah,* he told himself. *This is Vancouver we're talking about, not Toronto. It doesn't get cold enough for the pipes to freeze.* Did she ever get out of bed? Is she getting her period, does she need tampons?

He was almost afraid to go look.

Jessie was trying to regain her strength by doing pushups on the throw rug when a low rumble started up the driveway. She paused at the top of her extension and stared wildly at the wall. This was a sound she knew well.

While her children were with her, she heard it almost every day. Now, though, it was a scream in the wilderness.

The first thing Jessie thought when she heard large tires crunch their way up the gravel drive was *I appealed to these people to save my babies.*

The second bone jarring thought was *my God, please let my babies be okay. Let them be with their father. Let these people have taken them to their father. I beg you, God!*

She'd spent hours agonizing over Emily-Grace. The little girl was such a sensitive little thing. Jessie already knew her daughter was deeply affected from the screams she herself unleashed in futile attempts to escape their prison. She ached for the certainty of knowing her child was okay.

She wondered now if both of her captors were returning, or just the one who usually lurked on the other side of the damnable mirror. She knew from the first terrifying glimpse into her SUV's rearview mirror, and from the quick snatch of her children when David was sick, that there were two— a man and a woman, judging by their physiques the day they took the kids from her desperate grasp. For certain, it was the man who hung around most times. The woman was smaller, and her boots made a different staccato footstep on the floor above, and on the wooden stairs.

Soon, Jessie had her answer. The heavy boots came down the stairs, slowly this time. Tentative.

Jessie stood and faced her prisoner. She held up a sign she'd made from the torn back cover of one of Emily-Grace's coloring books, a newer book which was found in an earlier basket of food and sundries Jessie relied on. She'd written on the inside flap. Her message read, in large block letters, *I WILL NEVER GIVE UP.* She waited a few moments before grabbing another hand-scrawled sign from the Formica table—*THEY WILL NEVER GIVE UP EITHER.* Her third sign read *YOU WILL GO DOWN.*

Sparks blazed from her eyes while Jessie stood and faced her invisible menace, feet planted and biceps twitching. It was a while before she heard the man move. When he did, it was another five minutes before a juddering *crriinnch-thud* alerted her to the deadbolt's release on the back door.

Jessie had not felt the sun on her cheeks or felt fresh air waft through her hair for two weeks. She was rationing her food but stocks were low. But she didn't consider those things as she pulled her way hand over hand up the stairs. No, the only thing in her brain was an irrational, desperate hope— *is he letting me go?*

At the top of the stairs, she turned the knob on the heavy door and, heart racing, pushed it open. The day was grey but still the daylight was blinding. She had power, she had electric light, but daylight has a different power— an orange intensity in opposition to the blue-white of indoors.

When she peeked around the door, her heart crashed and, with it, Jessie's hope for freedom—today. Her kidnapper had already disappeared around the back corner of the small house, as evidenced by the disturbing click of the gate. He'd left a basket, finally, stocked full, according to the odd bulges here and there. Blue and orange Kraft Dinner boxes sticking out of the top were enough to sink Jessie's newfound courage and determination. What she would give for Pad Thai, or even just a mixed greens salad! Almond milk, feta cheese, Baileys in her coffee! Coffee…well, she dismissed that thought. She had given up coffee for her pregnancies and subsequent breastfeeding. So that was just wishful thinking. But it was part of her collective past, and damn it, what she would give for a decent hand crafted mocha from ROAM.

Grasping the heavy basket, she hauled it just inside the door. At least it was full. There was some level of compassion or at least hope here…the two weeks she was alone, inside, banging her head against the wall from sheer loneliness some days, and from a heartbreaking lack of human touch, was apparently being compensated for here, today. This couldn't go on forever. Emily-Grace was a smart little thing. She would give something away to whoever had her…if…well, just if.

Outside, sucking the invigorating air into her lungs, Jessie started walking around the perimeter of the small yard. Eventually she broke into a gallop. Raising her head high, she screamed at the empty air. For twenty minutes she jogged, first one way, and then she whipped around and ran counter-clockwise. She jumped on the picnic table, broke into one of her pop songs, and practiced a few salsa moves she'd picked up one night at a Cuban dance club in Miami. The darkness did not sway her when the sun's curtain fell in an hour. Two weeks inside, to Jessie, meant a long time outside.

Finally, chilled and tired, she turned and faced the thick steel door again.

From the second floor of the house, Morgan stood behind a curtain and watched indecision sink his captive's shoulders. Fear played across Jessie's features, spreading like the cracks in a twice-tapped hard-boiled egg. Two weeks trapped in a bleak basement without another soul to talk to, to be responsible for, to distract from the terrifying truth of reality by games and children's songs…to touch, to hold, to love…

She was afraid to go in for fear of being locked in again. Morgan watched Jessie make the choice—he knew the second it was made, because her expression switched gears instantly, going from hardened to downcast as if she were once again putty in Morgan's hands, a willing pawn in his and Nadia's sick game, if only to eat, to sleep, to buy time.

Shivering, she stood for minutes before finally bowing her head and entering. Closing the door behind her, Jessie paused at the top of the stairs and listened for the diabolical telltale clank of the deadbolt. Cocking her head, she tried to discern approaching footsteps, as she had many times before, but the guy was, intentionally, a silent walker, it appeared. Only at the last second did Jessie ever hear him. More than once, she'd tried to shove the door open, to eyeball him, to catch him and demand answers, but he obviously anticipated such moves and was always quick to respond. Now, the lock slid into place as it always did, a fearful cowardly move by a manic man, in Jessie's opinion.

Dragging the large overfull basket down the stairs, Jessie told herself she was grateful. *I have to think positively,* she said. *I have to believe this will end, and that it will end well. I have to believe my kids are okay. I have to.*

Emptying the basket only took minutes. To fill the time, to have some control of her circumstances, Jessie placed every container in a tidy row on the counter. Lined up like soldiers, they stared her down—brown beans, instant rice, pads, tampons, toilet paper, paper towel, and more; bananas, apples, orange juice, milk.

When she reached the bottom of the basket, her fingers touched something new to this ritual. She looked down. *Paper. There is a piece of paper here.* She sucked in a breath. A message? Glancing towards the one-way mirror, Jessie swallowed. *Please,* she begged the unseen watcher, whose heavy boots down the wooden stairs announced his arrival a moment ago. *Please let this be good.*

Taking the paper towards the mirror, Jessie sat below it, where she knew she couldn't be seen. It was an 8.5 x 11 sheet of computer paper, apparently blank on at least the outside. She could see print through the page, but Jessie was afraid to look. Instinct told her whatever was on this page was monumental, that it meant something. That it would affect her time here, in this godforsaken place.

Stirring up her courage, Jessie started unfolding the paper a tiny bit at a time. She started at one corner and, damp fingers trembling, gently pulled it down until she could see letters. A gasp caught in her throat. What she had before her was quite obviously something printed from a computer, from an Internet site. The first word she saw was *Home*. That, alone, was enough to jar her into frantically unscrambling the remainder of the paper.

Spread before her, held between clammy, quivering fingers, was her family.

Oh, God, she moaned. *Oh, God!*

The headline read *Sawyer Children Return Home*. Below that was *Josh Sawyer Takes His Babies Home From Hospital*.

The entire article was there for Jessie to savor, to read slowly, with painstaking attention to each and every word. But first, there were the pictures to inhale, to suck inside her soul, to energize her for the fight she knew remained.

The images were in full color. Scanning them quickly at first, Jessie felt she'd arrived at the Christmas tree on Christmas morning—so many gifts, where to start?

The largest photograph was taken outside the Alberta Children's Hospital. It was quite obviously the product of some gathered paparazzo, a typical static shot of a moving group of people who Jessie knew had learned over years of practice to ignore, as best they could, crowds of curious photographers.

The first people Jessie's eyes landed on were Charles and Deirdre. They were walking behind Josh, she knew, but she couldn't look at him yet. He was the prize. Her eyes on him would wait. No, she had to run her fingers over each beloved person in turn. She started with Charles, on the inside, who was walking with one arm around his wife. And, holy of holies, in Charles' other strong arm he was carrying Jessie's baby boy. David was alert, responsive, adorable. His blonde hair was blowing in an unseen breeze, but only the bangs—he was warmly dressed. A winter hat was fastened tightly under the baby's chin; a matching coat covered the chest Jessie last saw struggling through pain in order to rise and fall.

Dee's finger was ensconced in David's as she walked alongside. Both Charles and Dee appeared exhausted, done in. Old. Their hunched over postures and the shadows under their eyes clearly telegraphed their mixed relief and worry.

Relief, too, washed over Jessie. Her shoulders shook but stopped when a moment of clarity hit her. Frozen, frantic, she searched the article for a date. Was it even real, or was it photo shopped? Wildly, the pale eyes darted back to Charles and Dee. They looked like shit. She decided the picture was current. The date at the top right corner told her the article was published *today*. She'd been marking the passing days on the side of the maudlin kitchen cabinets. Jessie knew the date, she knew she'd missed Christmas with her family…she knew a new year had kicked in with her in prison, basically. And so here, beneath her fingers, was her family—as she knew they looked *today*.

A cry escaped her lips when she let her eyes finally rove up to Josh, who had their daughter safely wrapped in his arms. Walking ahead of Charles and Dee, alongside Ulysses, whose right arm was draped loosely but cautiously around Josh's waist, her husband was there, in front of her, alive, well, and carrying on. His lips were pressed in a tight line and his layered hair was gelled back over both ears, with the exception of one rogue piece that lay over his left cheek. It wasn't the usual strand Jessie knew drove Josh nuts, it was on the other side, but it was adorable and real, and she gasped when she ran a quaking finger over it. He was unshaven, but only for about three days, she thought, as she studied him, longing for a touch. Oh, to share laughter again with that man, to squeal in feigned annoyance and tell him to stop teasing her when he pressed his hard stubble against her cheek!

He was wearing one of his leather jackets, a tan one he got at a vintage place on Granville in Vancouver; falling loosely over his hips and ending mid-thigh, it was one of Jessie's favorites, reminding her now of their happier days on *Drifters*, when he wore it a lot. She stared at every pixel in that photograph, her eyes landing on Josh's jeans and wishing for more, because the picture was what in film parlance Jessie knew was called a 'cowboy shot,' taken from the knees up. So she couldn't see the boots or square-toed brown shoes she thought her husband might be wearing, and it frustrated Jessie not to see all, not to have all, *of him.*

She wasn't aware she was gulping back sobs until she had to angrily chide herself for allowing tears to fall on the page. The wet spots had the power to dilute the images of her loved ones, so Jessie moved the paper higher in front of her, but then she could hardly see it for crying.

Emily-Grace, she gasped next. First she traced Josh's strong firm arm around her child's bottom, where he was holding her upright, and then Jessie let her finger draw up alongside Emily-Grace's back, and over to Josh's left hand, with which he was attempting to shield his daughter from the obtrusive media.

Finally, she allowed her eyes to land squarely on his. She brought a hand to her lips then, and covered her mouth. Jessie saw what she expected to see— a hopeless, wounded pain. The chocolate eyes were dim, sad, sorrowful. Jessie searched them for some sign of hope—there was none. There was no stubborn pride apart from the way he tried to protect his child from the press; there was no light, and there was no *fuck you* meant for Jessie's captor. There was only hurt and a fierce dark look that screamed *leave us the fuck alone.*

It hurt to see that; it killed Jessie to see such despondence in the eyes she loved to climb inside. But then…what scared her even more were her daughter's eyes. They were haunted by the same pained look. Emily-Grace was twisting around, looking forward, and for once Jessie was glad the photographer managed to sneak his or her long lens around Josh's protective raised hand. For she was able to discern the angst in her daughter's eyes, but she was also able to see the pretty blonde ringlets, the little pink mouth, the delicate fingers, the pale round cheeks.

Dee must have dressed the kids, thought Jessie as she sobbed, studying the little girl's padded denim jacket, cute matching 1920's cloche hat, corduroy print dress, and red leggings. Emily-Grace was wearing her favorite boots, too, a pair of red cowboy boots Jessie got her on tour in Texas. And she was clutching a new doll, one that Jessie saw with delight was a guitar-playing redhead.

Jacob, she mouthed, lips twisting in gratitude up into a desolate, sad, half-grin.

Oh God, she gasped again, closing her eyes and looking upwards. Clutching the paper to her chest, she mouthed a silent prayer—*please please please let me be with them again, please please please, God.*

I trust you, she added. *I trust you, God.* And a sense of peace passed over her.

It was so strong Jessie's eyes flew open and her head bounced back to its normal straight gaze. The message was profound. It drifted over her in one glorious wave, and it said *Yes.*

Okay, Jessie responded. *Okay.* And she even managed a small smile.

Then she bent her head, stopped the steady flow of tears, and read the accompanying article. In it, she learned her son had pneumonia and was being released after two weeks in the Alberta Children's Hospital. *What? Alberta? Am I in Alberta?* There were no noticeable mountains outside. Jessie did not see anything except a high fence, trees, sun, moon, sky, and clouds. She could be anywhere.

The story of how the children were found was illuminating. The woman who found the children was interviewed. Surprised, Jessie was stunned to see that she was a police detective's attractive ebony-skinned wife; she had kind eyes, according to a smaller picture attached to the article. The woman told how she stumbled upon the children in a Calgary park, how scared the little girl was, and how sick the baby appeared.

Jessie read about the family's Christmas in the hospital—how Kayla, Paul, Zach and Hilary and their children, arrived for a belated celebration, and that Steve, Sophie, Charlie and Jane took part as well. Jacob was not mentioned.

Josh was quoted, briefly, in reference to Jessie's continued disappearance. He said only *there is always hope.*

For me, Jessie whispered inwardly. He said that for me. For that's what she had said to him all those years ago when she first bent down in front of his wasted, hopeless eyes outside Charlie's club, when he was perched amongst the fetid debris of other peoples' dinners.

"Babe," she whispered to him now, "don't give up on me. Please don't ever give up on me."

She went to sleep that night with the picture of her family pressed to her chest. And, for the first time, before lying down Jessie looked directly at the mirror and breathed, "Thank you."

~ ~

Within a week, Jessie was struggling with a new challenge. She had been trying to express milk from her breasts so she would still be able to feed David when she had him in her arms again. But it wasn't going so well. Now, her breasts were becoming painfully engorged. The milk wouldn't express, and the effort to try to make it express only ended up frustrating Jessie.

It was one more step backwards. It was one more sign that she might die in this dank basement, lost and alone. Breastfeeding her baby was important to Jessie, for all kinds of reasons—immunity, intimacy, you name it. And the opportunity to do so was coming to an abrupt and painful end.

The discomfort was profound. Even walking to the bathroom hurt. Push-ups, jogging, were suddenly no longer options. Standing under a warm shower, Jessie tried to get her milk to let down. But the effort was futile. Instead, she sat on her butt in the bathtub, let the water from the shower run over her, and cried, lamenting the loss of this sacred ritual with her baby.

During the day and at night, she set wet towels in the freezer. After thirty minutes or so, she placed them against the swollen breasts. The coolness offered some relief, but not nearly enough. Painkillers were not made available to her. Jessie didn't need to wonder why, for she would have devoured entire bottles many times in the last few weeks.

Then, abruptly, the pain stopped. And so did the milk.

Another opportunity to bond with her baby was lost.

Curled up into a fetal position in bed, Jessie ached to know how he was doing, and how Josh was coping with the two children. What was David feeding on now? Was he completely better? When would she see him again? Babies grow so much in their first year. He was six months old at the time of the abduction. He would be eight months now. Before he got sick, he was starting to crawl. He could be walking before Jessie saw him again, if…

…*if* she saw him again.

Chapter Eight

$\mathcal{N}$adia first sank her hooks into Josh at a gathering at La Casa.

It was a mid-January belated Christmas celebration. All of the security team was invited, and asked to bring their significant others. No one batted an eyebrow at Morgan for bringing who he told them was his 'stepsister.' However, a lot of eyebrows were batted at Nadia because she was, well, Nadia.

She glided into the home on silver Jimmy Choos, in a tight-fitting red sequined number that barely covered her thighs. The men at this party were accustomed to well dressed, dazzling women, but still, Nadia attracted a lot of stares. Her coffee skin seemed to glow, and the dark eyes were sensual and expressive. Lips of burnt-red glittered under the light and, when she spoke, she was confident and articulate, profound and aware. But, most of all, she appeared to be a listener. Not distracted by the business around her, she was attentive to whoever fired dialogue in her direction. She stood with a hand on one hip, sometimes, so as to appear even more focused.

Her introduction to Josh, who had his daughter in his arms at the time, was brief, but it made an impression. Nadia had a way of sucking men into her fold. She knew the actor would take some work, but she was prepared. When the opportunity presented itself, she met Morgan's wary eyes. He was standing just behind Josh at the time, and so he sucked in a breath, stepped up, gestured to Nadia, and introduced the two.

Josh was whispering to Emily-Grace. A cherubic angel in a red velvet gown with a wide bow at the waist, a pout was creasing her lips as she fingered the soft silk of her father's loose tie.

Just before Morgan's intro, Nadia caught Josh saying, "Daddy will come lie down with you."

"Ah," Nadia smiled widely after the introduction, "is someone ready for bed?" A delicate hand floated on the air between them and brushed shiny high-glossed nails against the child's cheek. Emily-Grace recoiled, and clutched her singer-dowwy tighter.

Josh sighed. He loved having his daughter around but she was desperately afraid to go to anyone but him or Jacob. And she rarely spoke. He had started taking her to a child psychologist, partly to help her adjust, and partly to see if the man could cajole any truths regarding Jessie's whereabouts out of her. Now, at this party, Josh was almost eagerly awaiting Jacob's arrival so the guy could hold Emily-Grace for a little while.

He responded to the beautiful woman in the slinky dress. "She is, but she's fighting it. She's a little too attached to her daddy these days."

"That's understandable," Nadia cooed. "She's had a rough time of it."

With her head pressed against her daddy's shoulder, Emily-Grace was surreptitiously watching Nadia. But the young woman wasn't concerned about being recognized. Even during the eleven-hour drive to Calgary that time, she was careful to wear her balaclava when she faced the girl. And she was certain not to speak, even during bathroom breaks, which she only took by the side of the road. She never stopped in a public restroom, and even gas breaks were rushed and hurried. Morgan had purchased a car seat for Emily-Grace; this they positioned behind the driver's seat so the child couldn't see Nadia through the rearview mirror. It was a quiet drive. Emily-Grace slept some, and otherwise never made a peep. Her baby brother slept almost the entire way. Nadia had to crank up the radio in order to drown out his wet, gurgling breaths.

Now, the woman responsible for kidnapping Josh's wife and children graced him with a wide smile.

He looked twice at her, thinking he saw kindness there, only Josh didn't know it was the put-on kind. But he nodded towards his daughter and said, "She'll fall asleep in a bit. Then I'll take her upstairs to bed. Carlotta's up there with David, she'll watch over her."

"And Carlotta is…? Your nanny, I presume." *This is so easy,* Nadia was thinking. He's walking himself right into my arms.

"No, uh, actually no, I don't have a nanny. I guess I need to get someone, though. I'm going back to work next week."

"On *The Wyatt Boys*? In Toronto?"

"Uh, yeah." Josh glanced towards a chorus of *heys, about time you got here's*, and slaps on the back. Jacob had arrived, his hand tightly wrapped around the fingers of a sweet-looking petite brunette. Josh stared.

Nadia was annoyed. She had to speak twice.

Josh finally turned back to her. "Sorry. What was that?"

"Oh, I was just saying if you're looking for a nanny in Toronto, maybe I could help out. At least for a little while. I live there. I'm between jobs at the moment. And your kids are adorable."

"Uhhhh…really?" Nadia had Josh's attention now, partly because of the way a tattoo moved up and down on her partially exposed left breast when she breathed. He tried not to look. But, inadvertently, Josh caught himself wondering what it said. He could only make out the letter *D*, which soothed him in a way because he figured it was a boyfriend's name. And the last thing he needed—or even remotely wanted—was female distraction. Not now, when his kids needed him and while his wife was still missing.

He asked about Nadia's experience with kids. A flicker of something passed through her eyes at the question—sadness, maybe, Josh thought— but it was quickly replaced with a soft light.

"Oh, I love children. I have friends with children, and I grew up working class, so, well, you know what that means—lots of babysitting! And I have First Aid, too, with CPR training, so…I could likely handle it. Not forever, Josh." Taking a chance, Nadia grazed one shiny blood-red nail against his forearm (and later swore she felt him quiver underneath her touch). "A few months maybe. Long enough to get you started in Toronto, maybe."

"You're, uh," Josh looked to his side. The quiet bodyguard was listen- ing. Tilting his head, Josh gestured towards him. "You're Morgan's sister?"

"Stepsister." Nadia held up an arm. "Different color skin. Our parents were one of those mixed marriage types. I was six and Morgan was eight."

"Parents…were?"

"Yeah. They died. About ten years ago now. Car accident."

"Ah." Josh soaked that up. This woman understood tragedy. Maybe she could help his daughter...? Josh's arms were getting heavy. He glanced over at Jacob. With a final look at the exquisite Nadia, he said, "Can I call you tomorrow? I mean...if you're serious, I'd say you're hired. Morgan's a dependable kind of guy. I'm guessing his stepsister is as well. Uh...what's your name again? Sorry. My mind's a sieve these days."

"Nadia," she purred, leaning in closer so her dress gaped slightly open.

Josh couldn't help it. He looked down, and swallowed. The first letter was a D, all right. He could almost see a dark nipple beneath Nadia's black camisole. Ducking his head, he reddened.

She caught the look, and soaked it up. "We can have coffee, if you like. Maybe at that place Morgan says you like? ROAM?"

"Okay," Josh agreed as he started to move away. "I'll get your number from Morgan tomorrow. In the meantime, I need to see if Jacob's up for a cuddle with my little cling-on, here. I'll see you, Nadia."

"Yes, you will," she almost moaned in anticipation, under her breath. "And I will see you, Josh Sawyer." When he was no longer within hearing distance, she smiled deliciously at Morgan. "Well, looks like I have a job. He walked right into it."

Morgan shot his wife a disdainful look. And then he turned his eyes to Josh and his daughter. After all, he was hired to watch over them. And Morgan took his job seriously.

Jacob was only too happy to lift Emily-Grace out of Josh's fatigued arms. "Hey, beautiful," he crooned. "Write any new songs for me lately?"

Groaning, Josh stretched his arms. "She's getting heavy in her old age."

Steve wandered up behind him and clapped Josh on the back. "This little Sawyer is totally crushing on you, Ryan." He tweaked Emily-Grace's cheek. "Aren't you, my darling girl?"

A hefty yawn was Emily-Grace's response. She snuggled into the safety of Jacob's neck and closed her eyes.

Josh glared at Steve. "Thanks for that, Steve. Seriously."

Beaming, Jacob grinned. Adjusting his stance, he loosed one arm from Emily-Grace, reached beside him, and took his new girl's hand. "Josh, Steve, this is Rachael. She's one of Charles' new sound techs down on Robson."

"Nice to meet you," offered Steve companionably. "Although you might want to avoid this guy. He's got a rep for…" Bending forward, he whispered, "STD's."

"Oh? Which one?" was the gal's sharp response. It was accompanied by a friendly set of upturned lips.

Steve didn't miss a beat. "All of them."

Which resulted in hearty laughter and a few knowing smirks.

After Josh shook Rachael's hand, and gave Jacob a *this one better stick* look, Jacob spoke directly to Josh. "Who's the siren?" He nodded towards Nadia.

"My new nanny, apparently," was Josh's serious response.

The statement was greeted with an uncomfortable silence.

Incredulous, Steve filled the pause with, "Seriously?"

"What?" Annoyed, Josh grabbed a glistening glass of champagne off a passing tray.

"Duh," put in Jacob.

Steve eyed the bubbly drink gripped tightly in his friend's fingers. "Nannies are supposed to be grey-haired and have lip hair." Two long fingers pantomimed where the lip hair would be.

Jacob focused a sullen stare in Josh's direction.

Josh read his mind. "Screw off, Ryan. Maybe I need a good lay." He glanced down at his daughter. She was sleeping, finally, as evidenced by the even rhythm in the rise and fall of her chest. Slightly embarrassed about the impulsive remark, Josh's eyes slid over to Rachael. "My apologies."

Jacob's new gal threw up her hands. "I'm not even listening." Waving to Charles, who was across the room deep in conversation with Charlie and his father Jack, she squeezed her new boyfriend's free hand. "Back in a minute, Jacob. I'm just going to say hello to Charles."

Taking advantage of her departure, Steve and Jacob eyed Josh, who caved under their scrutiny.

"Why not?" he muttered, eyes narrowing. His voice was thick. He was tired. It was tough, being a single dad all of a sudden, especially with a child suffering from some form of PTSD. Especially with…a constant never-ending overhanging uncertainty and grief. "Am I not allowed to get laid? It's not like it will mean anything." Pointing the champagne flute at Jacob, he bristled. "You can bet *he's* getting some tonight."

"And we've long established that I am not married to your wife. So I am free to do as I please." Adamant, Jacob was kinda pissed at Josh. However, he was astute enough to discern the red-rimmed eyes and frustrated stance, as well as the hasty manner in which the man was consuming his champagne.

Steve noticed as well. But he stayed silent.

"So," Josh said, lifting his daughter from Jacob's arms so he could take her upstairs and release her into Carlotta's care for the evening, "I'm open to suggestions on the statute of limitations concerning sex for men with missing wives." Moving towards the hall, he threw an arm out to his side. "Anytime. Just throw me some numbers, boys." Backing away, he disappeared around the corner.

"Fuuccckkk," breathed Jacob. "Jesus, that guy. He's a fucking mess."

"He's a time bomb," ascertained Steve darkly. "And he's going to go off, Jake old buddy. I suppose he might as well burn off some steam, as it were."

Unbelieving, Jacob stared at Steve. "Sure. So when Jessie comes back she once again knows her husband lasted, what, just over two months after she disappeared? She'll be thrilled. Oh, but then they'll split up so I can have her. I see what you're saying. I'm all for it. Jesus."

With that, he abruptly left Steve's side and joined his date over by Charles.

Steve watched him go, then pilfered a smoked salmon cucumber canapé from a nearby table, popped it into his mouth, and spun around to find himself locked in Nadia's dark eyes.

She never wavered. With a shiver, Steve looked away, towards the hall where Josh was no longer visible.

"Time bomb," he mumbled. "Just hope when you go off I'm around to see you through it, buddy."

Turning back to the party, he took a long, deep sip of his own champagne, and wandered over to annoy Jacob some more.

Chapter Nine

Josh set his baby boy down on a spread of brightly colored jigsawed rubber mats in the playroom on the upper level of his and Jessie's home. The child was on his hands and knees. Forcing a smile as he watched his son try to coordinate his limbs into crawling, Josh was knocked over by a desperate ache that almost tore him in two. Soon David would be crawling full out—another landmark baby moment Jessie was missing.

Sophie and Steve were in the room, sitting on the floor against the inner wall. Steve had a hand in his wife's. They all chuckled as David raised his little bum in the air and crept forward.

"You need to do something about your kid's hair," Steve teased Josh. "That longer piece in front—he's starting to look like his redneck dad."

"He's adorable," smiled Sophie. "Big eyes, and look at those dimples. He'll have a girlfriend by the time he's three."

As if on cue, the baby peeked up at her, all wide-eyed and innocent. Smiling widely, he rocked back and forth on his hands and knees.

Letting go of Steve's fingers, Sophie moved to her own hands and knees and crawled towards the baby, as Josh dropped down by Steve against the wall and loosely draped his arms around bent knees.

Facing David, Sophie lovingly told him, "Yes, I'm talking about you. You Sawyer men are charming brutes."

"Hey!" called her husband. "Watch it, Miss." He pointed to himself as she looked back over her shoulder at him and winked. "You own this. I have ownership of the words charming and adorable."

Laughing, Sophie bent down on her forearms to play with the baby.

Behind David, Emily-Grace was walking around an invisible eight-foot circle. Leaning in slightly, she was moving quickly, red tights slipping a little on the mat, singer-dowwy dangling from her outside hand. Babbling away, she was off in her own world.

When she stopped circling, Josh glanced over at her. He watched as she bent over and placed both hands on a rubber mat, and pointed her bum up in the air so that her body formed a small triangle. Josh made a mental note to someday teach her not to stick her butt in the air when she was wearing denim mini-skirts, like today. Idly, he wondered what other female things he would end up having to teach her.

Steve caught the hard look, and he followed his friend's stare to glance over at Emily-Grace. "Toronto will ease things, Josh. You'll be busy."

"It just blows my mind that nothing's turned up, Steve. Nothing. I can't stand the thought of leaving here. If she's in Vancouver..." He drifted off.

"If she shows up in Vancouver, we can be here in a few hours."

"The thing is...I can't even be angry at her. Like before. All I can do is worry myself sick." Sucking on his bottom lip, Josh started rubbing one thumb anxiously over the opposite thumbnail as he watched his daughter lay on her belly and stretch her head up towards the ceiling. She was still babbling incoherently.

Sophie noticed her, and turned curiously back to Josh.

"What?" he asked.

Sitting back on her knees, she pivoted her shoulders around to the little girl again and cocked her head. Oblivious to the watching adults, Emily-Grace rolled onto her back and brought her knees a hip's width apart up to her bum. She planted her arms on each side of her body and raised her hips in the air. The babbling stopped, and she inhaled.

Sophie crawled over to her. "Honey," she asked gently, "show me downward dog again."

Emily-Grace brought her butt back to the mat and regarded Sophie carefully. Then she rolled back over, brushed damp hair away from a cheek, and did her triangle pose again.

Astounded, Sophie gasped lightly and looked hard at Josh. "When did you teach your daughter to do Yoga?"

"What?" Blankly, his gaze drifted to his daughter as she came out of her three-year-old version of the well-known Yoga pose and watched her daddy.

Emily-Grace got back on her belly and lifted her chest off the floor again. When she came back down, she said clearly, "Wook, Daddy. Baby cobwa."

The room was quiet, with the exception of David's happy gurgling. Josh felt his chest freeze. He was afraid to breathe. "Who taught you Yoga, Emily-Grace?"

From her position on her belly, his daughter said in her soft, whispery voice, "Momma." She stood, while Sophie clapped her hands over her mouth and Josh bit his bottom lip harder, and she told her father, "After bweakfast we awways do Yoga. Momma say we need do our exacise."

"Momma?" asked her daddy, his breath coming in small gasps. "Every day?"

She nodded.

"Where, Emily-Grace?" asked Steve, as Sophie bent before the little girl and carefully yanked her cotton sweater down over the waist of her small skirt. She stayed by her side, an arm around the child's waist. "In a play-room like this?"

Wary at the adults' attention, Emily-Grace wrinkled her nose before shaking her head. "By the stwove. In the wittle house."

"What else was in the room?" This was Josh, unmoving, his words emerging in a quaking voice. He didn't want to scare his daughter with any kind of urgency, but hell, she rarely spoke, and even taking her to a child psychologist and to see Trudy as well got nothing out of her. This was an opportunity he didn't want to miss. This was an opportunity he *couldn't* miss.

"Bed," she murmured, now acutely aware of the importance of the conversation, despite her young years.

"What did you eat?"

Steve and Sophie held their collective breaths and listened.

"Kwaft Dinnew." The little girl was almost afraid to say more. Her daddy was wiping at tears now, and his voice shook when he spoke.

"Oh," Josh said, a little curve on the corner of one lip. "Momma must not have liked that very much, sweetheart."

"Momma said when we come home she need to put money in the sweaw jaw." She moved to her daddy then, who was looking at her through such sad, misty eyes. "Daddy, when Momma come home?"

Josh widened his knees so his daughter could stand closer to him. He placed his big hands on her waist. "I don't know, baby girl," he answered honestly, trying to remain strong for his daughter. But he couldn't prevent the choking sobs engulfing him now in giant waves. He knew his raw emotions scared her, but he was powerless here, now.

Emily-Grace moved both palms over his stubble and peered at him intently. "Daddy, Momma say be stwong. She say you tell Daddy be stwong."

"What, honey?"

Josh heard a movement to his right. Steve was crawling over to Sophie and drawing her into his lap.

"Wh-when did Momma say that, honey?"

"At the wittle house when they took me and David away. When the big doow cwose and Momma not come."

"Oh, God," came a muffled voice that sounded like Sophie's.

"Okay," Josh said. Wiping at his tears, he tugged his daughter closer for a kiss. "Okay. Do you know how beautiful you are, Emily-Grace? Do you know how much your daddy loves you?"

Small arms wrapped around his neck. "Emiwy-Gwace wuv Daddy too. And David. And Momma."

"We'll get her back," Josh whispered in his child's ear as he struggled to remain composed. "Momma's okay. We'll bring her home soon. I promise."

He prayed it was a promise he could keep.

A knock came at the door. It was Ulysses. "Guys? We should hit the road."

They were going to Toronto, so Josh and Steve could get back to work shooting *The Wyatt Boys*. Morgan and Ulysses were accompanying them on the trip, and Sophie was coming for the weekend, mostly so she could help with the children. Josh was finding her to be a sweet companion for Emily-Grace, and he wished the mild-mannered blonde could stay for the duration of the shoot. At least he would have Morgan's stepsister for a few months— she was officially starting on Monday.

Standing, he scooped up his daughter. Sophie bent to pick up David, but Steve stopped her. He picked the baby up instead.

"No lifting," he told her. Meeting Josh's eyes, Steve grinned.

"Really?" Josh asked, glancing at the diminutive Sophie, who was rather flushed all of a sudden, he noticed. "You guys are expecting? When?"

"Yep." Steve juggled the baby in his arms and bent forward to give his wife a quick kiss. "June."

"June. So you're…" Josh did a quick calculation. "So you're four months?"

"Yeah, about that," breathed Sophie, glancing at Steve. She touched her abdomen. "I'm just starting to show."

"You know, I'm not gonna break. You could have told me."

Steve adjusted the wiggly David before he answered. "Never quite seemed like the right time, bro."

"No, I get that, it's just…" Josh gulped. He changed tack. "I'm happy for you. For both of you. Really. That's great news." Moving to Sophie's side, he brushed his lips over her cheek, then turned to go without looking at Steve.

Exchanging glances with her husband, Sophie gave Steve a little push. Grimacing, he moved forward and followed his friend out of the playroom and down the stairs.

"Josh, look. I know you and Jessie planned on having a big family. What Emily-Grace just said was encouraging. There's hope, man. Let's just focus on that, okay? I'm going to call Matt and fill him in, if that's okay with you."

"Yeah, you do that, Steve." Josh set his daughter down on the main floor of the home and looked around him at the assorted baby accouterments Sophie helped him pack earlier. Morgan was there, grabbing another load in preparation for travel. Josh handed him a baby seat. Sucking on a corner of his lip, he placed his hands on his hips and stared at the overwhelming amount of stuff Jessie usually dealt with when they travelled.

A small tug on the side of his jeans got his attention. Steve wandered off to a seat at the kitchen island and put in a call to Matt.

Josh knelt down before his daughter.

"Daddy, whewe we go?"

"Toronto, sweetheart," he said, eyes softening at her fearful expression. "Daddy has to work."

"No. Miami." She stomped her foot.

"Not this trip, honey." Smoothing her fine hair back from her face, Josh

75

resolved to get Sophie to show him how to make those hair thingies work. The one he put in this morning was coming loose. Now, Josh tried to fix it, but it ended up looking lopsided.

"Yes, Daddy. Miami."

Uh oh. Josh eyed his daughter. Was there a three-year-old hissy fit coming on? "Grammie and Grampie are coming next week. They'll take you swimming in the hotel pool, honey."

"Miami." Crossing her arms, Emily-Grace mustered up all of the spite she could find and glared at her daddy.

"Soon," he answered, giving up on the hair. "I promise."

"I want Momma."

So do I, thought Josh. *Damn it.* He put both hands on his knees and, wincing, forced himself to a standing position. Ignoring his daughter, he glanced at Steve, who was bouncing David on his lap while chatting with Matt. Sophie was going over their things.

Morgan came back in and grabbed a large bag Josh was using as a diaper bag. The bodyguard met Josh's eye, but looked away quickly as, with his other hand, he plucked a suitcase from the luggage pile.

Huh, thought Josh. *How long has this guy been with us? And he still can't look me in the eye?*

Soon they were at the airport. Emily-Grace had resorted to regular hopeless wails that were quickly grating on Josh's nerves. He nudged her up the steps and into the jet. Sophie found a seat and pulled the child into her lap, speaking softly to her in a soothing tone as the wails faded into more of a hiccuppy cry.

Groaning, Josh wandered down the short aisle. Behind him, Steve touched Sophie's shoulder and said, "Be up in a minute," and then he dropped into a wide leather seat opposite Josh.

"The police are really drilling Caryn and Eric," he stated candidly. "Matt said they were brought in again today."

"I know," Josh replied quietly. "She called me yesterday and begged me to call off the witch hunt."

"What'd you tell her?"

Shrugging, Josh bit off, "I told her I had no fucking idea whether she and her creepy old ex have anything to do with Jessie's current unknown address."

76

With a brush of a thumb and finger against his two-day whiskers, Steve took this in. "Apparently Eric admitted it was he who released that first photo online. Not Caryn."

That was news. "Really." The surprised comment emerged bland and empty, leaving Josh's eyes devoid of emotion. "Like I fucking care at this point." Turning his head, he stared blankly out of the jet's small window. "And how's Matt's golf game?"

"You need to let this attitude shit go, Josh."

"Do I." Josh watched as, outside on the tarmac, airport crew prepared for takeoff.

"You don't get a free ride in the asshole department just because—" Steve sucked the end of the sentence back.

"Hmmph." Josh whipped his head around and narrowed darkening eyes at his friend. "Because why, Steve?"

"Don't be an ass." Hoisting himself off the seat, Steve did a 180 and left Josh alone for the duration of the flight.

Later, struggling to get the kids settled on his own, Josh finally lost it with Emily-Grace. He had fed the kids but not himself, and he was hungry. He knew the others were down in the dining room, but Josh was doing his best to get the children on a regular bedtime schedule despite the crazy hours he knew he would be working. Pissed at what he thought was Steve's crass judgment, he stubbornly refused Sophie's offer of assistance in tonight's bedtime routine. Emily-Grace was tired and still out of sorts. David was adding to the general sense of confusion and loneliness by whining and shaking the rails of the crib the production had supplied its lead actor. Giving in to irritated nerves resulting from his children's anxiety, and to the constant cloud of grief haunting his every breath, Josh yelled at his daughter.

She was complaining again about Miami, which he damn well knew meant sunshine, music, and Momma, which was annoying enough, but when Jacob's name slipped between her lips, Josh set the child roughly on her bed, crossly demanded she go to sleep, stormed across the room, and ungraciously slammed the door behind him.

Dropping onto the sofa, he hung his head in his hands and tried to shut out the forlorn sobs dripping through the wall of the small bedroom behind him.

Emily-Grace's hurt, wounded cries undid him altogether. "I want Momma, I want Momma, I want Momma."

"So do I," Josh choked along with his daughter. "So do I."

Chapter Ten

*B*y the time Monday rolled around, Josh was more than ready to bring the new nanny on board. Nadia arrived at the studio in a flurry of gifts and snacks for the kids, with coffees for her and Josh held high in a tray in one hand.

"Go," she demanded when he stood unmoving at the door of the small playroom Jon had set up for cast members' kids. Laughing, she somehow found the audacity to push Josh through the door. "We'll be fine. Come check on us after blocking if you want to."

Josh was afraid to leave the children. Yeah, the weekend was rough, and Emily-Grace had reverted to her soundless aching wide-eyed stare, but still, Josh felt fear grip his stomach at the idea of leaving the kids, even though they were in the same general studio area as he—just upstairs, in fact—and they were secure. Thanks to Jon, their grandfather, anyone with nefarious intentions would have to get through a gauntlet of security first.

Finally, Jon himself hurried by on his way to set, a handful of notes clutched messily in one hand. The producer grabbed Josh's elbow as he passed.

"Come," he commanded. "They need you."

So do my kids, thought Josh. He met his daughter's pale eyes briefly. She was wearing that lost look he saw so often in Jessie's face in the old days. His stomach churning, Josh knew Emily-Grace was already behind the eight ball in the realm of life. But Sara and Kevin were driving in from Peterborough later. Maybe they could at least cheer her up, although the families had not visited a great deal over the past few years, so he knew it might take

Emily-Grace some time to warm up to Jessie's half-sister. But still…Sara was family. Emily-Grace would somehow, on an intuitive deeper level, know that.

With a huge sigh drawn from the depths of his toes, Josh sent Nadia a dejected, hopeful look, and nervously slapped the doorframe as he left the playroom.

‿ ⸒⸑

At the end of the week, Josh stopped and considered that the whole first five day adjustment thing had gone much better than he initially dared dream, and Nadia was a tremendous part of that. Emily-Grace was responding to a routine, and the presence of steady women in her life seemed to be helping. Dee had arrived, her patient insistence on order and generous cuddles immeasurable treasures for the two small Sawyer children, and Sara had driven to the city twice to spend afternoons with the kids. But Emily-Grace's steady rock, at least in terms of consistency, was quickly becoming Nadia.

The coffee-skinned beauty was also rooting herself as Josh's anchor. Within the week, he realized her presence was a breath of fresh air. She was glamorous, even-tempered, carefree, and even joyful. Her steady company allowed him permission, finally, to exhale.

Friday night, after reading to Emily-Grace while Josh rocked his son to sleep, Nadia appeared at the door of Josh's bedroom. After tucking David into his crib, Josh had stepped out of the baby's room and started putting away laundry Nadia did for him earlier in the day. He had moved his family into a larger suite in season two, still in their usual Toronto hotel, but on one of the top floors. Emily-Grace and David each had their own room. There was a separate living area and even a decent kitchenette, complete with an expensive Italian espresso machine Josh rarely used but which he knew Jessie would have broken in on the first day.

There was enough space to bring Nadia in to assist with bedtime, which Josh was still adjusting to on his own, and she seemed willing to stick around in the evenings, so he pushed aside the others' vociferous disapproval and went for it. Captivated by her flowing presence in and around him and his children, and growing increasingly pissed off and recalcitrant around Steve and the other cast of *The Wyatt Boys*, Josh was starting to do two things—one, gravitate away from everyone else, and two, gravitate towards the exotic woman to whom his children seemed to be adapting so well.

Now, spotting the nanny at his bedroom door in the semi-darkness, he eyed her gratefully.

"She dreaming of sugarplums and fairies?"

"I think that only happens at Christmas," Nadia teased, coming further into the room and taking a pile of T-shirts from his arms. Moving into the nearby walk-in closet, she set them on a shelf. Languorously running a finger over the cotton tees, she rotated around on one heel and peeked up at Josh from beneath long eyelashes. Toeing a foot behind one ankle, Nadia thrust her chest out just enough to coerce Josh into noticing.

She was wearing a tight white scoop-necked T-shirt and faded jeans that hugged her curves viciously. Before her was a man accustomed to regular sex, and who, these days, simply ached for connection.

"I guess I should go," she cooed, but Nadia didn't move except to sway her hips just enough to make Josh's heart start to pump a little more quickly.

Josh knew her game. Women came on to him all the time. His lips parted as he let his gaze drop to the inked D visible on Nadia's left breast.

"What's the tattoo say?" His voice came out gruff, low. "Is it your boy-friend's name?"

"Noooope," she told him slowly. "My son's. He died." That moment, when she actually spoke some truth to Josh, was the closest Nadia came to crack-ing, to almost giving up her and Morgan's sick game. Normally she was a stone wall. She had no emotional connection to Jessie's plight, or to Josh's. But she had an emotional connection with a dead child, and the admission almost opened her up. *Almost.*

"Oh. I'm real sorry, Nadia. Really." *Ah, another tragedy. She and I are allies in this stupid life thing with all its pain.* "What was his name?"

Licking her lips, Nadia allowed a tiny curve to form there, and she stepped forward. Placing a finger inside the T-shirt, just over her breast, Nadia pushed the fabric down, just far enough for Josh to see her son's name and age tat-tooed there—*Darin5.*

What he also saw was a gorgeous brown breast, including the areola around the nipple. His breath caught. Josh was fed up, tired, lonely, and disgusted with the world. He was overwrought with responsibility and a constant worry for his children's continued safety, and with grief for his missing wife. So when Nadia grasped his forefinger by wrapping her hand around it and gently squeezing, then lifted it towards her breast and ran his finger over the tattoo, he sucked in a breath and let himself *feel*.

She moved his finger over her warm skin a few times, cautiously watching Josh's eyes as she did so; watching the dimness in them flicker and ache and want, and then she inhaled slowly so her breasts moved, and she pushed all of his fingers further down her top, just inside her bra. Nadia knew the moment he touched her nipple, not only because she felt his energy charge through her, but also because of the way his body hitched and moved just the slightest bit. And because of the way his breathing quickened.

Josh had yet to meet Nadia's eyes—his were glued to the sizzling heat of her skin underneath his now more deeply probing fingers. But her intent was clear.

She voiced the intent anyway, only she turned it around on him, in a soothing, husky murmur. "It's okay, baby. I know you need this. Let me do this for you."

Of all people, Caryn flashed through Josh's mind then. The lust, the white skin, the desire…Jessie's image and essence did not cross his mind. He buried her, like a bad memory, down a deep well. He couldn't bring himself to think of her, no, he just let his shadow side take over; he let it deal with his wants and needs and the hurts that needed easing by a woman such as the sensual creature in his closet.

Nadia was now close enough to Josh for him to place both of his big hands on her hips. Her heated breath moved up his cheek, landing by one lonely eye as his hands somehow found her elbows and slid up her arms. Murmuring softly, she brushed her lips against his cheek, causing sweet little anticipatory vibrations to scatter over Josh's body that, at the same time as they excited him, massaged balm into his open wounds.

Closing both eyes, he let her minister over him; he let her murmur and touch and guide his right hand up under her top, and Josh's eyes flicked open when her hands abandoned him, but no, it was okay, she was just reaching behind her back to undo her bra. Josh allowed himself to look back at her breasts then, and the erect nipples peeking through her T-shirt, which he ached to stretch out his fingertips and touch.

Removing the bra entirely, Nadia dropped it on the floor of the closet, so her hands were free again, but Josh didn't need her help anymore.

Sliding one palm up inside her T-shirt, Josh's breath was ragged when he thumbed Nadia's nipple for the first time. He moved around there, his other hand on her waist, sliding back and forth, the fingers wanting to slip inside the waistband of her jeans. Still, he did not meet her eyes, he didn't want to *see* her, he just wanted to *feel* her. Josh *needed* to feel her.

Gripping the bottom hem of her top, he pulled it up over her head, and suddenly this gorgeous creature was exposed in front of him. Bending over her, Josh slipped a nipple in between his lips. He sucked hard, using his hand to grip her more firmly and bring more of her inside his mouth, and when he started to tongue her there she cried out, a moan that came from somewhere deep inside and that longed for more from this larger-than-life film and TV star.

Nadia yanked Josh's T-shirt over his head and grabbed his belt buckle, pulling him towards her. She palmed his rough cheeks and lifted his mouth to hers, and sucked on his bottom lip before desperately tonguing him.

His wide leather belt was deftly unfastened by her small, groping hands; she undid the button of his jeans, then, and slid down the zipper. Nadia's searing touch was inside Josh's boxers in a second flat—she gripped and massaged him hard, forcing him to groan and huff and duck his face into her neck as a wild, reckless pleasure consumed him.

His knees were giving way, so Josh took that as his cue to lift Nadia and bring her to his bed. Roughly, he laid her on her back and yanked down her jeans. There was no tenderness and no delay in Josh's now urgent quest for release—he moved hard and fast, palming her panties hard enough to make Nadia gasp and moan and widen her legs for him.

Arching her back, she grasped both of her breasts, massaging them underneath his probing hands as she rounded her back in ecstasy.

Moving down her body, Josh saw only white light, white heat; there was only a deep need here tonight with this woman he barely knew, who was, this week, a sort of mother to his lonesome children.

When he pressed his tongue to her, she grasped his head and moved back his roguish hair so she could watch the sweet pleasure ease from his searching, desperate lips into her body. As the erotic sensations deepened and spread, Nadia shook her head wildly from side to side; she rocked her hips into her lover, arching her back wider, her own breath shallow and quick, her quaking body desperate for release.

She came loudly, moving her hips hard against him, and he soaked up her wetness before driving himself into her. When his body let go, Josh melted over Nadia with a vigorous groan and a few last intense thrusts.

And then, with the release of months of pent-up pain, came a release neither he nor Nadia anticipated. It came from someplace deep within his soul, a place where Josh had buried debilitating grief and love for a woman who, at this moment, he missed so desperately he thought he would explode.

Burying his face in Nadia's unfamiliar neck, Josh breathed in a spicy perfumed scent that was foreign to him, then he wrapped his arms around her and let his grief be known. It came in giant, hulking sobs, and lasted until Josh had nothing left to give the universe. It made his muscled body crumple and rock and ache and seize, and it destroyed Josh's heart even further, adding another layer of stone over the few layers he'd accumulated over the last few months.

She responded with soft caresses and tender touches, whispering false hope and hollow love in his ear.

When he finally quieted, empty and ashamed, drained, Josh slipped from his lover's grasp and made his way into the bathroom. He couldn't look at himself in the mirror. Instead, he grabbed a glass and heaved it towards his reflection.

"Fuck you!" he cried as his image shattered, the mirror's crystal shards sharp and menacing in the dim light. "FUCK YOU!!!"

In the bedroom, Nadia rolled onto her side, clutched a pillow, and smiled. "Got you," she told the darkness. "My broken man. It's all uphill from here, Josh Sawyer."

Reaching for her jeans on the floor nearby, she retrieved her cell phone from a back pocket.

Her text to Morgan read simply *I win.*

Chapter Eleven

"He's going to be walking before you know it."

Jonathon was leaning against the doorframe of the studio playroom watching his grandson hang onto a chair and try to pull himself up to a standing position. David's hair was getting longer, the fine blonde strands straight as a pin.

"He reminds me of you when you were a baby, Josh. Stubborn and insistent. He'll work at standing by himself until he gets it." Jon brushed long fingers through his snow white mane.

"Thought you weren't around much in those days." Josh's tone was harsh and biting. He was losing patience with absent parent thoughts and stories. In his period wardrobe for the 1920's show, which today consisted of trousers and suspenders over a white Henley shirt, and his hair slicked back and cheeks stubbly, all Josh needed to make him downright threatening was the usual holster and gun from the props department.

Regarding him in silence, Jon's eyes roving over the ever-present worry lines creasing Josh's forehead went unnoticed. Josh was fixated on his girlfriend of now a few months, who was sitting on one butt cheek on the floor by Emily-Grace, helping her place large baby farm animal pieces in a wooden puzzle.

Nadia looked up, and met Josh's solemn stare. She smiled affectionately, but he didn't return the pleasantry. His lips were slightly curved down at the corners, the usually warm chocolate eyes now dark and foreboding.

Jon brought him out of wherever sinister place Josh had momentarily disappeared.

"I was around some in your first few years. It was after Wes lost that fire

85

department show, when he moved back home for a while, that I got the boot." Clapping his son on the shoulder, Josh's biological dad turned to go. "Let's have dinner tonight, okay Josh? After wrap?"

"Nadia and I have plans," was Josh's subdued response. "We're getting that sitter Jessie and me…" He swallowed, catching himself, and shifted his weight to his other foot, "Uh, the one we used to get last season. Nadia wants to try that new Italian place down by the CN Tower."

Of course she does, Jon caught himself thinking as his blood pressure spiked. *It's the most expensive place in the city.*

Expensive plans aside, the Sawyer nanny was frowning at Josh now. Any reference to Jessie…well, he recognized the slip immediately, so Josh avoided her glare.

Steve was upstairs too, just down the hall chatting with one of the production's office assistants, who was coordinating travel for him to fly back to Vancouver the following weekend. He tensed when he saw Nadia approach Josh at the playroom door and wrap her arms around his waist. He saw Josh lay his right hand over a bare arm, and meet the woman's eyes. She was talking in a low pouty voice so Steve couldn't make out what she was saying, but her downcast eyes were pretty damn clear, especially as the tension in Josh's posture suddenly made his back stiff as a board.

As Steve eyeballed the couple, Nadia leaned into Josh and kissed him, longingly and lovingly, which seemed to relax him as his other hand went around her waist and crushed her body against his.

Sickened, Steve looked away before turning to go. Just before he hit the landing for the stairs ten feet away, he glanced around again, disgusted, curious, in time to see Josh say goodbye to Nadia. Scowling, he watched as Josh strode down the hall towards him.

Josh slowed when he read the blatant disapproval on his friend's face, and he dropped his gaze to the industrial carpet beneath his feet. As he passed the production office on his left, Josh noticed more uncomfortable stares following him. The office folks adored Jessie, everyone did, and no one was even remotely impressed that he was messing around with Nadia.

Josh shoved the thought away. Who he got involved with was his business. Screw the ignorant buzzards.

Steve and Josh had four scenes together that day. Their chemistry on camera had long been established with the three *Drifters* seasons, but since coming back to *The Wyatt Boys* this year, things were off. As professionals, there was some relief for Josh—and Steve as well, who felt the acute pain of Jessie's absence too—in disappearing inside the fictionalized story of wealthy prohibition era rum runners. But as an actor, Josh's emotional touchstones—the techniques he employed in pulling up the emotion needed to play his part—were off balance, crooked, too deeply buried to access for fear of where they would take him if he had to go there.

So, these days, Josh was working on a more surface level, unable to communicate with his co-star even on a visceral level, and so his performance suffered. What it meant was take after take, and an increasing impatience on everyone's part. The crew was feeling the fallout, people were tense, and through the long days Josh found himself ducking his head and sucking in his breath more and more, aware that he was the object of their pity and scorn.

And so, near the end of this seemingly endless day, he lost it.

His target was himself, but his arrows were aimed at the camera operator, whose annoyance with Josh missing lines—again—was voiced through quickly dropped hands, a twist of his neck so he could glare behind him at the episode's mid-fifties director, who was standing nearby in front of a video monitor, and a loud obnoxious *hummpph*.

Steve knew it was coming. As the day progressed, he was witness to the pressure building on set, and especially in his friend's eyes, the same way the little kids in the upstairs playroom stacked their blocks, higher and higher, unwieldy chunks of pressure each fitting crookedly on top of the other.

Steve prayed they'd get their day shot before his friend exploded, before the blocks were flung violently to far-off corners. But the pressure was too much—the blocks had reached their limit. First there was the twitching nerve on Josh's cheek, then Steve noticed a constant clenching and unclenching of his fists. There was also the habit Josh had picked up of late of avoiding everyone's eyes by staring downwards, and then, the final straw—a rapid look in the camera guy's direction, and a black *I fucking dare you* stare.

The set dec department wasn't impressed. Today, the production was shooting in a space designed as the Wyatt Estate's formal front room, which was lavishly dressed with actual antiques, including a rare mantel clock with a bronze statue of a cowboy resting on top. Set dec watched as their usually genial actor—with whom many of them used to share jokes, laughs and dinner—in two steps, using his arm as a crowbar, swiped the antiques with a hard left and sent the clock and the bronze flying.

The production still didn't have the scene in the can. The crew on set that day, which numbered almost seventy when you counted interns, froze, almost afraid to breathe, as a man they felt they no longer knew fired imaginary bullets into the cam-op's exasperated hazel eyes. And they listened, stunned, each with one ear cocked, as Josh lit into the man with both guns blazing.

"You fucking asshole, you want to try this? You want to come out here in front of everyone and be a trained monkey for a day? Huh? Get out from behind that big camera where people can actually see you? No? Maybe it'd be good for you. In fact," eyes raging, Josh scanned the room of shocked faces, "all of you should try it."

Ruthless, he picked out a guy from the props team. "Earl, you're about my height. If pukeface here doesn't have the guts, maybe you should play my part. Pretty sure my wardrobe would fit. Here." Josh whipped off the dove-grey double-breasted jacket he was wearing for the scene. "Try this on. See if it fits. I'm taking a goddamned break."

Dropping the blazer in the dazed guy's arms, Josh stormed off the set, past Steve, who he didn't bother looking at since Josh figured what he would find would be disapproval and loathing.

He was wrong. Steve ached to reach out to his friend, to pull him close in a big hug, even. To try to make things go easier at a time when the world around them was confusing and strange.

Jonathon was on set, watching from the perimeter. As a quiet murmur started around him, he eased his way over to Steve, who, eyes afloat, was staring hopelessly at the door through which Josh just disappeared.

Jon shuffled his feet before speaking. "I think I'll give that counselor he and Jessie were seeing a call."

"No point," Steve told him directly. "He's been to see her. Trudy's husband Frank sat in with them too. Frank told Charles and Dee that Josh is just in a real bad place right now. That he's trying to function but he can only manage it on some peripheral level." Sighing, Steve shoved both lanky hands in his pants' pockets. "To be honest, Jon, I don't even recognize him. Since he took up with Nadia, it's like he's been completely sucked into some dark abyss."

"I can't help but notice he's been drinking."

"So far it's only a few beer a night. Maybe that's one good thing about Nadia, at least. She seems to keep that in check."

"No comment." Jon watched as a delicate Asian woman from his set dec department lovingly picked up the bronze cowboy and cradled it in her graceful fingers.

"Looks like we're taking five. Or thirty-five," Steve said drily. "I think I'll see if Josh's brother Zach has any coffee accounts in Toronto in need of a site visit."

Steve didn't bother going to check on Josh right away. He figured his friend would either be in the playroom with Nadia and his kids, or in his dressing room. *Also,* he thought with a heavy heart, *the guy needs some time to cool off. Even if I do drop in, it's not like we know what to say to each other anymore.*

But in ten minutes, after he got Zach's downhearted confirmation that he'd book a flight from Seattle to Toronto within the next few days, Steve found himself outside his co-star's dressing room. He hesitated before knocking lightly.

It took Josh a minute before he said, "It's open." He knew it was either Steve or Jon at his door and, despite not wanting to see either of the men, he had cooled off enough to realize he had to finish this shoot day…in front of all those staring, judgmental eyes. The alarming thought got his heart pounding in his ears again, and made his palms all sweaty.

When Steve entered, Josh forced himself to face him. He was sitting on a small bed placed in the room for his benefit on days when lighting was taking forever and nighttime sleep was elusive. Knees bent, arms draped loosely over them, he was the picture of doom.

Apprehensive, Steve creaked his tired body down onto the sofa across the small space from Josh.

"That was quite the show, Sawyer." He imitated Josh's on-set arm swing.

"Irreplaceable antiques and all. You might want to apologize to Daphne. Pretty sure she's in tears on set right now."

Josh didn't say anything. He just turned his head to the side and stared at a small hole in the wool blanket folded over the foot of the bed.

Hesitant, Steve went on. "Although I'd say you got back at Gallant. He's gonna have to do a creative reverse for continuity in case some viewer in Greenland is keeping track of the set dec on this show."

"Get to the point, Steve. Although I already know what you plan to say so maybe we should just skip the little 'poor Josh' song and dance."

"Actually, you're getting laid regularly these days, so I can't say I feel too damn sorry for you."

"What does everyone have against Nadia?"

"I don't know, Josh. Any idea?" With that sarcastic query, Steve sat back and laid an elbow over the backrest of the small sofa.

A shrug of the slumped shoulders telegraphed Josh's thoughts, which were basically *I don't really care.*

Steve illuminated him anyway. In a subdued voice he said, "It's only been a few months."

"Five now," Josh said, snapping his head around to face Steve. "She missed David's first birthday. He'll be walking any day now. She's losing her daughter, too. We all are. Or haven't you noticed, being so focused on the imminent arrival of your own kid and your own perfect little family?"

"So that's how it's going to be now, is it Josh? You're so damned angry at the world that everybody in it is a target?"

A flicker of the old Josh seeped in then, as the slumped guy on the bed faced his best friend. "I can't do this, Steve," he announced. "A second time. I can't...sit around and wonder if she's alive again, or if she's ever coming home. I can't always be wondering if that girl walking down the sidewalk in front of me with the brown boots is Jessie! Hell, every time I look at Emily-Grace and wonder what the hell she knows that the rest of us don't, I feel like I'm gonna lose my mind. Like I want to pick her up and shake some truths out of her! My own daughter."

Trying to get a grip, he looked away again. Then, facing the hole in the wool blanket, Josh's words were frank and final. "I choose not to do it again.

I'm moving on. Nadia's a part of that, so the rest of you may as well just get used to her."

"Nadia is a gold digger, Josh—you have nothing in common with her. If you want to move on, at least find someone who is more in tune with you."

"I had that. I'm not interested in forming deep attachments to anyone, Steve. Not anymore. This cast and crew included."

"Oh, so this is just about sex. And by cast and crew, I'm assuming you also mean your best friend. And your father."

"Jonathon is my father just about as much as Gallant on camera is. He missed all the good stuff."

"You know he's here for you."

"And you," Josh pointed a finger at Steve. "You just sit there judging me. But you have no idea what my life is like right now. Or what I need."

"Maybe not." Green eyes flashing, Steve stood to go. "But I do know one thing. I know what Jessie needs. She did not choose this, Josh. Not this time. She has to be going crazy, without you, without her children. She needs us to believe in her. To keep hoping, for *her*. What she doesn't need is you fucking your children's nanny and treating everybody around you like they're the ones who've stowed her away, wherever the hell she is. That's what she doesn't need."

"You almighty prick." Josh stayed seated on the bed, but his eyes were crazed now, after the heated emotion of the long day. "Aren't you just a god-damned social conscience? Supporter of runaways and victims of violence?! Why do you think they gave the kids back, Steve? Huh? Half-assed, as it were, if you consider my daughter is not what she used to be, a happy little girl whose laughter buoyed you when you had a bad day, who could turn your mood around with a look in your direction, huh? Who now is just vacant half the time, 'cuz I guess it runs in the Wheeler blood and all, but still…"

He was choking now, supremely pissed at Steve for accessing the part of him that so desperately hurt, for making him feel something he didn't want to, that ruthlessly sliced him in two. The last part of the sentence was a pained whisper.

"Why do you think the kidnappers gave the kids back? Huh? I'll tell you why. It's because she's dead, that's why. Jessie was no longer able to care for her children. That's what Emily-Grace saw that upsets her so much when we try to get her to talk about her momma. She saw her die. This time Jessie's dead. She's not coming back, Steve. She's not. Not this time. We couldn't be that lucky…twice."

"You bastard." Coiling his fists, Steve prepared to strike. "How dare you. Jessie's your wife! You don't give up on her until you know for sure! Until there's proof!"

"I have proof!" Josh cried, thumping his chest with one trembling fist. "You know what it is, that proof? I used to be able to feel her, *before*, you know—that stupid telepathic kind of shit you always teased us about! And I can't feel her anymore, Steve. I can't. And that only means one thing." Josh summoned the courage to say it, and then he spit out the terrible words. "She's gone."

Unable to bear the weight of the intolerable declaration, Steve crumpled. But the light in his eyes where Jessie Wheeler was concerned was not yet fully extinguished, as it seemed it was in Josh's sorrowful gaze. He rallied. "No," he said definitively, drawing himself up to full height. "No. You're the one who's dead. *You* gave up. *You* died. Not Jessie."

Swinging around, he shoved open the door with both fists, pitilessly thinking he couldn't give a damn if he ever saw Josh's shadow darken his door again.

Two days later, Zach arrived, but all Josh's brother saw was the same guy who, after a terrible accident on a motocross course years ago, had disappeared into himself in much the same way, and who was quickly spiraling downwards until he would soon only crawl on the base level of society, with garbage and worms and creepy black bugs. Josh was largely uncommunicative, and Zach left Toronto with the thankless task of having to tell Hilary, Kayla and his own sprouting youngsters that the light that came back in Josh's eyes after he met Jessie Wheeler…was now irrevocably buried and gone.

Chapter Twelve

$\mathcal{N}$adia started making scenes of her own around the Toronto set. The unwelcome antics started with her bringing the children down from the playroom so she could watch some of the shooting. Take after take was ruined when David cried or gurgled, ruining the sound recording. Emily-Grace was never a problem. The child was removing herself from reality more and more lately. She always stood silently at Nadia's side, a good little girl who never seemed to want to be held by her father anymore.

Jacob was on set the first day Nadia had a hissy fit. He had his girlfriend with him—Rachael, who Josh first met at the Keating home in January. She was a steady rock for Jacob—easy-going and interested in producing music, a musician in her own right, and at the time an employee of Charles Keating. Rachael was, Jacob told himself, almost his twin. They shared a silly sense of humor, and for Valentine's Day she made him a tray of cupcakes decorated overall with an iced pink message—*Love u forever.* He was starting to think she was a keeper.

Now, Jacob stood with his feet a hip's width apart and silently watched as Josh made his way to Nadia, quietly took her elbow, and removed her from the set. Jacob couldn't hear what was said, but whatever it was, it was not accepted graciously. Nadia threw a hissy fit in front of the children and in front of the crew. Finally, she turned to leave.

That was the moment both Emily-Grace and her father spotted Jacob.

Somewhat apprehensive, when he found himself locked in both sets of Sawyer eyes, Jacob waved.

Josh nodded back at him but he didn't make his way over. He knew Jacob had a guest spot to shoot for the series for a few weeks, so the guy's appearance was not a surprise. What did, however, surprise Josh—as well as Steve and Jon and everyone else on set that day—was Emily-Grace's reaction.

The quiet child had always been close to Jacob. But she hadn't seen him in months, not since January. It was now late April. She had barely spoken over the last many weeks, and clung to no one, with perhaps the exception of Nadia at times, and her baby brother, whom she watched over like a little mother. Now, her singer-dowwy dangling from one hand, she left her nanny's side and started walking towards Jacob. Picking up her pace, the little girl ran the last twenty feet, blonde ringlets waving in the slight breeze created by her rapid movement.

Jacob met her halfway. Scooping her up, he swung Jessie's daughter around.

Trembling, she clung to her mother's good friend, tears leaking from both lonely eyes.

"Miami," the small lips whispered into his neck. "Miami."

"I know, baby girl," he answered softly. "I Miami you, too."

Grinning through the wetness unleashed by his own eyes, Jacob held Emily-Grace away from him so he could see how much she'd grown; so he could discern how hurt she still was after all these months without her glorious momma's golden light around.

He was taken aback at her sallow, vacant appearance. But Jacob swallowed the shock and turned the child around to meet his girlfriend. Emily-Grace averted Rachael's gaze and buried her face in Jacob's neck, refusing to see anyone but him.

Nadia stormed by and shot him a dirty look. "Bring her up to the playroom when you're done with her, will you?"

Like an old toy, he thought. He'd been talking to Charles over the last few weeks. There were serious discussions in the works about Charles and Dee taking over stewardship of Josh and Jessie's children. Even Steve, Zach, and Hilary agreed it was likely for the best. Kayla was mute on the subject. Always her brother's biggest fan, next to Jessie, she refused to believe Josh was so far gone that he couldn't care for his own babies.

Now, holding the little girl and spying the fear and sadness in the diaphanous, pale eyes, and feeling the shaking arms around his neck, Jacob couldn't help but agree. Sighing deeply, he looked up to meet Josh's hard stare.

Josh spoke without greeting either Jacob or Rachael.

"She shouldn't have been on set. There was some serious cursing and grown-up stuff happening on camera. Nadia was wrong to bring the kids down. Emily-Grace got a fright."

Placing a hand on his daughter's back, Josh cringed when she tried to squirm away from him. Jacob noticed but was wise enough to remain silent.

Josh bit the corner of his lip. Curt, he nodded at Rachael, then dropped his hand from his daughter's back and strode away.

"Sweet Jesus," Jacob murmured as Steve approached. "It's like a whole different dimension."

And it was, with Jessie gone. All these months, it was like without her light the golden fairy dust was gone. Everyone's lives were hollow.

Jacob suddenly had a surreal moment in which he realized the full impact on all these people's lives a few years earlier, how scared they must have been then, as well, when Jessie was gone. It hurt his belly to think of it, and he wrapped his arms tighter around the little girl who so clearly desperately missed and needed her momma, the momma who would have never these days willingly left her family—Josh—behind.

Burying his face in the pretty blonde ringlets, Jacob didn't answer when Steve said hello.

Chapter Thirteen

Jessie plunked a few notes on the Gibson, then she jotted some lyrics in green crayon over a drawing of a unicorn that Emily-Grace missed coloring when she was with her. But her heart wasn't in the music. It was April now, and although she'd long ago stopped making marks on the cupboard to acknowledge the passing days, Jessie knew it was spring by virtue of the one sweet blessing in her life these days—Sakura trees exploding in gorgeous pink bloom around the back fence. Some weren't as high as the fence, but if Jessie squeezed her eyes by one of the cracks between boards, she could see the blooms. And when she stood in the middle of the small backyard and looked up, she spied them just peeking over the fence, as if they were saying *see, there is still beauty in the world if you look for it.*

Now, though, she was running out of steam. She was forgetting to write notes to her captor to tell him what she needed, what to load into the daily basket. Jessie only bothered showering once a week or so, when the ripe, rank smell of her dirty skin and clothes reminded her of how she felt, like some disgusting bottom-dweller with no future.

On the good days, she was able to tell herself she was lucky, that there were political prisoners in the world kept captive for years in worse prisons, and still their will to survive triumphed over evil. Also on those days she could feel a divine presence somehow seeming to egg her on, that sent new tunes to write, new lyrics to sing. Sometimes Jessie thought the muse was her father. But sometimes that was her undoing, too.

Because the more she thought about her father, the more she considered Heaven, and dying. Seeing her dad again. Her thoughts passed to George and

Martha. Because of their advancing ages, they weren't long for this earth. Jessie would go to Heaven and hang with them, and…

Blissful sighs escaped her lips when she pictured her tousle haired teen boyfriend again. Sandy…and their skinny, freckled friend Rachel. *What sheer bliss to be with them again.*

Jessie knew she was in trouble when she spent entire days in bed making up stories about her old friends instead of thinking about Josh and her children.

The downhill slide actually came along pretty quickly for Jessie. She was doing okay with her songwriting, brief outdoor runs around the yard, push-ups and Yoga. But then one day another story from the Internet was delivered in print via the outdoor basket. Initially grasping it with a desperation that sucked the breath out of her, thinking it was another photo of her children and Josh, and maybe even Jacob this time, it ended up being an image and article with the power to destroy the little will and hope Jessie had left.

It was Josh, all right, but not the Josh she knew. This man was angry, according to the dark eyes and downturned lips. He was facing the camera this time, so she could clearly see the fury playing beneath the surface of those perfect eyes, on the lips Jessie loved to tease with a finger and then her tongue.

Worse? He wasn't alone.

On his side was a woman whose hand he firmly held, an East Indian woman, it seemed, a real beauty, in fact. The woman was clearly his, the photograph said, and…worst of all, she was holding the hand of Josh and Jessie's daughter. Not Josh, no, he wasn't grasping the child's fingers in his. This stranger was. And Emily-Grace was the one holding David's hand.

Jessie's baby was standing upright. He was walking.

Why the children weren't on Josh's side was not a mystery to Jessie. She discerned instantly, by virtue of her husband's angry countenance, that he was not the father they all knew. That he was likely barely being a father at all to these two children he cherished so deeply. That he was a skeleton only, and his soul was missing.

Yet…he had a new woman. Josh was moving on. Again. Michelle crossed Jessie's mind.

Unbidden, she recalled some of Jacob's last words to her.

When he cracks, and he will…I'll be waiting.

"I don't want to go back," Jessie cried into her pillow that night. "I want what I had. I can't do this anymore."

Great heaving sobs consumed her then, at least what was left of her. She had a few lucid moments left, like today's, when she tried to write songs and play the Gibson, but they were now becoming few and far between.

One day she just stopped living altogether. Jessie stayed in bed and asked death to come. She didn't beg—not at first, at least. But then…yes.

On such days, Morgan sometimes saw a smile crease his captive's face. He wondered where her mind was taking her. He had no way of knowing she was playing guitar at ghostly campfires on Folly Beach in Charleston, and that her father was across from her.

But he knew one thing—she was slowly dying.

~~~

Nadia came out to Vancouver with Josh during a break in shooting.

The writers were cautiously scaling back their lead actor's part in *The Wyatt Boys*. As the show's creator and executive producer, Jon supervised and wrote with the team of writers, but he was unable to meet their eyes when they suggested new actions for Josh and he felt he had no recourse but to shake his head *no*.

Today, a late April day, her last day in Vancouver on this trip, Nadia pointed a rented car towards Langley. She arrived in a rush of heels and elegance that Morgan found off-putting. Chewing on his lip, he leaned a hip against the main floor's stove in the small house and listened to her ramble on about the virtues of life as Josh's woman.

Below, lost in a stupor, through the increasing fog in her muzzy mind, Jessie thought she heard a woman's voice in the house again. She imagined she heard her captors making love somewhere above her. She imagined she heard them fighting.

The inside door opened at one point and the woman tiptoed into the room. By then, Jessie was too far gone to even bother raising her head. The woman bent over her. She was wearing the usual balaclava, and she didn't speak. Through the vague eyeholes in the creepy black knit mask, she peered at Jessie. Her dark eyes were searching, but they were devoid of substance.

Like Deuce's, Jessie was able to discern through the haze of muzz and fog permeating her meager existence these days.

As Jessie lay on the bed with one elbow crooked underneath her head, the mystery woman roughly grabbed her hair and pulled her wan face back so she could take a better look. The woman's low top sagged open. Somewhere in her addled mind, Jessie's unfocused gaze picked out a tattooed name scripted across a breast—*Darin.* Or *Darins*? Absently, she thought it read *Darins*, which seemed an odd name.

Moments later, the woman teetered around on one high heel and left the room.

Jessie couldn't muster up enough energy to give a sweet shit. Closing her eyes, she floated herself back to the beach.

~ ~

Nadia said her goodbyes to Morgan that day.

"I've had it. I'm done. I like my new life, and I'm staying in it."

She was standing across from him in the ratty seventies décor upstairs kitchen. Hands on her hips and one knee bent, she was presenting such a haughty stuck-up arrogance that Morgan wanted to slap her. But he didn't. Instead, he stood staring blankly at a woman he thought he knew, but whom he now realized, after the last many months of watching her with Josh, was someone who had taken on a new role—the partner of a film and TV star.

Disgust lined his broad face.

"This was supposed to be a game, Nadia. A challenge. Which you won a long time ago. It was supposed to be something to spice up our marriage with, to feed your sick need for fantasy."

She wiggled her left finger at him. A diamond ring flashed in the scattered sunlight being diffused in the ugly kitchen. "Josh and I are getting married. As soon as it's proven Jessie's no longer an issue."

"Uh-huh. And how do you propose we—" Morgan's eyes widened. "No fucking way."

"She's dying anyway, Morgan. She can't even lift her head off the pillow. When's the last time she ate anything? Or pissed in the toilet? It smells like goddamn piss in there."

Pausing, she softened. "Look, honey, I know this is more than we bargained for. I know you care about her. But trust me, this is for the best. There's no way we'd get out of this mess now without someone eventually figuring things out. For one, your grimy fingerprints are probably all over this place. The way I see it, we have no choice but to cover our tracks by cutting and running."

"I always wear gloves here," Morgan bit off before a new thought sliced him in two. He shifted his feet before glaring at his wife. "Not you, though," he said darkly. "You're not going to cut and run."

Shrugging in that stuck-up way of hers, Nadia responded recklessly with, "Why would I? He's every woman's dream. I like being Josh's girlfriend, going to the fundraisers and awards shows in haute couture gowns and being photographed and featured in all the fashion blogs."

"Even though they all label you a nasty gold digger? And say he's some kind of royal asshole?"

"He's never hurt me. I'm not afraid of him. He's putty in my hands as long as I take care of his kids."

"So you're walking out of this. You're MY goddamned wife, Nadia."

"I'm not stupid, Morgan. I know what this was. It was some kind of twisted gift. You went along with this bizarre game as some kind of sick exchange for the loss of our child. Our lost family for Josh and Jessie's real one. That doesn't make you much of a husband, in my books. In my books it just makes you weak, as if you can hide behind Darin's death by virtue of shrinking in a corner, not even caring that I'm out there grabbing at a whole new brass ring! Well, I've got news for you, Morgan. I don't want to be married to a weak man." Her cocky, narrowed stare was accented with a *huff* and a quick twist of her hips.

At the mention of their son, whom neither discussed, ever, Morgan went cold. His heart turned to ice. Speechless, he could only stare at the large diamond on his wife's finger.

Nothing was forthcoming from Morgan's lips, so Nadia jumped in again, chin raised defiantly in the dusty air and red lips curled in a malevolent downwards sneer. "Yes. I'm leaving you. You and me are done. But you know something? This isn't news. The truth is, we were done that awful day when our boy was diagnosed." Pausing, Nadia's voice changed to one devoid of emotion. "I bought some gasoline. I'll leave it on the porch. It'll speed things up. I'm off. We're flying back to Toronto tonight."

Turning to go, she flipped back around at the last minute. "Oh, and Morgan? You might want to quit your job."

His wife's sardonic smile was the last thing Morgan saw before she left and he went ballistic. Mocking his failure to rescue their son, blaming him, Nadia's righteous, soulless face hung there in the lifeless kitchen, taunting him, a final ode to a marriage that started to flounder the instant a doctor shocked it into decay with very bad news.

Morgan paced the old linoleum for hours, wringing his hands through his hair and muttering incoherently to himself. In the dismal early light of the next morning's tentacled pink dawn, he made a decision drawn from the bottomless well into which he'd fallen.

Before he ended his and Nadia's vicious game, though, Morgan decided he had one last gift to give his boss. Not once did he consider he was also gifting himself.

Morgan didn't plan it, but he saw through the one-way mirror that Jessie must have been having some kind of nice dream, because she was mewling a little on her back on the soiled bed, and the filthy jeans were undone. Her fingers were underneath the waistband, and Morgan saw the ache in the parched, twisted lips.

Clearly, he knew what she wanted. In fact, he thought it would be a nice way to go, for her to really *feel* one last time, to have a man fill her up. Over all, Morgan didn't give a shit who she thought he was, in her delirious state. But he felt he owed her something. He refused to admit it had anything to do with his own desires…months of watching her, or years, if you counted the time before he and Nadia stole Jessie and her children away from their superstar celebrity lives.

As Morgan watched, slightly dumbfounded and overtly aroused, on the bed he saw Jessie rhythmically moving her hips. He wondered if it was Josh she was thinking about. Realistically, he supposed it was. Or maybe Jacob. That wouldn't surprise him, given the way she sometimes gazed at the guy, obviously awestruck and captivated by his blue eyes and pouty tunes.

Placing the balaclava over his head, Morgan grabbed a few lengths of rope he kept for such an emergency, and he strode angrily towards her, entering through the thick inside door Nadia used earlier.

Jessie was too ill and weak now to fight him, but Morgan didn't want to take any chances. He was on her before she realized anyone was even in the room. One knee atop her thighs forced her legs to remain still while Morgan trussed Jessie's wrists and tied a few loops around the hollow 1940's headboard. Then, cursing Nadia's stupidity and his own inability to save anything worth saving—a child, a marriage…Jessie—he yanked off her jeans and panties and tied her ankles, each separately, forcing her legs apart. He tied off the ends of the rope lengths at each corner of the foot of the bed, just underneath it, around the metal legs.

And then Morgan took his time with Jessie because he knew, he just knew, she was so out of it she wouldn't really understand that the person on top of her, making love to her, simply touching her after months with no human touch at all, was not her husband. Caressing the pretty, pale face, settling his frustration and anger somewhat, Morgan gently lifted Jessie's top, pulled the balaclava up a bit, and brought his lips to her nipples. He sucked on the delicate pink parts of her, each in turn, moaning at the feel of her damp skin beneath his lips as he knelt over her and moved his mouth down her body. When he forced himself inside this woman the world mourned, he cried while he thrust again and again, partly for her pain and the deep loneliness he witnessed almost daily from the other room, but also partly for the loss of Nadia and Darin in his own life, for his own deep loneliness, and for Josh, Emily-Grace, and David, who he knew would never recover from what started as a vicious game, but seemed would now end as a heartless murder.

Morgan also cried for his own love of this woman beneath him, a woman who was always nice to him, who loved him in her own kind way, and who he used to watch with a simple joy and longing while she played with her children, or while she stared in adoration at the husband she loved with her entire soul, or while she sang to audiences of thousands.

Jessie orgasmed underneath Morgan. It didn't take long, she was already ripe for the picking, Morgan knew, because she was giving herself a head start while he was still grabbing the bits of rope. It took him a little longer because she felt different to him, different than what he was used to, at least. And because there were still some nerves on his part, despite the total losses he felt consuming him today, and the total sense of desolation and longing for a life he knew he could now never again have.

When he did finally erupt inside her, he stayed there for a while and tented his arms around his boss like he supposed her husband did after they made love, and despite the soiled bed and the soiled rotten stench of her, and the aching loss in his boss' eyes, he pulled the balaclava up further to give his mouth even more room to play, then Morgan bent to her neck and kissed her there, underneath the greasy hair, and loved her anyway.

A disembodied voice called him back to reality.

"Why?" was the extent of what it had to say. One word. One tiny, hollow, simple questioning word, which hung in the dank air to haunt Morgan for the rest of his life.

Yanking the creepy mask back down over his chin, he slipped away without answering. He left the ropes. He left her half naked. Morgan was done. One set of fingers was still doing up his jeans when he grabbed the first red plastic container of gas. He sobbed like a baby the whole time he spread it around the first floor of the house.

The match was lit at 5:54 a.m. He dropped it, then stood outside and watched the flames take hold, before Morgan hauled his exhausted spirit into his pickup truck and drove away.

Chapter Fourteen

$\mathcal{A}$ farmer on his way to a rented field across the road spotted the first plumes of smoke. The red headed thirty-something guy was young, agile, and quick—he grabbed his phone off his tractor's console and immediately punched in 911.

When sirens came blazing up the rural road, they passed Morgan. He glanced behind him once but kept driving, knuckled hands white on the wheel and tears streaming down his cheeks.

The fire trucks screeched to a halt outside the one-and-a-half story nondescript beige house.

"Anyone inside?" called the chief as he approached the farmer, who was leaning against his tractor idly watching dirty smoke spirals trail off into the sky.

The crew rushed around setting up their hoses and preparing to battle a fire that was, in all likelihood, already well underway and set to demolish the home with a few well-placed licks, spits, and sparks.

"I don't think so," the farmer responded casually, crossing his arms as he leaned back. "The people who rent the place are only here off and on. Thought I saw the truck yesterday, but maybe not. Maybe it was the day before. Suppose you better look, though."

The chief sent his boys in. They came out right away. "Not happening, Chief," the first guy said, shaking his head.

"Okay. Give 'er a check 'round back, will you Danyluk?"

The chief, a solidly-built dark-skinned man of African descent, firm in stance and definitive in authority, glanced around to the main engine, a ladder truck. His crew was quite capably handling things. Looking sideways at the farmer next to him, who pulled out his cell and started filming the fire, he asked, "YouTube? Lotta my fires are on there now. Crazy shit. People like to watch someone else's hard work burn. Weird."

He was starting to walk away when one of his guys hollered from the far side of the house. "Chief? S'like Fort Knox back here. Big fence and solid doors. But Danyluk's gone in the basement. Seems like there's an apartment down there. Smoky, he said, but he had a feeling."

"Gotta listen to your gut when it comes to this shit," the chief muttered. He strode towards the side of the house. The gate floored him. It was a thick, tall door with a deadbolt on the outside, completely out of place in such a rural setting. "What the hell?" he mumbled.

Just then his young Ukrainian guy, Danyluk, came running through the gate, which a ponytailed gal dwarfed by her flame retardant suit was holding open for him. He was carrying someone wrapped in a stained beige comforter—a woman, judging by the long hair drifting dispiritedly over the ground. She wasn't heavy, the young guy wasn't struggling under her weight, but at first glance she appeared lifeless, although the chief was encouraged when he spotted one arm dangling beneath the quilt clutching a soft doll with dark hair.

"Here we go," he declared to no one in particular. "Shit." Glancing behind him, he stared at the road towards the wail of a high-pitched siren announcing approaching EMTs. They were at least a minute away.

"Over here," he demanded sharply of his guy.

Danyluk complied, and laid the prone woman on new tufts of spring grass. He had placed his oxygen mask over her face but she was grabbing and clutching at it. She was trying to speak, but the words were obviously a struggle. Pale and thin, sallow, the woman was by no means well even *before* the fire. The men turned their noses up at the acrid smell of urine wafting up from her body.

As one side of the soiled covering fell away, the chief noticed that, with the exception of a light tank top, the victim was naked. Grabbing the comforter, he draped it over the woman again, but she was struggling against him, seemingly unconcerned about her modesty at the current time.

She was desperate. He knew that look. The chief swallowed a sense of alarm he knew well.

There is someone else in that house. A child.

He noted the doll. The house was already creaking and groaning and starting to splinter. Danyluk, the hero, was poised on one knee ready to go back in. The chief shook his head. *No. Too dangerous.*

But that wasn't it. There was no child inside, but it took a few moments to figure that out.

The woman was finally managing to find the words. "My children," she was crying hoarsely between coughs. "Are they okay?" Approaching hysteria, she was fighting against the men, grabbing first Danyluk's arm and then clutching the chief's heavy jacket. "Please tell me they're okay."

Young Danyluk was staring at her now, at the startling pale eyes. His gaze darted to the plush doll in the woman's hand. This was a doll he knew well. These were eyes he recognized. They graced the news a lot last fall and over Christmas.

"Jesus Christ," he stammered, to the chief's astonishment. He placed his big hand behind the head of the woman he'd just rescued. "What are your children's names, ma'am?"

"Emily...Emily-Grace," came one stammered name. "And...and David. Please!" She gripped his forearm. "Please, are they okay?"

On some level, at least, Jessie knew the children were okay. At least when she saw them in the printed Internet picture, which featured them on Nadia's arm, they were. But in her delusional state, which to Jessie made things still dreamlike and unreal, she needed to hear it.

At that point the chief thought the children were likely still in the house. A familiar crunch tore at his heart. But even he, a man who rarely listened to the gossip news or watched TV, recognized the names of the two very famous children.

It hit the chief like a ton of bricks, then. The woman his young rookie just rescued from this home, a rundown old beige house in Langley, B.C., a short drive from the old *Drifters* set where she once worked—was Jessie Wheeler.

The red headed farmer filmed the rescue.

Within an hour, his video was all over the television news, and all over the Internet.

Chapter Fifteen

In the playroom on the second floor of the Toronto studio, no one was speaking. Jacob was singing, though, in a low tone, as he sat cross-legged on the rug across from Emily-Grace, his hands in hers. She was responding to him, not quite smiling, but regarding him in a worshipful way, eyes alight for once. To Josh, who was crouched down by David handing him blocks to stack one on top of another, his daughter and Jacob were in their own little world. It seemed music had the power to reach the child. Music had the power to offer her comfort. Music had the power to heal.

Rachael had flown back to Vancouver a few days earlier, but Nadia was there with the kids. She was also fetching blocks for David, sitting delicately on one butt cheek as she always did, in a very good mood since she and Josh had snuck back to the hotel in mid-morning for a quickie, despite how tired they were from their rather sleepless all-night west-to-east flight.

Charles and Dee had graciously taken the kids for a few hours that morning—they were in the city on business but stayed an extra day to see the children and to try to convince Josh to let them take Emily-Grace and David back to Vancouver for at least a few weeks. Now, after only a brief few hours with the little ones, they were on their way to the airport to board the jet. The power couple did offer a certain respite to Josh after his all-night flight, but he, in the end, flatly refused their offer. He was afraid it would turn into a battle for custody. Things were that bad.

Charles and Dee left the studio incensed, already missing the baby and three year old they considered their grandchildren.

In the playroom, Josh had his back to the door. He twisted around when he heard footsteps approach and stop behind him. The footsteps were Jon's and, when Josh looked from the expensive shoes up to the face of the man who owned them, he felt his throat close over. Something was wrong. Something had happened. Jonathon was struggling to speak. The man's thin lips were quaking.

Josh's dad managed one word—"Josh." He waved an arm towards his office down the hall.

Jessie. It had to be. A new terror struck Josh. If this was about his wife, what was the news going to be? He knew if it was bad, if it was…final…he would not be able to handle it. He would collapse, close his eyes, and want the world to end. If it wasn't…

His breath started to come in small, short rasps. He let his gaze come back around and, his mind whirling, he stared at David's blocks. The baby knocked over the pile he was building. They were all over the place. They were just sitting there, waiting to be picked up and put into some sort of order. A white gauze covered Josh's eyes. Shaking his head, he blinked, and then looked up.

A few feet away, Jacob had turned his head towards the visitor, also. And now he was staring wide-eyed at Josh. When their gazes connected, white lightning seemed to crash wildly from one set of eyes to the other and back again. Instinctively, both men knew whatever painful truth Jon was holding was about the woman they both loved. They were powerless to move.

Nadia sensed it too. It was tough for her to sit there in silence and not gloat, although she wanted to. Instead, she made a move to go. Jacob eclipsed her. He touched her shoulder as Josh, too, finally stood.

"Stay with the kids, Nadia," Jacob insisted. He rested a hand on Josh's shoulder and, with a last frightened glance towards Emily-Grace and David, he and Josh followed Jonathon down the hall.

In Jon's office was a 17-inch iMac. He turned it towards Josh, who stood, brown booted feet planted a shoulder's width apart, a few feet in front of Jacob. With a finger, Jon clicked the mouse.

A video started to play. It was a TV news report, taken in front of a smoldering pile of lumber and cement blocks. The title across the bottom read *Langley, British Columbia.* A woman reporter started to speak.

A woman was pulled out of what used to be a house here at approximately 6:30 this morning B.C. time, just moments before the structure collapsed. A representative from the Langley fire department said a young rookie entered the home through a back door and made his way through thick smoke to find her lying on a bed in what appeared to be a basement apartment.

Amateur video started to play as the reporter continued her story. Incredulous, unable to breathe, Josh and Jacob watched as a fireman came running around the burning house with a limp woman in his arms wrapped in a comforter, a doll clutched in one hand. As they came closer to the camera, an oxygen mask covered the woman's face, but the doll was unmistakable—it was a Diana doll like the one Emily-Grace was missing. The actual live audio was unheard under the announcer's voice, but the guys could see the woman struggling to remove the mask.

The announcer cleared up the mystery of what the woman was trying to say.

This woman had one thing on her mind—she wanted to know if her children were okay. She told the firemen their names were Emily-Grace and David. It is believed, incredibly, that Jessie Wheeler, the missing singer and Oscar winning actor, and wife of Josh Sawyer, also an Oscar winner, is the woman who was rescued from this inferno. This has not been confirmed by the police at this time. The woman appeared to be very ill and is also suffering from smoke inhalation and minor burns. Apart from giving the children's names, I'm told she was unable to communicate with the firemen. She has been transported to nearby Vancouver General Hospital in what is reported to be critical condition. Is this Jessie Wheeler? Time will tell. But one thing appears to be certain. Whoever this woman is, she was locked inside the home by a massive deadbolt on the outside. And she is very sick.
Hannah MacCallum, CBC News, Langley, British Columbia

"Langley…?" Josh turned to Jon. "Fucking Langley?" He was white.

Behind him, Jacob was gasping for air. He grabbed Josh's arm. "We have to go. We have to go!"

Jon stopped him. Collecting his wits, he took a deep breath. Staring at

Josh and wondering why he was just standing there, stone cold sober with an impenetrable mask on his face, Jon said, without losing his son's gaze, "Hold on, Jacob. I caught Charles and Dee. They're at the jet and they're watching the video now. I called Matt, he's getting in touch with the police. We don't know yet if this is Jessie. There have been other false alarms. Hype over her disappearance is huge in Langley because of the *Drifters* set. We need to be prepared to move, but we also need to wait for Matt's call."

"But…Jon…"

Jon held out a palm to Jacob. "Sit for a minute, Jacob. Wait. There was no way to tell from that amateur cellphone video if that was Jessie or not. Matt won't be long in finding out. Josh," Jon continued. "Son, I'm sorry if this doesn't turn out to be her and I've brought you in here and run you through this roller coaster. But I think it might be. Emily-Grace's doll…her hair… you need to be prepared."

Still a stone wall to Jon and Jacob, inside, Josh was fighting to stay in control. Finally he spoke, just a murmur, really, but loud enough for the men, and Steve, who came careening down the hall and into the room, to hear. "It's her," he said, starting to crumble.

"H-how?"

Jacob answered for him. The singer was crying. Pointing a trembling finger to the screen, he moaned, "The fucking noose." At Jon and Steve's confused looks he added, "The goddamned $ 23 000 Tiffany & Company engagement ring."

It was, indeed, a unique and unusual ring. It was exquisite. Jacob stepped forward and clicked on the mouse. He moved the video back to a point when the rescued woman's left hand was struggling to pull off the oxygen mask. The ring was not large in the frame, but it was certainly big enough to see, especially when the image was static.

It was Jessie's ring all right; the one Josh gave her that magical Christmas Eve when he first proposed.

And now it was in a hospital in Vancouver, on the finger of the woman Josh loved, who was listed in critical condition and who, unbelievably, likely just spent the last six and a half months locked in a basement apartment located just down the road from the *Drifters* set.

Chapter Sixteen

He had to tell Nadia. While Josh walked on shaking feet down the hall, he kept his emotions at bay. He had to. His children were in the playroom with her. Jon's cell rang while Josh was passing Steve, who was leaning on the doorframe, wide-eyed and anxious. Josh heard Jon say, "Yeah, the boys saw the ring on her finger. They think it's her." After a pause, he heard, "Sweet Jesus. Okay. All right. Matt, can you fly up to Van? Please? Charles asked me to ask you. We'll meet you there, the jet's fueled and ready anyway since Charles and Dee were just heading back."

After that, Josh tuned his father's voice out. Watched by Steve, whose eyes he could feel boring into his back, he stepped into the playroom.

He couldn't look at Emily-Grace or David yet. Not until Nadia was gone, out of sight. She stood and faced him.

"I'm sorry," she said, reaching for him. "I'm so, so sorry, Josh."

Confused, he grabbed her elbows and held her away from him. "Wh-what?"

Upon realizing what she said, Nadia recovered quickly. She'd almost let the cat out of the bag, per se. "It must be something bad. The—the look on Jon's face. That's all."

His mind was a mess. Josh was all over the place. He wouldn't remember her saying that for months. For now, he held Nadia back and, while Emily-Grace watched, he told her to go home.

"Wh-why?" she asked. "It's Jessie, right?"

"It's Jessie," he answered definitively. "I have to go." He sucked in a breath. "Nadia, I'll call you. We'll sort this out, okay? But right now, I just have to go."

111

"No! I'm coming with you." *She's dead, right? But...the fire...how could they know so soon the body was Jessie?*

"That's not gonna happen, Nadia. You're staying in Toronto." Josh's voice was all thick and gummy now, and he could feel a desperate moisture trying to leak through his eyes. Caryn's comment from so long ago haunted him. *I'm an iceberg. And I'm melting.*

He wanted to tell his kids. He wanted to get on the jet and see Jessie in person. And there was that new terror, too, the one the reporter called 'critical condition.' What the hell did that even mean?

Dropping Nadia's arms, he spoke gruffly. "Go home," he said again, demanding she listen. "I'll call you."

She understood then, still not that Jessie was alive, but that there would be details he would have to attend to. And press, and...well, it likely wouldn't do to have the new girlfriend at the old wife's funeral. Nadia nodded. "Okay."

Swiping at his eyes, Josh finally turned to his uber-sensitive three year old, the child who never wanted her daddy to read to her, or play with her anymore. The one looking at him now from behind Jessie-eyes, too scared of her father's visible emotion to set down the little book she was holding on her lap while she pretend-read to singer-dowwy.

Steve had followed Josh down the hall. With a firm grip, he grasped Nadia's elbow and led her out of the playroom.

Vaguely, as Josh bent before his daughter, he heard Steve say, "Let's find you a ride home, Nadia."

Now, Josh studied Emily-Grace for a long time before he could speak. He brushed a strand of hair back from a pink cheek. Then he searched her eyes and wondered how much to tell her. How much could she possibly understand when the reality of the situation was just dawning on him?

"Sweetheart," he started. "We'll go on the jet with Grammie and Grampie, okay? I think you would like that."

The child's soft eyes generated hope. *Gwammie and Gwampie. Love. Hugs. Safety.* "Now, Daddy?"

"Yeah. Right now." Oddly, their hotel suite crossed Josh's mind. Were there things he would need to pack? Under no circumstances did he want to go back there right now...he just wanted to get on the jet and go see...

Emily-Grace rose first, carelessly pushing the book off her lap. She clung to the singer-doll Jacob gave her and looked at her father, who stood as well. Then Jacob came to the door, slowly, scared. Emily-Grace went to him and raised her arms. He picked her up.

Turning around to look at him, Josh sighed deeply. He raised both hands out to the sides. "I don't know how to do this, Ryan."

"Do what?" Jacob asked, still trembling. "It's simple. We go, we see, we help."

"Nadia." It was a whisper.

Regarding him critically, Jacob's lips twisted into a weird frown. "Don't f-n tell me you give a sweet shit about f-n Nadia." He spit out her name as if it was poison. Picturing the video image of a very sick Jessie, all Jacob could think was *fight, Jessie, fight.* He knew damn well what heartache she would face if Josh chose Nadia. But…why would Josh do that?

"No, I mean, I do, I just…I don't have anything left, Jacob. I'm barely hanging on. I don't know how…I mean I just don't know…how…" The stone wall started to break. Josh stared at Jacob. His daughter was in the guy's arms. David made his way to his daddy and pulled on his pant leg. Josh was crying openly now, but he knelt down and scooped up his son.

Emily-Grace watched for a moment and then scrunched her eyes tight, buried her face in Jacob's neck, and started to hum softly.

Josh finished his earlier thought. "What if she…" He swallowed, and stood blinking back tears as he dared Jacob to say what he couldn't.

"She won't," is what Jacob demanded of the universe that day. "She won't, because she's alive now, and she's made it this far, and this fucking nightmare's gonna end." He glanced down at the little girl whose humming was eliciting vibrations against his neck. "Sorry, EG. I owe money to your swear jar now too, okay?"

She showed no sign of hearing him.

Heavy footsteps hurried down the hall. "C'mon boys. Josh, Jacob, we'll have someone from the office go to your suites and gather some things for you, and send them out on a commercial flight. Charles and Dee are waiting at the jet. Where's Steve? Let's roll."

Forty minutes later they were at the airport, and were versed on what

Matt knew, which was that Jessie was dehydrated and malnourished. But she was alive.

The flight was more excruciating than waiting for Emily-Grace's birth. There was a lot of silent hand holding (Charles and Dee), and anxious, guarded looks (Steve and Jacob). There was also stony, frightened silence (Josh).

When they landed, Ulysses was cursing Morgan. He had wanted the kid to provide a second vehicle for the large group. Dan had a car there, waiting, but Morgan was, uncharacteristically, not responding to texts or calls. In the end, Ulysses rented an airport limo and chauffeur to go with Dan's vehicle, and the group made their way to Vancouver General.

At this point, after so many months of turmoil and torture, Josh couldn't think straight. His anger consumed him, Nadia's sizzling touch consumed him, and beer and whiskey were his newest friends. He was isolated and alone. In a weird way, Jacob seemed his only friend at this juncture—well, not friend, exactly, but compatriot, at least, in some odd quest.

No one thought Josh deserved to be the first to see Jessie. But he was her husband, and so a kind doctor took him to the ICU while Deirdre cuddled little David, and while Jacob continued caring for Emily-Grace.

Jessie was asleep, her left arm and leg and an area of her left cheek bandaged. The doctor explained that she had second-degree burns but that they were miniscule in size and would heal. The greatest risk was infection, but they would do all they could to prevent any such occurrence. The biggest issue was the dehydration and malnutrition.

"But not months worth," he added, knowing Jessie's story as well as anyone. "It looks like she just lost her steam in the last few weeks or so, Mr. Sawyer. Prior to that, she must have been able to take care of herself." He pointed to the various tubes attached to Jessie's body while Josh stared, hands thrust deep in the pockets of his tan jacket, trying to be impassive. Trying not to feel. Trying not to crumble.

Josh couldn't look directly at her while the doctor was in the room. He was a louse. He had given up on her. He had, for the most part, given up on their kids. He was using Nadia—for her body, for sex, as a security blanket, as a drug, as a babysitter. But on some weird level he also cared about the woman. She was an even-tempered date, and although Emily-Grace seemed to just put up with her, as of late, she was good to the children. Josh didn't feel he belonged here, in this room, with a very ill woman he felt he betrayed the moment she went missing for the second time.

After the doctor left him alone with his wife, Josh stood unmoving until he heard a movement in the bed. He looked down.

She was awake. And she was watching him process this—his missing/found wife. His very sick, looking like hell, detached and lost missing wife, in fact. Jessie's eyes were glazed—from drugs, loneliness, a dream state, you name it. But she recognized him, although she couldn't make her mouth work enough to speak.

Still, when Josh's eyes met the sea-pearl blues he loved, the old connection was back. She seemed to be trying to focus on him. He felt the invisible wire and its electric blue light traverse between them. His iceberg melted just a tiny bit more. Josh tried to make his feet move. They refused. He was standing at the foot of Jessie's bed, his own mouth struggling to find the words, any words.

Finally, he reached out a hand, and let it lead him towards her. There was a large chair by the bed, from which a nurse had been monitoring Jessie before Josh's arrival. Collapsing into it, Josh buried his face in his wife's side, grabbing at her left hand but trying not to hurt it, because it was her burned arm. *Burned?* The whole thing was, indeed, some damnable nightmare. How did the fire start? That information was not yet forthcoming.

"Jessie," he managed. "We're going to have a lot to tell our grandchildren one day."

If we survive this, he caught himself thinking. *If we get through the new agony this latest saga has unleashed. What new trauma has this released,* he wondered. *What new hell have you endured?*

Lifting his head, Josh let his eyes drift over to hers. She was watching him, still. Lifting his right hand, he gently brushed the backs of his fingers over the edge of the bandage on her cheek. There was that old lost look in her eyes, the one from the old days, only...only something was different. Something about the way she was looking at him...judging him...Josh wasn't sure if he actually saw it or just felt he deserved it, but it seemed that through the fog

115

of despondency and drugs, there was anger there. And hurt. He wanted to ask her if she knew…about Nadia. But obviously this wasn't the time.

All the same, he felt a wall come *chunking* up between them, crashing there like the old walls in the Maxwell Smart spy TV show after the spy himself walked by.

Then Charles and Dee were at the door. They, too, were struggling to stay composed. Charles had wrestled Emily-Grace from Jacob, and Dee had David nestled in her arms.

From Jessie's perspective, which on that first day was very much a dream-like floating observation point, it was weird to see these people. *Are they even real?* She spent so much time lost in her fantasy of going to Heaven lately… with Sandy, Rachel, her father…that she was very detached from these still-living people. Until…until her daughter saw her and jarred her back to a brief reality.

"Momma. Momma!" The child knew her mother immediately. She knew her momma was sick…Jacob had explained that very carefully, but Emily-Grace didn't care. She wiggled and wiggled until Dee set her on the bed with a tearful admonishment.

"Be careful not to hurt Momma, she has some boo-boos." Dee had set her down on Jessie's right side. Emily-Grace was suddenly inconsolable. She dropped to all fours and crawled up to her mother's side, wormed her way in between Jessie's arm and body, and sobbed.

A tiny smile lit up Jessie's face at that…at the touch and at the feel of her daughter's hair, and at the little body cuddling up to her. In a hoarse whisper, she uttered her daughter's name. "Emily-Grace. Momma's girl."

In that brief lucid few minutes, there was something Jessie didn't understand, though. Charles and Dee were there, fawning over her, relishing her safe return, but although Josh was in the room, they were ignoring him. He had sequestered himself into a chair against the far wall while everyone else took turns coming to see her. The only one who acknowledged him was, surprisingly, Jacob. By then, Charles and Dee were in the hallway talking to a local detective.

"Hey," was Jacob's tender greeting to her as he bent and kissed the damp forehead. Jessie noticed him lay a gentle hand on her daughter's quavering back. "I knew you'd come back," he murmured. Gesturing to Josh, he said simply, "He needs you."

A grunt from the far wall accompanied the remark.

"Shut it, Sawyer," was Jacob's attempted lighthearted response to that. He grinned happily at Jessie. "I mean it, kid. We've got work to do. We've got music to write."

At that, Josh hauled himself away from the wall. He stood back from Jessie's bed and frowned at Jacob. Then he studied Jessie's eyes and wondered how lucid she was. *Not very*, he thought, so he said aloud, "Jacob's finally gone and got himself a woman."

Her expression flickered at that, and Josh was certain he saw hurt in the pale eyes he loved. But he went on anyway, stupidly and without regard for her feelings, should she actually understand. "So do I, in fact."

The silence was thick and heavy. Then Jacob rubbed Emily-Grace's back a little harder and said, "Well done, Sawyer."

The next voice to break the silence was Jessie's. Despite the surrealism of being out of the tiny basement suite for the first time in six and a half months, and of finally tasting freedom and seeing her children again, she was able to fully discern the deeper meaning behind Josh's admission. She also understood now why everyone seemed to be shunning him.

And she knew what he was really telling her. It came to her with the same tone and meaning as a voice being ruthlessly yanked away from her through a thick steel door. In Emily-Grace's language.

I lost. I hurt.

Josh was her husband. She met him in a pile of garbage outside Charlie's club at a time when his eyes looked similar to the ones watching her now, wanting her to be angry, to hate him the way it seemed everyone else did now. But, as Jacob watched, Jessie buried her own disappointment and pain in the midst of her drugged and lonely purple haze. She reached her burned arm up and waited for Josh to take her hand. When he did, he was choking, struggling, fisting away tears.

"I know," she said. She couldn't say more. The words were not available to Jessie on that first day. But her eyes—her soul—said more. They softened noticeably. They sent him love. And so he calmed.

It was one of those rare, beautiful moments Jacob would remember forever; that allowed him during the tough days to come to calm himself and know without doubt that what Jessie and Josh had went beyond anything anyone else could ever possibly hope to understand. That they were connected so deeply in and around each other, neither time nor distance could ever hope to pull them apart. So deeply in love were they, for so long now, built on a deep friendship and trust, that Jessie's simple touch and tender look had the power to undo many hurts.

And now, Jacob stood silently apart from Jessie as Josh melted in his wife's gaze, and collapsed again, into the closest chair this time, where he could once again bury his face in her side, just like his daughter on the other side of his wife, and cry until he was dry.

And so it was that Jessie met Jacob's eyes then, and smiled sorrowfully at him, wanting to ask him so many questions, like *why is Josh not holding his babies,* but instead sinking into that healing place again where a golden light welcomed her on a sunny beach.

Chapter Seventeen

*E*arly the next morning, in a private boardroom the hospital made available to their celebrity visitors, Charles pulled Matt, who had just arrived, and Ulysses, who was at the hospital all night, into a corner. He sat on the edge of the long, rectangular table and twisted his torso so he could see two uniformed policemen outside the room, chatting with a female detective. Making a small *harumph* sound, Charles pressed his lips together and fixed his gaze on Matt and Ulysses, who were sipping on hot Starbucks coffees kindly brought to them by Sophie.

"All right," he started. "Deirdre's in with Jessie. I don't want her hearing more gory details than she has to. Tell me what you're thinking."

Ulysses glanced sideways at Matt before focusing on Charles. "I'm thinking this isn't over."

Matt placed a hand on his hip and turned towards the side wall, away from the men. Over the last few years, before that terrifying call from Jessie, life had been so peaceful. Busy, yes. Doing security for Kelly Reilly was insane at times, but at other times there were golf games with his brother, dinners out with family, Christmases with Michael and Kelly...and, for the most part, life was on an even keel, for once. No Jessie angst, no worrying constantly over her mental health, no watching for signs of trauma to reappear. Now it would start anew. Not just her, either. Charles told him earlier that Josh was in a bad state and, sadly, Emily-Grace was suffering too. Then there were Charles and Dee to consider, along with Steve and Sophie, Charlie and Jane...it was like Jessie was in the center, surrounded by concentric circles that represented the people in her world, who were all suffering on some level.

And someone out there very likely still wanted the singer dead.

He looked back to Charles and wondered what the man expected of him, if anything. They had barely spoken over the last few years. Their friendship was toast, as far as Matt was concerned. But they were still family. Somewhat estranged, but still…all those years with the Keatings…and then there was Jessie.

That scream coming through the phone last November had him waking in a cold sweat for a long time afterwards. It chilled Matt. It haunted him. It taunted him. Until she was well enough to talk to the police, no one knew what she really went through in the Langley house. On some level, Matt didn't even want to know. It was like going on roller coasters with his daughter. You didn't really want to ride the things, but you knew you would be missing out if you didn't. If you walked away, you'd be wondering what the hell you just missed.

Sure, Matt was no longer in the Keating employ. But he was still family. He needed to know. And he would help where he could, *if* Charles was okay with him sticking his nose in this new mess.

Charles softened when he saw the tough emotions play across his old friend's face.

"If you want to cut and run, Matt…I get it," he offered sorrowfully.

"What if I want to stay? Not to work. Just to…talk to Jessie. To see what's up."

"I'd like that, Matt. And I know Deirdre would too."

"And Jessie," added Ulysses. "She'll be real happy you're here, bro."

"What do we know at this time?" Charles asked, abruptly bringing them to the task at hand, the relief at having Matt nearby almost choking him. He missed the guy. He missed his friend.

Ulysses started. "The house was rented under a name that has proven to be a fabrication. It was a 'cash only' deal, brokered by a woman over the phone who got the place reference free because the owner knew it was a dive. He wanted it rented, and she offered to pay a full year in advance. The guy never met her in person."

"She paid without meeting him?"

"Apparently she left the money in a manila envelope in his post office box. The owner is a Korean guy who flips houses—who picks up properties, then fixes and resells them, hoping to make a quick buck. There are at least a dozen of these ramshackle homes listed under his name. He got the cash rent on this place and then took it off his radar, according to the detective."

"Never dropped by to make sure the place was okay? Some landlord."

"Slum landlord, you mean." Matt shifted his weight and turned to Ulysses. "The farmer said there was occasionally a pickup truck in the driveway."

"Occasionally. But apart from seeing the driver from a distance, and ascertaining it was likely a guy, he didn't give it much thought."

"How occasionally?" Charles asked.

Ulysses eyed Charles carefully. "Sometimes he wouldn't see it for two weeks or more at a time."

Matt pondered his old boss to see how he was handling that shocking news.

The older man swallowed past the bile rising in his throat. "So she was alone for long periods. Not much wonder she's so thin."

"He must have fed her something. And the kids were in good shape over-all when they were found, at least in terms of body weight."

"If they were even together."

"Evidence seems to suggest they were, at least for part of the time. Emily-Grace learned a child's version of Yoga, Steve said. From her mom."

"So no luck tracing the owner of the truck or who was renting the house."

"Who set fire to the house, you mean." Matt's words were subdued.

"There will be a police presence at the house for the next while, Matt," Ulysses offered, scratching his chin thoughtfully. "They'll be watching in case the guy decides to sneak back for a peek at his handiwork."

"To see if she's dead, you mean."

Charles sighed. "Guessing he already knows she isn't."

"Which brings us back to Ulysses' first comment. This likely isn't over."

The men were silent then, as they contemplated the alarming verity of that statement.

"We might need to get Susanne back full time." Charles was speaking to Ulysses, but hoping Matt was paying attention.

He was. A low rumble announced the clearing of his throat. "I can help. If you'll have me."

Crossing his arms, Charles turned to him. "At the top of this conversation you said you weren't interested in working, Matt."

"Maybe some. Not full time. I can fill in a few shifts, at least."

"Can you start today? Morgan texted an hour ago. He's out with the flu."

"Flu?" Matt wrinkled his nose. "The kid do okay over the last few years?"

Shrugging, Ulysses answered, "Yeah. Fine. He did his job. Jessie likes him okay. He's not super social. Never brings his wife to any events or anything."

"He's married?" Surprised, Charles sat back and stared at Ulysses. "I don't think I even knew he was married. For some reason I assumed he wasn't."

"Their home is in Toronto. But Morgan was usually with Jessie, in Miami or on tour, not with Josh in Canada. There hasn't been much opportunity to bring his wife around."

"Remind me to get to know my staff a little better, Ulysses. Anything about you I should know?"

"Yeah. I'm hungry." The good looking dark-skinned man clapped his boss on the shoulder. "Let's take a break, boss. We'll get some breakfast and go over this. There are enough uniforms around here to keep an eye on our girl, and Big Dan's outside her door as well, so I think we can safely head to the cafeteria for some eggs. You in, Matt?"

A quiet nod prefaced Matt's hesitant movement towards the door. As Charles joined him, clapping him on the shoulder as they walked, their eyes met briefly in unity. The small gestures were enough to push the old hurts under some invisible rug, at least for the time being.

With that, the investigation into Jessie's captors began, both on behalf of the police, and via the Keating camp.

The first person Matt considered was Morgan.

And the first person he crossed off his list, due to seemingly sufficient alibis, and Jessie's trust in the guy...was Morgan.

Chapter Eighteen

A few days later, Jessie was feeling the benefits of increased nutrition and hydration. Still very sick, she was at least more fully lucid now. When she got Jacob alone around 11 one morning, she whispered on a voice hoarse from disuse, "He had a hard time of it."

Jacob was sitting on the edge of the hospital bed, facing Jessie, subtly playing with the fingers of her uninjured hand. "He's angry, Jessie. He got angry before the kids came home. And then he got even more angry."

"How angry?"

"You saw him. You saw his eyes. A part of him died, Steve says. He shut himself off. Self-preservation."

"What do you say?"

"I say I'm glad you're back."

"Why isn't he interacting with our kids? Why aren't Charles and Dee talking to him?"

Jacob sighed. "This is too much for you right now, Jess. Just rest for a few days, okay? The hard stuff can wait."

"The police want to talk to me again."

"Yeah. Everyone's curious. You've only given them the basics so far, I hear." Through searching eyes, he peered cautiously at her. "How bad was it?"

"Thought you said to save the hard stuff for later." Her eyes were glistening. "I gave up. I wanted to die, I was so fucking lonely." Exerting a little pressure on his fingers, Jessie soaked up her good friend's essence, reveling in the sheer warmth and pleasure of desperately missed human touch.

Extending his other hand, Jacob touched her cheek, the unhurt side. "You were in a basement apartment. All that time?"

"Yeah. Completely alone once the kids were gone."

"Your voice…is that why…?"

"I sang a lot. But after a while I just stopped using it. I just talked in my head. To dead people."

"Not to us?" A sudden ache crushed Jacob's heart.

"At first. But then it hurt too much, y'know?"

"I know. Damn, I missed you." Bending forward, he brushed his lips against Jessie's forehead.

"I missed you too, Jacob. Although I guess with me gone you finally got yourself more than a warm body, huh? Someone whose PMS you can stand?"

His cheeks pinked up at that. Jacob picked a place on Jessie's arm to stare wordlessly at while she softened.

"Babe?" She nudged him gently. "Aren't you going to tell me about her? What's her name?"

"Ahhhh. I guess I figured we'd have to do this sooner or later." Groaning, Jacob half-faced the woman he loved. "Her name's Rachael."

"Ummm. Good." The gossamer eyes glistened at his obvious happiness as far as this new Rachael gal was concerned. "That's a good name."

"I know," he replied, finally meeting her gentle gaze straight on. "Same as your friend in Charleston, right? I thought that too. I thought maybe it was a sign or something."

She smiled, although it hurt to think of him with someone else, even after all this time. "I'm sure it was, Jacob. Or is."

"Rachael works with Charles. He hired her in December—he's got her working as a recording engineer on Robson."

"Oh! So she's a…she's a musician?" *Ouch. Why does this hurt?*

"Yeah. She is, actually."

"Are you writing with her?"

"Not so much writing as recording. She has some cool tricks up her sleeve."

"I bet she does, hmmm. Enough to keep my boy happy, anyway, huh?"

"She's nice, Jess. You'll like her."

"Bring her in. I'd like to meet the woman who finally stole my sweet Jacob's heart."

"Hey, it's not like we've got plans to get married. But maybe some day. I dunno."

"I'm glad."

Sitting back, Jacob lifted Jessie's knuckles to his lips. His eyes melted, and got that inquisitive look that sometimes worried her.

She frowned. "What?"

He didn't want to ask. But Jacob knew it, too, would come up at some point. "Your dad's Gibson," he started slowly, watching the pretty eyes to see if this was something she'd considered. "The fire…"

Turning her head away from him, Jessie struggled against the mist that seemed to be a constant presence in her eyes these days. Slowly, she drawled, "I know. That lovely awareness hit me around three this morning during some poor nurse's profuse apology. I don't know which hurt more, the loss of the guitar or her turning my skinny arms black and blue in search of usable veins."

"I can guess which hurt more." Jacob's troubled gaze was accented by a loving pressure on Jessie's fingers and a tender brush of his thumb against the back of her pale hand.

Looking back at him, she mumbled, "Looks like I lost a lot of things while I was squirreled away."

"If you're referring to Josh, Jessie, he isn't going to stay with Nadia. All they had was sex. Trust me."

"Thanks for that. Jesus." A heavy exhalation accompanied the curse. "I don't know, Jacob. I know he sees me, but…I know what he's thinking, you know?"

"And what might that be, oh little telepathic one?"

"He's thinking he's not strong enough. For us. For me and the kids. To protect us. He's pulling a Matt. Honey…you have a girlfriend now too. I feel like time got put on hold for me while everyone else carried on with their lives. Sophie's having a baby next month. Everyone's moved on."

"Charlie's the same."

She couldn't help but smile. "Good old Charlie."

"He'll be back in Vancouver in a day or so. He's been shooting in France."

"I heard. The big goofball. He called yesterday."

A shuffle at the door alerted them to a detective's presence. Sticking his head in the door, the forty-something man looked at Jessie inquisitively.

Waving him in, Jessie spoke to Jacob. "He's been hovering. I guess I should do this. I mean *really* talk to these guys." Sending him an imploring look she asked, "Jacob...will you stay with me while I tell my sordid story? And will you find Matt and tell him I'm ready? He went for a coffee in the cafeteria."

"Of course," Jacob replied, kissing her knuckles again, as his heart started to pick up its pace. In all honesty, he, like Matt, was afraid to hear what Jessie had to say. But Jacob could lose his mind with grief for her pain later. For now, he was here and he had to be strong. It was late morning. Charles and Dee had already visited with the kids, and Steve and Sophie had ducked in, but Josh had yet to appear. No way was Jacob leaving Jessie if her husband wasn't going to be around to support her.

"What about Josh?" he couldn't help but ask, though. "Wouldn't you rather he was here for this?"

Shaking her head, Jessie fought back yet another onslaught of hard emotion. "Might be days if we decide to wait for him."

A flicker in Jacob's eyes radiated his sorrow at that harsh truth. "Okay, kiddo. I'll hold your hand, then. But you'll owe me."

"And what would that be? That I owe you?"

"I'm sure I'll figure something out." He grinned and winked, then went to the door and signaled again to the cops. "She says she's ready." In his heart, he wondered. But the thing was...would Jessie ever be ready?

Matt came back then, too, so Jacob didn't have to round him up. Jessie's old security knew this 'telling' was imminent, so his coffee runs were brief. Striding definitively into the room, he dropped with a grimace into a chair near the bed.

"How're the burns?" he quietly asked the reflective patient as the detectives got themselves sorted.

"They hurt like hell when the nurses change the bandages. Dee's ordering me some hyaluronic acid from Prince Edward Island that I can put on them when I get home. It's made by a company called Quannessence—they produce it at a spa we went to when we were on the island, Mystical Touch. There's supposed to be lots of moisture in it, so it's good for burns."

Could have been worse, Matt's caring eyes said. *Thank God.* She would scar, but the burns weren't bad enough to require skin grafts, and the scarring would likely be minimal.

Adjusting her butt on the bed, Jessie shrugged absently as Jacob moved to re-position the snowy pillows. "I'll heal, Matt," she said idly, avoiding his concerned stare. *Maybe.* Josh flashed across her mind. He should be here. *I want him here.*

Running a finger across her top lip, then pinching the bottom lip hard and continuing an anxious squeezing movement as she spoke, Jessie glanced at the open doorway before she started her tale. Prompted by the detectives, she started the traumatic telling with the abduction. Since Jessie hardly remembered any of it, her words were brief—an annoying van blocking her SUV, a smashed window, a scream from Emily-Grace in the back seat, a sickening wave of terror…black balaclavas, fighting off some strong guy, a rough grip on her arm followed by a sharp jab, and then blackness. A horrible headache when she came to.

Grabbing Jacob's hand, Jessie gripped his fingers tightly while she recalled the terrible day.

The hardest part during the telling came when the female detective asked gently whether she was sexually abused during her forced confinement. The woman knew there was semen found during Jessie's physical examination.

Unable to look at the silent Jacob or brooding Matt, Jessie admitted it only happened once. The last morning.

"He was saying his goodbyes," she breathed quietly. "He set the house on fire right afterwards."

"What makes you think he set the fire, Jessie? As opposed to it being accidental, I mean." The detectives knew. They had already shared that information with Charles Keating. Matt knew. Jacob knew. But all of them wondered if her captor had said anything to Jessie beforehand, whether he told her why.

"I heard him going through the house," was her horrific response. "Spreading liquid. I could smell the gas."

"Fuuuccckkk." Jacob couldn't hold it in. "You knew he was lighting the house on fire. While you were in it."

Matt's reaction was similar—overwhelming shock and disgust crossed his face as he moved to the edge of his chair and un-clasped and re-clasped his hands, the iPhone he was using to record the session perched next to him on the wooden arm.

"Not just that." She swallowed. Eyes drifting over to the female detective who was doing most of the questioning, Jessie squeezed harder on Jacob's hand. She blinked. "He, um…he left me tied there. To the bed. I can't imagine why, except that maybe he was in such a hurry to get out of there that he didn't want to deal with untying me. It wasn't like I was going anywhere, even if I had been more lucid at the time. I'm kinda glad that cute fireman had a knife handy." Gulping, she inhaled slowly.

"If I ever get my hands on this guy—"

"Hey," Jessie breathed, a hard stare landing on Jacob finally. "You're already my hero, Jacob. Stay outta this one, okay? I don't want you anywhere near this maniac. And, yeeaahhh. The thing about the fire is…I knew and I didn't know. I wasn't all there, Jacob. I was off on a beach somewhere with dead people, remember?"

"Still…geez, Jess…"

The moisture in his eyes was hard to take. Jessie lifted his hand, breezed her lips over the back of it, pressed it against her cheek, and morphed her hard look into a more caring one. "I'm here, babe. I'm fine."

"Uh huh." Sure, she was talking the talk, but Jacob could see the anxiety leaking through Jessie's tough demeanor. And he could feel the clamminess in the hands nervously clutching his. *Leave it to Jessie,* he thought. *Trying to be strong for the rest of us. But she's gotta have a breaking point. She has a lot to grieve.* He knew the loss of her dad's Gibson guitar would destroy her once she had time to really process it. And where the hell was Josh? He was also aware that her husband's pronounced absences from Jessie's bedside were playing on her mind. The guy had only been in for an hour yesterday, and so far today he had yet to darken her doorway.

Under his breath, Jacob cursed Josh and made a mental note to donate to the Sawyer family swear jar. Emily-Grace was policing him on that account.

The female detective broke into his thoughts. "Jessie, you told us there were two people at the house sometimes. And two who took the kids, that time. Did you ever get a closer look at the woman? Or…hear her voice, maybe?"

Sighing, Jessie reflected for a minute. "She actually came into the room at the end. I think maybe she was just getting a closer look because I…well, I hadn't moved in a while. I had given up, you know? So I was off in my dreamland, or fantasyland, I guess, I don't know for how long, how many days… and somewhere off in the distance I heard the door opening. The interior door, not the back one the guy usually unlocked and left food by."

"Did you get a look at her?"

"Her body, I guess, not her face, they always wore those knit masks. The balaclavas I mentioned earlier. Black ones."

"You told us she was slim-ish." The woman was both recording the interview and writing notes. She flipped back over the written notes now. "Curvy, you said. What was she wearing this time?"

"Ummmm…" Jessie thought. Vaguely, she recalled dress pants, heels, and a silky top…a tight one…a scoop neck. She inhaled sharply. Everyone's shoulders perked up and they looked at her expectantly. "She had a tattoo. On her breast, her left breast. It was a name, her husband's maybe? Likely his name, I guess, since I heard them making love…I think…above me. The creeps." She forced a sardonic grin in Jacob's direction. He rolled his eyes.

"What was the name?"

Her face falling, Jessie paused. "I don't know. I could only make out a few letters. A 'D' and a small 'a'…" Bitterly recalling the woman lingering in front of her, she added, "I hope it wasn't David."

It was a tough interview, but Jacob's presence helped Jessie get through it. And having Matt nearby was a blessing Jessie cherished.

After the others left, Jacob kissed Jessie's cheek and headed out to the lobby to give her a chance to catch some zzzz's before the Keatings came back with the children. The only way they managed to convince Emily-Grace to leave her momma at all was by promising the little girl two visits each day.

In the lobby, Jacob was surprised to spy Josh sprawled out in a chair, half-asleep. He approached slowly. Lately, the guy's temper was on a short fuse, and Jacob wasn't about to light a match and set him off.

"What's up, buddy?" he asked warily, taking a seat across from Jessie's husband.

"Not much," Josh answered, his voice sharp-edged and guarded. "Just needed to sit a bit."

"Not sleeping, huh?"

"What gives it away? The bloodshot eyes or the glazed *fuck me* look?"

Jacob wisely chose to ignore the attitude.

After a moment, Josh calmed his nerves enough to ask, "How do you think she's doing?"

"Put it this way. Her new favorite song is 'It's a Wonderful World.' Suffice it to say she didn't get out much."

Just drive that dagger deeper, Josh scowled wryly.

"Still in touch with Nadia?"

"Yup."

"Why." It wasn't a question for Josh. It was Jacob simply asking himself why.

But Josh answered anyway. "I can't deal, man." Wiping sweaty hands on the thighs of his jeans, Josh regarded Jacob. "They wanted her dead."

"And she isn't."

"Exactly."

Jacob let that unsettling thought percolate. "She's your wife, Josh," he tried. "And what about your kids?"

"I lost them already. A long time ago. Or haven't you noticed? So now I'm on the outside looking in, and it's like a fucking time bomb, waiting and wondering, Jesus. My wife, my kids. You oughtta know what that's like, Jake old buddy, the whole waiting thing."

"Asshole. And that goes for whichever reference you're pulling out of your ass now, Josh, the whole nasty Deuce McCall business or the waiting for Jessie thing." Jacob fidgeted with his fingers before lying back in the uncomfortable waiting room chair and resting one ankle over the opposite knee. He turned a corner in his mind. "So you're gonna pull a Tom Ryan and disappear, huh? I'd think you knew better."

"I didn't say that."

"You don't have to. I can see it in your eyes. But I think you're forgetting something."

"What?"

"Jessie. Who she is. How you guys met, all that bullshit. I saw the way she looked at you when you told her about Nadia. And I saw you 'get it,' Sawyer. She's always had your back."

"That's what you're not getting, Ryan. I know she has my back. But the thing is...I don't have hers. Everyone judges me for everything I do, every choice I make. I'm tired of it. I'm tired of the stares and the whispers and the Josh Sawyer pity party. Not to mention the Josh Sawyer loser party." He made an L out of his thumb and forefinger and placed them on his forehead.

"You can't leave her."

"I don't know if I can do it. This living in fear thing, waiting for the other shoe to drop? Waiting to lose what my brain thinks I already lost? I honestly don't know. The pendulum has swung and I'm on the other side now."

"With Nadia."

Josh shrugged. "With Nadia."

"Just try. Okay? For her? For what she's been through?"

"Funny, I thought you'd be all over her, Ryan. Now's your chance."

"I've got someone who loves *me* the most now. Why would I give that up?"

"Because," Josh stood. "She's not the one *you* love the most. I'll see ya."

Watching him, Jacob called out, "You're going the wrong way, Sawyer."

Josh wheeled around but kept walking backwards. "Relax, Ryan. I'm just getting a coffee. I'll be back."

He did come back, but not until after he saw Charles and Dee come and go with the kids. By then, Jessie was settling into a serious funk.

When she heard Josh's quiet booted footsteps come down the hall, she straightened, and lay back on the pillow. Swallowing uneasily, she waited.

"Hey."

"Hey." He stopped briefly inside the door and studied his pale wife. Making his way over to the big chair, Josh dropped heavily into it with a big sigh.

"Sooo...I've been told I should be able to go home in a few days."

"S'good." Eyeing the bandages on her arm, Josh asked, "Are you sure?"

"Yeah. I'm sure." She paused. "You're not, though, eh?"

He blinked. "We'll figure it out." Josh averted his gaze, though.

"Who the hell are you playing these days, Josh? Like…who the hell are you?"

That hurt. Jessie could tell she got through to him with that one by the way the beloved lonesome brown eyes flickered and faded.

"I met someone," was his response as Josh licked his lips nervously. "I've been with her for four months, Jessie. It' not that easy to just end things, you know? Just like that?"

"Because your missing wife came home." It was a whisper.

"Everything's changed."

"Like what?"

"Like Emily-Grace. Or haven't you noticed? Gone is our beautiful little happy daughter."

"I noticed." Guilt sliced Jessie through the gut. All those locked-in screaming furies…

"And Charles and Dee. They were waiting for the other shoe to drop from the time I went nosing around into your past on East Hastings. I'm sick of it."

"Yeah," Jessie breathed slowly. "I see that, Josh." She raised a finger and pointed it at him. "And you've changed."

"I just want different things now."

"Not your kids?"

"Sure. I want my kids." Raising his coffee cup, he pointed it at her. "They just don't want me."

At that, she smiled, just a little. Melting in her luminescent gaze, he swallowed back the hurt.

"C'mere," she said. "Please."

It took him a moment, but then Josh hoisted himself up out of the low slung chair and made his way to his wife's side.

She inched over. "Lie down with me. Please, Josh."

He hesitated. But then Josh set his coffee cup down on a nearby hospital tray and eased himself onto the bed, being careful not to jar her sore spots.

Jessie reached her good hand across her body and grasped his warm hand. Smiling, she held his gaze. He was angry, all right, she could see that the fire was burning deep, but he didn't look away. Small mercies.

"I'm going to bring you back to me," she murmured. "Because I love you, Josh. Always and Forever, we said. We promised, remember?"

Subdued, his lips parted at that proclamation. "I love you too, Jessie. But I'm scared."

"Of what?" she whispered tenderly, fingertips landing lightly by his eye, his cheek.

Hesitating, his answer was crackly. "Of everything."

She kissed his fingers, one at a time. "You remind me of someone, Josh."

"Mmmm?" He was feeling a little sleepy now, in the safety of his wife's arms. "Who's that?"

"Me," was the loving word that sent an exhausted Josh off into a quiet slumber.

Jessie brushed her pink lips against her husband's forehead, his cheeks, his lips, his eyes. "I love you so much," she breathed into his ear as he dozed off. "And I will fight for you, Josh Sawyer. Come back to me."

A few days later, Josh got up the nerve to call Nadia and break up with her.

On a sunny late spring morning, when the blue waters of English Bay sparkled crystalline with promise, while the fat brown robins sang inspiring songs of peace and hope, he took his wife home.

Chapter Nineteen

Incensed, Nadia threw her new iPad on the couch in Josh's Toronto hotel suite. It bounced, and would have hit the floor had Morgan not vaulted forward and caught it.

"You lame screwball asshole! You were supposed to finish the job! Now where do you think I stand with him?"

Carefully, Morgan set the iPad down on the coffee table. He had tapped on it first to see what set off his semi-estranged wife. Disgusted, he'd discovered the reading material that pissed her off so royally was another of those ubiquitous gossip sites—the Internet was open to some sensationalist story about the whole dramatic Jessie Wheeler rescue. Most reporters were hailing her survival as miraculous. The freelance reporter who scribbled this article and sold to this particular entertainment biz site was obviously staunchly in that camp.

Facing Nadia's wrath, Morgan seethed. "You weren't supposed to take it this far."

"And why not, Morgan? I like wearing Vera Wang. I like sparkly things. I like jetting privately between Toronto and Vancouver. And I particularly like sexing that man!"

Ouch. "He's not yours to sex, as you put it!"

"The hell he isn't!"

"He isn't! He never was! He was just fucked up over Jessie!"

"Get out of here." Her voice was a growl.

"Not until we sort this out, Nadia. I told Ulysses I was sick, that I had a bad flu. But if I quit my job now they'll start putting two and two together.

I need to get back to work, to suck it up for a few weeks, or a month even, and then quit. And I need to know what you plan to do."

"Well, for one, I'm not moving back home."

"You think Josh will keep this luxury suite for you? I highly doubt that! It's only his for the duration of the production, anyway, and he'll be wrapping in a few weeks."

"I'll get him to buy us a condo."

"Why, so you can be his mistress? His concubine?" Morgan was near tears with frustration. Damn, this woman infuriated him. "He's never leaving Jessie! Ever! The two of them are—"

"Were." Her eyes snapped fire. "Not are."

"Well, they were perfect together. Head over heels in love. And they'll get back to there once things settle down and she's feeling better."

"No they won't, because he's coming back to me. I'll make sure of it."

"How? Seriously, Nadia, how?" Flinging himself onto the couch, Morgan shot her a bitter look that said *good f-n luck with that.*

"Easy," was her quick answer, accompanied by a haughty shrug. Dark eyes narrowed, she scowled down her nose at him. "You'll see." Nadia paused before continuing. "And if for some inane reason it doesn't work, then I will see that this thing ends once and for all."

"When did we become murderers, Nadia? Darin dies, and we die too, is that how this goes? So we're capable of killing someone else? An eye for an eye? Jessie spends time in cancer wards. With children. She's a good person. She cares."

"This," she stepped around the coffee table to Morgan and flicked his chin with her shiny red nail so it caught in the light and flashed wickedly, "was never about Jessie. Was it, Morgan?"

She left him sitting there wondering who the hell she even was anymore, before Nadia tossed in, "And oh yes, by all means go back to work. We wouldn't want them thinking *you* had anything to do with Jessie's disappearance now, would we?"

I'm sunk, Morgan thought. *Sunk. I can't win with this crazy woman.*

As he left the suite, slamming the door behind him, Morgan retrieved his cell phone from the chest pocket of his denim jacket. A few thumbed letters, and he had a text ready for Ulysses.

Feeling better. Need me?

Heart racing, breath held, he raised a finger over it and counted to three before closing his eyes and poking *send.*

~~~

Jessie thought everything was going to be okay when she heard Emily-Grace's sweet laughter coming from the living room. The child's bell-peal amusement was genuine and unexpected, given her usual silent countenance. But now she was in the next room with her father, and she was laughing. Not loudly, and not effusively, but still—laughing.

In the kitchen, where she was cleaning up their evening meal of Mediterranean chicken and rice (heaven, compared to Kraft Dinner and hot dogs!), Jessie tilted her head to listen. She tiptoed around the half partition separating the two rooms and rested a hand on a shelf where family photos stood gathering dust. Josh was seated on the large couch, his pretty daughter on his lap. Standing to one side of him was the baby, now fifteen months old, rambunctious and busy. Josh was trying to keep David from toppling off the edge of the couch while, at the same time, entertain Emily-Grace with videos on the iPad.

"What are you watching?" Jessie asked with a smile. Clicking an invisible camera, she froze the moment in her memory bank. Josh rarely seemed interested in the children anymore, at least no more so than with a passing detachment, or in doing more than the necessary everyday duties like changing David's diaper or getting cereal for their daughter. He rarely sat and played with them, in fact he rarely sat at all.

Josh's anxiety was getting the best of him. Now, Jessie was quietly pleased to see him spending time with the kids, and he even had Emily-Grace laughing. A hint of a smile colored his lips as well, not a big one, but a tiny one was better than nothing.

I'll take it, Jessie thought. *I'll take any happiness at all I can get out of this man.*

Josh looked up at her now and started to speak, but Emily-Grace leaned back into his chest, peeked up at her momma, and interrupted with, "Nomena song." A quick pointy finger floating towards the screen accompanied the announcement.

"Hmmm?" Crinkling her brow, Jessie wandered over. She half-knelt on the couch and drew David onto her lap, leaning against Josh at the same time, but he recoiled and pulled away.

"Oh," was Jessie's knee-jerk reply as a dull ache instantly waylaid her heart. "The Muppets. Menomenah. Animal's pretty funny, huh, sweetheart?" The words were thick and wounded, spoken without a glance in Josh's direction.

She sucked up the hurt and settled back to watch the silly video with her family. When it was over, Emily-Grace demanded, "Again," and so they ended up watching it three more times. Even little David settled against his momma's chest and laughed along with his sister.

When Josh took the kids upstairs for baths, Jessie disappeared back into the kitchen to finish drying the dinner dishes. Twenty minutes later she heard his footsteps on the stairs. Their two cherubic angels were dressed in warm onesies with their wet hair combed back. Josh had Emily-Grace by the hand, and David in his arms. As Jessie lifted her son from her husband's arms and sat by the island with her baby cozied up in her lap, she voiced something to Josh that had been on her mind since she was released from hospital.

"I want us to see Trudy together. Instead of alone, like we've been doing."

Pausing, Josh waited a moment before setting Emily-Grace down on the stool next to Jessie. The little girl picked up a small spoon and started picking away at a bowl of cut up apples and raisins her mom had sprinkled with cinnamon and set on the island for her.

"Okay," was Josh's quiet reply. "When?"

"Tomorrow."

"Fine. What time?"

"Two. Charles and Dee will hang out with these two yard apes. They can help Dee in the garden."

"Harumph. Good luck with that."

"So you'll be around?"

"When?"

Frustrated, Jessie almost dropped David's spoon, which she was helping him steer into his mouth. "By like one or so, before the appointment with Trudy. It'll take us some time to get to North Van and then downtown."

"Okay. Fine."

That was about the extent of their conversation. In truth, Josh rarely met Jessie's eyes these days. But she relaxed now. Tomorrow would reveal some of what was troubling her man, she hoped.

But the next day, by one o'clock, Jessie still hadn't heard from Josh, who had gotten in the habit of leaving right after breakfast and taking off for the day, sometimes on the Harley, and sometimes in the King Ranch.

Grumbling, Jessie packed up the kids and drove to North Van anyway, tailed smartly by her security for the day, a darkly brooding Morgan. Her cell bleeped as she was approaching Burrard. Stopped at the light, she peeked at it.

Will meet you there

"Okay," she mumbled to no one in particular. "At least he's coming."

At La Casa, generous hugs were the order of the day, although both Charles and Dee masked their disappointment at Josh's absence from the little family unit. They knew better than to ask *where's your husband, Jessie?* because they knew a stony silence would be all they would receive in return.

Trudy's office was spacious and still verdant. When Jessie first saw her after the woman moved from Charlottetown to Vancouver, she had teased her wholeheartedly.

"You must have hired a gardener to drive all these plants across Canada, Trudy! Did he have a refrigerated truck?"

Trudy liked her plants and trickling water fountains. To her, they were life. To Jessie, they were familiar—cues for healing.

In the last month, visiting Trudy twice a week, Jessie couldn't agree more with the calm therapist's chosen surroundings. Everything was richer to her now—the deep colors of nature were more saturated than ever. When Jessie walked by the plants, she took the time to lightly finger each delicate leaf, each appealing flower.

To Josh, who—today—had met his wife downstairs in the lobby of the Vancouver sky-rise where Trudy shared an office with her husband Frank, the actions were just another knife thrust in his heart. Subtly watching his wife so gently finger the leaves, and then run her hand under the cool trickling water of the mini-fountains, was like being on the receiving end of yet another twist of Deuce McCall's jagged-edged dagger.

Trudy saw the heartbroken thoughts play across Josh's face when she ushered the couple into her private office space. The old comfy Charlottetown wicker was gone now, so Josh and Jessie approached large boxy modern chairs that Trudy thought were more 'hippie city appropriate.' Josh waited until Jessie was seated comfortably before sighing his tired body into position himself.

"Is there any place special you'd like to start today?" Trudy asked as she settled herself across from the dejected couple. She took note of the fear in Jessie's eyes, and the amber flames flecking through Josh's.

He raised his hand, which surprised Jessie. Raising her eyebrows, she glanced over at Josh.

"I'll start," he offered, avoiding Jessie's curious gaze.

This morning after he left their UBC neighborhood home, Josh had cruised the Harley up Cypress Mountain, which overlooked English Bay and Vancouver. He had stopped at his and Jessie's favorite old rest area, where they once made love in those surreal first weeks of their affair, during the shooting of *Drifters'* first season. That's the kind of thing Josh did every day now when he left the home he was finding stifling, and which was making him more and more anxious. He drove and went to cafes, then drove more and went to more cafes; sometimes he went to places he and Jessie now considered sacred monuments of their relationship. Yesterday he even got the nerve to drive out to Langley. Like it or not, the rubble now encircled with yellow tape—where Josh's kids and Jessie were kept against their will—was part of that history now.

With both Trudy and Jessie's eyes on him now, Josh spoke, his voice hoarse and musty. "I used to have this dream. Before Jessie and the kids were...taken."

"The golden field." Jessie knew the dream. She had it once herself. She knew it by heart.

"Yeah," Josh replied. "I never thought to tell you about it before, Trudy, but it's on my mind a lot these days."

"Why, Josh?" Trudy probed gently. "And before you tell me, I know about this dream. Jessie told me. I hope that's okay, but she felt it was important."

"Oh. Okay." He still didn't look at his wife but Josh knew what he would see if he did—a hopeful sadness. A fading light. "It's just...after they went

139

missing, I always thought this dream was about that, you know? But now I realize…it's about how I feel now."

"And how's that, Josh?"

"Separate." He cleared his throat. "Apart from them."

"From…?" Trudy wanted him to say it.

"From…my family." Even saying it hurt. The word just felt wrong, like Jessie and the kids weren't his anymore.

"Why do you feel separate from them, Josh?"

"You know why."

"Because their whereabouts were unknown. And it rocked your foundation out from under you."

He paused. "And because I started a new life."

"With…another woman."

"Her name is Nadia."

Beside him, Jessie hung her head and cringed. She knew Josh wasn't with Nadia these days. But she was aware that he was still messed up over the woman. And she knew he called her—he didn't even try to hide the calls from his wife. He just went out to the pool or he sat in the back office while she read to Emily-Grace and David. Always, she could hear the low rumble of his voice, but Jessie never tried to discern exactly what he said, although by Josh's defensive tone it seemed Nadia was often pleading with him.

"We've talked about Nadia in our sessions before, Jessie. Josh maintains he is not with this woman now."

Although I bought her a condo, Josh was thinking.

"He maintains the relationship is over."

And a Gucci bracelet.

Trudy waited for Jessie to speak.

"I'm glad," was all she said, wringing her fingers.

"Josh, what else do you want to say about this dream of yours?"

A low rumble announced the clearing of his throat again. "I think it was always a sign of things to come. That maybe I am meant to be separate from them."

"From your family."

"Yes."

"No." This came from Jessie, who was sitting childlike, both feet on the floor, ankles turned over sideways, shoulders slumped, and hands twitching in her lap. She looked at Josh, a stricken panic in her eyes. "No. I'm not giving up on us, Josh."

Her husband refused to look at her. He couldn't. "In the dream, Trudy, Jessie and the kids are so happy. They're walking through this amazing field which is like the fields of gold she sings about, and they're happy." He sucked in a breath. "Without…me."

"I could never be happy without you, Josh. Ever."

Finally, Josh twisted around a little so he could better see his wife.

And so she could see him.

After spying mostly only darkness and shame in his eyes these last weeks, Jessie was touched to spy the old hurt there now, the old agony she saw lingering in his soul that long ago night in Charlie's garbage.

"You remember when you met me?"

No wonder, Jessie thought. *He's remembering that night, how he felt…*

She wanted to reach out and touch him, to move that favorite rogue strand of hair behind his ear, to brush her fingers against his cheek, anything…just to feel her man under her skin again…to hope he would take her hand like in the 'before' days, and maybe kiss her knuckles…but she didn't. Jessie knew he would shrink away from her touch. And she didn't think she could handle that right now.

"'Course I do," she said, eyes swimming.

"I was dealing with a drug addiction then, Jessie. And I've got an addiction again now that I feel powerless to let go of."

"Alcohol," she whispered, almost…almost hopefully.

"No," he said.

Trudy knew. Josh knew she understood. He almost felt her collapse under the weight of it, because for certain Trudy saw other men confess such things to their wives in this very same chair. It must be a heavy weight to bear.

"Nadia," Jessie said for him so he wouldn't have to.

"I'm losing my mind right now, Jessie. I was someone else while you were gone. I couldn't bring myself to think about you at all once I got the kids back. I couldn't. I'm sorry. So I buried myself in something that consumed me. And now I don't know how to climb back out."

"If we started having sex again…maybe…"

Josh looked her in the eye. "When I think about having sex with you, all I can see is her."

Even Trudy couldn't bring herself to respond to that heartless admission.

"Well," Jessie breathed, her heart starting to pound in her ears, "I guess we're even for the Jacob comment, huh? Finally? Got a few good orgasms out of her, did you? Like…maybe five or six a night? Or should I say 'a time?'"

"That's not fair."

"Personally, while you were fucking her I did pretty good with my finger. Had to do most of my work in the bath, though, because, well, there was that nasty business about the one-way mirror facing the bed. But whatever turns your crank, right, Josh? Jesus."

Standing quickly, Jessie rounded the chair, gasping.

Josh rose too, while Trudy quietly scraped her chair back a bit and watched.

"You asked me to come here today with you. I figure it's as good a time as any to be honest with you, Jessie. I have been telling you since you got back, I had to *bury* myself in order to survive, and now I'm in so fucking deep a hole I don't know how I can ever climb out. I'm sorry if it's not what you were hoping for here today, but it's all I've got."

"Would you rather I didn't come home, Josh? Huh? Do you wish I'd died in that godforsaken inferno?" Jessie poked a finger in his chest, repeatedly and with enough pressure to make Josh yelp and back up. A heavy mist covered her baby blues as the power of the urgent words demanded a new truth. "Do you think about that sometimes, like at three a.m. when you're sleeping in the guest room and going to the bathroom to make yourself come while you picture her fucking herself at the same time?"

At his shocked expression, she cried, "Yeah, I heard you one night last week when I got up to check on the kids, you were talking to her, I could tell she was on the line, and you made me sick, the two of you make me so goddamned sick!"

Throwing his arms open wide, Josh ignored her and whirled around to face Trudy. "What am I supposed to be doing here, Trudy? Huh? You think you can fix this? Because I think we're done. That's what I think." He turned back to Jessie. This time his eyes were pained and his voice was hoarse. "I think we're done."

"No," she demanded, fists curled and knuckles white. "We are not done, Josh. You and me. I will fight for you until the day I actually do die. And then some. You are everything to me. Every day in that disgusting prison, what do you think kept me going, huh? Thoughts of you, that's what! You are what gave me the strength to keep on keepin' on, for one more day, when I wanted to die. And now by some God-given miracle you are standing here in front of me, a real live Josh, one made of flesh and bones, not the image I had in my head for so long of the guy I couldn't touch…and I am not letting you walk out that door and go back to some…*whore*…who gold dug her way into your life! Speaking of which, I saw your credit card statement for last month, I know about the fucking diamond bracelet from Gucci, and I know it didn't end up on my wrist, but I don't care. She will never have— with you—what I have. *Have*, Josh. Present tense. Including two beautiful children, by the way."

He was quiet now. Pleading. "She's a drug, Jessie. An addiction. I can't let her go."

"Then I'll do it for you. Tell me how to find this Nadia chick."

"Not happening, Jess."

"Bullshit. Stop fucking calling her, and tell me where she is!"

"I don't know who I am anymore, Jessie. I don't recognize myself."

"I know who you are, and for now maybe that's enough!"

A dark silence met Jessie's weary plea for him to understand.

"Please, Josh. Please." Mascara trails were forming under Jessie's eyes now, creating little black rivulets that made her appear ghostlike, to Josh, which is what she was to him, in part—still a ghost. One he'd buried in his mind and was now afraid to face.

Trudy stood now and quietly approached the two.

"After a trauma is not a good time to make life-changing choices, Josh. Give it a few months, okay? Please. Come sit."

Josh focused on the mascara trail under Jessie's left eye. "I can't even look at you," he admitted, his voice expressionless, the darkness in his eyes morphing to a dim vacancy. "You're not real to me. And when I look at Emily-Grace I see your eyes. So I can't look at her, either. You're all just ghosts in a goddamned graveyard."

On that final eerie proclamation, Josh let his numb gaze drift over Jessie's face. Reaching out a finger, he trailed it slowly down the blackness beneath her right eye. She grabbed his wrist and bent her cheek towards him, closing both eyes as she did so, but Josh sucked in a breath and yanked his hand out of her grasp.

Then he rotated softly on one black motorcycle boot and left the room, closing the door behind him with a quiet grace and decorum he couldn't even begin to feel.

Jessie held her own. She accepted Trudy's hug, sat back down in the big chair, and bent over as she waited for an attack of nausea to work its way through her body. "I'm trying so hard to help everybody else, Trudy," she sobbed. "To help them adjust and get through their own pain...the children, Jacob, and Steve, Charles and Dee...but I can't seem to help him— or me. At all."

Trudy's gentle wisdom was welcome, a soft, misty yellow light in the midst of a raging sea. "You can't help him, Jessie. He needs to figure this out. With my help, if he'll let me. There's only one thing you can do besides take care of yourself and those two gorgeous babies of yours, and that's love him. That's it. Until he comes around."

"*If* he comes around."

"You can do this, Jessie. Maybe even just agree to a trial separation, if that's what he thinks he needs."

"No. Never. Like six and a half fucking months wasn't enough?"

"He needs to sort his demons out."

"Is there rehab for this? There should be rehab for the spouses of missing women. For the ones who find an immediate replacement. Those guys."

"If he leaves, you work on yourself. On finding peace. You don't need to lie sobbing on a bathroom floor. I mean, do that for the first day, fine, but then get up and keep going. Find reasons to make each day worthwhile. I guarantee it will get easier, one day at a time."

"This sucks."

"Yes."

"Oh Jesus, Trudy. That was heartless of me. You've been through it. I'm sorry. I suck."

"Yes, but Jessie…Frank and I are back together now. We're happy. There is such a thing as a happy ending even when you can't even begin to see it. Trust me."

Breathing in to a count of six, Jessie closed her eyes and said a silent prayer before raising her head up from between her knees and facing Trudy. "You know something? You're the best. You know that?"

"I've been told." Trudy's tongue-in-cheek declaration was accompanied by a small laugh.

"I hope by Frank." Jessie eased herself out of the low chair and reached for her friend. Another genuine hug did wonders for her hurting soul.

"Every day," was Trudy's contented response. "And his praise usually comes with a glass of Merlot or Shiraz. And sometimes chocolate."

"And I hope sex."

"Hmmm." Arm in arm, they were walking to the door now.

"What?" Jessie stopped and looked at Trudy.

"Josh sleeps in the guest room?"

Jessie's shoulders sank. "Yep. Every damn night."

"Have you tried climbing in there with him?"

Making a face, Jessie emitted a sarcastic growl. "Sure, next time I hear him on the phone with her I'll just barge in."

"There might be something to that, honey. See you in a few days. And call me in the meantime if need be, okay? You have my number."

"Okay. Thanks Trudy. Luv u. I really do."

Down in the underground parking, Jessie spied Josh's Harley. It was still there, silent, unmoving.

"Huh," she said under her breath, wrinkling her brow. She had come downstairs with Morgan, who had followed her and Josh upstairs earlier. Turning to him, Jessie sighed. "I guess Josh went for coffee."

Morgan's face was white, his skin sallow. He just blinked back at his charge. He couldn't hear Josh's thoughts in Trudy's upstairs office, but if he could have, they would have been an echo of his own. Jessie was a ghost.

145

She was not supposed to be here. Shivering at the accumulated remembrances of her screaming in anger at him, pounding her fists on the mirror, and responding to his possession of her body, Morgan absolutely could not meet Jessie's eye.

Focusing on his rather green countenance, she twisted her lips in curiosity. "You okay, hon? Still recovering from that nasty flu?"

He had been working on the Keating side of things lately, and so had not been spending much time with the Sawyer family. Today was one of the first times Morgan was alone with Jessie since…well, since. And as luck would have it, he knew exactly where Josh was at the moment. He wasn't having coffee. Jessie's husband was with Morgan's unofficial ex-wife, who was also supposedly Josh's ex-girlfriend.

And chances were he would not be coming home tonight.

Chapter Twenty

After the appointment with Trudy, Josh was a mess. His day was toast. Trembling from the toes up, he wandered the sidewalk in a dark haze, muttering to himself until he met up with Nadia, who had flown in a few days earlier but whom he had yet to eyeball. In truth, Josh had not seen her since the day he first left Toronto. He'd gone back to finish *The Wyatt Boys*, but Jessie and the kids were with him. So the two did not meet in person. Now, anxious, nervous, and confused, he felt so displaced and disassociated from the world and his place in it that he could barely walk straight.

Immediately after leaving Trudy's office, Josh had dropped into a liquor store, where he picked up a 2-4 of Granville Island Pale Ale and a bottle of Jim Beam, *as a final ode to Jessie*, he told himself.

Then he walked three blocks to Nadia's hotel. He ducked his head going in, mostly because he was used to hiding from the spotlight, but it didn't matter. People pointed and whispered anyway.

In her suite, Nadia was secretive, mischievous. Accepting the alcohol with a graceful flourish, she easily drank her share—she never had any problem keeping up with men. Her suite was large, but was not even a remote strain on her pocketbook, since her famous actor boyfriend was paying for it.

Meeting Nadia was like taking the first sip of a highly anticipated desirable Rwandan roast; it was an inaugural puff on a cigarette, a premier slug of whiskey. The second Josh wrapped his arms around his lover's waist and inhaled her scent, he felt his body sigh and give and, along with it, he knew the instant his soul closed completely over in some vague attempt at protecting his heart. He wanted her immediately, to ease the ache, to still the pain, to be a place to pour the bad parts of himself into.

But she placed a graceful finger on his bottom lip and begged him to wait. "Let's drink first," she said, winking mysteriously in his general direction.

So they did.

Nadia asked him how things were at home, how he was feeling.

"You look like hell," she tossed out a little too casually, noting the scruffy unshaven cheeks, the dark circles under Josh's eyes, and the tremors in his hand as he raised the bourbon to his lips.

"I'm fine," Josh muttered, sucking back the drink in big gulps while, at the same time, inadvertently turning away from the poison fluttering dark nails and long eyelashes at him.

She tried another tack as she picked at the label on her ale bottle. "The condo's decorated and furnished. I think you'll like it. I stuck to black leather, like in your media room. So you'll feel more at home."

Josh didn't answer.

"I bought some plants. Plants always make a place feel more alive, don't you think? Josh?"

He paused, the glass halfway to his lips. Then Josh brought it the rest of the way to his mouth as he shoved the remembered mess of his and Jessie's meeting in Trudy's office jungle aside.

"I can keep plants alive, Josh." *Not my child, but plants I can do.* Nadia ran a finger down the front of his button up shirt, following it with her eyes, and licking her lips in anticipation. "I can do a lot of things Jessie can't do, actually."

Josh whipped his head around then as his protective bubble burst. "Can we keep Jessie out of this?"

"Ohhh," Nadia pouted. "I'm sure we can, baby. Come. Come with me. I have a surprise for you."

By then, Josh was stumbling drunk. In his brittle mental state, it didn't take long, and it didn't take effort. All it took was most of a bottle of Jim Beam.

He followed his lover willingly.

She started by taking his hand and pulling him up off the couch. As she led him to the bedroom, Nadia was almost purring. "You're gonna like this, darlin.' I promise you."

It took a moment for Josh's empty eyes to adjust to the dim aura of the bedroom—the curtains were closed, so the light couldn't get in.

Taken aback, he could, however, make out a vague shape on the bed— there was someone there…a woman. He struggled to focus his eyes. Behind him, Nadia lightly punched a dimmer switch on the wall and slowly moved it upwards.

"Honey," she said to the girl on the bed, "your biggest fantasy is about to come true."

Josh stared, the last bit of bourbon creating little wavelets in the glass he was holding as he weaved and tried to maintain his balance. Although she was swimming in his vision, he could tell the woman was young, maybe twenty or twenty-two. It seemed apparent she was a professional sex worker—she was wearing a tight white blouse unbuttoned to her navel, with no bra underneath. Pink nipples were visible through the sheer fabric. Below, white lace panties beckoned Josh. The young woman's legs were already spread and waiting as she leaned up on one elbow, licked a finger, and slipped it inside her panties, watching him all the while with parted lips and 'come hither' eyes.

Turning, planning to leave the room, his stomach heaving and that miraculous door behind which he thought he tucked Jessie and the kids sliding open every time he lost his balance, Josh moaned.

"Fuuuccckk." Self-loathing was well intact in his aching soul that day.

Nadia stopped his exit with her glistening nails, silky coffee skin, rounded body, and dangerous eyes. Her fingers deftly undid Josh, one button at a time, as he wavered between sanity and insanity, and between simple longing and deceitful lust. She took the glass from his hand, but not before Josh downed the last bit of the bourbon.

He was still wearing his motorcycle jacket. She pushed it off his shoulders, and it slid in a heavy warning *shufft-thud to* the carpeted floor. Then Nadia opened Josh to the room by pulling back his shirt. She moaned at the look and feel of him and the way his strong abs tensed under her touch as she rubbed her hands up and down his warm stomach and chest.

Smiling wickedly up to meet the dim, hazy eyes, she undid the top button

149

of Josh's jeans before sliding down the zipper. Gripping her lover's shoulders, she pointed him towards the bed.

The girl was mewling plaintively now, as she moved her hips up and down and begged this man to touch her. "Please," she whispered. "Please. Now."

He couldn't stand it. Hell, he was already so far across the line of no return that he was never coming back, as far as Josh was concerned. He remembered a similar feeling, only the lust was for drugs—heroin, cocaine, ecstasy, percs. Quick pain equals quick pain removal.

The dissolution of grief. The end of fear.

For a time.

Josh took what was given to him, hard and with his shoulders straining from the effort. First he palmed the girl roughly, on the outside of the white lace, while beside her on the bed Nadia stripped and crooned, "She's so wet, Josh, she's ready for you, take her, baby. Take her."

Then he ripped the panties off and started tonguing where they used to be, grasping the undulating thighs and pulling the unfamiliar body closer to where he needed it to be, while the girl moaned loudly, arched her back, and lifted his hair so she could watch Josh pleasure her.

Nadia undid the hired girl's top one button at a time, in the same manner in which she undressed Josh, then she took the girl's fingers and rubbed them against her, first outside and then inside her panties. Bending over her plaything, Nadia brought her lips to a nipple and sucked hard while the girl explored, probed and played.

When Josh couldn't stand it anymore, he stood and pulled his jeans down over his hips so he could be free to enter the unknown woman on the bed. She was begging him anyway now, mewling and moaning and crying for him to go inside, and he was only too happy to oblige. But after he came hard into her, with the room spinning and Nadia coming beside him (why?), and the unfamiliar body under him and a despicable guilt assaulting him, Josh choked and fought for breath.

He cried, the same way he did the first time with Nadia, for everything that was lost, and found, and lost again—for Jessie, for Emily-Grace, for his baby boy. He sobbed and choked and tried to steady his breath, but the heaves were coming from deep inside his belly and so he was incapable of gaining control until Nadia removed the girl from the room, laid down behind Josh, and soothed him until he calmed.

He slept, then, and didn't get dressed and go home until dawn.

When Josh entered the house, Jessie was up with David in her arms. Her pale eyes were red-rimmed and puffy.

"You're drunk," she said softly. "I heard the bike, Josh. But you're drunk. You drove drunk."

"Yeah, I drank a while ago," he said by way of explanation, averting his cloudy gaze from her penetrating stare. "So I'm okay. Just tired."

"Okay," she said, only half accepting that as she watched him stumble into the kitchen for a glass of water.

Thrusting a glass under the faucet, Josh filled it to overflowing, almost desperately sucked its contents back, and turned and leaned against the counter, wiping a wrist across his lips and staring despondently at his toes as he did so. The rogue piece of hair Jessie loved slipped out from behind his ear, almost hiding him from her fearful scrutiny.

Jessie carried the baby into the kitchen and set him on the counter next to his father. She stood there and held David while Josh studiously avoided looking at either of them. The toddler reached out and grabbed a handful of his daddy's hair, as if he somehow knew he needed to hold on to this man with all he had in him.

"You smell like sex," Jessie said faintly, without judgment.

"Yeah, well, you would know, wouldn't you?" was her husband's terse response.

She was silent but unable to keep the seemingly incessant tears from pricking at her eyes.

Finally, Josh turned to her. His eyes were blank. "I have to go back to TO today. I'll get a commercial flight."

"Oh," she gulped. "I thought you were done shooting for the season."

"Jon needs some pickups," he said, a flicker of deceit crossing his somber face. After kissing his baby, Josh touched Jessie on the right arm, and rotated her towards him. Her tears killed him.

Leaning forward, he kissed her with lips that still tasted of the young woman on the bed. She was sickened, but his vacant, tired eyes frightened her, so she refrained from tossing out words, any words, that might send him tumbling down the abyss over which he seemed to be so carefully balancing.

"Goodbye," he managed. "I'll come back when I'm finished the pickups. We'll talk then. Okay?" The thoughts sputtered out, unbidden and with no depth to them. Josh only spoke them to cover Jessie's stunned silence, and to try, somehow, to ease his conscience. He was also reaching for a modicum of hope to add to this unplanned parting, despite his earlier terrifying declaration at Trudy's office and the accompanying, smothering numbness that had overtaken his soul.

Josh stumbled to the stairs, dropped his black leather motorcycle jacket about halfway up, laid down fully clothed on the guest room bed, buried his face in a pillow and, with a desperation born of almighty loss, begged the universe for help.

Chapter Twenty-one

*T*wo weeks later, Sophie had her baby. The infant was a healthy eight-pound boy she and Steve called Caleb, for Steve's grandfather. Jessie went to see them at home when the baby was five days old.

They settled on the floor in the living room of Steve and Sophie's condo, so Steve could lie on his front to play with David while Emily-Grace and Sophie built a princess castle out of blocks. Jessie held Caleb, and fawned over how tiny he was.

"They grow so much in their first year," she said, as a cloud passed over her face. She'd missed a good chunk of her baby boy's first year. Looking up at David now, she couldn't get over how much he looked like Josh. Their son's hair was so long now, and so blonde, and his eyes were chocolate brown like his dad's. But David's were happy eyes, not sad and lost like his father's, these days. Somehow, the child seemed to have bypassed the agony haunting the rest of the Sawyer household.

Steve saw the wistful look. "The old man didn't come with you?" he tried, unsuccessfully trying to ease into a conversation about how Josh and Jessie were doing as a couple.

"He's still in Toronto," Jessie replied, attempting unsuccessfully to hide the deep despondence clouding around her like a thick, dopey fog. Averting her eyes from Steve, she wiped a small trail of spittle off the new baby's tiny chin.

"Still?" Steve was hesitant. He glanced over at Sophie, who sent him a warning look.

"He said he had pickups for *The Wyatt Boys.*" Forcing her gaze upwards, Jessie met Steve's eyes. "Why?"

Her good friend eased his body up, tucked his long legs underneath him, and sat cross-legged in front of Jessie. He wondered what to say.

The rather harsh buzz of the intercom saved him from responding. Steve jumped up to answer it.

"Yo!"

A deep male voice drifted up to them from down in the lobby. "Steve? Is this a good time?" The visitor, who wanted to meet the new baby, was Jonathon.

Jessie crinkled her eyes at Sophie. "Shouldn't he be supervising the pick-ups?" Eyeing Steve, she added, "I figured Josh had a lot left to do, since he was away so much at the end. When I came home."

But Steve's gentle flecked green eyes told her otherwise, when a ripple of uncertainty passed quite clearly through them.

Jonathon was at the door then, and so Jessie rose alongside Steve to greet him. The producer enthused over the baby in Jessie's arms before meeting her eyes. When he did, his were so much like Josh's that Jessie had to keep herself from gasping. The man was kind—he had always been more than fair to all of them on *Drifters*, and he was Josh's real father. Jessie wanted to collapse in his arms, and melt into his snow-white hair. Besides Steve, he was the closest person to her husband. Kayla was on tour in Europe, Zach and Hilary were in Seattle, Maggie was in New York, Carter and Sue-Lyn were in L.A., and Charlie and Jane were back in France…Charles and Dee did not factor into the equation at all.

"How…how are the pickups going?" Jessie managed to croak, as she rotated at the waist and handed Caleb over to his mother. She slipped her hands into her back pockets, braced herself, and faced Josh's producer-father, who was bent in front of his grandkids, giving and accepting hugs.

"Pickups?" Jon frowned. He clued in rather quickly, though. As he stood up from the kids, Jessie watched fear pelt down his face like rain shadows on a window. He shook his head, his lips moving as he tried to work out what to say.

"Okay," she answered for him softly as a harsh new reality worked its way into her numb bones one at a time, like molten lava from a volcano. "Okay." Stooping, she started gathering the kids' toys. "Emily-Grace, it's time to go, sweetheart. Grab singer-dowwy."

Sighing, Steve followed Jessie to the door. He grabbed her bicep, but she threw him off. She couldn't look at any of them. Instead, juggling a toddler in her arms, a diaper bag over one shoulder, and a clingy three year old at her side, she grasped the door handle and tried to escape.

"Jessie—"

Whipping around, Jessie lit into Steve. "It's been two weeks. He hasn't called, and he hasn't texted. I'm not stupid, Steve. You know something? I may as well still be locked in that godforsaken dungeon. Because being on the outside sucks a hundred times more!"

After the door slammed behind her, Jonathon regarded Steve with a mixture of trepidation and guilt. "I don't know what to do, Steve. I never got to raise the kid in the first place."

"Is he at the hotel? Still? I thought the production wrapped all the suites."

"We did. He bought a condo somewhere."

"Uh huh. I see. Bastard."

"Does it matter where he is? Really? I mean, as far as Jessie's concerned?"

"Does the word abandonment mean anything to you, Jon?"

Behind him, Sophie cringed before chiding her husband. "Steve, Jon paid for his sins a long time ago."

Jon frowned. "I was forced away from Josh when he was a small boy, Steve. I didn't abandon my kid." *Not then,* he was thinking, as guilt sliced him in two.

"I was talking about Josh." But Steve was firing daggers at Jon. "We need to find out where he is, Jon. Jessie didn't give up on him when she first met him, and we're not giving up on him now. We've got to help him work through this. We can't let him go under."

"I hear you, Steve, but I mean it. I'm at a loss here. He was nasty on the shoot, even cruel sometimes, and we let it go. But now…"

"Like it or not, Josh has a wife and little kids. And he needs to be a part of their lives, Jon. Do you want him missing out on everything you missed out on?"

Jon's guilt found a voice. "He's off my show, Steve."

That silenced Steve. Then he almost gagged. "What?"

"He's done. I have financiers. I had no choice."

"We're green lit for another season and you're firing your lead actor?"

"He's a mess, Steve."

"He's your son!" Steve looked over at his own new bundle, blissfully asleep in his mother's arms. He couldn't imagine giving up on him—ever.

"I'm not abandoning him. I'm just taking him off *The Wyatt Boys*. Call it tough love."

"I call it disgusting. I'm disappointed in you, Jon. You suck."

But Jon was not the rock Steve thought he was. The rigidity of his posture and suddenly blurry eyes told the actor exactly how well Jon was dealing with his son's current struggles.

"I don't know how to help him, Steve."

"You didn't come here to meet my kid, did you, Jon?"

"I suppose the answer to that would be 'not entirely.'"

Puffing up his cheeks and exhaling slowly, Steve nodded. "Okay, fine. I'll play the heavy. Send me into battle. But first, one of us better figure out where the hell Josh's love nest is. So we can burn the goddamned thing down."

He glanced down at the floor by the door. "Oh, shit," he said. Moving forward, he leaned over. When he stood back upright, singer-dowwy was dangling from between a thumb and two fingers. "She must have dropped it when Jessie grabbed her hand."

"Oh, no," breathed Sophie, picturing the agony Jessie would be dealing with tonight when her little girl started missing the only thing that truly offered comfort these days. "I'll take her over in the morning, Steve. I should drop in anyway and make sure Jessie's doing okay. Besides, it's time to get out for a drive. I'm going stir-crazy in here." She met her husband's eyes and frowned. "I don't know how Jessie is even remotely sane right now. Six months in that place and this is what she comes home to?"

"One thing I can say about her," Steve said sorrowfully. "She's sure used to handling shit alone."

"She's got Trudy. And us. Jacob too. She's not as alone as she used to be."

"Try telling *her* that."

He turned to Jon, who had wordlessly watched the exchange, and offered the man a beer.

As Charles Keating's good friend, the producer was loath to admit Steve was likely right. Accepting the beer, he settled in to discuss, in deeper detail, exactly how worried he was about his son, Jessie, and his grandkids.

The next morning at eleven, Sophie pulled up behind Jessie's SUV at the UBC neighborhood house and flipped off the ignition. She moved to grab her baby's diaper bag, which had Emily-Grace's singer-dowwy sticking out of an exterior pocket, when she froze. Cocking her head towards her window, she pushed open the driver's side door and listened.

It was a warm day. There were windows open in the modern, boxy house. And from one of the upstairs ones, David was screaming bloody murder.

"Well that's unusual, even for him," she thought. She shrugged it off. Babies got mad, they screamed, they cried. Idly, as she gathered her things and released the baby's carrier from the back seat of her car, Sophie wondered what set him off, and why Jessie hadn't managed to calm her son.

Morgan was there, ankles crossed, biting chunks off a protein bar while leaning against the trunk of the grey Audi sedan Ulysses wanted him to use when they were in Vancouver. The Audi was parked next to Jessie's SUV. Sophie didn't know the guy well at all, and he gave her the heebie-jeebies, as she'd told her husband on more than one occasion. Now, she wondered what was up, but she realized he likely always did his watching from the exterior of the home, otherwise what would be the point?

"Hello, Morgan," she tried kindly. "Sounds like someone's having a bad day. I hope this little guy is less inclined to screaming fits."

He just looked at her in his odd way, and then stretched his head over to peek inside Sophie's baby carrier. She held it up and turned it ninety degrees so he could better see the baby. Something crossed Morgan's face then— a look Sophie didn't quite know how to interpret. Sadness, longing...anger?

"Do you and your wife have kids?" she asked.

It took him a minute to respond. "No," was his raspy answer, but Sophie swore his eyes flickered when he spoke. She exhaled slowly after passing him, and headed towards the house. He was a weird one, in her opinion, he didn't seem to have a lot of the usual social graces, but heck, at least he was here, keeping an eye on Jessie and her kids.

Her ballet flats trod lightly down the flagstone steps and the gate clanged shut behind her, before Sophie started frowning. Reaching her free hand up to her long, sleek blonde ponytail, she furrowed her brow. The toddler wasn't silencing, even a little. David's little lungs sounded like they were bursting. *Put that kid in opera lessons,* she thought.

Weirdly, when she went to knock on the patio door, Sophie noticed it was open. Before sliding it the rest of the way, she fingered her cell phone in the left pocket of the diaper bag, then pulled it out and held it in her free hand. Later, she would say she just had a feeling…

Finally getting up the nerve to slide the door further open, she entered, slid it shut behind her, and then set the baby carrier down by the coffee table in the large living room. Tiptoeing around it, she inhaled, and immediately coughed. Her nostrils were picking up a strange smell, like burning rubber and plastic. Moving around the half partition to the kitchen, she was startled to find Emily-Grace standing on a high stool she apparently dragged over from the other side of the kitchen island.

The little girl was stirring something on the stove, and the burner was on.

"Honey?" Sophie's heart was racing, but she sucked in a breath and tried to remain calm. "What are you cooking? And where's your pretty momma?" *Please God let Jessie be okay.* She knew her friend was in a bad place right now, but Sophie did not think Jessie would harm herself. Yet…there was also still this threat hanging over her head, this idea perpetuated by the police as a result of the way Jessie was found, that someone still very likely had it in for her. But Morgan was just outside…

Oh God, Sophie thought, her mind taking a quick right turn at the sight before her. *Emily-Grace is cooking a car.*

Sure enough, as Sophie delicately removed a wooden spoon from the child's hand—from a child who at eleven in the morning was still in her pink nightgown—she looked down to see a large red plastic car covering the base of the pot. The toy was liberally sprinkled with pepper.

Flipping off the burner and shoving the pot away from the heat, Sophie searched the small girl's silent, pale eyes. "Are you hungry, sweetheart? Have you eaten today?" A quick scan of the kitchen island didn't reveal any dirty plates, but that didn't necessarily mean anything. She looked back at

Emily-Grace, who was wringing her little hands and trying to speak as her eyes flooded.

"David keeps cwying."

"I hear him, sweetheart." Gently, Sophie lifted the distraught child into her arms. "Let's go get him, and check on Momma, okay?" Again she thought of calling Steve, but David's plight seemed more urgent.

Silent tears were rolling down Emily-Grace's cheeks now. Sophie had to lean in to hear her next words. "Momma's sick."

Almost tripping on the stairs, Sophie's throat closed over as she digested that. *Sick? Sick how, exactly?*

She found Jessie first, in the children's playroom, scrunched up against a wall, knees drawn up to her chest, and hands over her ears, wearing the same clothes Sophie saw her in yesterday. She appeared to be all cried out.

"Okay, Emily-Grace, why don't you go into David's room, and I'll meet you there in a second. I just want to talk to Momma." Sophie set the little girl down in the hall, and watched her pad into her baby brother's room while looking back at Sophie as she moved, face stricken and eyes worried.

Sophie moved quietly into the playroom and bent before her friend. She forced Jessie's hands away from her ears and was heartsick at the pain she saw in the piqued face.

"Oh, honey," she breathed, sliding down alongside Jessie and pulling her into her arms. "It'll be okay. I swear."

At the kindness in her friend's expression, Jessie collapsed into tears again, and buried her face in Sophie's lap.

After a bit, Sophie said, "I'll be back, honey. Let me get David. Okay?" *And Caleb too,* she thought, nervous about leaving her newborn unattended downstairs.

In David's room, she talked softly to Emily-Grace while the toddler's cries quieted into hiccups. "Let's change him real quick, okay sweetheart? Can you help me find everything?"

The little girl turned out to be a real help, soundlessly handing Sophie a diaper and a few baby wipes, and soon a deftly changed baby was in Sophie's arms.

"I get dwessed too?" Emily-Grace hopefully asked her momma's kind friend.

"Yes, baby, sure, why don't you pick out an outfit and I'll help you?"

"Okay." Emily-Grace dashed into her own room, opened a few drawers, and pulled out leggings, a pink cotton sundress with a white lace collar, and socks and underwear.

Sophie took the leggings and laid them back on the child's unmade bed. "It's a hot day, darling. Let's leave those. I don't think we need socks, either. Do you have sandals up here?"

When the kids were dressed, Sophie peeked back into the playroom. Jessie was curled up in a fetal position on the floor.

"Okay," Sophie told Emily-Grace. "How about I call Caleb's daddy? We'll get him to come over and give us a hand with breakfast, okay? Or lunch, maybe," she added idly, glancing at the time on her phone. "But for now, you and David can go in the playroom with Momma, but play quiet and let her sleep. I have to go downstairs to get Caleb. I'll be right back, sweetheart."

The kids did as they were told, while Sophie jogged downstairs, anxiously rubbing her ponytail with one hand while holding the phone to her ear with the other. Just as Steve answered, she looked up and gasped, startled.

Morgan was in the living room, and he was holding Caleb.

"He was starting to fuss," the usually quiet guy sputtered nervously. "I didn't think you'd mind."

"Oh! Uh…no. Of course not. Um, just a minute, Morgan." She could hear Steve on the phone saying *Sophie? Everything okay over there?*

Turning her back to Morgan, Sophie said quickly, "No, Steve, can you come over? Right away? Jessie's had a meltdown. She needs us."

"Meltdown?" Steve dropped the script he was reviewing onto the cushion of the wicker loveseat on which he was sitting on the outside balcony of his and Sophie's condo overlooking Vancouver's False Creek and its quaint paddle boarders, sailboats and kayaks. "How bad, Soph? Should we be calling an ambulance?"

He was already up and on the way.

"No, I think she's okay, well not okay really, but…just get over here." Sophie could feel herself breaking down. Her friends' pain was too much. Josh and Jessie. Collectively. "Steve, the kids were still in their pjs, not fed, and I don't even think she got David out of his crib at all this morning.

Emily-Grace was on a very high stool at the stove cooking a toy car! And the back sliding door was open, there's no cover on the pool, and Emily-Grace could have wandered out there instead of deciding to cook a car, and—"

"Stop, Sophie." Steve's tender voice was silk and honey. "Emily-Grace did not fall off the stool, or wander into the pool. I'm on my way."

When she turned around again, Morgan was watching her, still with Sophie's brand new infant in his arms. If she knew what he was thinking, she would have ached for him, because even though he gave her the creeps, he was, at heart, a man in pain.

He was thinking *she's got it all—a husband who loves her, a new baby, money...and I have nothing. No wife, no child, and soon no job.* Now, he just ran his tongue over his lips to summon up enough moisture so he could force words from his mouth, and he handed over the baby.

"Here," he said. "He seems better now."

"Hmmm, he is." Sophie forced a smile. "You have a way with babies, Morgan."

He shrugged. "I better go back outside. Just thought I'd check on things in here. Is Jessie..." He let the words drift off.

"She's not having a good day, Morgan. Steve's on his way over. We'll deal with it."

"All right." But Morgan didn't move.

After bending and grabbing the diaper bag, Sophie headed back to the stairs. Making the assumption he was worried about Jessie, since he was her closest security over the last few years, she called over her shoulder when she realized he wasn't moving. "We'll call you if we need you, Morgan, okay?"

He didn't answer and, when Sophie got halfway up the stairs, she glanced back over. He was gone, although he left the sliding door open so the breeze was flowing in, setting the gauzy white summer curtains dancing.

She shivered.

In the playroom, Sophie found a child's small blanket and laid Caleb on it. Peeking over at the kids, she saw that they were fine. Emily-Grace was moving a My Little Pony around, babbling softly to it, and David was playing with his blocks. She handed singer-dowwy to the little girl, who accepted her with a tiny pleased and grateful smile.

Sophie touched Jessie's back. "Honey? Steve's on his way over, okay?"

Jessie didn't move. Sophie sat in silence, watching her baby sleep and praying his life would be all toy cars and chocolate fudge.

When Steve finally ripped into the driveway in his updated sporty Audi TT, Sophie was relieved. He bounded down the flagstone steps and into the house, and was up the stairs in two seconds flat. Running a hand through his blonde hair, he quickly assessed the situation—a heartbroken friend, a scared wife, a sleeping newborn, and two hungry, frightened children.

"Soph," he suggested softly, taking charge, "why don't you take Emily-Grace and David downstairs for some grub? I think Jessie and I need to have a heart-to-heart."

With a ping in her own heart, Sophie pushed aside the wee bit of jealousy that always took her over in times like these, when Jessie needed Steve who, Sophie knew and understood, was really the singer's best friend apart from, well, Josh, who was apparently AWOL in Toronto with his sleazy girlfriend at the present time. Or Jacob, who was touring somewhere in the southern States.

"Come on, kids," she said, holding out a hand, leaving Caleb with her husband, since the infant was comfortably asleep. "What do you like to eat?"

"Not Kwaft Dinnew," was Emily-Grace's honest response. "Ceweal."

As they disappeared around the corner, Steve sighed and lay down on his side facing Jessie, who was lying on her right side with her head resting on one folded elbow. Wiping a few strands of hair out of her eyes, he ascertained from her breathing that she wasn't sleeping, but the pale eyes were closed.

"Jessie, you will get past this. You will. I promise you."

Her eyes fluttered open. With equal parts angst and equal parts sheer hopelessness, Jessie regarded her good friend. The sea-pearl eyes were adrift. "Not this time," she croaked. "Not this time, Steve."

"Nadia's nothing. She's just a diversion, Jess. He needs some time."

"It's not this Nadia woman that's freaking me out, Steve. It's not." The tears were trickling freely again now.

"Then what is it, kiddo? Because I can only imagine how bad that hurts right about now." He implored her to listen, to let him offer the best comfort he could at such a terrible time.

"It's *him*, Steve. I know him. I know him." She buried her face in her forearm and sobbed freely. "I could care less about some woman who I am pretty sure means shit all to him."

Tentative, Steve brushed the hair back again. "I know you do, Jessie. I know you know him. More than anyone. But he's changed. This last time… it was like something switched off in him."

She whipped her face back up to her friend, and he used his fingers and one thumb to wipe away the salty streaks on her flushed cheeks. "He's hurting, Steve. He needs me. *Me*. I'm the only one who can…who can reach him, y'know?"

"I do." Sadly, Steve smiled. "We all do. But…"

"But what, Steve?"

He sighed. "Jessie, I…" Struggling with the words, he spoke slowly. "I think maybe you can't help him this time. And I think you know that. I don't think anyone can. I think Josh needs to help himself. And to be honest, I'm not sure if he's up for that right now."

"Why *not* me?" It was a whisper. But Jessie knew. She didn't need to hear Steve's answer. She *knew*. And that's why last night and today hurt so bad.

"Because you need to take care of yourself, little girl. You're trying so hard to figure everyone else out, and to help everyone else—the kids, Charles and Dee, Josh…that you're not taking care of yourself. You need to take care of yourself. Because, Jessie…he's killing you. What Josh is going through right now is destroying you. And I think you know that too."

The tears welled up again. Jessie lifted her left arm, the one still healing from her burns, and gently rested her hand on Steve's elbow. "I do," she sobbed. "I do know that. He's more than I can handle right now."

"Jessie, you left the sliding door open. To the pool. Sophie found your daughter at the stove. Cooking. With a burner on. Standing on a stool, by the way. Your children need to be fed, and David is still in diapers, which means, well you know what that means."

Closing her eyes, she inched closer to him, just so she could cry into her good buddy's chest and feel the closeness of a real live person, a good trusted real live person, again.

He heard Jessie's muffled voice as her words vibrated against his chest. "It means I'm a terrible mother. That's what it means."

"It means you're in rough shape, girl. You've had a rough time of it. You need some time to heal."

She was silent, reflective. And finally—honest.

"We're done, then. Josh and me. Aren't we, Steve?"

"You need to put yourself back together, Jess, before you can even consider trying to be there for him. You're like Humpty Dumpty. You've had a great fall."

"I'm not sure Humpty Dumpty ever got put back together, Steve."

"Bad example, then. I need to work on my nursery rhymes. Cut me some slack, my son's not quite a week old yet."

"I wouldn't have believed it, Steve. I never thought Josh and I would ever lose each other this way."

"Me neither, Jessie. Me neither. Not after…"

"Not after everything, eh?"

"It doesn't mean you have to give up on him, Jessie. Not entirely. And I pray you don't. I don't want to see your fairy tale end. But for now…" Wrapping his arms around her, Steve whispered into Jessie's ear. "Yeah. You need a break to help yourself get well. And while you're doing that, I'm going to see if Charles and Dee can take the kids for a few weeks, okay? Just so you can have some time to figure things out. Emily-Grace and David need some stability, Jessie, okay? In a home they know, where they feel safe." He leaned back far enough to see the tortured eyes, but relaxed a little when a slight nod acknowledged her agreement.

He added, "And I'm calling Maggie. I'm sending you to New York to be in a different environment, with someone not exhausted from a newborn's beck and call. Okay? Although Sophie and me will be down to visit and we'll Skype every day."

"All right, Steve. Okay."

"Okay."

Steve kissed her forehead and held Jessie for a while, before he eased her up, turned her away from him, and maneuvered her into her bedroom towards the ensuite bath.

"Get cleaned up. You're on the move again, Jessie Wheeler."

As she stepped under the hot water, Jessie responded softly to herself, "Wheeler-Sawyer."

And then she bowed her head and prayed.

Later, she stood at the playroom door and stared into it. Once such a happy place, this room now felt haunted. Her eyes caught one of Emily-Grace's old adorable crayon art drawings from before they were abducted, from before life took such a dark turn. It was rough, but despite the shaky lines it was quite clearly a bright yellow sunshine, and a colorful rainbow.

Wandering over, Jessie traced it with a tired finger. She turned and looked around. A box of crayons presented itself at a small table a few feet away. Selecting a red one, she gripped it between her fingers and wrote across the bottom, *always and forever.*

Then she let the crayon slip from her grasp. It landed on the floor with a tiny but menacing *thwunk*.

Shrinking into herself, Jessie pinched a thumb and forefinger into the outer corners of her eyes, and left the room.

Chapter Twenty-Two

The thing about the new condo in Toronto was that it was right down-town, within walking distance of not one club, but many, including a slick new number called Nightbird that, by the time Josh arrived, Nadia had already christened, and christened well. She took him there on his first night in the city. They weren't alone—there were a few crew there from *The Wyatt Boys* who Nadia had gotten to know over the course of the season, and who liked to party. The most notorious of this group was a transplanted Newfoundlander who could out drink and out curse any of them.

Penney, as they called him, was the show's unofficial social coordinator, although his paid wage on *TWB* was in Transport. He arranged the bowling (and the drinking), the sleigh rides for the cast and crew's kids (and the drinking), and just, well, the drinking. An affable kind of guy, not particularly good looking but definitely full of Newfie charm, he was an easy party pal for Nadia. Their season was done, despite Josh's outright lie to Jessie about shooting pickups, but Penney and some of the other guys were sticking around Toronto to work on an upcoming film.

In a way, Josh found himself glad to have Penney and his pals along. The guy wasn't into coke or heroin or any other 'really damaging shit,' as Josh told Nadia right from the get-go he wanted nothing to do with. Just good 'ole plain Molson Canadian, and sometimes a good 'ole American Budweiser—those were Penney's standbys. At Nightbird the first night, the guy seemed tuned in to Josh's state of mind somehow—maybe that was also Newfie charm—and so he stuck by Josh at the bar.

He was frank. "I gotta tell ya Josh, I'm surprised to see you here. It ain't none of my business, but I'm damn surprised."

They were sitting at the bar with their backs to it, facing a number of bouncing heads and flailing arms on the dance floor. Penney had to shout over the bomp-bomp-bomp of the techno dance tunes.

"You're right," responded Josh, sucking back on his Bud. "It's none of your business, Penney." He was reminded of Manny on the Virginia shoot a few years back—nosy crew. Annoyed, he grunted.

"I'm not dissing Nadia, she's great, a helluva lotta fun, but—"

"I said it's none of your business, Penney. Let's just have a good time and the hell with the doomsday shit, okay?" Josh's eyes flashed.

Raising an arm, Penney backed off. "Don't take a shit fit, Sawyer. I was just gonna say if you need a pal in the city, I'm your guy. S'all. Hate to see ya get all fucked up here and have nowhere to go, no one to hear yer story, that's all."

That comment almost caved Josh. In a way he thought it might be alright to have someone on the perimeter of his life to talk to, especially a well-liked guy like Penney, whose easygoing Newfoundland heritage made him a friendly and popular guy amongst both cast and crew of *The Wyatt Boys*. But Josh just nodded and said a quiet, "Thanks." And he stared straight ahead and watched Nadia under the ethereal neon club lights.

They'd gone to dinner at the Italian place she liked, first, her sequined cocktail dress with its strapless sweetheart neckline absorbing all the male eyes within viewing radius. The fancy little number was short, and showed off the diamond Gucci tennis bracelet she tossed around on her wrist in front of everyone's faces. The neckline was low enough to see the top letters of her breast tattoo—*DarinS*. Now, at the club, she was gyrating on high wide-strapped Jimmy Choos she sweet-talked Josh into buying for her earlier in the day—her fifth pair on his credit card in the last month. He'd switched to a brand new card after buying the tennis bracelet—he didn't need Jessie stumbling across the statement.

Jessie…he pushed her tragic eyes out of his mind, ducked his head, and exhaled with a low *pffft*. He felt like shit for lying to her, but after last night with Nadia in Vancouver, Josh was too messed up to even think about sticking around. He needed a break. He needed some time to adjust to the fact she was home, and he needed Nadia's body to ease the pain.

To Penney's credit, he stayed alongside while Josh drank himself into oblivion, and he held his hair back while he puked. The guy even helped Josh and Nadia stumble home, partly because he, too, was drunk and wanted a place to crash.

The next morning, they hung out and laughed about the night before, but by noon more *Wyatt Boys* crew arrived after hearing there was an unofficial 'post wrap party wrap party' happening, and soon a two week bender was under way.

In truth, Josh was so caught up in the hype and decadence he barely saw Nadia. Part of him thought she was glad of that; he knew she detected the ennui in his eyes and the ache in his soul. And she seemed to sense he needed some space. But on the nights when she did come to bed with him, they did what they did best, 'til dawn usually.

As good as it was, sex with her now, for him, was leaving a big 'ole hole in Josh's heart. Nadia was a siren, a goddess even, in her new designer dresses and fancy shoes—hell, she was a siren before the expensive clothes. Men flocked to her. But there was something missing in her, Josh knew now. She was all about the partying, the sex, the men, the clothes. She was all about the game. And she had won him back—he figured she knew that now, or thought she knew that, maybe. But he was messed up, at rock bottom, lonely and aching for something—someone—he missed so bad for so long that he could barely manage to zip his jeans up after a piss. So after sex, when he was coming down from his orgasm and she was already climbing out from under him to go clean up, he squeezed his eyes shut and begged the universe for more, for someone to hold and love and caress and laugh with, the way... well, the way he and Jessie used to.

Josh wanted Jessie. In his *soul* he wanted her. But he had no idea how to open himself back up to her, how to dive inside the sea-pearl eyes he loved... how to empty his spirit crushing agony from that very bad day when she and their children disappeared. He didn't want to feel that agony again—the loss, the sheer hopeless terror...but that came with Jessie now. It was part of Josh's family. The horror of their abduction was now inextricably intertwined in the fabric of all their souls.

After the partiers fell asleep in his condo in the wee hours of each dawn, soaking up his generosity, Josh stepped over their bodies and went out on the balcony to stare at the busy cityscape around him. He took a beer with him, always, but as the days went on he realized it didn't seem to matter how much he drank. He got drunk at first, but then he always seemed to plateau. He couldn't drown all of the pain through alcohol or through Nadia. And it was killing him. He needed to go further down. He needed a bigger high.

Fourteen days in, he broke his own cardinal rule by casually asking one of the crew known to do a little coke to see if he could round some up. The guy came through, showing up at four o'clock on a Friday with the coke and a few friends to share it, once again on Josh's dime.

Penney showed up at ten. By ten-oh-five he was recalling Josh's words that first night at Nightbird —*it's none of your business.* But Penney knew Jessie, he knew Steve, he knew Jonathon, and he knew Josh's kids. And he recognized a man in desperate pain when he saw him.

He left the condo, texting Steve before he reached the elevator. *Think u better come get your co-star.*

Steve got the text an hour after he put Jessie on the jet. He had her kids in her SUV—his Audi TT was a two-seater, and he needed the car seats anyway. He was on his way down the 99 from the airport. The plan was to take the kids to La Casa, where Charles and Dee would meet him around ten. They were at a charity event in Kelowna, four hours drive away, but planned to get away as soon as they could. Steve had called them at two. It was now six p.m. He hoped they would arrive soon.

Checking his text while stopped at a light, Steve got chills.

He glanced at the kids in his rearview mirror. Emily-Grace worried him. She was still hiccupping with sobs now, after saying goodbye to her momma. The separation might be necessary for Jessie's mental health, but hell, after this little family's forced confinement and distance from each other, it sure as hell wasn't easy. And *Jessie* was barely functional—how do you explain such things to a three year old?

"It's gonna be fine, honey," Steve called back to the little girl. "Tonight, you and me and David are gonna hang with Carlotta. She's making us pizza. You like pizza, right?"

"Momma," was all the child said, wistfully turning her head away from Steve's voice and staring through tired eyes out of the window.

Steve knew part of the issue was the SUV. Emily-Grace did not have good memories associated with this car. She still awoke screaming from God knows what—being ripped apart from her mother, Jessie's self-confessed rants at the one-way mirror, and definitely from the tire iron crashing through her mother's driver's side window last November. It was difficult to get her in the SUV, period, and now today, after seeing her mother enter the jet and not take her, she was inconsolable.

The whole damn shebang tore Steve's heart in two. And now this text from Penney...what the hell was Josh up to now?

He didn't answer Penney until he got a chance to hand the kids over to Carlotta and find a quiet place from which to text, which happened to be La Casa's first floor washroom. Through the door he could hear Carlotta trying to sooth Emily-Grace, and he was glad to have her help carry this newest Wheeler-Sawyer drama. The maid was a tried and true member of the Keating clan, and a sweet soul Emily-Grace knew and loved deeply.

Steve's text to his *Wyatt Boys* crew friend read *What the hell's he into?*

Instinct and Josh's past led Steve's mind immediately to some diabolical substance. Heroin? Jesus. While he sat on the toilet seat and waited for a response from the east, his hands went clammy and he could feel his heart trying to physically break free from his chest.

He got dingbat Carew to bring coke to tonite's party

"Oh fuck. Josh, you ass." Steve hung his head between his knees until lights stopped flashing before his eyes. He raised his phone and typed.

Jesus Penney I have a new baby I can't come to TO right now straighten him the hell up

He needs someone to kick him in the ass and let's face it I'm only Transport

Don't play the crew card with me, TWB would fall apart without u, who needs cast?

Ha ha funny guy, get ur ass here Steve. I mean it. UR wife's amazing. She'll understand.

She's gonna cut off my balls and hang them from the CN Tower

Just come. Plz

It wasn't like Penney to sound desperate.

"Oh Jesus," Steve said again. "Will this nightmare ever end?"

He stood, set his phone on the vanity, took a piss, washed his hands, and left the bathroom.

On the one hand, he was relieved to see Carlotta sitting on one of Dee's fancy chairs by the kitchen island, rocking Emily-Grace and singing to her. David was playing with Tupperware at their feet, trying to build something. Steve bent down by him and smiled sadly as he tried to help him build. The real victims here were not Josh and Jessie. The real victims were the children they loved beyond measure, who now were relegated to the care of three worried sixty-somethings.

When Charles and Dee arrived near eleven, Steve was in the media room waiting for them, rather pissed, in fact. Carlotta was upstairs sleeping in a rocking chair, with a dozing Emily-Grace in her arms. David was asleep in the crib the Keatings kept at La Casa. Steve's own baby was home where he wanted to be; the infant was sleeping in a bassinet by Steve and Sophie's King-sized bed.

He stood to greet Jessie's pseudo-parents.

Dee started with an apology before he had a chance to speak. "Sorry, Steve, we got away as soon as we could. Bridge traffic was a nightmare. Taylor Swift's show got out just as we hit the city. You know the drill."

Charles was not apologetic. He was just concerned. "So we'll have some visitors for a bit?"

Biting off his frustration, Steve muttered, "Yeah, thanks for getting the jet ready. I sent Jessie off with Morgan. Maggie's meeting them at the airport."

"We'll give her a few days then, and fly down to see how she's doing."

Deirdre touched Steve's arm and motioned for him to sit. She dropped down into a seat as well. "What happened today, Steve?"

A long, tired face preceded his explanation. "She had a meltdown." Briefing the power couple on the state Sophie found Jessie in earlier that day, Steve was cautious. "It started yesterday," he admitted. He sucked in a breath before continuing. The truth would only serve to nail Josh's coffin shut a little further. But it was going to come out to this couple sometime. "She found out Josh isn't in Toronto for *Wyatt Boys* pickups."

They reflected on that, Charles *harrumphing* and Dee sinking lower into the fancy chaise. Not that they cared much about Josh, Steve thought. But it was obvious Jessie would not respond well to Josh's trip to TO.

He waited.

Charles started. "I am going to hang that boy's balls from the rafters, Dee, I swear."

Mutely, Steve considered his and Josh's balls hanging all over Toronto would not likely fare well with the locals.

Her throat constricting as she imagined Jessie's state about now, Deirdre stood. "I need to go see my grandchildren," she said in a cloudy voice. Touching Steve's arm again as she left the room, she managed to add, "Thank you, Steve. For everything. I know you'd likely rather be home with your new baby. This isn't easy for any of us."

Watching Steve as Dee made her 'gracious-under-the-circumstances' exit, Charles considered the actor's countenance. "What aren't you telling me?"

Adjusting his seat on the deep chaise, a long exhalation accompanying it, Steve decided the truth was the order of the night. Not that Charles would care, but…he dove in anyway. "Did you know Josh bought a condo in Toronto? For Nadia?"

Charles' shoulders sank. "Jessie knows this?"

"Yes. She does now."

"I suppose that makes sense. Before Jessie was rescued—"

"He just bought it last month."

"Then I see why Jessie lost it today."

"She loves him desperately, Charles. But I think she turned a corner today. I think she's done. You and Dee need to know she's done. Because after the hell of being confined like that, and raped, and hearing the guy slosh gas around above her, I am pretty damn sure the last thing she expected was to come home and have to face the end of her marriage to the guy who pretty much saved her in the first place, back when we were all making *Drifters*."

"She's going to need some help getting through this."

"Not just psychologically, Charles. These beautiful kids could be yours for a while. Are you prepared for that?"

"Of course. Dee's over the moon. She's been worrying herself sick over them. We need them here where we can see them on a day-to-day basis, so we know they're okay."

"Emily-Grace…she was inconsolable when Jessie left today."

"God, that child is three. And already her world is a disaster." Melting down to the arm of the chaise, Charles took a deep breath. "Consistency is likely best thing for her right now. And I'm sure Jessie will take a week or so and then come back. Emily-Grace will get lots of love here, Steve. She'll be fine."

"And Josh?" He swallowed. Not that Steve thought Josh should be around his kids anytime soon, anyway.

Shaking his head, Charles hesitated. "I don't know, Steve. I'm not going to keep the man from his children. But we might need you or someone the children know to mediate visits. I personally don't care if I never lay eyes on him again."

"There's more, Charles." *Since you already hate the guy,* he bit off to himself.

"Let me guess. He got Nadia pregnant."

"Geez, I hope not. Lord. No, he, uh…I got a text tonight from one of the crew Josh is, uh, hanging out with."

"Don't keep me in suspense, Steve. Spit it out."

Steve hesitated. Then he dove in, and buried his friend even further. "He's doing coke."

"Ah. So he's gone from drowning himself in liquor to disappearing into hard drugs. Good for him. We'll just bury him with the other friends he used to party with before he met Jessie."

"Jesus Christ, Charles. Have a fucking heart."

"I'm sorry, Steve. I am. That was uncalled for. I know he's your friend. I know Jessie loves the guy. And there was a time I really liked him too, but he's trouble now."

Steve stood and turned his body to face Charles square on. He was tired, he wanted his wife and baby, his heart ached for everyone around him, and now he had to get on a plane, fly across the country, and try to talk some sense into his best friend. He didn't need Charles' judgment stabbing him in the back all the way to Toronto.

"He's not...'trouble' now, Charles. He's *in* trouble. There's a goddamned difference."

"What he does when he leaves his marriage officially is really not my business, Steve. I'm sorry things went down this way, but we all went through hell when the kids and Jessie were taken. The rest of us aren't shooting white powder up our noses. And we're still capable of taking care of Emily-Grace and David!"

"And the rest of you are so in love with Jessie that when she was missing, for a second time goddamn it, you buried yourself so deep you couldn't find your way out? You insulated yourself with a warm body and sex and alcohol, and cursed everyone around you because it hurt too much to acknowledge that you hurt?! Like Josh had to do in order to survive?!"

The emotion of the hard day was taking its toll. Steve was damn tired of picking up the pieces. He grabbed his phone from where he'd set it on the cushion, and moved to go.

Charles grabbed his arm. "Stop. Steve, I'm sorry. But we do love Jessie. It killed us."

Studying the charcoal shading under the man's eyes, and the new wrinkles at the corners, Steve acquiesced. "I know you do, Charles. But you have Deirdre and she has you. I have Sophie. Charlie has Jane. And even Jacob has someone now. Who did Josh have? Huh?" He let that sink in before adding, "Give him a fucking break. And keep your promise. At least let him see his kids."

At that, he turned and left the home.

There was one light on in the room. Charles pondered Steve's words before twisting around and reaching to flick it off. When he did, and the room was dark, he collapsed onto the chaise's center cushion. "This is too much," he moaned. "I owe Josh nothing. Nothing!"

His intestines clenched at the thought. Over the last many years, Jessie was a golden light. Her life, with her husband and her children, was pure, simple joy. Josh was everything to her. He brought her that joy. So many times Charles remembered seeing them lost in each other's eyes, backstage at concerts, at dinner, sitting by the pool, cuddling in the jet, wherever. And now, he admitted, that light would be extinguished. He remembered the girl he and Dee rescued—the quiet waif who was almost afraid of her own shadow. There wasn't much light in that girl's eyes, either. Yet they brought beautiful music out of her soul.

Would she get past this? Was there a breaking point for Jessie Wheeler? *Yes,* he thought. *She has a breaking point. And she's reached it.*

Groaning because his knees hurt as he stood, he limped to the stairs. It took him a while to make his way to the top.

But when he got there, Charles hesitated before going in to the children's room to see his wife. He had to swipe at a few tears first. It wouldn't do for Deirdre to see her anchor cry.

Chapter Twenty-Three

Thank God for small mercies. Steve slept on the plane, better than he had the last few nights with the new baby at home, even. Still, when the commercial airliner landed, he was a sleepy mess.

Grabbing his bag at the carousel, he headed towards the car rental area. An SUV was waiting for him—he'd booked it while waiting for his flight in Vancouver.

This was a drill Steve knew well. After a number of seasons on Jon's hit TV show, he was very familiar with Toronto, often renting vehicles rather than taking rides with the show's transport department.

Before leaving the parking area, he plugged the address of Josh's condo, provided earlier by Penney, into his phone's GPS. It was a forty-five minute drive. There was satellite radio in the car, so Steve found a rock station he liked, a classic one where he figured he would not be plagued with one of Jessie's mournful ballads, and he cruised onto the 401.

The dash on the car read 11 a.m. when he slid into a street side parking space a block down from Josh's place. Vancouver time, it was only eight, but Steve was accustomed to making this time adjustment so he tried to make himself appear more awake than he felt.

He texted Penney. *Here. Let me the fuck in.*

The genial Newfie was waiting for him. *Say pretty please*

But he stepped out from a building down the way and waved at the blonde actor.

When Steve reached him, Penney was bleak.

"Not a damn thing I could do to remove Nadia, Steve. And I don't think

Josh is budging. You may have just flown across the country for no damn reason."

"Oh, I have a reason," was Steve's fiery response. A wide yawn accosted him, but he could feel adrenalin start to work its way through his body. "Let me at him."

Raising his eyebrows, Penney asked, "Am I gonna need to call the cops?"

"The firemen, maybe. The ladder truck." Steve decided if anyone was hanging Josh's balls from the rafters, it was gonna be him. But hell if he'd help the guy get them down.

"Huh?" asked Penney, his mouth twisting in confusion.

"Never mind. Which one?" Steve stood poised at the buzzer panel and looked for Josh's name. "Of course," he muttered under his breath. "It's not gonna be here. The damn love nest is in Nadia's name."

Penney pushed a button and the voice of one of the *Wyatt Boys* crew came through the speaker. "This better be the pizza guy."

"Yeah, I'll bring you pizza," retorted Penney. "In your big wet dream, Hoozer."

Soon he and Steve were outside Josh's door. Steve didn't wait for Penney's good graces. He had a new baby to get home to. Raising a fist, he hammered on the door.

"Sawyer, open the damn door and let me in. I've got a sharp knife, and I'm coming for your balls before Charles Keating decides to cut them off with a dull razor."

The heavy door swung open, and Josh stood there glaring. "What the hell are you doing here, Steve? You're not invited to this party."

Marching past him, Steve flicked a finger against his nose. "You might want to get some of that nasal mist stuff. Looking a little red there, Josh."

"Ow! Fuck off!" was Josh's reply, as he glared at Penney. "Traitor," he spit at him.

"Get dressed," Steve demanded, waving an arm at his friend and co-star. "Take a fucking shower first. You stink. We're going for a walk."

Hung-over and sick, Josh didn't move until he caught the fear in Steve's eyes. As he did, two thoughts hit him—one was, *is my family okay? Jessie?* The second was, *didn't Steve and Sophie just have their baby?* He vaguely recalled cheering one night at one of the clubs when someone on the crew got the text from Steve.

He hedged. Should he say something or wait for Steve to tell him? Taking the coward's way out, he moved towards his bedroom.

Naked, Nadia was sprawled out on the bed, snoring off her liquor and coke. Josh stepped past her discarded designer gown and soaked himself in the shower.

Steve's here. Shit.

But inside, a tiny glimmer of hope took hold. Josh was so lost, so scared and confused. The coke last night terrified him. Sure, it was awesome, it took away the ache for a few hours and they partied til dawn again, but overall Josh well knew what dark road it led to. And already his stomach was a mass of pain again. It seemed like nothing he did had the power to ease the dark ache.

Thank God Steve's here. Thank God. I'll go home with him. He'll help me get sorted. God, please let him help me…

Twenty minutes later, he and Steve were at a park down the street. It was a warm summer day but a soft misty rain was falling. Neither guy had a decent coat on, so they got wet, but at least the moisture kept any potential curious staring locals at home.

Steve started. "I have a kid. I have a kid now, and he's seven days old, and my best friend missed out on his birth."

Josh was silent.

"So, instead of being home with my brand new son on his one week birth-day, I am here in Toronto with said best friend, who apparently doesn't give a shit about anyone but himself." Inside, Steve knew he was being hard on Josh, but he was tired and pissed. And worried. He wanted to see where this would go.

"I'm done here, Steve," was Josh's unexpected answer. "I'm done."

"Meaning…?" Steve wondered if he was going to have to call an ambu-lance and get Josh committed to rehab, or to a psych ward. But Josh illumi-nated him real quick.

"I mean with Nadia. With beer, with whatever. I just…I needed to do this, I needed the space to see…" He gulped, knifed a hand through his hair, and didn't bother enlightening Steve further. The guy well knew. "Just…I know what a dick I've been, Steve. It's just…it's so hard, you know? I need to go back to Vancouver. I know that now. I need to try to be the guy Jessie needs me to be."

Almost laughing, Steve guffawed, "Really? Now? After treating her like she's the plague, all of a sudden you're ready to be the perfect husband again? Get over yourself, Josh."

"I mean it, Steve. I'm so fucking lost I can't find my own asshole. I'll go see Trudy and sort through this shit. I'll be there for Jessie and my kids. No more drinking. No more Nadia."

Oh Jesus, thought Steve. *No you won't. You'll keep drinking. Or worse.* The accumulating mist wasn't enough to hide the glistening sheen in his green eyes. Steve was standing three-quarter on to Josh, ahead of him, twisted around a little. He turned his head away now, unable to face him. He counted to ten, and then turned full on to give Josh news he knew had the power to send him more fully under.

"You think Jessie still believes you're in Toronto shooting pickups? Huh, Josh?"

A confused flicker crossed Josh's eyes. "What? Yeah. Why wouldn't I?"

"You been in touch with her at all, buddy?" Shoulders and chin raised, Steve prepared for the worst.

Josh swallowed and blinked. "No. Not for a few days."

"Not for two weeks, Josh. Not for two full goddamned weeks."

The friends were now facing each other like in one of *Drifters'* old-fashioned gunfights. They could almost hear an invisible someone standing close by counting their paces. Soon they would be forced to draw their pearl-handled Colts on each other. But for now, neither of them moved.

Josh's voice was quiet, subdued. "She'll forgive me. She understands. I know she does."

"That's how it works, huh buddy? You stomp all over her for weeks on end, after the hell she went through, and think she'll turn the other cheek?"

"She knows me. She knows how hard this was for me. Her, the kids…in one fell swoop they were gone…and the lunatics are still out there, wanting her dead for all we know!"

"You're right about that, Josh. I'll give you that. Jessie knows how hard this has been on you. But you know what else?"

Without speaking, Josh angled his head, raised his own chin a little, and listened.

"I think there's a limit to Jessie Wheeler's capacity for pain. Not everybody thinks that, because despite the hell she's been through time and again in her lifetime, she always rallies. Even when she was missing we all said 'no worries, Jessie's the strongest person we know, she'll be strong, she'll get through this.' But you know what, buddy?"

Steve had to pause for a breath. He was keyed up, and blood was pounding in his ears. After a moment he continued, repeating himself so he could be sure Josh really got it, pointing a finger at his friend as he finally unleashed the raucous thoughts that had bounced around in his brain all the way from Vancouver to Toronto.

"There's a limit to Jessie Wheeler's capacity for pain. And it wasn't Deuce McCall, and it wasn't this asshole who trapped her in a dungeon for six months, raped her, poured gasoline on the floor above her head while she was tied up, and then lit a goddamned match! No, Josh. It's you. It's watching you suffer. It's watching you in pain. That's her limit. And you know what? She's fucking reached it."

Swiping at a stray tear, he waited for Josh to clue in.

It took him a few seconds, but even then Josh didn't want to believe it. "What do you mean she's reached it?"

"I mean she's not in Vancouver anymore. After Sophie found her on the floor of your kids' playroom while Emily-Grace cooked a car on the stove and, thankfully, avoided slipping out the open door into the pool, I booked her a trip to New York. On the Keating jet, thankfully, because no way would she have been able to handle commercial travel, commercial travel's a bitch these days,—"

"Steve! Focus."

"Oh, this from the alcoholic coke addict—"

"I did coke once," Josh growled. "Last night. And I have no plans to do it again."

"Okay, well good, because you're not likely to see your kids again if you keep that shit up. Oh, and Josh, they're not with Jessie. I took them to Charles and Dee, who I'm sure won't hesitate to sue for custody should things heat up any further."

"Why aren't they with Jessie?" Josh's voice was small, childlike, as the nightmare he was engrossed in since November just continued circling and circling around him like a flock of buzzards.

"Didn't you hear me, Josh? Didn't you fucking hear me? Jessie's barely capable of taking care of herself right now! She knows you bought a condo for Nadia! And she knows why—because you're so fucked up right now you don't know if you're coming or going! She can't stand to see you like this. And she can't reach you."

"I told you, it's all good, Steve, I got it out of my system, I'm going to figure this out!"

"No, Josh. You're not. At least not anywhere near Jessie. She needs time away from you."

"Like she hasn't had enough fucking time? Like six and a half goddamn months, maybe?!"

"She's done, Josh. She's done. And not the way you tell me you're done."

"What do you mean, done? Like what, she's divorcing me or something?"

"Something like that. Yeah. That's exactly what I mean." It was a stretch, maybe, because Jessie hadn't exactly voiced the nauseating word, but Steve had looked into her eyes before he put her on the jet, and what he saw was simply a very bad ending. He sure as hell didn't see hope in the pale baby blues.

"Why are you doing this, Steve? I thought we were friends."

"Then I guess you just answered your own question, friend. Would you rather have heard this from a lawyer, Josh? Or from Charles?"

"Jesus Christ, Steve. This just gets better and better."

"I'm sorry, Josh. I am. But it's too little, too late, you know? You've got to deal with this shit you're buried in. All of it. The booze, the drugs, the way you've been ignoring how much all this shit hurts by insulating yourself in anger and in Nadia. And you need to leave Jessie and the kids alone until you do it."

"There's one problem, Steve." The truth of his new reality was now sinking in. Josh was struggling to stay on top of his frayed nerves, but tears were threatening him too.

"What's that, Josh?" It was killing Steve to see his friend in so much pain. And he had just knocked him down even further.

181

"Jessie." Crumbling, choking, Josh widened his arms. They floated at his sides, pulsating a little as he trembled, as if they had nowhere to go, nowhere to land. "She's my rock. I can't do this without her."

"You might have wanted to consider that before you lied to her and flew back to Toronto to party with Nadia. In the love nest you bought for her. Jesus, Josh, what the hell were you thinking?"

"I have a feeling you know, Steve."

Taking this in, Steve considered Josh's comment. "Yeah. Yeah, buddy. I guess I do."

Moving forward, he rested a steady hand on Josh's quaking shoulder. "You guys got eggs in this neighborhood? A guy gets hungry after taking the red-eye to try to rescue his friend."

"You call that a rescue? Telling me my wife is leaving me?" Josh pressed his thumb and forefinger to his bottom lip, and squeezed tightly, but he rotated on one heel and started to walk next to Steve.

"I call it a mercy mission. And I'm your angel of mercy." Steve kept his hand on Josh's shoulder while they walked. Lowering his voice, he softened his next words. "I'm not leaving you alone through this, Josh. I know you're in a bad place. And I'm sorry about Jessie. But you're not alone, okay? Kayla and Zach too, and the rest of the gang, everybody's worried. They're all hoping you get through this shit intact."

"That's what she said."

"What?"

"Jessie. She said she wasn't leaving me alone. But she is." Slumping along a bit further, Josh added, "She told me she would fight for me. But she isn't."

Steve couldn't keep a bitter edge from coloring his voice. "After you abandoned her and the kids to fuck off with Nadia, if Jessie's got any fight left at all, Josh, well…she needs it for herself right now. You get that, right? Tell me you fucking get your own insidious part in all this."

They were silent. The question went unanswered.

Josh spoke next. "I got an email from Jon. I'm off *The Wyatt Boys*."

Another bullet, thought Steve. *How much more can this guy take?* Toning his anger down, he managed to sound sympathetic about this particular blow. "I heard. I'm sorry."

"My own father fired me. Through a fucking email."

"He had no choice, Josh. You destroyed some rare antique clock because the camera guy looked at you sideways. Among other things."

"I'll get help. I swear."

After a bit, as they crossed the street to head to a nearby restaurant, Steve said, "Caleb. That's my kid's name. Caleb. In case you are even remotely interested."

"Oh. Cool. Good name." Josh sniffed and wiped his nose. The rain was intensifying.

"Come home, okay Josh? Come back to Vancouver with me and let's figure something out. Come meet my kid."

"I dunno, Steve. Maybe in a few days. I dunno, now. When I saw you I thought maybe, yeah, but now I dunno. I'll see, okay?"

"That's the best you got?"

Josh paused. "Do you think I can get her back?"

"Not in the immediate future, Josh. No. I don't." At his crestfallen look, Steve added, "I'm not gonna lie to you."

"Some angel of mercy you are."

They went indoors out of the rain, ordered eggs and bacon, and shot the shit about their other friends until the sun came out, glistening and hot, leaving steamy moisture rising from the sewer grates. On the way back to the condo, they walked through the steam. It left wet trails on their skin.

To Steve, it was soothing and somewhat ethereal.

To Josh, it felt like he was walking through hell.

Chapter Twenty-four

Kelly got the news to Jacob five minutes after she found out. She and Michael had hooked up with Jacob in Savannah, Georgia, to entertain on behalf of *Mystic Nights* at a Domestic Violence awareness concert. The morning after the concert, they were planning to meet for breakfast in their quaint Bed and Breakfast, the luxurious Hamilton-Turner Inn. Set amongst the beautiful magnolias and live oaks in Savannah's Lafayette Square, the historic 1873 mansion seemed apropos for the telling of monumental news.

Kelly bounced into the dining room ten minutes after the boys, her iPad held gaily in one hand. Holding it high, she turned it towards Jacob and pointed at the screen.

"Guess who's splitting up."

"Uh, I dunno, Kelly, Ike and Tina Turner? Oh no, pardon me, that was before you were born." He sometimes got tired of Kelly's propensity for drama, and even Michael focused on his coffee and smothered a small laugh at Jacob's quick retort.

"Always the comedian, aren't you, Jacob? Well, you won't be laughing when you hear this."

Michael reached towards the chair next to him, and dragged it out so his wife could sit. Once she was seated, she wriggled into a more comfortable position in the large chair, and settled her gaze on Jacob. He seemed to sense what she was going to tell him, for his coffee was halfway to his lips, frozen in place, as he waited to hear the words.

"Josh and Jessie. That's who. It's all over the news today."

Jacob set his cup down without taking a sip. He couldn't speak.

Michael saved him. "What?"

He took the iPad from Kelly and read the Huffington Post article she had open, which mourned the couple's break-up since their union seemed so hard won. But the writer also acknowledged the traumas the couple recently experienced, with the abduction of Jessie and their children, and how Josh moved on with Nadia at a time when the rest of the world was still hoping Jessie would be found.

Kelly eyed Jacob warily. "Now's your chance, Casanova."

Finding his voice, Jacob said hoarsely, "This is gonna break her heart, Kel."

A dark shadow crossed Kelly's face. She glanced at her husband, who smiled sadly and took her hand.

"I know," she said to Jacob. "Although since Jessie was the one doing the breaking up, maybe she'll get through it okay."

"Wh-what? She ended it?"

"According to, well, everyone, yes. She did. She called it off and went to New York to stay with one of her *Drifters* friends for a bit." Cradling her head sideways, she studied him. "Why is that so surprising? It's not really a secret he was seeing someone else before she was found."

Considering the number of times he saw magic float between Jessie and Josh's eyes over the last few years, most recently that first day in the hospital, Jacob was floored. "No. That can't be right. Josh was hedging, but Jessie—no. She would never give up on him. It'd have to be pretty bad for her to let him go."

"Well then, I guess it was pretty bad, Jacob. I'm sorry for her. I really am."

"Me too."

They finished their meal before Jacob sprinted up to his room and scrolled through his own iPad for news of the break-up. The most shocking statement he read was about Jessie not taking her kids to New York with her. He had to read it twice. *No way,* he muttered to himself as he sprawled out on his bed and selected another entertainment gossip page to see if everyone was reporting the same news.

Like a sinking boat in troubled water during a storm, Jacob's spirit plummeted. If Jessie broke up with Josh and went to New York without her kids, she was in trouble. Big trouble. Serious trouble. *Enough trouble not to feel up to calling her best friend to tell me,* he thought.

185

A call to Steve confirmed it. Jacob paced his grand B and B bedroom as Steve filled him in. At the end of their call, Jacob asked for Maggie's address.

He was met with a lengthy pause. "I don't think that's such a good idea right now, Jacob."

"What? Why not? She and I are close. I want to see if she's okay."

"First of all, she's not okay. Obviously. Second, yeah, you two are close. And she doesn't need to be distracted by you while she's trying to figure things out."

"I have a girlfriend," Jacob offered, more convincingly than he felt.

"That's enough reason to stay away from Jessie. Rachael's sweet, Jacob."

"Steve, please." This time, Jacob didn't hide the angst in his voice. "I need to see her."

A long, exasperated sigh was Steve's response. "Look, I'm in the middle of this thing, okay Ryan? Josh is my best friend. Jessie is one of my best friends. You? Not so much."

"Geez, tell me how you really feel about me."

"I'm just saying you have been a thorn in Josh's side all along. He's suffering through his own version of hell right now, and he doesn't need you crawling into Jessie's bed the second he steps out of it."

"Seems to me he hasn't been in it for a while, anyway, Steve. And you know, Josh may trump Jessie to you, but to me, she's everything. She's everything, Steve." He couldn't keep a tremulous timbre from sneaking into his voice. "I'm just saying I care about her in a way none of the rest of you can even imagine, because I knew her at a time when she was this sad lonely punk woman in Scotland, and I fell in love with her then. When she was nobody special—well, not famous, I mean, to me, at least. But I knew what Josh meant to her then, even though I had no clue who the ring around her neck represented at the time. And, Steve? I know what he means to her now. And that's why I need to see her. Because there's no way in hell she's okay right now, and it scares the hell out of me." Jacob sucked in a breath before adding, "And you don't hold the all-exclusive rights to her, Steve. *Especially* because Josh is your best friend."

The line was silent. Then Steve sighed and said, "All right. But Jacob— consider how messed up she is before you try to jump in her bed, okay? Not just for her sake, or Josh's for that matter. But for your own. Consider yourself warned."

"I just want to see her, Steve."

"I know, man. I get it."

Immediately, Jacob switched his airline destination out of Savannah from Vancouver to New York. When he arrived at Maggie's place, the kindly *Drifters* star the other cast considered a good friend and a kind of older sister, who now lived and worked in New York primarily in the theater scene, greeted him with a relieved hug.

Morgan, who was peeling an orange, sat on a stool at the kitchen island and nodded in silent greeting.

Maggie jumped in right away. "I know how the others feel about you being here, Jacob, but they don't have a very depressed woman hiding in their guest bedroom at the moment. I'm glad you came."

She took his duffel and guitar and set them aside. "Can I get you anything? You must be tired."

He hardly heard her. Hands in his pockets, Jacob was scanning the apartment for signs of Jessie. "No, it's okay. I'm good, thanks."

"She's in the back bedroom, Jacob. Down the hall to the right. Apart from getting up to pee, she hasn't left it since she arrived Friday night. Since it's now late Sunday, I'd say your first challenge is to get her to at least eat something."

"I'll make her some chocolate chip cookies." Jacob tried to grin, remembering good times in Scotland in a tiny Edinburgh flat, which now seemed like eons ago.

"I was thinking more like salad or soup, actually." Maggie smiled at him. "Ah. I see. Singer humor. Never did understand you music types. You mind if I go out? This babysitting gig is hard on a girl accustomed to her daily Hot Yoga class." She looked at Morgan. "Although this nice guy didn't seem to mind doing a few coffee runs for me."

"Sure, Maggie. I'll keep an eye. We'll be fine." Jacob's eyes were glued to the door at the far end of the hallway, although he could see, from his peripheral vision, Morgan's unnerving singular gaze on him.

Maggie couldn't help herself. She hugged Jacob a second time, and he actually took one hand out of one jeans pocket and half-hugged her back.

"I mean it, Jacob. It's good you're here. I know you're close."

A pink rose flush crept into his cheeks. "Thanks Maggie," he said, while staring at the floor.

After the door clicked shut behind Maggie, Jacob moved to the right towards a decent sized open concept kitchen. He rummaged around a few cupboards until he found a glass, and then he helped himself to some water from a Brita pitcher in the large fridge.

He turned to Morgan. "Into the breach," he said nervously.

Summoning up his courage, Jacob made his way on tiptoes down the hall.

Straightening, eyes narrowing and lips curving down, the orange in his big hands forgotten, Morgan watched him go.

Raising a fist at the door, Jacob knocked tentatively. When Jessie didn't answer, he slowly pushed the solid wood door open and peeked in. It creaked and she moved, so Jacob knew she was awake. He made his way to the bed, and gently eased himself down behind his good friend.

Stirring, Jessie raised her head off the pillow, but she was facing the opposite wall so she couldn't see him.

Placing one arm around her waist, and then subsequently raising that hand to brush sweaty hair back from her forehead, Jacob whispered tenderly, "I'm here, Jessie. You're not alone."

She had known instantly that the body spooning her was Jacob. Jessie remembered well the feel of him, and his faint green apple scent was always his shadow. She found the hand brushing back her hair, and pressed her own against it. Kissing it softly, she drew it close around her body.

"Jacob," she murmured. "So glad. So glad you came."

"Of course," was his subdued answer. "My girl's hurting. Where else would I be?"

When she didn't say anything else, he snuggled closer and buried his face in her hair. He was tired and wanted sleep. In this semi-dark room, with his arms where they always longed to be, around Jessie, Jacob felt himself drifting off. He startled when he felt her shoulders shaking.

Lifting his head to lay his warm cheek against her wet one, he asked, "What can I do, Jessie? What can I do to make all this bad stuff go away?"

Without answering directly, she spoke of the one thing he knew would eventually catch up with her. "I'd ask to sing with you but I don't have my dad's guitar anymore. The Gibson...it's gone. It's gone, Jacob."

He knew she was mourning so much more than just the Gibson...her father, Josh...likely all of the losses in her life, which Jacob was well aware always haunted Jessie when she was down.

"I know," he murmured, as she rolled over on her back to face him. He pulled her into his arms and rocked her while she cried. For him, there was no greater pain than to hold the woman he loved together while her world fell apart. "I know," he repeated, unable to keep from sobbing with her.

When she quieted, Jacob lay next to her and wiped away her tears. "Beautiful girl," he started, cobalt blue eyes probing her lighter eyes, "I know we can't replace your dad's Gibson, but we can find one of the same vintage. With the same feel and the same sound, you know? We'll go looking around New York tomorrow."

"Why'd he have to go and do that, Jacob? Why?"

"Josh? He was missing you. He was scared. He disappeared every bit as much as you did, kiddo."

"Not Josh. That's not who I mean."

Quizzically, Jacob squinted a little at her. "Who, then?"

"The fireman," she moaned, hopelessness consuming her. "Why'd he have to take me out of that burning house? I wish he didn't. I don't want to be here anymore. I want to die, Jacob. I want to die." Once more, she collapsed into sobs that felt like they were ripping her in half.

A tremor started in Jacob's toes then, and traversed up his legs and spine in frightening tingles. "No," he begged her. "No. Lots of people have shit in their lives, Jessie. You have to believe things will get better."

"I keep thinking about my mother, Jacob. How she disappeared somewhere in her mind and how afraid I've been that someday it would happen to me too. That I would disappear. But you know what? I keep trying to. I keep trying to disappear for good, Jacob, but I can't! I can't disappear! I want to, so bad! But I can't!"

Gasping for breath as he held her, Jacob breathed *nooooooo*. Closing his eyes, he implored her to listen. "Thinks will get better, Jessie. I promise."

"I don't want them to. I just want to go away."

189

"No, baby girl. No more running." Inside, a thought took hold that Jacob wished could come true. *I would give anything to see her happy again. Anything.* He even told the universe he would rather see her back with Josh than see her in such despair, despite his own not-so-secret longings. "No. Tonight we sleep, and tomorrow we start fresh. We'll find you a new-old Gibson, and we'll Skype your kids, and we'll go get ice cream at that Serendipity place you like. You hear me? And no more bad thoughts. The world would be a sad, sad place without my Jessie in it."

She hiccupped as her crying calmed, and turned her face to his. "Your Jessie, huh?" The limpid, pale eyes searched his. She let a finger trail down his cheek.

Steve's words echoed in Jacob's ears. He wanted to push them away, to ignore the warning, but he had more than one heart to protect here. So he heeded Steve's cautionary vibe. "Beautiful girl," he whispered, "whether or not you and I ever get together again, you will always be my girl. Always."

A wistful smile encouraged him. "I like the sound of that," she murmured, wiping away the salty trails on Jacob's ever-bristly cheeks. "Thank you, Jacob."

"You know I love you," he said softly. "So much. Now go pee and let's sleep. Tonight there will only be sweet dreams for you, Jessie, I promise. I'll keep the bad ones away."

She did as he asked her to, before snuggling back under his arm. "I feel better already," she told him as he pulled a quilt they found lying over the foot of the bed up over them. "And I love you back."

The words *always and forever* almost slipped out. But no, they couldn't. They were for another man who, right now, was likely stumbling around Toronto, lost and drunk. *Without me,* Jessie thought as a new wave of pain clenched her sore belly. *Without his babies.*

But, in the safety and comfort of Jacob's arms, bad dreams did indeed remain elusive that night. Instead, Jessie dreamed of her father. He was playing her—no, his—Gibson.

She woke up smiling.

Chapter Twenty-five

The next day, Jacob kept his promise.

Jessie nudged herself off the bed, stretched, showered, and managed to choke back a half slice of dry toast and a few sips of oj. Waving a solemn hi to Morgan, she hugged Maggie, whispered *thank you*, and disappeared for a bit with her best buddy.

She and Jacob passed a sunny day wandering the streets of New York, followed at a distance by Morgan who, in truth, and unbeknownst to anyone else besides his ex, had orders to protect Jessie from, well, himself.

The co-stars and friends were in search of an old 1985 J-45 Gibson. Pawn shops, music shops, and Internet ads led them on an easy exploration of some of New York's best kept secret type shops. In late afternoon, they found what they were looking for in a tiny, dark music shop only two short blocks from Maggie's building.

"I think it's meant for me," Jessie murmured as she drew a finger down an aged fret. Smiling sadly at Jacob, she hoisted the Gibson over her shoulder and strummed and picked a few phrases, cocking her head to better admire its sweet, pure sound. "Two blocks from Maggie's place. Weird."

Jacob insisted on making the guitar his gift to her. While he paid for it, she wandered the shadowy shop and let a finger make tiny tracks in the dust on some of the older guitars lingering in dark corners. Absently, she was wondering who once played these lonely instruments, and where—clubs, weddings?—when her cell phone bleeped. Thinking it was likely Dee, whose frequent worried check-ins were starting to become annoying, Jessie sighed and reached for her phone. Retrieving it from a large front pocket of the leather aviator jacket she was wearing, which she bought at a vintage shop that day in honor of her dad, she froze when her eyes landed on the display.

It was a text from Josh.

Pls can we talk

Another followed close behind.

I need to see u

While her heart did a double take, and then about five somersaults, she peeked over her shoulder at Jacob, who was sweetly chatting with the ancient stringy-haired hippie behind the cash. Poising both thumbs over the miniature keyboard, Jessie considered what to text back. After a brief pause, she typed in *always and forever,* and hit 'send.' Then she sent a second text—*just not now.*

A click of a fingernail on the phone's side button sent it to 'silent' mode. Casually dropping the cell in her pocket, Jessie accepted the guitar case from Jacob. He held up a smiley-faced sticker the old guy had by the cash register, *for kids,* Jacob said. Together they stood the guitar case up on its base, and Jessie placed the sticker around where the old one would have been on the case of the lost Gibson.

Laughing, trying to hide her pounding heart, she ducked behind Jacob and asked the older fellow for a few more, *for my kids.*

Happy, or at least enjoying a temporary respite from the worst of the crushing pain, Jessie ducked under Jacob's arm. Together, they sauntered back to Maggie's place. Suddenly the world didn't seem like such a desperate, dark place.

Behind them, Morgan walked at a distance, unnoticed and unseen, as he was trained to do.

In Toronto, Josh hung his head and wished he could disappear. His rogue hair fell from behind his ear and hid his cheek from Nadia's constant scrutiny. Josh didn't bother tucking it back where it belonged.

~~~

"Hey, Rachael?"

Outside Maggie's building, Jacob took advantage of a few free minutes to call his girlfriend and give her the heads up. It was Wednesday, and although he'd texted her a few times, he hadn't called since his arrival in New York, so he knew she'd be wondering what he was up to. His schedule was free until the next Monday, at least in terms of promotional work commitments, so he thought he would stay in New York until then. Common sense prevailed, which had Jacob deciding those plans needed to include Rachael.

When he reached her, the phone was quiet. She was waiting for an explanation.

Already Jacob and Jessie had been spotted together in the city, sauntering down streets in Greenwich Village, and standing with awed respect at the Strawberry Fields John Lennon Memorial in Central Park. This was hot news in the fast-paced cutthroat world of entertainment biz gossip. The photo that bothered Rachael the most clearly showed Jacob's arm flung cozily over Jessie's shoulders as they strolled down Broadway. As they walked, his lips were brushing her left ear; it wasn't a stretch to imagine that he'd just whispered something apparently seductive or, at the very least, funny, as he was sporting a wide grin. Jessie, her right hand raised and clasped comfortably in his at her right shoulder, was blushing and grinning as well, and her head was slanted towards his.

The gossip blogs took no time in establishing the two as a couple. Rumors were rampant that they were together before Josh and Jessie's breakup, and maybe even in Miami during the shooting of *Mystic Nights*.

So now, with his phone pressed to his ear, clasped in a sweaty palm, Jacob had some fence mending to do.

When Rachael finally responded with a quiet, "I'm here," a nauseous wave swept over Jacob's stomach, but he wasn't entirely sure why. Was it because he knew he was pushing the boundaries of his relationship with Rachael? Or was it because Jacob knew in his heart he was having the time of his life hanging out with Jessie?

He answered with a, "Hey, what are you doing for the next few days?" *Might as well try to bypass any drama*, he was thinking.

"I guess that depends on you, Jacob." The ennui coloring his girlfriend's voice was not lost on him.

"Charles and Dee are coming to New York tomorrow. I'm not sure if he's told you, but Charles is calling in some favors with music biz friends of his in the city. He's renting us a studio and some musicians for a couple of days. I'd love it if you came down. Come see how they do things in the Big Apple."

SUSAN RODGERS

She pondered the offer. At this point Rachael had yet to meet the famous Jessie Wheeler and, after having seen the woman's hand grasping her boyfriend's, she wasn't sure she wanted to.

"I don't know, Jacob."

He tuned in. "Look, Rachael, I know stuff's all over the net with me and Jessie. But it's just friendship, I swear. You know she's my best friend." Catching himself quickly, he corrected the statement with, "One of my best friends."

"Social media world doesn't think you're just friends."

"Social media world is full of crazy people wanting to get the next big scoop. Jessie and me know what's up."

"Jacob...when we got together we swore we would never lie to each other, right?"

"Yeah, Rach, we did. And I haven't."

"Honey, the way you look at her tells me otherwise."

Digesting that information was difficult. Jacob knew where he stood with Jessie and, if he thought he had a shot with her at all, he would have dropped Rachael like a child drops a hot french fry. But she was a good woman, and they shared a lot of musical interests. She would be a good partner to him if Jacob could somehow make it work—the whole 'loving one woman and trying to get over another' scenario.

He countered. "Jessie and I have a history, Rachel. We're super close, I admit it. But I haven't slept with her since the day we broke up. Not in Miami, not in Vancouver, and not here in New York. I swear."

"You haven't *slept* with her."

He spoke carefully, choosing his words with caution. "Not in the Biblical sense, Rach. No. I admit when I first got here she was pretty messed up, though, so I did sleep *beside* her. But not in a sex kind of way."

"Uh huh." Rachael's sarcasm was biting. In Vancouver, where she was sitting on a stool in the middle of the Robson Street studio staring at a large framed publicity photo of Jessie, Rachael was chewing thoughtfully on a strand of hair.

"Buy it or not, it's the truth. And I've been wanting you to meet her. You'll love her. The two of you will hole up in a corner and talk music for hours, I swear."

"She's a pop star, Jacob."

"Ouch. Try telling her that. Jessie sings a lot more than just pop. Her music goes a lot deeper than that. Today we were even messing with a funk tune, it was hilarious."

"You were playing music today. Having a *hilarious* time, as you say. With the supposedly heartbroken Jessie Wheeler."

An exasperated exhalation rocketed through the connection to Vancouver. "You're killing me here, Rachael. I thought we weren't going to do that whole 'crowding each other' bullshit." The last sentence was uttered in Jacob's customary pout, which Jessie had not once heard coming from him since their initial confab Sunday night on the bed in Maggie's spare room.

Rachael's response was a deep sigh.

He tried again. "Music is a way to bring Jessie out of the pain, Rach. You, of all people, oughtta get that."

"Um humn. Sure."

His girlfriend's rather plaintive tone immediately wormed its way annoyingly under Jacob's skin. Breathing in, he took the high road. "Just come to New York. I'll set it up with Charles so you can travel with him and Deirdre on the jet. You won't have to worry about a thing."

"So we'll get a hotel, then?"

At that, his voice caught.

Truthfully, Jacob almost had a panic attack at the idea of leaving Jessie at Maggie's place without him. He was feeling very comfortable there, too damn comfortable, really, with the gals and the rather weird silent, watchful Morgan. The idea of leaving Jessie, even for just a few sleeps, started his heart racing. Jacob was well aware it was his presence that was bringing his friend around. The last thing he needed was for her to step backwards into the dark abyss in which he found her buried a few nights earlier.

Yet he caught himself swallowing, then announcing more amicably than he felt, "Yeah, we'll do that. We'll get a hotel."

And so it was that Rachael arrived on the jet with the Keatings and Jessie's children on Thursday morning, a week after Jessie found out Josh was not in Toronto shooting pickups for *The Wyatt Boys*. Initially, Rachael found herself uncomfortable around the famous actor and singer, but she soon realized, especially upon witnessing Jessie's true sorrow and emotion upon first spotting Charles and Dee and her children, that this was in fact a woman suffering very real pain at the dissolution of a relationship she cherished.

When the emotional reunion settled somewhat, Jacob took Rachael's hand and shyly introduced her to Jessie.

"This is my girl," he said, looking down, cheeks a little hot, before he had the guts to meet Jessie's eyes. When he finally glanced back up at her, he searched her baby blues for a thousand unsaid words, and watched as she swallowed an invisible chunk of ice in her throat before forcing her gaze away from Jacob and over to his girlfriend. Thankfully, it seemed the new girlfriend was oblivious to the waves of heated energy traversing between Jacob and Jessie.

He was right about one thing. Once the girls got chatting, music proved its weight in gold, and there was a lot to talk about. They hit it off immediately, Rachael finally starting to relax with toddler David sitting in the crook of her crossed ankles, playing with a padded baby book, while Jessie snuggled her clingy daughter, who was spending her evening silently begging for hugs, hugs, and more hugs from both her momma and Jacob.

Carlotta was along on the trip as the designated meal prep help, and so what Charles and Dee nervously anticipated would be a painful gathering turned out to be genial and even fun.

After dinner, Jessie and Dee bathed the kids, shepherded them into their pajamas, and handed them over to Jacob and Rachael to play with for a few minutes before bedtime. Dee took advantage of a few minutes alone with Jessie, ushering her back into the bedroom where she spoke candidly.

"It's nice to have Jacob around, honey, isn't it? He brings out a light in you I haven't seen in a very long time."

"He's a good distraction, Dee." Jessie was just being honest.

Together, they started unpacking the kids' clothes and sorting out travel bedding. For Jessie, folding baby clothes was now a treasure. No longer would she take such seemingly mundane duties for granted. She lifted a handful of baby shirts and pressed them to her nose. Inhaling deeply as David's sweet baby scent traversed its way directly into her heart, she closed her eyes and dreamed of the old days. *Before.*

Momentarily, forcing her eyes open, she sighed and dropped the small pile onto the bed, then chose a white T-shirt to fold.

"Have you heard from Josh?"

Jessie stopped folding. The tiny T-shirt in her hands remained suspended while she pondered what to say.

"Yeah, I have, actually. Just a couple of texts, though. That's all." A thought occurred to her, and she glanced over at Dee, who was scanning the room looking for a place to deposit a stack of diapers. "Have you?"

Holding the diapers in one hand, Dee moved a few books around on a shelf. She set the diapers down, moved them into position up against a Neil Simon play, and faced Jessie.

"We have. Not directly, though. It seems Steve is the unfortunate middle man in all of this."

"Oh. I suppose. What did he want?"

"Josh wants to Skype with the kids. That's all."

"He doesn't want to see them?" She couldn't bring herself to look at Dee.

"Not right away. He's still…well, he's still in Toronto, Jessie."

"Oh." The old agony came rushing back, like a swollen river in spring. Jessie laid a hand over her suddenly aching stomach.

"If it's any consolation at all, hon, Steve says he's ending things with Nadia."

Starting to fold rather hurriedly now, Jessie shrugged, trying to appear nonchalant. "Is he. Again. I see. Doesn't matter, anyway, Dee. Anymore."

They folded and sorted and organized wordlessly until Dee again broached the topic of Josh wanting to Skype the kids.

"How do you feel about that?" she asked. "Josh communicating with the children, I mean."

"They're his kids, Dee. He has every right to have contact with them."

"Does he?"

Finally, Jessie turned to face Dee. "Is that what this is about, Dee? Whether or not Josh deserves any kind of access?"

"We do need to sort these things out, Jessie. And we need to bring in our lawyer and formalize your separation. Sooner rather than later."

"I'm…I'm not ready for that yet, Dee."

"Well, we have to at least sort out custody of the children, then. How is this going to work? With us…and with Josh?"

Sighing, Jessie wheeled around and dropped her butt on the edge of the bed. She fingered a toy tiger David seemed to enjoy lugging around and torturing. It had lived on Jessie's pillow for ages; Josh bought it for her at some market years ago. A little ragged now, it was a sorry barometer for how she was feeling. Lightly touching the droopy tail, Jessie wondered whether Carlotta could put a few stitches in it so the baby wouldn't inadvertently pull off the tail and choke on it.

She spoke to Dee from beneath damp eyelashes. "I think as far as Josh goes, at least let him Skype the kids for now. Just make sure you or Charles talk to him first so you know he's sober." It hurt to have to add that. Shoulders slumped, Jessie stared at her toes.

Dee was trying to be sensitive so she lowered the urgency in her voice, but the words still came out clipped. "All right, Jessie. We'll do that. And we'll keep the kids for as long as you need us to. You just say the word. Us old fogies are exhausted, but we are loving having your gorgeous children around to keep us young."

"I'm sorry about all this, Dee. I really am. I'm feeling better, at least… I feel like I can cope on some level now. But I guess the real truth will come out when Jacob leaves. He's a breath of fresh air."

"Jessie…about Jacob…"

"Nothing's happened with him, Dee. He and I know our limits. I'll be careful, I swear."

Gently, Deirdre appealed to Jessie's good sense. "Please do. Be careful, I mean. And may I add I'm glad. We don't need any more broken hearts."

Surprised at the way Dee seemed to read her mind, Jessie bit her lip and nodded. But as much as she liked Rachael, she was jealous as hell of the girl's arrival today. Jessie knew Jacob wasn't hers to hoard, like some prized toy…like the tiger in her hands. But these last few days…she sure as hell wished he was.

A tiny tinkling laughter came from the direction of Maggie's big front room, followed by Jacob's voice in some song type parody. Jessie pictured him, sitting cross-legged on the floor with her daughter nearby, holding up

Emily-Grace's singer-dowwy. He would be making the doll move and dance while pretending she was singing.

Inclining her head to listen, Jessie felt a warmth soak her belly she hadn't had the sweet pleasure of feeling in, well…months.

"He's so good with her," she murmured to Dee, who fought a rising panic at the way Jessie was smiling now, lost in either Jacob's knack with her distant daughter, or with the welcome tinkle of Emily-Grace's joy, for once.

When Jessie looked up at Dee, her eyes were shining. Which conflicted Dee even more.

The older woman reached out and touched Jessie's cheek, then flipped a long curl back behind her ear. "Honey," she smiled, "let me put these things away. You go enjoy your children."

And so, with a grateful hug, Jessie left her and joined the fun in the front room. Soon there was rowdy laughter from everyone, Jessie included, in a big old heritage building in New York.

The gentle, golden light from whence the laughter emanated—on which the gathered friends and family were happily focused—originated from, not surprisingly, a once lonely guy who, at one time, made a living playing guitar in a dusky Scots pub. Here, now, he was enjoying his best gig ever. One of America's much-loved singers / actors, he had grown accustomed to playing for thousands. Today, though, the rewards were a million-fold more as he easily urged oft-buried laughter from a sad, shell-shocked child.

And that humble accomplishment, to Jessie, succeeded in further cementing her love for a man she already adored, but whom the universe, in all its wisdom, was screaming at her not to touch.

As if he could read her thoughts, Jacob, while singing to Emily-Grace with singer-dowwy at his fingertips, met Jessie's grateful, dreamy gaze. His smile was genuine, his cobalt blue eyes flecking happily as they danced. He looked away before she did, but not before a pink flush spread across Jessie's cheeks, and not before the pink in Rachael's faded and disappeared.

Chapter Twenty-six

The next day, most of the group made their way to the studio Charles rented for Jessie and Jacob. After a bit, Deirdre saluted her goodbyes and drifted off to explore the city with Carlotta, Ulysses and the kids. Maggie said her *so longs* and flitted off to a rehearsal for her new play, while Morgan set up camp in the control room with Charles, Rachael, and a local engineer.

In the studio, Jessie and Jacob made magic.

They recorded a song they wrote together earlier in the week, after Jacob bought Jessie the new-old Gibson. It was a haunting ballad, a 'Jacob and Jessie special,' that spoke of bad endings and new beginnings. The first few times they rehearsed the piece for the hired studio musicians, who would anchor the song with background drums, bass, and keys, the watchers were moved to tears. Goosebumps flitted up and down Morgan's legs, while Charles sat back with glorious satisfaction and counted his money.

Rachael watched in stony silence.

What she was quickly discerning about Jessie and Jacob was that they shared some secret language, almost. When they sang, they rarely looked away from each other. At Maggie's place, Rachael's observant eyes had lit upon many little intimacies the two had never quite seemed able to let go of after their break-up a few years back. A hand on a thigh as one reached for the butter, a little squeeze of a hand when one walked by the other, a knowing glance and tender smile for no apparent reason…not to mention a deeply shared love for a haunted little girl.

It was obvious they were deeply connected. But the calm, loving manner in which Jacob protectively carried Emily-Grace around and let her sleep on his shoulder, was the deepest layer apparently winding he and Jessie in and around each other, beyond their music, even. It was disconcerting, to say the least. And now, in the studio, it was downright terrifying for Rachael, who had come to love Jacob in her own way, for his forlorn puppy dog eyes, his sweet temperament, his shy approach to fame, and for his rich musical talent.

She did not count on having to witness his love for Jessie Wheeler here, today, in such a public forum. Last night hurt enough. Now, though, the ballad drove it home. The song was sensual, filled with longing, and wrapped in grief. Recognizing it for what it was, which was a way to help Jessie let go of Josh, Rachael tried to accept it and, as a recording engineer herself as well as a musician, she even reveled in its technical highs and lows, and in its powerful message. But she felt utterly betrayed by Jacob and his *we're just friends* line.

Charles noticed.

He touched Rachael's shoulder lightly and said wisely, "Musically they're good together, Rachael. But what you see out there in the studio stays out there. Or on the stage, whether it be on a *Mystic Nights* set or during a performance. Although I admit there were times I wished things were different."

"I understand," she replied, before adding, "but I beg to differ." And then Rachael left the studio for a ten-one washroom break.

She did come back, telling herself she wasn't comfortable with the easy rapport between her boyfriend and Jessie. Nor was she even remotely calm when it came to the easy glances and intermittent touching. But, at the same time, she was curious enough about Jessie herself not to want to pull a hissy fit and walk out. So Jacob's girlfriend stuck it out that day. In fact, she hung out in New York with the Keatings until Sunday, at which point she rather succinctly removed her man from under Jessie's grasp, by taking him back to Vancouver with her.

⁓ ⁓

Jessie was devastated the day everyone left. Maggie found her sitting alone on the couch in the front room, counting her losses again.

"No," she demanded of Jessie. "Don't do this to yourself. You will stay here for another few weeks, and then you will fly back to Vancouver, pick up the pieces and move on."

"I feel like my heart has been ripped open again, Maggie. This place was so full of laughter this afternoon, and now it's, no offense, kinda like a morgue. The light is gone."

"It was fun, wasn't it?"

Winking at Jessie, Maggie reached for her iPad, which was sitting on the coffee table in front of them. She selected a file and tapped on the *play* arrow. A video dance party came to life.

Unable to restrain herself, Jessie burst out laughing. She pointed at the screen. "That's us! Doing Zumba this afternoon. Who filmed that?!" Her brows knitted together in curiosity.

"Charles filmed it!" Maggie roared. "Emily-Grace needs to be taking dance! Put that kid in dance! Look at her!"

A new glow lit up Jessie's sea-pearl eyes. "Yeah, she's really something, isn't she, Maggie?"

The little girl was wearing a pink tutu with a matching pink T-shirt and leggings. In the video, she was imitating her momma, who was trying to show her how to gyrate her hips in the Cuban style. The result was a radiant child who Jessie eventually picked up and swung around. Overall, mother and daughter had enjoyed a glorious—and very much healing—visit.

Nodding towards the screen, Maggie gestured to Jacob. "I'm putting this on YouTube. America's favorite singer is one helluva sexy man, and I admit the guy has 'the' touch with music, but he sure can't dance."

Now it was Jessie's turn to howl. She and Maggie were in fits of laughter over innocent Jacob's doe-eyed concentration.

"The man cannot salsa. Period! Emily-Grace schooled him!" Maggie was unapologetic.

"Geez, you'd think after all that time in Miami he'd have glommed onto that move!" Softening, Jessie added, "He's something though, Maggie, isn't he?" The words were not really a question that required a response.

Reining in her hilarity, Maggie tucked an arm loosely around her guest's shoulders. At the same time, she sucked in a quiet breath and avoided saying what she knew Dee had already said to Jessie, about the rather real possibility of more hearts breaking should Jessie and Jacob hook-up.

They watched the video until the end, giggling at Charles' tongue-in-cheek criticisms of their dance moves as he filmed them.

Removing her arm from Jessie's shoulders, setting the iPad on the coffee table, Maggie point blankly steered the conversation towards Josh.

"Is it really over, Jessie? And by that, I mean do you really want it to be over?"

"The truth?"

"Of course. Always. We go way back, you and me." Smiling, Maggie hugged her old co-star.

"I don't. Want it to be over. In any way, shape or form. I love him, Maggie. From the first time I looked into his eyes, I loved him. And I know he loves me back. Still."

"I thought I heard something discussed today about lawyers."

"You did. Charles is on the bandwagon. Dee mentioned it the night they arrived, but I put her off. But as you can see, Charles has all the power in our little made-up family when it comes to any legal stuff."

"Don't do it, Jessie."

"What?" Backing away a little so she could see Maggie better, Jessie tensed. "Don't do what?"

"Don't divorce him. Not yet."

"You still believe in us." A wetness in Jessie's eyes was captured by the dim floor lamp at Maggie's side.

"Of course I do. Don't you? At least a little?"

Biting her bottom lip, Jessie almost gasped. Maggie's reaction to this whole mess was certainly optimistic. And Jessie needed optimism, but she let Maggie in on her thoughts first.

"You know I do, Maggie. But I can't help but subscribe to Steve's wisdom when it comes to Josh, at least on one front. He's changed."

"Well, then," was Maggie's simple answer, which was delivered in a loud whisper accompanied by a big smile, "change him back."

Jessie's tearful reply was layered with hope. "Maggie? That's the best idea I've heard in a long, long time."

She lay down with her head in Maggie's lap, and let her friend entertain her with stories of theater life in New York until she fell asleep, uplifted by the sweet sound of friendship, and buoyed by the heart-healing warmth of love.

Chapter Twenty-seven

The next time her children came to visit, Jessie twisted a dishtowel in her hands while Charles set them up to Skype their father.

"We finally agreed to once a week, Jessie," Dee explained while, after Charles dropped down onto Maggie's couch, she set one child on each of his thighs, then handed him the iPad. "Why don't you and Maggie take some time and go for a walk? We just want to catch Josh now, if we can. We're trying to stay on a regular schedule for the kids' sake."

"No, it's okay, Dee," Jessie admitted with a shrug and a sigh. "I want to see this. I want to see how he handles the kids, what he says to them. I mean... Skyping with a three-year-old and a toddler? Good friggin' luck."

"He does okay," was Dee's honest response. She gestured towards her husband. "He really does. With Charles' help, Josh manages to keep the kids interested. The calls are short, though."

"I want to talk to him after, Dee. Charles, let me talk to Josh after, okay? When the kids are done?"

Charles and Dee were both quiet, then. But Charles nodded. "If you're sure."

It had been a month since the break-up. Other than the two texts Jessie got at the guitar shop, she hadn't received a single message or word from Josh. Steve told her Josh's lawyer was on his back, advising him not to contact her, but she wondered. Also on her mind was Nadia. Was the woman still a part of her estranged husband's life?

"Not that it matters," she whispered under her breath, glancing behind her as the door to the condo swung open and Morgan sauntered in, Ulysses at his side. The two men wandered over to the refrigerator and helped themselves to filtered water.

The Skype call came in, loud and abrasive, jarring her. Then Josh was there, head and shoulders only, although a forearm appeared when he reached out and adjusted his screen. He was tired, apparently, judging by the stooped shoulders and bleary eyes, but at first glance at least he seemed sober.

"Hey there, Emily-Grace," he started, as the little girl sank deeper into Charles' lap, clutching singer-dowwy and whispering a lonesome, "Hewwo, Daddy."

Their call was, indeed, short, as Dee had suggested it would be. It hurt Jessie's heart to see her daughter's reticence towards her father. David was better, but he was still small. Josh was emotional, although he tried to be tough in front of Charles, who insisted on supervising the calls.

Before Charles slipped away with the children, he told Josh to hang on.

Emily-Grace spoke up. "Momma wants to Skype, Daddy." Pointing to the screen, she looked up at her momma. "Heah, Momma. Daddy's wite heah."

Wringing her hands, Jessie smiled softly at her daughter. "Thanks, sweetheart. Go with Grammie and Grampie now, and brush your teeth. Momma will come in to read with you in a few minutes."

After the kids scooted off down the hallway, Jessie eased down onto the couch and picked up the iPad. For the first time in six weeks, she pondered her estranged husband's features.

"You look like shit," was the first comment she found the courage to force between dry lips.

Josh sat back a little and let one corner of his lip turn up. Wiping a thumb and forefinger over his nose, he laughed a little—well, more of a chuckle really, but almost a laugh, albeit it seemed to be a nervous one. Without meeting her eyes he managed, "Thanks. I guess I deserve that. I can't say I've been sleeping all that well."

She resisted the urge to bite off *why, too much sex? Too busy giving Nadia multiple orgasms?* Instead, Jessie inhaled slightly. "So you're still in Toronto?"

He understood the subtext, and paused. "Yeah."

He still hadn't looked up at her. In truth, Josh was afraid to. He thought he might break down the second those hurt pale blue eyes searched his.

"Okay," was Jessie's subdued response to his admission.

"Look, uh…do you think we could talk? In person?" Finally, with a heavy sigh, Josh forced his gaze upwards.

What Jessie saw in his eyes, and what he saw in hers, crushed both of them equally. Their first meeting in the garbage—which consisted of two very lonely people—was no less painful, no less fraught with hurt and grief.

Jessie's lips moved, but no words came out. The old agony was there, the old longing, the old exquisite need to hold this man and pare away the things that tortured him. These eyes, tonight, were the ones she knew. They weren't the angry dark eyes from six weeks ago.

Josh struggled, too, and sucked on a lip while he watched his wife assess the wicked accumulation of sorrow now drowning him on a day-to-day basis.

She ignored his earlier question. Here in front of her, at least on some level, was the man Jessie vowed to love always and forever. She needed to know….well, she needed to know.

The words were slow, swollen with anguish. "So do you want me back at all, Josh? Us? Even a little bit?"

He didn't hesitate. "I didn't want you gone in the first place, Jessie. What I said in Trudy's office…I was just scared."

"But you're still with her."

Sideways from Jessie, in the open concept kitchen across the hall, Morgan cringed.

Stuttering a little as he considered what to say and how to say it, Josh spoke quietly. "N-not..not like you think."

"How, then?"

"Just like…I dunno…I don't know where else to go. I don't know what to do. Jessie…" He was appealing to the Jessie whose heart and soul he cherished, who Josh *knew* loved him.

She cut him off. "You're not doing so well, though, are you Josh? Still?"

"No. No Jess, I'm…"

Rubbing his rough cheek, Josh glanced away as he grappled with the heavy feelings. When he looked back at her, Jessie had to clutch the edge of the couch to keep from collapsing.

*Such pain in those eyes…maybe I should…*she pushed the thought away. She had to.

He licked his lips this time, and rapidly brushed his thumb and forefinger over his nose again. The simple honest query from the woman he loved—who knew Josh the best, and who once told him *there is always hope*—was searching his eyes with longing and worry. He wanted to climb inside her and curl up in her soul where he could feel safe, in a place where Josh knew she would curl around him, and hold him so he could stay buried forever.

He finished his thought. "I'm so fucked up, Jessie. I'm so fucked up right now," were the words that floated from his lips to her ears, from Toronto to New York. They were thick like mud, and dripping wet.

"Babe," Jessie started, but she couldn't finish.

He choked a little, but pulled himself together. "I need to see you, Jessie. Please. In person." *I need to hold you.*

"Most people around me don't seem to think that would be a good idea."

"Most being…?"

"Maggie's rooting for us."

"Maggie's…oh. Okay. So that's good, then."

"She's the only one."

"I get that. I fucked up. I fucked up and I'm sorry."

"Meaning…?"

"Meaning we need to talk, Jess. I want to sort through this mess and make it go away."

"Then go back to Vancouver, Josh. Get outta Dodge, as they say. Let her go."

"She's on her way out, Jessie, I swear. She's going."

"So why are you still there?"

"I think…" The voice got thick again. "Like I said. I'm scared to move."

"You need to get help, Josh. Check in to Rehab. Sort out this addiction." *To Nadia? To booze?*

"You gonna tell me there is always hope again?"

"Ha. No."

"Why not?"

"Because I'm not sure there is. For us, I mean."

"You asked me if I wanted us back together. Our family."

"Call me curious. Doesn't mean I think we *can* be back together."

"Awww Jess…please…I need you. I fucking need you so bad."

"Don't do this, Josh. Please." Jessie was swiping at her eyes now. "You need to go home, to see Trudy. To be around Steve."

"What if I told you I don't even know what home is anymore?"

"I'd tell you I don't know either."

"Will you let me know if you figure it out?"

Jacob flashed across Jessie's mind. Sweet, kind, so amazing to make music with…great with the kids…"You might not like the answer."

Josh was silent. He let his gaze drift over his wife's features—so pretty, so natural, so…sad.

"Don't give up on us." It was a whisper. "Please."

"I didn't, Josh. You did. I only made the choice you didn't have the courage to make. That you started to make, but ran away from committing to. That we needed to make."

"Jessie, please. I know you don't want this. You don't want us to be done. In my heart I know this."

"What I want is what we had. And it went out my smashed car window."

"We'll get it back."

"Take some time, okay? We'll talk again, Josh. We've got things to sort out for the kids, anyway."

Footsteps echoed in the hallway behind Jessie. Dee touched her on the shoulder. "Emily-Grace wants her story, Jessie, but her eyes are closing. Can you at least come say goodnight?"

"Okay. One minute, Dee."

Dee tiptoed away.

Jessie studied her husband again. She tried to lighten his load as he pressed his thumb and forefinger into the corners of both eyes again.

"Did Emily-Grace tell you she does Zumba now? You should see her moves. She's got the salsa down pat."

It worked, at least a little. His laugh was quiet, but it was there. Josh peeked up at her from behind his hand, which was still pressing away the moisture leaking from his eyes.

"She did. Yeah. She said Grammie thinks she should take dance."

"She's pretty cute in her tutu. She wears it all the time."

"I bet. Send me some pictures, will you Jessie? Please? Until…until I can see her again."

"Okay. I will." *I'll send him the Zumba video with Jacob in it. That'll help.* Mutely, Jessie reprimanded herself for the cowardly silent sarcasm.

Just then, Josh turned his head slightly to the left and looked behind him. A set of glossy red nails landed on his shoulder, preceded by the ricochet of heels on expensive flooring. He glanced back at the screen, but trained his eyes on the bottom frame of the monitor.

A face ducked into view. Nadia.

"Hello, Jessie. How's New York?" Nadia smiled her winningest 'I-fucking-own-him-now' smile.

Unprepared for this addition to Josh's call, Jessie was immobilized. She stared at the perfect coffee complexion, the low cleavage she could see just behind Josh, which was the top of the woman's right breast, and at the sultry, sensuous lips. Nadia moved and, with a smirk and a satisfied *humph,* let the high-gloss crimson nails slide off Josh's shoulder. She disappeared from frame. Something about her appearance bothered Jessie, but she wasn't sure what. Just some niggling feeling…

Josh looked up then, and the sudden hard stare threw Jessie. Recoiling, she caught herself thinking *where is the sweet man appealing to me for reconnection? Where are those beautiful liquid chocolate brown eyes?*

Now, the eyes were dark, devoid of light. They were guarded and afraid.

With Morgan still listening in curious judgment in the kitchen, Jessie voiced a few final words to her husband before disconnecting the call. "I love you, Josh. Always and forever. You know that." She choked her way through one last biting phrase, echoing the one she texted the day Jacob bought her the Gibson. "Just can't be now."

When she touched 'end call' on the screen, Skype went blank, Jessie's aching heart closing over with it. Easing herself off the couch, she padded down the hall to go kiss her daughter and son goodnight. She didn't look at Morgan or Ulysses on the way by.

In Toronto, Josh sat and considered for a minute, biting his nails, before he opened Safari and booked a one-way trip to Vancouver.

From his silent perch at Maggie's kitchen island, Morgan watched Jessie handle closing the Skype call. He spent his time inside and outside the condo, sometimes just outside the door, sometimes inside where he could grab a snack, a break, a coffee. Now, he drained his water, watching Jessie's back as she moved towards her children.

Ulysses was across from him, curiously watching subtle hints of anger and pain flicker across the guy's gym-chiseled features.

He's too emotionally involved with Jessie, Ulysses was thinking. *The guy never says a word, but it's clear he suffers for her, like we all do.* In particular, the guy seemed to hold his breath when Nadia came into frame. *What the hell was that about?*

Ulysses resolved to switch Morgan off with Dan, who mostly spent time with Charles and Dee and the kids, and sometimes with Jacob. He considered that maybe even Susanne might enjoy some time in New York. At least this would lessen the intensity for Morgan, on these difficult days when sometimes it seemed all they did was watch Jessie suffer.

Morgan caught on that he was being scrutinized. The big guy rotated away from Ulysses' thoughtful stare, and retreated back out into the hallway.

Chapter Twenty-eight

"You're going back to Vancouver? Are you sure that's such a good idea?" A red silk negligee highlighting her curvaceous body, Nadia was sitting on the edge of the large bed watching Josh toss jeans and T-shirts into a suitcase.

"Just for a bit, Nadia," he replied, unable to meet her eyes.

"I'll come with you."

"Not this trip." He added, in a subdued tone, "I need to see my kids. I need to check the house, meet Steve's kid." Josh also wanted to see his sister, Kayla, who was back in the city on break between gigs. *And maybe Charlie*, he thought, as a small lighthouse beacon that cried 'old friendships and good times' tweaked somewhere in his heart.

From the moment he booked the trip last night, Josh felt the small guiding light intensify somewhere off in the distance. It was tiny, and there were choppy waters from here to there, but still…it was there. He knew Jessie lit that eternal light—she did years ago for him, and suddenly, through the fog, after hearing her voice last night, after seeing the sea-pearl eyes he adored, he detected it in himself again.

Josh pictured her now, her lips pressed together in a thin line, the nails of one hand digging into the back of another as she poured her soul back into him during last night's Skype call. And he knew now, beyond the shadow of a doubt, that the light he was missing and refused to see all this time, out of fear, was hers.

As he closed his suitcase and zipped it up, Josh forced his eyes on Nadia. The nerve on his cheek twitched.

"Nadia," he started.

She raised a palm towards him, cutting him off. "No."

Josh was tired. "I want her back, Nadia. I want my family back. We always knew she might be found. We—I—hoped."

"Don't even think about breaking up with me, Josh. Again." A dark warning blazed across his lover's cheeks.

"I can't do it, Nadia. I can't keep burying myself in beer. In you. I lost my job on *The Wyatt Boys*. Did you know that? No. Because we don't talk. We party. We evade. And the way you spend money, and the way my career seems to be nose-diving, you won't want me for much longer anyway. You'll move on to your next big prize."

"No. I won't. I want you."

"You want the life I can give you. You don't give a sweet shit about me."

Truth sputtered in Nadia's eyes. But she countered. "I'm not letting you go. Not without…" She ran a long nail across her top lip, and then across her bottom one.

"Not without what, Nadia?" Josh's eyes narrowed as he grabbed the suitcase off the bed in one hand, and his green vintage leather jacket with the other.

"Not without a price, Josh." The words were laced with arsenic.

"What the fuck is that supposed to mean? If you want money, I'll gladly give you some."

"I'm not your whore."

"Aren't you?"

After a moment in which her eyes shot death rays into his, Josh shivered. Wheeling around, he started to move towards the door. "So long, Nadia. Good riddance."

"You'll be back. You'll be back when your precious Jessie disappears for good."

Halting in his tracks, Josh half-looked back over his shoulder. "You might want to think twice before making those kinds of dirty comments, Nadia. Or Matt and Charles Keating'll be down your fucking throat."

That shut her up. But the second the door slammed behind Josh, Nadia texted Morgan.

Game on again, Morgan. I want this over.

If Nadia couldn't have Josh, Jessie Wheeler sure as hell wasn't getting him.

Not that the little bitch wants him back anyway, Nadia thought, viciously throwing a bottle of Josh's aftershave onto the floor, where it splintered and broke, oozing liquid onto the high-gloss ceramic. *Jessie's all over the net with her little boy toy.*

But she underestimated the love Jessie had for Josh. Nadia didn't consider how intrinsically and deeply linked the two were, almost as if they were one.

Jessie wanted him back, all right. She just couldn't have him.

At least…not yet.

Staring at his cell phone, Morgan felt his heart constrict. He thought about what to do. Should he text back? Any texts coming and going from his phone were subject to scrutiny, he knew that, and so in the end he chose not to answer what others might think was a rather cryptic text. Not that he would ignore its message, no. It would haunt him for the rest of his life.

Now, he considered what might have driven Nadia to write it. It wasn't until that evening that the motive behind it was revealed. He was sitting at dinner with Ulysses, eating Carlotta's delicious spicy lasagna, when Charles, in the adjoining front room, mentioned to Jessie that he'd received a text from Steve earlier in the day.

"Josh is flying home," the producer said abruptly.

"Oh," was Jessie's surprised 'what-the-hell-do-I-say-to-that' response.

In the kitchen, Morgan tensed.

"He wants to see the kids."

"Cool. Let him." But her heart was suddenly doing its dip-swoop-dive thing. She swallowed uncomfortably.

"Are you sure, Jessie?"

"Yeah. Of course."

"We need to get some legalities sorted out. It's time. You don't want him running off somewhere with those children."

"He wouldn't do that to me."

Charles eased onto the arm of the couch next to Jessie, where she was on her iPad listening to the ballad she and Jacob recorded a few weeks back.

Scratching notes about adding strings and auxiliary percussion, and maybe even a few background vocals too, Jessie was focused and determined. Until Charles' rather interesting announcement, that is. It quickly and succinctly threw her for a loop.

Down the hall came hoots and hollers of joy. "Dee and Maggie must be *in* the tub with the kids," she tossed out as an aside.

Morgan angled his head towards them, aware of Ulysses' presence nearby, but he relaxed when the black-skinned man seemed oblivious to him. Ulysses was chatting with Carlotta, seemingly lost in a discussion over the merits of homemade tofu.

Charles let Jessie's comment about the kids' bath time slide, and tried to refocus her. "He's not necessarily thinking straight these days, honey."

"He's still in there somewhere." Picturing Josh's tortured eyes on Skype last night, Jessie hunched herself lower into the couch. "Behind all those layers of protective misery he's shrouded himself in."

"Jessie…"

She looked up from her work. "We just have to dig a little deeper to find him, that's all." *Like all the way to China,* she caught herself thinking.

"I'm booking a meeting for next week. I want you to come back to Vancouver for a bit. We'll talk to Steve or Hilary and make sure Josh gets the heads up so he can apprise his lawyer as well."

"Can't wait to rush this through, can you, Charles? You'll have us divorced in a month."

"I'm looking out for your best interests, Jessie."

"No, you're looking out for your best interests, Charles."

"I'm not talking about your career. Your career is well established. You're fine."

"Am I?" She chewed thoughtfully on her lip while she regarded her producer and pseudo-father. "Although it's not my career I was thinking about, Charles." She nodded towards the laughter coming from the direction of Maggie's large washroom. The sound of Emily-Grace's obvious unrestrained delight was a shiny jewel in Jessie's heart.

"Those children have had a rough go, honey. We just want them to have some stability. Listen to your daughter. She's happy. She's laughing. She doesn't need a father who is struggling with addictions and a hell of a lot of personal demons coming back into her life and messing her up."

"What she doesn't need is to be kept from her father."

"I don't want him trying to take the kids, Jessie. Even for a week at a time. Even for two days." Throwing up his hands in frustration, Charles seethed. "Josh is not capable. I don't trust him."

It's not Josh I don't trust, thought Morgan, grimacing. Groaning inwardly, he glanced down and couldn't help but notice his reflection in the large dessert spoon by his plate. It was distorted. He didn't recognize himself.

Sighing, Jessie lifted her feet up onto the coffee table, and crossed her ankles. She laid the iPad at her side. "I'm well aware that you and Dee are doing an amazing job with Emily-Grace and David, Charles. And I am eternally grateful. But they're our kids. Josh and me. I'm doing a lot better, and I think it's time I start taking them back for a week or two at a time. And you know, Charles, that I hope Josh starts doing better too. The dust is settling, so to speak, after the hell of last winter."

"The hell of last winter is not over, Jessie. Don't try to pretend it is." Charles' serious countenance chilled Jessie.

She blew a quiet *ploomph* through pursed lips as Morgan straightened. "Okay, so I have a feeling you're not just talking about healing here."

Charles waited for her to voice her thoughts on the silent background menace that still had them all walking on eggshells.

Finally, she did. "I can't live my life in fear. I did that before, for far too long."

"I know, honey. But the kids…"

I am not going to hurt those children, Morgan fumed.

"You think they are safer with you and Dee. But you're only human, Charles. You're not a shield."

"I have access to a fenced-in home and security."

"So keep security on Josh and the kids again. At the UBC house."

"It's not just the one issue, Jessie." Charles was getting frustrated. "With Josh, it's everything."

"Fine. I'll come to Vancouver. Set up a meeting. But be fair to him, okay? I think I got through to him last night. I think he'll go to rehab or at least to see Trudy and Frank for help. I think he's ready."

"Is that why you're hesitant to see this lawyer, Jessie? Why you're balking about formalizing your separation?"

"Oh, Charles," she replied sadly. "Of course it is."

"You're thinking about taking him back."

Shaking her head slowly, Jessie whispered, "Not at the present time." The old haunted Jessie was back, the pale eyes large and luminous.

He echoed her. "Not at the present time."

"I love him, Charles."

Guffawing mutely, Morgan added an addendum to her thought. *Apparently you're not the only one.*

Reaching out, Charles tenderly ruffled the auburn-tinted curls. "That's what scares me," he admitted. "Love does weird things to peoples' minds. It has the power to destroy our reason."

No shit, Dick Tracy. Morgan would have been enjoying his silent part in the repartee, were it not for the fear slicing his heart at Nadia's nefarious intentions.

"You, my friend, are looking at it entirely the wrong way." Smiling, Jessie got up and leaned over to give her producer a big hug. "I love you too," she said, and straightened, a rosy blush on her cheeks. "And I still feel very reasonable. Reasonable enough to know I am missing a lot of bath time fun at the moment, in fact."

Bending over, Jessie grabbed the iPad. With a smile, she thrust it into Charles' hands along with the scratch pad she was using for notes.

"Here," she insisted. "Tweak this ballad and make another billion. This one'll chart at number one in twenty countries within a few months. Mark my words."

With that, Jessie sauntered off down the hallway, whistling. Both Morgan and Charles watched her go, each lost in their own worries as far as Jessie Wheeler was concerned.

When she peeked in through the bathroom door, Jessie found her kids wearing soap bubble hats, and the people who created them, soaking wet.

David squealed when he spotted his momma. He grabbed a clump of bubbles and laughed joyously as he squeezed them into submission. Jessie's heart clenched at the sight of Josh's eyes—in miniature—filled with pure bliss.

Oh my darling David, she begged him. *Stay innocent. Stay pure. Stay safe.*

She let her gaze drift over to Emily-Grace. The little girl was watching her momma too, but in a wise way that made Jessie feel as if the child was a thousand years old.

"Hi, baby girl," she whispered. "Can Momma get in on the fun?"

The gentle smile with which she was rewarded warmed her soul more than any amount of money or fame ever could.

"Yes, Momma. I make you soap eahs. Okay?"

And Jessie Wheeler-Sawyer, international superstar about to chart at number one in more than twenty countries singing a ballad she wrote with Jacob the day after he encouraged her back to the land of the living—after mourning the dissolution of her marriage to a man she loved beyond all measure—knelt by the tub, bowed her head, and cherished the delicate feel of small angel hands molding feathery soap bubble ears over her messy locks.

Chapter Twenty-nine

Kayla bounced over the flagstone walk and let herself through the small iron gate at Josh and Jessie's UBC house. She found her film and TV star brother on his hands and knees scrubbing the toilet in the master bedroom's ensuite bath. When she knocked on the door and peeked in at him with a woeful smile, he sat back on his haunches, wiped a wrist across a sweaty forehead, and allowed himself a melancholic grin back at her.

"Missed you, big brother," Kayla beamed, stepping into the room as Josh stood and reached for her. She grasped him tightly, wrapping both arms around his waist. "I've been so worried about you."

Holding his sister away from him a little, Josh sized her up. "Nice hairdo, kid." Kayla's usual blonde hair was fringed with an exotic lavender.

"Got a tat, too," she grinned, flipping around and lifting her two layered tank tops.

Silently, Josh read it. The maxim *If music be the food of love, play on* was inked across her lower back. In a delicate script, the tattoo was accented with eighth and quarter notes.

"Jessie would like it," she mused shyly as Josh chewed on his lip picturing Jessie getting a similar tattoo.

"Yeah," he finally agreed. "She would."

"So," Kayla breathed, shrugging up her shoulders and looking around. "Doing some spit-shining, I see. Never quite saw you as the domestic type, bro."

"Well, speaking of Jessie, she's coming back to Van in a few days. I want the place to look good."

Regarding him carefully, Kayla noticed that her brother had shaved, and he seemed a little lighter here today, in mood and temperament, than last she saw him. His clothes were clean, the brown eyes clear and focused, and his hair was longer than he usually kept it, but washed, at least. Steve had warned her that Josh wasn't always at his best these days.

"You look good, Josh."

"That's what they all say." He allowed a light to flicker in his chocolate eyes as Kayla laughed openly.

"You planning to clean all day or do you want to take a drive?"

"Where to?" Josh was already placing the toilet brush back in its holder.

"Well, I was thinking to North Van, actually."

He hesitated. "I don't think they'll have me, Kayla. They want to wait until after we sit down with our lawyers and hash out some custody agreement."

Her voice was soft, but gently encouraging. "When's the last time you saw your babies, Josh?" Kayla was standing with both hands in her back pockets, rocking back and forth slowly.

The nerve on his cheek twitched. "It's been a while," he admitted, shoulders slumping. "Too long."

"You need to see your kids."

"I don't see Charles going for it."

"Let me call Dee. She can be reasonable. And I can't see Charles keeping you from your children, anyway. He might be a crusty old bugger on the outside, but the man's a softie on the inside. Otherwise Jessie would have walked away from him ages ago." Starting to back up as she searched for Deirdre's number on her cell, Kayla added, "We can visit the kids at La Casa. We won't take them anywhere." She stopped moving, reached forward, and slapped her brother gently on one arm. "Anyways, they're my niece and nephew. And I miss the hell out of them. I got some stuffed animals for Emily-Grace and David in Copenhagen and I want to hand them over before I decide to let them live on my bed for keeps."

Frowning, Josh shifted his feet.

Kayla lowered her voice with a smile. "Big brother. We'll stop at Toys R Us on the way, okay, so you can get something for them too. Now grab a hoodie, it's cool out there today. I'll call Dee."

To Josh's surprise, it turned out La Casa's matriarch was amenable to the visit. He wondered what kind of reception he would receive from both her and the staunch Keating clan protector, Charles.

At least Jessie won't be there, he thought. *I can only handle so much today.*

Truthfully, although he wanted the house to look good for Jessie when she returned in a few days, part of the reason Josh was housecleaning was in order to keep his hands from shaking and reaching for a bottle of booze. Josh figured he could use old-fashioned willpower and lots of activity to keep the demons haunting him at bay.

Fueled by hope and the desire to hold his wife in his arms again—to wrap his arms around her waist, and to breathe in the sweet love he so desperately missed—he was also driven by the passage of time as a healer, by the families he saw in the park, and by the hurt in the pale eyes he loved.

La Casa's sunshine yellow reassured Josh that good times were once had within its hallowed walls, yet at the same time the site of the quaint Spanish Villa creased his face in fear. Inside, Dee answered the door, as nervous as he, Josh thought. She didn't hug him as she usually did in the days before things went bad. Instead, she smiled wanly at Kayla and gestured down the long hall to the back sliding door that led to the pool.

"The kids are in for a swim, despite the coolness of the day. They love the pool. Charles keeps it fairly warm because he knows he can't keep them out of it." She was talking fast, filling the blank spaces with words, any words, that might make this meeting with Josh go down a little easier.

Outside, Josh was happy to spy Carlotta's young grandson frolicking in the pool with the kids. To his surprise, Charles was in there too. The older man had all three children in a high-sided inflatable, and was towing them around the shallow end.

Josh couldn't avoid smiling. Glancing over at Dee, he relaxed further when she winked at him; she was obviously happy to see that the old darkness usually hovering over his head like some sinister black cloud seemed to have faded.

"He's a kid at heart," she offered by way of explanation, nodding towards her husband.

"Humph! Men. They all are," Kayla added brightly, bending over the edge of the pool. She waved the two stuffies she'd bought in Denmark during her last tour as a background dancer. A third was in her hands as well; she'd just picked it up at Toys R Us for young Eric, who Dee had advised was also at the house today.

David saw the toys first. Instinctively knowing one of the proffered stuffies was for him, he waved at Kayla.

Spite creased Charles' face when he spotted Josh, but he towed the kids over to the side of the pool anyway.

Kayla squealed happily when David plummeted into her arms. With Dee's help, Eric maneuvered his body onto the deck just fine, but Emily-Grace stayed put, warily giving her daddy anxious stares and wringing her small fingers. She couldn't help but rather wistfully study the ballet doll he held up for her to see.

"She has a pink tutu, Emily-Grace," Josh told her gently, giving her the chance to come to him. "Just like yours, Momma says."

"Wike mine," she said, pointing to her chest.

With a sense of regretful longing, Josh touched the top of his son's head as Kayla held him. She was laughing at the child's infectious enthusiasm and good nature, and at the simple fact that she was now soaking wet. A heavy sigh accompanied Josh's pensive study of his son's intelligent eyes and enduring innocence. Turning his gaze towards his daughter again, Josh inhaled slowly, then knelt by the edge of the pool and reflected on the damp curls and worried Jessie-eyes.

"Hey, baby girl," he murmured, a slight downturn to his lips. "You got big."

"Hewwo, Daddy," she whispered, still not making a move to come to him.

With a cursory nod, Charles greeted Josh finally. "She's swimming a little now. Dog paddling, but still…I qualify that as swimming."

"Really? Wow." *God this hurts. I've missed so goddamn much with these kids.* His eyes were moist, but Josh made a valiant attempt to push the ennui away. Today, thanks to Kayla, he would not think about having to bury his pain. He would not consider drinking at all; not even one beer or glass of the potent old standby, Jim Beam, would wet his lips. "Can you show Daddy, Emily-Grace? I'd love to see you swim."

Shyly, she nodded, fluttering her small eyelashes adorably as Charles lifted her out of the floatie and placed her belly-down in the water. He stayed close by while she demonstrated her new skill, spitting out bubbles and working her arms and legs in a furious dogpaddle.

"That's really something." Josh grinned. "You're a real little fish, sweetheart."

Then, it seemed like his daughter, like her mother before her, recognized that something was different about daddy now. Genuine warmth bathed Josh's eyes with light here, today. When he held up the ballet doll again, she reached for it.

Charles boosted his granddaughter out onto the pool deck, where she stood before her father and looked nervously at him before reaching again for the doll. Delight lit up the rosy cheeks when she had it in her hands where she could closely study the pink tutu.

"You know," Josh said to her, still at his daughter's eye level, "your Aunt Kayla here is a dancer. I bet she can teach you some good Zumba moves."

"Zumba?" A wide smile creased Kayla's pretty face. "Okay. A little hip thing here, and a pelvic thrust there. I can handle it."

Emily-Grace's eyes lit up even further. Unasked, her small arms wound their way around her beloved daddy's neck. Josh picked his firstborn up and turned away from everyone's prying eyes, the same as he did in the hospital the night his children were returned to him months ago. But this time he choked back his tears. He didn't want to scare Emily-Grace. He just wanted to love her, to cherish this brief time with the children he and Jessie shared.

"You are so beautiful," he told his daughter, wiping a few wet blonde curls away from his daughter's forehead as she admired the new doll.

Charles glanced over at Dee, and frowned. She smiled a little and shrugged.

Kayla drove them to action. "My adorable nephew's lips are turning blue. How about we get these kids warmed up?"

In a second, Dee was by her side with towels for all three children. She took charge of Eric while Josh and Kayla ran Emily-Grace and David up the stairs to find warm clothes.

They met afterwards at the kitchen island for hot chocolate Carlotta gladly prepared for them—her special child-friendly 'lots of chocolate and marshmallow' recipe. Afterwards, Charles and Dee took some time to work on business affairs while Carlotta supervised the kids' playtime with Kayla and Josh.

At one point, Charles checked on them, and took Josh aside. They stood at the door to the first floor room Charles and Dee were using as a playroom.

"You're all set up with a lawyer, Josh?"

The skin on the back of Josh's neck prickled. "Yeah. I've had someone lined up for a bit. One of Charlie's guys."

"All right. Good. We're set for next Wednesday, then?"

"Sure. No problem." Inhaling deeply, Josh couldn't look at the man. "Jessie will be there too?"

"Yes, she's agreeable, as are the rest of us. As long as one of you remains sober and the other remains strong enough not to cave."

Considering that, Josh bristled before asking, "You think she might? Cave, I mean?"

"You are her weak spot, Josh. But I have a favor to ask."

Oh, here it comes. "What might that be, Charles?"

"Don't let her."

Josh exhaled deeply. "Our relationship is between us."

"You're not fooling me here today, Josh." Charles morphed instantly from the fun grandpa in the pool to the shrewd businessman Josh knew him to be. "You only left Nadia a few days ago. Prior to that, as far as anyone knows, you were still drinking and carousing. Although I admit I'm glad, for the sake of these kids, that you're looking a little better today."

"Spying on me, huh? Again? Stalking me?" Josh continued to avoid Charles' eyes by choosing to watch Kayla accept a plastic teacup from Emily-Grace and pretend to sip from it. Kayla was wearing a silver plastic diamond-encrusted crown; Josh's daughter had her favorite pink tutu positioned around her little girl waist.

"Concerned for you. Put it that way." Charles turned to his estranged son-in-law, forcing Josh to meet his steady gaze. "Josh, we want this transition to be as smooth as possible, for all of you. Don't make it harder by pretending you can just flip a switch and be the man Jessie needs."

"What if I can?" The actor spoke quietly, as if even he wasn't sure he could follow through with those powerful words.

"I don't want to see her hurt anymore, Josh. No more. She's had all she can handle."

"How is she doing, Charles? Really, I mean."

"She's singing this weekend. Getting back in the saddle, as it were."

"Oh? Where?" A quick pulse started in Josh's neck.

A quiet *mmpphh* preceded Charles' next grumbled phrase. "Dee has the details."

In other words, thought Josh, *none of your fucking business.*

Emily-Grace chose that moment to jump up from her tea party to show her daddy the new Zumba move Kayla taught her earlier. "Wook, Daddy!"

Despite the intensity of their conversation, both Josh and Charles had to smile at that.

"Just like Auntie Kayla, huh? You're a beautiful dancer, sweetheart." Taking advantage of the perfectly timed intervention, Josh moved into the room and swooped his daughter up into his arms. Joy lit his cheeks, the stilted conversation with Charles pushed aside for the moment.

"Jus wike Momma, too," was the serious answer that came from between Emily-Grace's tiny pink lips, as if she needed to be certain her silly daddy would not forget her precious momma.

"Yes." A twinge in his belly accompanied Josh's response to that comment, which had the power to almost derail him entirely. "Just like Momma." He couldn't help but add, in a hushed tone so only his child could hear, "Just like your beautiful momma."

Emily-Grace smiled gratefully in her wise, cherubic, three-year-old way.

After dinner, Josh couldn't hide his gratitude when Dee asked him if he wanted to stay until bedtime. At Kayla's pleased nod, he took the time to read to his children. Positioning David on his lap, he sighed heavenly as Emily-Grace snuggled into his side. The little girl had warmed up to her daddy throughout the afternoon and dinner. Now, she couldn't keep her curiosity at bay. While her daddy read, she pointed at the colorful baby animals parading across each page, and asked quietly whispered questions. Eric had departed earlier, with Carlotta, who had the evening off.

"This is a keeper," Kayla said, watching joyfully. Aiming her cell phone, she snapped a photo of Josh with his kids and emailed it to his account so he could print it at home.

From the hallway, where they, too, were reflecting with mixed emotions on the renewal of Josh's relationship with his children, Charles spoke quietly to his wife.

"Has he asked if he could take them home tonight?"

"No, Charles. Not that he would really have to ask, you know. He *is* their father. And nothing's gone through the lawyers yet."

The producer *harrumphed*, loud enough for Kayla to spin around and wonder what the power couple was discussing. Carefully eyeing her, because in no way, shape or form did the Keatings need Josh's sister reporting anything untoward about this visit to Jessie, Deirdre added to her husband, "I think you can give Josh some credit, Charles. He knows he's not ready to take them home just yet. Actually," she added thoughtfully, "I think he knows the children aren't ready for that yet. So stop your grumbling and just be thankful we've all had such a good day. Josh seems to be coming around. Look at Emily-Grace. That beautiful child needed this time with her daddy."

At her wise words, which in some ways were a thinly disguised reprimand at her husband's quick tendency to attack Josh in whatever way he could, Charles settled. He left Josh to his babies, and disappeared into his office to work.

Later, on the drive home, Josh reflected on his afternoon's awkward conversation with Charles at the playroom door. Kayla was driving, and so he was sitting quietly, staring out of the window, watching the world slide by.

"You gonna be okay, bro?" Suddenly Kayla wasn't so sure taking her brother to see his kids was such a great idea. Josh was awfully subdued now.

He twisted his head to the side to ponder her. The soft brown eyes were infused with the old sadness. "Charles said something about Jessie singing this weekend." At Kayla's hesitation to respond, he added, " I know Dee told you about it after dinner. I heard the two of you talking. It's a fundraiser, right? In New York."

A nervous jitter made its way up Kayla's spine. She shrugged, hoping a nonchalant response would be enough to telegraph to Josh that it was no big deal, even though it was a huge deal, since Jessie would be singing live for the first time since prior to her abduction.

"Yeah," she finally admitted. "It's a domestic violence fundraiser shin-dig Maggie's involved in. Kind of a chain thing. Jacob sang at one already in Savannah."

"Hmmm."

"No, Josh." Kayla hated to admit it, but it would not be a good idea for Josh to show up. "You can't ambush Jessie at a charity function. Wait until she comes to Vancouver next week. Talk to her here."

He knifed strong fingers through his layered hair. "What if I don't want to wait until next week? What if we can come to some sort of truce before all these lawyers get involved?"

"The lawyers are already involved, Josh. It's a done deal. It's just a sepa-ration, anyway. Custody stuff. Everyone's being reasonable, just run with it. You and Jessie can talk and maybe sort out the deeper issues later. But stay away from the fundraiser. Please? I beg you. That's not the time and place to corner Jessie."

Josh looked at her wistfully. "She'll be singing, Kayla."

His baby sister smiled sadly and laid a hand over his. "I know, honey. I know you love to watch Jessie perform. But the last while has been more than a little crazy, and neither of you need the heartache. Besides, she and Jacob are doing, like, a 45 minute set."

"So?"

Puckering her lips, Kayla pondered what to say. She spoke cautiously. "Josh, have you been on the net at all?"

"Not much, no." A heavy sigh spoke legions for the obvious reasons why.

"She's been spending a lot of time with him."

"Mmpph," was his wounded response, which effectively ended the sib-lings' brief conversation during the drive back to the UBC house.

At home, after chatting a little more about the fundraiser, and hugging Kayla tightly goodbye in gratitude for her wise presence and sheer effer-vescence on what ended up being, for the most part, a magical day, Josh dropped into a chair at the kitchen island and tapped on Steve's name in his iPhone contacts. When his friend answered, he jumped on him. "I have a favor to ask."

Detecting a certain urgency in Josh's voice, Steve bent his head to listen over the sound of his fussy infant, with whom he was walking the floor. "What's up, Josh?"

"Kayla says you're going to New York for the weekend."

Steve's blood pressure shot up while his tone skyrocketed downwards. "I am."

"To the domestic violence fundraiser?"

Pause. "Yup."

"Kayla says Sophie's not going."

Longer pause. "No, a family thing came up. She's staying in Van. Josh, I know what you're getting at, and I'm not giving you Sophie's ticket to this extravagant bash."

"Steve…I need to see her. I need to see Jessie."

"You don't deserve to see her."

"So glad to have you on my team, Steve."

"Have you even been away from Nadia for two days yet, Josh?"

"I was there in body, not in spirit. I couldn't face Vancouver, it was just too much, you know?" Josh wiped sweaty palms on his jeans. "I just think if I could talk to Jessie in person we might be able to salvage a seed of hope here, Steve. For the sake of the kids, even."

"I don't know, Josh. I don't have a good feeling about you having your first face to face with Jessie in public like that. Call it intuition."

"It might be the best way—we aren't likely to get into a pissing match with Charles and Dee's hoity toity friends around."

"Fuuuck, Josh. I don't know. Don't put me in this position. I beg you."

"Look, I wasn't ready, Steve. Before. It was too much, when she first came back. It was so fucking…it was so fucking messed up, the way she got rescued from that inferno that, may I remind you, some crazed psycho set. Even now, I know there are things Matt knows that he's not sharing. It's like, if I let myself remember the fear and, and *feel*, I just want to sink to the ground and bury my head, like that big bird—"

"Big Bird's on Sesame Street." Steve's attempt at humor was dry and came out cracked.

"Oh f-off, Steve. You know the bird. An ostrich. That's it." Emily-Grace's sweet innocence consumed him then, as he remembered her wide eyes and a small finger pointing out baby animals earlier. Josh filed away a plan to show his daughter a picture of an ostrich some day. *She'll like that,* he thought absently.

Steve was hesitant. "Josh, I know this whole thing has been a shit parade, for both of you. I'm glad you finally left Toronto. But maybe you should give Jessie a wide berth. For now. Until she can at least picture you without the image of Nadia and that Gucci bracelet you gave the woman instantly burning her retinas."

"Steve...Kayla says Jessie and Jacob are all over the Internet, together. I might still have a chance if I can get her attention now. While it's still early."

"Ahhhhhh. You piss me off, Sawyer. Damn it." Steve considered that comment. He might actually be doing Jacob a favor if he thwarted any attempt at him and Jessie finally hooking up. He sighed deeply. "Maggie says they are not together, Josh. Jacob's still seeing that Rachael gal. Ahhhh, my nerves."

He adjusted the baby and the phone to opposite sides, and stopped during his walk by the refrigerator, where his eyes landed on a very happy cast and crew photograph from *Drifters,* season two. Josh and Jessie were in each other's arms; she was practically in his lap, for that matter. Jessie's eyes were shining.

"Okay," Steve capitulated, aching to see that golden light in the baby blues again. "Against my better judgment...okay. You can have the ticket. But only because some sick part of me thinks there's still hope for you and Jessie's fairy tale magic."

Josh's soul-felt thank you catapulted through the connection. "Thanks, Steve. Seriously. And please...don't tell Jessie. I don't want to stress her out by my coming. I'll just stay out of sight until after she sings, and then I'll see if she'll talk to me."

"She'll talk to you, Josh. But I swear to God if you hurt her again, I might not."

"Promises, promises. When are you flying down?"

"I'm going on the jet with the Keatings. I suggest you book a commercial flight."

"All right. Will do. And Steve?"

"What." Already Steve was regretting his choice. His stomach was suddenly doing somersaults.

"Thank you, man. I mean it."

"Harumph." The grunt was accompanied by a mournful wail courtesy of Caleb. "Geez, I hope that doesn't mean you know something I don't," Steve muttered under his breath to his infant son. He gazed at the tiny flailing fists. "Are you psychic, little guy?"

"What?"

"Not meant for your ears, Sawyer. Me and the kid are having our own private confab."

"Ooo-kayyyy…."

"I'll see you in New York, Josh."

"Yeah. I'll see you, Steve."

When they disconnected, Josh sat at the island and reflected on the unexpected treasures of the day. It seemed things were finally back on track. It seemed there was, in Jessie's old wise words, suddenly hope again.

Saturday found Josh on a plane to New York.

Saturday night found him at the fundraiser.

Midnight found him in a dingy bar with Steve and Charlie by his side, completely and overwhelmingly lost—again.

Chapter Thirty

It started out okay. He dressed carefully, to blend in with all the society geeks and freaks Josh knew would be at the fancy soiree. But nerves got the best of him.

"Just one drink," he told himself, "to help this go down easy."

But one turned to two and two to three. By the time Josh arrived at the Ritz-Carlton, he had a good buzz on.

Security was on high alert. But since the whole Deuce McCall mess, Big Dan had a soft spot for Josh, so he let him pass without more than a raised eyebrow. With a flick of his thick fingers, Dan lined up an escort for Josh. The actor was taken to a seat at the bar in the back of the richly adorned gold-walled ballroom. Settling in, Josh was relieved. He could watch Jessie sing without her becoming aware of his presence.

The night might have gone down okay if Dan had the sense to see that Josh was escorted somewhere other than to the bar. But in the past, Josh had spent lots of time in bars without imbibing, so Dan rather naively thought the guy could handle the temptation. Like many of those gossiping about the Oscar winning actor these days, he figured the stumbling-over-drunk Josh was the one who showed up at events with Nadia, not this forlorn guy whose plaintive voice and melancholy eyes said he just wanted to sit quietly and watch his wife sing.

For the most part, Josh sat sipping ginger ale at the mahogany bar unnoticed, since lots of patrons were on the move and he wasn't necessarily on anyone's radar. But that changed after the divine five-course meal was consumed, when Jessie took the stage with Jacob.

An absorbing thrill started flowing throughout the elaborate room at first sight of the musical couple. It commenced at the white linen-ed front tables and worked its way back, spinning almost like a gentle windswept twister, its golden fairy dust landing on each table separately, and then anointing every privileged guest in turn. In their Armani and diamonds, the elegant social-ites rose—one by one, like blooming flowers in dark earth—in a standing ovation before the first note was strummed.

Josh straightened to see over the heads of the appreciative audience as the last few stragglers dashed towards their seats to join in the gracious wel-come. Then, with his damp knuckles wrapped around a substantial crystal glass, which he paused halfway to his lips, Josh saw Jessie clearly.

Exquisite as always at this type of event, she was a vision in creamy Chantilly lace as she paused, standing, in front of a microphone, and smiled shyly at the fundraiser's attractive guests. Embroidered with flowers, pearls and crystals, the dress was a Zuhair Murad—Jessie and Sophie's favorite designer. Its lightly flowing hem brushed the tops of her thighs, and framed Jessie's décolletage in a wide diamond shape with tight, low cleavage over her breasts and a standing collar that teased her neck attractively. Delicate Manolo Blahnik snake embossed wrap heels completed the dazzling outfit.

Beside her, as Josh watched, Jacob swung his guitar over his shoulders, then bent an ear to Jessie's high-glossed lips as they prepared to launch their first tune of the evening. The two were apparently sharing some secret joke; if Josh could hear, he would be privy to Jessie teasing Jacob over his trendy slim Italian suit. The guy was even wearing a rare tie, as was Josh, although neither man wore their tie pulled tight.

Josh forced his gaze away from his girl. Pulse quickening, he craned his neck to see the Keating table. Jacob's girlfriend Rachael was there, in a slim black silk dress with cap sleeves and a square ribboned neckline, sitting proudly, her spine tall as her man took the stage. Charles and Dee were there too, eyes locked on Jessie and never wavering, as were Charlie and Steve, both minus dates for the evening. Maggie sat comfortably next to Rachael; now and again, she leaned in for a conspiratorial whisper.

Josh knew Emily-Grace and David were safe under the watchful eyes of Susanne and the care of Carlotta at the Keatings' hotel. Vaguely, as he waited for Jessie and Jacob to start their set, he wondered if he might get in to see his children at some point tomorrow.

All in all, since walking out on Nadia, his heart was starting to rebound. A sense of revived joie-de-vivre imbued Josh's soul, leaving him optimistic and ready for a paradigm shift. Over the past few days his spirits had lifted as if some unseen muse released a deadbolt on a steel gate and set him free. The fear and desperate gloom of the last many months seemed to be dissipating, like misty fog does in the heat of a new day. Josh wanted his old life back, and he wanted it back now.

Even drinking the ginger ale wasn't bothering him. Sure, he'd rather have a cool, crisp handcrafted beer, but Josh had Steve's voice from earlier in the day in his head—*take it easy, don't drink, and you'll be fine.* He'd had a few drinks at the hotel, to do battle with his nerves. They helped. Now, he must abstain.

He thought he would. Josh thought he would be fine. What he didn't consider was that murky fog sometimes lingers over unseen cliffs. Despite an evolving sun, there can still be hidden dangers.

Watching Jessie step to the mic in haute couture and four-inch heels, while Jacob accompanied her with vocal harmonies and guitar, was what sent Josh over the edge. The catalyst wasn't so much Jessie herself, although of course she was the magic around which everyone else revolved; instead it was the entire dreamy mise-en-scène.

Background musicians, including Jessie's standby pianist Christian, handsomely adorned in a black nineteenth century knee-length suit jacket, completed the stage ensemble. Silver spotlights enhanced with cerulean lights picked up the two lead singers, gracefully illuminating their every nuance, including every strum of Jacob's guitar and every sparkly snow-white fingernail of Jessie's as her fingers encircled the microphone while she sang.

The enchanting lighting design caught the wistful admiration and longing in Jacob's eyes as he watched Jessie sing, and the 'I'm-in-this-bubble-with-you' gaze she drifted right back at him. The music brought them there, and the sanctity of the stage—its distance from the Keating table where, earlier, they consumed their $1000 a plate dinners—kept them there, alone together in that trancelike fairy-tale place where playing music with a 'someone' each loved, and sharing that music with a faceless crowd, had the power to lift the couple to an otherworldly sphere.

The first few tunes were safe. Rousing pop tunes, they were fun and upbeat, intended to relax the watchers and bring them on board from the get go. Afterwards, the tunes delved into more serious issues, and elevated the stakes for both the singers and for those who knew them well.

Jessie always communicated through music. Lost in her bubble with Jacob, she thought tonight was a safe place to express tangled feelings about her recent separation from a man she loved, who she knew was still suffering from their small family's most recent trauma.

She thought wrong.

Jessie had no way of knowing Josh was watching her performance. If she did, she would not have chosen the pieces on her playlist.

It was one thing to sing them.

It was quite another to be somewhere in the eerie semi-darkness at a rich mahogany bar, soaking in the sorrowful lyrics and solemn melodies, knowing they were about mourning *you*.

The first song to hit Josh like a sucker punch in the gut was a fast-paced power anthem, almost. Jessie seemed slightly tense before she sang it, as she sucked in a breath and looked over the crowd towards the Keating table before inhaling deeply and singing the first note. It was as if she were seeking strength to give her enough energy to dispel the dark demons haunting her; by virtue of belting out this powerful tune, she was demanding liberation. The song took her to an extraordinary place; it was a physical release as much as an emotional one. It took everything Jessie had in her to get past the raw emotion it wrought and call up the power required to lay it down, but lay it down she did, in a way so overwhelmingly raw and grief-stricken and angry that she owned the grand ballroom and every captive soul in it.

She was not playing guitar tonight, Jacob was. A background musician was filling in the blanks, so Jessie, standing at the mic, did the usual thing when she finished. But she added an extra step, which, Josh noticed, she seemed to be doing now with every song. She took her time coming back from the power anthem—the pale eyes were unfocused at first, her breaths emerged like gasps, which she sucked in and out through short, quick bursts while one hand still gripped the microphone.

And then Jessie focused her gaze on Jacob.

Jacob was lost in that dreamy abyss too, so he was there for Jessie every time. When her foggy eyes came up, returning her hurting soul from wherever lost place her music took her, he called her back with his. First he sent her hope, with gentle, encouraging, loving eyes. Then, with a slight raise of his chin and a parting of Jacob's lips, he sent her faith.

It was a calling, in a way. It was as if he was saying to her, *I am here,* each time, after each song, as if Jacob knew she was lost at sea, and that he was her lighthouse, her beacon in the dark.

Yet…

After the power anthem, Jessie was obviously exhausted from the effort. As her chest heaved, she tried to get her feet under her, so to speak, before the next tune. On trembling legs she backed away from the mic, faced the elite audience, raised one arm, and bowed. Jacob leaned towards her and whispered something in her ear, which had Jessie instantly ducking her head and blushing. When she looked back up at him, her eyes were shining.

Clearly, she adored him. Clearly, he adored her.

Everyone in the grand ballroom noticed.

It got worse for Josh when the musical couple neared the end of their set and announced the premiere of a new ballad.

Jessie introduced the song.

"Thank you, thank you, you have been a wonderful audience tonight. So wonderful, in fact, that we have a very special treat for you. We would like to play a song we wrote together just a few short days after I, well, left my husband, actually. It's angsty and real and you might cry. I might too. Just sayin'."

She laughed then, a little nervous titter that echoed in diminutive waves around the capacious space as Jacob met her eyes and counted the band in.

Jacob's voice had the most beautiful, pouty, puppy dog tone. In this distinguished venue, with the mystical lights and the musical enchantment already entrancing the souls within, he rose to a flawless grace. Alongside him, Jessie, in the gorgeous floating chiffon lace, elevated Jacob's enthralling presence by focusing only on him for the entire ballad.

Even Josh could see, from his dusky bar-cave at the back of the elegant ballroom, how Jessie's pale sparkling eyes wandered up Jacob's form, wordlessly appraising the rhythmic way his body moved in expensive Italian fabric as the music lifted him, and the way he tensed his shoulders and squeezed his eyes shut to hit the lonesome melody's high notes as a capable hand strummed his hollow-body guitar.

Josh was uptight and anxious well before he landed at JFK earlier in the day. Now, he was downright unsettled. His main motive for coming here today was to see Jessie, to take her by the elbow and tell her he loved her. To tell her he was sorry for being scared, and that he wanted to try to reunite their family, to rebuild it after the hell of the last while. But now, as he watched his wife on stage with Jacob, lost in the musical bubble the two singers shared from day one, he couldn't help but be full-on clobbered by a growing anxiety.

Sure, the two were always close. Jacob had always been one step behind Josh, near enough to whisper silent threats in his ear, or to send Jessie downhearted looks that telegraphed his deep affection for her. Jessie, for her part, admitted her love for Jacob, even to her husband. But she made it clear the two had boundaries they had not crossed over the years since the Deuce McCall shooting. Yet tonight, something was different. Something had changed. The air between them on stage was electric. It was a silvery blue. And it was intoxicating.

It hit Josh like a bolt of supercharged lightning.

Jacob was Jessie's go to guy. He was her confidante, her touchstone. He was her rock. And Josh was a cement block dragging Jessie to depths she couldn't handle. He was a bottom dweller now, a loser, a worthless cheating sunuvabitch. He was what Charles feared he would be. He was what Charlie warned him not to become.

Jessie had gone to Jacob when she needed a friend, or he went to her, more likely; not that it mattered. It was crystal clear tonight that the two had each other's backs; it was so fucking clear, in fact, that they seemed barely aware of the other souls in the room.

A claustrophobic choking feeling accosted Josh; he looked over to Rachael to see whether she, too, had clued in to this new game. By her frozen posture and locked-in stare—no longer joyful and excited, but now disturbed and fearful—he knew she had. And for that, Josh was sorry.

But he was sorry for himself as well, damn sorry. And angry. Angry at his own stubborn refusal to be there for his wife when she needed him. Sure, Josh's reticence was based on fear, months of it—gob-sucking soul-eating life-crushing months. But Jessie got rescued. She was here. She was still a target, maybe, which terrified the hell out of Josh. But she was here.

Alive. Singing. Glorious, beautiful, dreamlike, perfect...

And no longer his.

He raised his hand to beckon the bartender. Josh ordered a beer.

It was a good half hour before Jacob and Jessie reappeared at the Keating table. That was plenty of time for Josh to down a few beers. Hell, not like anyone who spotted him bothered to even drop over to say hello—they waved half-heartedly like they understood his pain and his need to hide in the dismal bar away from the general population in the exquisite ballroom; either that or they pitied him outright. Even Steve and Charlie remained distant, *as if they might be tainted by their association with me*, Josh thought.

He was a leper. He was alone.

When Jacob and Jessie made their reappearance, they strolled in together to raucous applause. Both blushed and ducked their heads, shaking hands and accepting hugs on the way in. Because there were so many people now on the move as the stage crew set up for the next band, and people were taking advantage of the dead air in order to empty their bladders, Jacob and Jessie had to walk part way single file. From Josh's vantage point, he could see Jessie's fingertips floating behind her, lingering in Jacob's gently outstretched hand.

Josh ordered another beer. He tried to turn away from the ballroom and face the bar to sort out his confused and loathsome feelings, but he couldn't quite make the break. The agony was too close; time and distance and booze and Nadia did nothing to put a dent in the hole now deeply wrought in his heart. He wanted to melt, to sink, to cry, but he was humiliated to discover he was already as low as he could go, apart from climbing under the bar stool and crying like a baby.

Turning again, he fixed his gaze on Rachael. He had to sway a little from side to side and crane his neck in order to see her as the wealthy moved past in their haute couture and jewels. She appeared to be trying to be tolerant, to tell herself her boyfriend was just Jessie's friend, that nothing untoward was at play between them. Josh could tell that was what she was thinking by the way she sat with her hands folded in her lap, her back straight, as she politely nodded and smiled at the backstage tales Jacob and Jessie were no doubt enthusiastically sharing with the table.

Slipping off the stool, Josh gripped the edge of the bar with both hands. Staring at his fingers, he longed to intimately touch his wife with them again. Letting go of the bar, he teetered. But he managed to turn and face the ballroom. Piped music—languorous jazz—was filling the room now, as a black T-shirted crew rushed around the stage preparing for the next musical guests. Couples were on the dance floor. Charles and Dee were arm in arm, enjoying the sensuous saxophone sweeping over them; at the table, Charlie and Steve were leaning in cracking jokes at Jessie and Jacob as Rachael, lips pressed tightly together, wordlessly watched.

Josh approached, carefully trying to place each high-polished square-toed shoe somewhere that looked normal, so he wouldn't lurch and appear as stone drunk as he knew he was. The room was swimming…but there was Jessie—his wife, the mother of his babies—laughing, happy, a diaphanous cream-lace angel.

I need you, Josh ached. *Please don't give up on me. Please don't let me go.*

Steve saw him first. Instantly, he braced an arm against the back of Jessie's chair. Charlie looked up then, as did Maggie and Rachael.

Jacob was next.

Jessie was last.

Both Charlie and Steve rose. They approached Josh with subdued *hellos,* and tried to lead him to a nearby table. But Josh wasn't having it. He fought off their arms and called out to Jessie.

"Please, Jessie, I just wanna talk to you. Thassall. Please. One minute."

Slowly, shocked to see him, she stood.

Josh fought the shameful demons assaulting him earlier as he sat at the bar. He had to. He had to give it one more try, or else he knew he would lose Jessie to Jacob forever. Trying to bring her into focus as she rose, he thought *hell yeah, I knew you wouldn't let me down, you love me, I know you do,* but then she tipped her head away from him and walked a half dozen steps in the opposite direction.

Behind her, Josh saw Charles and Dee spot him. He could tell by the way Deirdre did that *oh my goodness* 'hands-in-front-of-her-mouth' thing that she was mortified at his appearance, but Josh fought off the unfavorable scrutiny and lurched forward towards his wife, only to be firmly held back by two people he used to consider his friends.

He got louder. "Jessie. Jessie! Please. Jus talk to me! Goddamn it, why won't you talk to me?!" He didn't realize it at the time, but others could see that Josh's cheeks were wet. He was unbalanced and unkempt, he had to piss like a racehorse, and his shirt was leaking out over the waistband of his pants, but he needed to get Jessie's attention, and that was all that mattered.

Finally, she turned to him.

The hurt and pain in her eyes silenced Josh flat. He swallowed and blinked helplessly. With her eyes, Jessie was begging him to leave. It wasn't hate he saw there, or even disgust or shame. For the next while he would recall the look, and even months later it would leave him reeling.

It was sorrow. A deep, desperate, agonizing sorrow, for the man Josh used to be before some crazy oddball snatched his wife and children away from him, destroying his sanity and breaking Josh down to his lowest common denominator. She was shaking her head at him now, from side to side, slowly, and then she was sobbing, great gulping gasps that took her breath away.

Wrecked, obliterated, Josh watched, held back by Charlie and Steve, as Jessie struggled to remain upright. As Jessie struggled to breathe.

Through this, Jacob remained seated, slightly slumped over, shocked at Josh's audacity in showing up here, drunk. Stunned by how low he had sunk. Amazed by his capacity to hurt Jessie again and again. He rose. He was standing between Josh and Jessie now, and so he ended up locked in Josh's hopelessly despondent eyes.

Josh sank lower than he ever dreamed he could go.

He begged Jacob. "Please, Jacob. Please don't do this. Don't do this to me."

At the time, Rachael wondered what the hell he was talking about, although later she realized she saw this coming all along.

Jacob blinked. He took a moment to digest what was happening. Across the table from him, still seated, shaken, was his girlfriend. Before him was Josh, Jessie's estranged husband and the father of her two children—the one man Jacob damn well knew Jessie desperately loved.

But behind him was Jessie, hyperventilating by the sounds of things or, at the very least, dazed and struggling to breathe.

He let his eyes drift away from Josh, and he turned.

Jacob was riding on the magic of a surreal set on stage with Jessie, lost in the music he and she captivated the world with again and again, in its power to uplift, to raise, to heal. He was on the crest of a wave floating towards perfection. He was buoyant. He was cool. And he was needed.

He did not look at Rachael. He did not find Charles and Dee in his peripheral vision. He just locked his eyes on Jessie, strode towards her, and grasped a trembling wrist with his left hand. With his right hand, he lifted her chin, confident and sure, and he spouted instructions at her.

"Look at me, Jessie. Breathe. Just breathe. Here. Look at me."

Within a few gasping seconds, she was able to do so. She was still shaking, and was bent over, but Jacob was trying to hold her up.

So she let him.

"Jacob," she gulped, "help me. I can't breathe." The sea-pearl eyes were afloat.

He held her wrist and chin more firmly. "You can breathe," he told her defiantly, shifting his weight hurriedly. "Trust me. Yoga breaths. Like you and Emily-Grace practiced. Come on Jessie, look at me. Just look at me."

It was only a few moments before she started to settle. Jacob had a power over her that night that no one else in the room could even begin to touch. And once those loving eyes captured hers during those difficult first few moments after Josh's drunken appearance during their magical evening, she belonged to them—if only for a time.

His power was once Josh's power. Jacob had forged a deep and earnest friendship with Jessie in the last few years, with all the music making and songwriting and television shooting on *Mystic Nights*. She was sorely in need of him when she first left Josh; he was her confidante and soul mate over the last few months, and now he was her pillar of strength.

A new ballad came on, an Eva Cassidy cover tune. The first few chords took Jessie by surprise—it was one of her favorite Eva tunes. Its simple beauty and ode to pure love was surreal in that space, at that time. The song was 'You Take My Breath Away,' and it filled every corner of that elegant, expansive room. Eva's voice was liquid honey poured over warm skin.

You watch my love grow, like a child
Sometimes gentle, and sometimes wild
Sometimes you just take my breath away

Jacob recognized the moment the universe was handing him. Wheeling slowly around, he led Jessie to the dance floor, which was about twenty feet away. As if he and Jessie were still on stage in their glorious bubble, he pulled her to him, his left arm behind her back, at her waist, and his right hand brushing rogue hair off her cheek. They waltzed slowly, his eyes lost in hers. As the tender ballad worked its way to a satisfying climax rooted in perfection, he let his lips brush her forehead, her eyes, the tops of her cheeks.

Her lips.

He kissed her sometimes anyway, light kisses, loving, tender, gentle little kisses. They were that kind of friends. But now, Jacob pressed his lips to hers and let them sweetly linger as Eva Cassidy's honeyed lyrics and nourishing melody floated in and around them. He let his tongue touch her lips, the bottom, and then the top, and he exerted a gentle pressure on her back in order to feel her against him. She was still gasping slightly from the effort to regulate her breathing, but Jessie was calming in his arms and under his loving ministrations. Jacob kissed her harder, then, so she would not mistake his love for her any longer. With his right hand he let his thumb brush her cheek, and finally, finally! He felt her melt into him.

Jessie responded to him now in a way Jacob had dreamed and wished for over many long sleepless nights when his desire was unbearable. She relaxed into him, placed both hands on his forearms, and moved to the music with him. Soon one small hand covered his on her cheek; she intertwined her fingers amongst his. The other hand she moved to his waist, hooking one thumb over his belt.

She kissed him back, hard now, lost in Jacob's power to protect and savor her. Jessie was in the bubble. No more sorrowful, hurtful, heartbroken Josh, no more Rachael hanging off the sleeve of Jacob's designer suit, no more nights lying next to Jacob aching for more, like the few times they were together these last few months with the kids, horsing around, playing, being respectful friends.

No, tonight was different. Tonight, everything changed.

And around them, the world imploded.

Rachael sat unnoticed until Maggie touched her arm, and then she screeched back her chair and tiptoed away.

Charles and Dee watched Jessie with Jacob before forcing their eyes sideways to land on Josh.

Josh shrugged off Charlie's hand first, and then Steve's. He watched Jacob do what he had the chance to do in other years but what he never had the guts to do. And Josh knew it was his own fault. Jessie was right. They were lost to each other the day some idiot smashed the window of her SUV. Because he—Josh Sawyer—couldn't cope. And because he—Josh Sawyer—pulled a Jessie Wheeler and ran away instead of facing painful truths that might have helped them overcome the devastating hurts of the last many months.

He watched his wife's body respond to Jacob and, instead of going after the guy and tearing his balls out, Josh let him have her. He knew how hard fought Jacob's battle was; he understood the depths of the guy's agony over the last few years. But mostly, he understood Jessie's heartache where he himself was concerned, and so Josh let her have what she desperately needed—a true and trusted friend she loved deeply. Someone who would treat her right.

She used to love me best, he thought drunkenly. *She used to love me more.*

He forced his feet to turn away. He forced his eyes to let go. He forced his legs to move. Then Josh was outside, with both Charlie and Steve by his side. Leaning against a wrought iron fence surrounding the property, he heaved until he thought he was going to turn inside out.

When he stood, Jacob was outside too, holding open the door of a Lincoln SUV Josh recognized as the usual car Charles Keating had been hiring to escort his charges the last few years. Jessie was at the car too, standing on her impossibly high heels, one hand resting on the door.

Josh straightened. She was looking directly at him. He thought he saw her shoulders cave. He thought he saw her melt. He thought he felt her silent pleading cries. He thought she might move towards him. By Jacob's nervous stance, it seemed he thought so too.

But she didn't.

Jessie ducked into the car then, and Jacob twisted briefly to regard Josh in his puppy dog gaze. Funny thing, though, Josh thought later, he didn't seem to be saying *good riddance* or *I'm the better man,* or *fuck you.* Instead, Jacob seemed to be saying, *I know I'm second. I know.*

Morgan climbed into the front seat and Josh saw him signal to the driver. As the slick black SUV pulled away, Steve laid a hand on Josh's shoulder. "Come on, buddy. Let's get you back to your hotel."

Josh backed away from him, teetering, choking on a heady cocktail of emotion and booze. He raised both hands so the palms faced Steve and Charlie. "No," he gasped. "No. I need to get drunk."

"You *are* drunk, buddy." Even Charlie didn't have the heart to pick on his friend tonight.

"I-need-to-get-more-drunk." Sobbing now, Josh bent over again.

Steve eyed Charlie, who nodded and gestured down the nearby sidewalk.

They stood one on each side of their friend, and slowly the odd procession made its way to a bar down the street. Inside, the guys let Josh get as shit-faced drunk as his body could bear, before taking him to their hotel and holding his hair back so he could puke his sorrow dry.

Chapter Thirty-one

*B*efore Jacob and Jessie left the ballroom, Maggie had placed her palms staunchly on Jessie's cheeks and asked, "Are you sure, honey?"

Jessie's silence was her answer.

"Jessie, Jacob is everything to you. If you...if you take him down this path and things go wrong, you could lose him. You know that."

Slowly, the wheels in Jessie's mind turned. Eyes widening, just slightly, she searched Maggie's kind eyes and whispered, "You still have hope for Josh and me."

"Oh, honey." Maggie held her friend away from her body and studied the confusion flitting across the pale eyes. "Of course I do. You and Josh..." She didn't need to finish the sentence.

"He's in such a bad place, Maggie. I can't go there. I am not strong enough," Jessie fist pumped her chest lightly, "to go there. I can't hold him up this time."

"And Jacob?"

"I love him, Maggie. I always have."

"But Josh..."

"Josh is in the stratosphere, you know? He is not of this earth, when it comes to me loving him. He is everything...and nothing." Fighting to push the raw image of her drunk husband out of her mind, Jessie added a post-script. "As much as I want him, it hurts too much to go there with him like this. I lost him, Maggie. He's gone."

"You could lose Jacob, honey."

"Not tonight. Not tonight I won't." Pulling herself gently out of Maggie's arms, Jessie backed away, towards Jacob, who was saying solemn good nights to Charles and Dee. "And tonight…I need him. I fucking need him, Maggie. So bad."

"Okay, sweetheart. I hear you. I do." Maggie nodded at her latest flame, a bald Pitbull-lookalike in a dapper charcoal gray suit. "I'll stay at John's. My home is yours tonight."

Her lips pressed together, Jessie tilted her head and said a simple, "Thanks, Maggie. Luv you. I mean it." They hugged and separated, Jessie holding her friend's kind gaze for an extra beat before she pivoted around and moved towards Jacob.

Watching her, Maggie sighed deeply. "Hearts are breaking already, honey. Namaste."

Later, at Maggie's place, Jessie allowed her friend's thoughts to roll around and around in her mind. She walked in before Jacob, who closed the door behind him with barely a backwards glance at Morgan, who watched it click shut before taking up a post leaning against the far wall in the hallway, from where he stared at the closed door.

Jessie stopped at the kitchen island, let her fingers trail along the edge, and turned to face her best friend, her savior over the last few months, her *Mystic Nights* co-star, her musical soul mate. A sad smile met his cobalt eyes.

He paused, unsure.

She reached a hand out to him. "C'mere, babe," she murmured.

Nervous, he took her hand. As far as Jacob knew, Jessie was saying good-night, like she did all the other long excruciating nights when he had to touch himself to still the ache. Jacob knew tonight was not a night he could lie next to this beautiful creature and watch her sleep. Not without touching her. Not without moving over her body and loving her the way he so desperately wanted to for so long now.

He inhaled slowly, and moved towards her.

Jessie reached for his other hand and exerted a small pressure on both. Her eyes were searching, wondering. *Maggie's right,* she was thinking. *I could lose him. Or…or maybe I could keep him. Maybe we can make this work.* Josh's raw pain creased her brow.

Jacob noticed. He exhaled to a count of five, lifted a hand, and brushed his thumb across her cheek. *It has to be tonight,* he thought. *If I am going to win her, it's got to be tonight.* The music, the madness, the euphoria…they were a lover's perfect instruments. He just had to play them…

"Jessie, I know I am not who you—"

She placed two sparkling white nails on his lips and shook her head slowly. "No, babe," she said, and watched as his expression crumbled. But Jessie had more to say. "Tonight is not about him. It's about you. It's about how I *feel* about you."

Leaning in slightly, she let her lips brush his. Jessie let her tongue slide over Jacob's bottom lip, and then his top lip. When he groaned just the littlest bit, his lips parted inadvertently, and she placed her palms over his stubbly cheeks and gently slid her tongue inside Jacob's mouth. The sensation, to both of them, was of an otherworldly plane; it was as if their senses were suddenly fully ignited, on the highest alert, as if every pore of Jessie and Jacob's skin was suddenly opened—wanting, electric, alive.

"I want you," she managed to whisper. "I need you."

Backing off, she kept hold of one set of calloused fingers and sent him her desire through softly aching eyes; he accepted the look with one of equal measure, swallowed, and let his best friend lead him to her bedroom.

Inside, they were too preoccupied to close the door, which was fine since Maggie wasn't coming home and the children were at Charles and Dee's hotel for the night.

Jessie slipped off the high heels and faced Jacob. She started at his tie, tugging at it until it loosened. He rested both trembling hands on her hips, and memorized every nuance of the face he loved—the flushed cheeks, the sensuous lips, the soulful eyes.

Tossing the tie on the bed, Jessie buried herself in Jacob's eyes and pressed her lips to his to say *this is what I want* before she unbuttoned him the way she always did back in their Scotland days. Starting at the top, she worked her way down his expensive black dress shirt. When she pulled the shirt open to the sides, she saw that he was wearing a white undershirt; she slipped her hands underneath it and felt his body tense instantly. He moaned at the sizzling sensation of those beautiful warm hands finally gracing his skin, closed his eyes, and let his head hang heavy in the curve of her neck before opening his lips and tonguing delicate trails over her skin in response.

At that, Jessie shivered. She arched her neck upwards as he moved to the little hollow there, and then her breathing changed as she pushed his shirt off his shoulders and pulled the white undershirt up and over his head.

There was that Celtic cross to think about now, to sink her long nails into. Jessie pictured it there, inked across Jacob's shoulder blades. He once told her she was his cross to bear; tonight she only wanted to be his lover, and so she pulled his body towards her so she could feel all of him against her. Pushing hard on his back, she moved her fingers over where she knew the cross marked him; she pressed down, deeply, and let her lips and tongue taste the salt on his neck while he started to move a little against her, small moans accenting the tiny movements of his hips as Jacob lowered one arm to her runner's butt and pushed her hard against him.

"Oh God, Jessie," he breathed into her neck, "I have wanted this for so long."

She was mewling against him now, tiny pre-orgasmic sounds that echoed his want and his need. Then, she stepped back and moved his hand over one breast. Lifting the hand, she kissed the fingers before closing her mouth over them and sucking and moving them in and out.

"Sweet Jesus," was Jacob's response as his knees melted. He let her play with him that way while he bent over her and slipped his other hand inside the diamond shaped neckline of the low cut dress. He let his fingers float languidly across the top of one breast before he slipped them further down to tease an erect nipple. She sighed and he felt her warm breath over his fingers as she placed her free hand over his, across her breast, encouraging him. Finally Jacob removed his other fingers from her mouth and reached around behind her. With trembling fingers, he located the zipper of the exquisite Zuhair Murad and pulled it slowly down. It made a soft unremitting *zzzz* sound as it loosened under his touch; other than that, there were no sounds in the room with the exception of their needy, raspy breaths.

Jacob slipped his hands inside the bodice of Jessie's dress then, and pulled it aside to free her breasts. He let the Chantilly lace and pearls hang at her waist as he slowly fondled one breast, and then the other, before he bent to her and drew a nipple into his mouth, massaging the lovely roundness of her as he did so.

The second hand responded to her mewling as well, first by fondling the nipple and roundness of Jessie's other breast, then by pressing against the small of her back, pushing her body against his own aching need, before Jacob suddenly plunged that hand down the front of Jessie's dress to feel a wetness between her thighs that increased as he sucked hard on her nipple and massaged her below at the same time.

Jacob was moaning louder now, completely unaware of the sounds escaping his lips as his desperate need to completely love this woman intensified. He moved the hand down her dress harder against her, slipped two fingers inside, and felt her grasp his wrist as she cried out and arched her back towards him. He played there, still sucking her nipple, until Jessie yanked at his belt, pulled down his zipper, and bent down on her knees, hauling his trousers down over his hips as she moved.

She placed a palm underneath his testicles first, gently scratching and then massaging, before her second hand grasped his penis and her lips closed around it. His hips gyrated harder as he tried to go as deep as he could inside that small mouth; Jacob was almost crying from the sheer bliss and bodily pleasure of being loved by the woman he desired so desperately for so long. Pulling her hair back from her face, he watched, gasping and grunting, as Jessie sucked on and massaged him, her own desperate moans vibrating through him and sending sizzles to every exposed pore and nerve on his body.

He couldn't stand it anymore. He was going to come then and there, and he didn't want to—there was more Jacob wanted from Jessie on this incredible night, so he eased her away before lifting her under the arms and forcing her onto the bed. She arched her back, spreading her legs for him as she slipped her hand down the front of her dress to keep the sensations coming, but Jacob didn't do what she expected. Instead, he moved over her and grabbed her roughly by one bicep.

"Roll over," he ordered her, gasping.

When she did as he asked, he quickly placed a strong arm around and under her abdomen, then used his free hand to pull her dress down over her slender hips and off her body. Moaning, Jessie was already spreading her legs widely for him, in anticipation of him thrusting hard inside, but Jacob bent to her first and tongued and sucked while fingering her instead, hard thrusts of two fingers that had her screaming *ffuccckkk!!!* in ecstasy, not just for the physical love, but for the complete faith and trust in his belief and soul love for her.

When he finally grabbed one breast and started squeezing, grunting behind her, Jessie knew he was close, so she helped her lover out and moved her body to meet his. Jacob pulled her more upright on her hands and knees, and then drove himself hard into the woman he moaned over during many hot, sleepless Miami nights.

"Jesus!" she cried. "Jesus! Oh fuck, Jacob!" was Jessie's instant reaction as an unequalled pleasure soared in and through her. He was careful to gauge her reaction, to see if she would tense up, but she didn't; instead, Jessie moved to meet and help him, and to increase her own pleasure by virtue of where she placed her body.

When he was ready to come, she was writhing against him, crying out and starting to orgasm. But he pulled out and brusquely shoved her over on her back again, before driving himself back into her to complete the job for both of them. Bucking against him now, Jessie dug her nails deep into the Celtic cross on his back before moving her hands lower and pressing hard against his buttocks to bring him as deep inside her as he could possibly go.

His muscles were fully taut, at their limit and beyond, so when Jacob let go with a huge cry and kept surging into her, Jessie wrapped her arms around him so she could feel his body give completely and pour everything he had into her—all those years of wanting, of loving, of hurting and needing. As he started coming down off the orgasm, and she from hers, he kept thrusting at her, wanting it all, wanting every last crumb he could take from her. Finally, Jacob sighed the last of his love into her, and settled over Jessie, his arms tenting her in a safe cocoon as she let her nails trace first the sweet, gentle curve of his hip, and then the nuances of his damp back.

They still moved together a little as they soaked up the afterglow of their coupling. Finally, Jessie pushed Jacob's face away from her so she could place her palms on his cheeks and peer into the deep abyss of those gorgeous blue eyes.

She was smiling wholeheartedly, genuinely, loving him for who he was, and even for who he wasn't. "Sweet Jesus, Jacob," she raved, tired eyes sparkling. "You are something else."

"Ahh," he grinned, his heart still racing. "So I shouldn't have performance anxiety? I did okay?"

She laughed outright. "I would say my four *fuuucckkks* and seven *Oh Gods* would answer that question for you!"

He didn't respond. Instead, Jacob's eyes took on a sweet softness that melted Jessie entirely. She let the backs of her fingers trail over his cheek, and then she lifted her head up to press her lips against his.

"I love you, Jacob. I always have, and I always will. You know that, babe."

Something flickered in his baby blues then, but she knew what it was, and so she told him, "I meant what I said before. This is about us, about you and me. Okay? Let the other shit go."

He allowed a small smile to lift the corners of his lips before exhaling deeply and pulling out of her. "You want to go again?" he teased. "See if you can up that *fuuucckkk* quotient?"

Their laughter was healing for both of them. But the best part of the coupling was the simple closeness they found in each other, a soul closeness that both Jessie and Jacob were in desperate need of, and one they could only ever find in each other. They lay together now, side by side, facing each other, and doing that thing new lovers do, just touching and tracing and admiring and adoring, and losing each other in the opposite searching eyes.

After a bit, as Jessie's eyes were starting to close, Jacob eased off the bed and retrieved his pants from the floor.

"Maggie's not here," Jessie told him softly, her voice whispery with the need to sleep. "You can walk around in your birthday suit, handsome boy."

"Aww, just in case," Jacob said. "It would feel weird to walk around out there with my thing hanging out."

"Oh, it's all shriveled up from overuse," she murmured from the bed, giggling. "No one would see it."

"You think you're so funny," he grinned, buckling up the pants. He bent forward and kissed her tenderly. "I'm just going for some water. I'll be right back."

"Bring me a cookie," she managed, trying to keep her eyes open but losing the battle after the emotional night. "Chocolate chip." Jessie forced them to remain open long enough to see Jacob leave the room. The Celtic cross arching across the muscles on his back danced in the dim light when he stepped out into the hallway. A tingle spread up Jessie's thighs and she shivered. "Fuuccckkk," she tittered to the pillow, blushing.

Jacob made it down the short hallway to the kitchen before he jumped, and stepped back suddenly. He was barefoot, and therefore quiet, so overall he wasn't surprised to see Morgan startle as well when they spotted each other, but still…only a few minutes before, he and Jessie were both less than quiet as they clung to each other in a soul-satisfying ecstasy neither had felt for some time.

"Jesus," Jacob said, as Morgan straightened. The guy's eyes freaked him out. Jacob was certain he'd heard, because of the way the security guy was regarding him now, his eyes hard, lips in a thin straight line, and his posture tense.

"Awww…" He let the sound drift off into a quiet *mmpphhff* as he moved towards the fridge, for some inexplicable reason afraid to turn his back on the solid, quiet guy. "Just getting some water," he mumbled.

Under his breath, Morgan added, *don't forget the cookie. Chocolate chip.*

He watched as Jacob grabbed two from the plate on the kitchen island. He, Morgan, was sitting there, pouting and feeling sorry for himself. Yeah, he was curious. He stood for far too long at the end of the hall and watched Jacob fuck Jessie solid. Did he still want her? No. Morgan didn't think so, although it was not an easy thing to watch Jacob roll her over on the bed and tongue her that way. At that point he'd even put his hand on the doorknob, and stepped towards the room, his pulse quickening.

But now…no. He wanted a woman, yes, but he wanted the mother of his dead child back. He wanted his wife back, with her sensuous curves and mocha skin. Those round breasts…and those dark eyes…Nadia was exotic, and always creative in bed. Now, she passed before his vision, but what came to mind was an image of her with Josh. The game had gone on far too long. It was over now, at least as far as Morgan was concerned, or at least it had evolved. Josh left Nadia only a few days ago, but already it made Morgan hopeful that she would consider coming back to *him*, to rekindle and reignite their marriage. Maybe they could even have another child, although he doubted she would go for that. Loving and then losing was far too exquisite a pain to even consider chancing that again.

The thing is, he'd gotten another cryptic text from Nadia today. Obviously she was still longing for Josh, but Morgan saw the guy tonight at the fundraiser, and he was such a mess it seemed improbable that he was entirely over Jessie. So that meant one thing. Nadia was not likely to get him back. But she thought she could. She still thought if she got rid of Jessie, her competition would be eliminated, now more than ever. And she knew Morgan wanted her back—he knew she was aware of his continuing devotion to her. So today's text was clear—*U get what u want if I get what I want.*

How to interpret that? *Well, maybe it means I have to share her,* Morgan thought, after analyzing the thing all day. *Although I doubt that will happen. Judging by the way Josh was so crushed at Jessie's dismissal of him in favor of an erotic night with Jacob, Josh will be destroyed once and for all, in one fell swoop, if Jessie is removed. So I will get Nadia to myself.*

But there was a price. He had to kill the singer, the woman he guarded so carefully from 'sick predators.' Like himself. He tried and failed the first time, so he would have to try again now. But he would have to think it through so he wouldn't be detected. He almost hadn't—he was so excited getting that text from Nadia today that, as he stood outside the bedroom door watching Jessie suck Jacob dry, Morgan held something shiny in his hand—a butcher knife that he only just returned to its wooden block in the last few seconds before Jacob's appearance in the kitchen.

He looked up at Jacob now. The musician was watching him carefully.

"You look tired, Morgan. You should get some sleep. Jessie and I are fine."

Straightening, Morgan simply eyed him back, and tipped his head in a small nod without losing eye contact.

Jacob took his water and cookies and headed back towards the bedroom. The Celtic cross on his back loomed large in the eerie dim white light. Morgan thought it would make a great target. He figured he would be doing Jacob a favor by killing him alongside Jessie. Otherwise the poor puppy would, like Josh, be instantly destroyed. Morgan wouldn't kill Josh unless...well, unless he caved and went back to Nadia. As far as Morgan was concerned, he wanted the bastard to suffer. He liked Jacob. His killing would be a simple and welcome mercy, if Jessie was gone.

Now, Morgan rose from his seat by the island. He heard the gentle click of the bedroom door this time after Jacob padded through it. Morgan made his way to the front door and eased it open. He thought again about Nadia, about her silky skin and those perfect breasts. According to today's text, there was a chance he might feel her writhing in his arms again.

If he killed Jessie.

He wanted Nadia back. What was it everyone credited Jessie for saying? *There is always hope.*

"Thanks, Jessie," he muttered, sinking into a chair outside Maggie's place. "I appreciate the hope."

Within minutes, he was asleep. There didn't seem to be a lot of point in staying awake since he was the person they all feared. And he wasn't going to act tonight. Soon, but not tonight. He dreamed of making love to his wife again, but her face turned to Jessie's underneath him at the house in Langley that morning, the morning of the fire. She was sick, she was delusional that day, even, but her body moved the same way he saw her move tonight under Jacob's hot touch. In his sleep, Morgan smiled.

In the bedroom deep inside Maggie's home, Jacob lay awake and pondered the strange guy as he watched Jessie sleep, her naked body lying overtop the covers, arms wrapped around a pillow. One breast was partly visible. He traced it with his finger, and then did the same over her hip, where he finally let his hand rest.

For sure Morgan heard us, he thought, chilled by the thought. It never even occurred to him that Morgan had watched their vigorous lovemaking. Still, he made a point to talk to Charles or Ulysses soon, or even Matt, since rumor had it Matt would be filling in a few shifts here and there this week while Susanne took a holiday. No doubt about it, Morgan creeped him out.

Shivering despite the warmth of the bedroom, Jacob let his gaze fall upon his lover's sweet face, which was partially obscured by her wild, loose curls.

"Babe," he whispered to her, knowing she couldn't hear, "I am so in love with you. Thank you for the best night of my entire life."

He thought silently that if it was all he got, it would be enough. To have the chance to hold her again, to love her again, to be loved by her again— it was surreal.

Jacob let his eyes close over as he felt his body pulling him towards sleep, like a ship being roped tightly to a pier. Despite telling himself one night was enough, he prayed that when he woke his beautiful Jessie would still be there, in his arms, in his heart, under his care. He inched closer so he could feel her warm breath on his chest.

He pictured Josh, desolate and lost, and wondered what kind of night he was having.

I'm not sorry, he whispered to himself as his own breath evened out.

And, finally, Jacob slept.

Chapter Thirty-Two

Josh spoke to no one the next morning, not to Steve, not to Charlie, and not to the waiter at the diner where he and the boys had breakfast. Instead, he just grunted and pointed, and avoided all stares. He forced down two bites of toast and one of bacon. Coffee was a chore. He got halfway through a cup. Orange juice was not an option.

Charlie and Steve indulged him. Hell, as far as they were concerned, at least he was here and not wallowing in self-pity with the covers over his head.

They put him on a commercial flight back to Vancouver later that day. He didn't even stop to see his kids—he couldn't. Emily-Grace's innocent eyes loving someone as despicable and loathsome as himself was not worth considering. Josh figured he'd save her the torture later on by cutting and running now.

He did manage to meet Steve's eyes before he turned to go through security at JFK. A lot was said in sadness on an invisible wire between the two good friends.

Josh added a spoken final thought, trusting Steve to understand. "Did you see them? On stage, and after? They're magical together, Steve. They always have been."

"Don't you dare give up on her, Josh. On the two of you. You both just need to chill for a bit and let the rest of the dust settle. You were doing fine. You were getting your shit together."

Gesturing to himself—scruffy, unshaven, hung-over—Josh almost laughed. "Look at me, Steve. Look at me." Backing away, his voice cracked with bitter, final words. "She's where she should be. I've got nothing good to give her. Nothing."

Steve grabbed his friend and pulled him close, sniffling before he let Josh go.

Josh couldn't bring himself to meet Charlie's eyes at all. But Charlie, too, showed his affection and concern for Josh by almost crushing his shoulder with one strong hand.

When Josh was safely out of sight, the guys retrieved Charlie's rental from the parking garage, and they nosed it towards Maggie's place. When they arrived, the condo was buzzing—Jacob and Jessie, Charles and Dee, Dan, Maggie and John, and Emily-Grace and David were all there, along with Carlotta, Matt—around whom they were all clustered—and Morgan, who was yawning in a corner.

A rousing greeting from the kids welcomed them—the little ones adored their parents' friends and so each immediately chose a guy to lift them up for some good-natured teasing. Eventually Maggie and John teamed up with Charles, Dee and Carlotta, and shuffled off to Central Park, with Dan overseeing the children's security. The others stayed back for coffee that Jacob and Charlie went off to fetch from the indie café down the street.

Jessie, Matt, and Steve settled around the kitchen island to wait.

"So…where'd you guys go last night, Steve?" Jessie couldn't delay the inevitable another second. She clasped her hands together and tried not to appear anxious, even though her insides were churning.

"Yeah. About that." Steve sucked on the inside of his cheek and glanced up at Matt, who had gotten the gruesome details from Charles earlier. "I'm really sorry, Jessie. He got in on the ticket Sophie wasn't using."

"Hmmm. I figured it was something like that."

He decided to test her, to gauge what she was thinking. "I think maybe I was hoping, you know? Although, thinking back, I should have known better. I know you guys are through—I know *you're* through."

"He was through first." It was a whisper. Running a hand through her loose curls, Jessie exhaled slowly through puffed cheeks. "Is he okay?"

Pondering her, Steve considered what to say. Finally, he chose honesty. He shook his head. "No. I don't think so."

"Ohhh." A glistening blade sliced another chunk off Jessie's heart. "That sucks." She stared at a broken nail on her left hand and wondered if she left the bit that was gone somewhere in Jacob's back.

Matt, leaning over the island on both forearms, spoke up. "Would Josh consider rehab again, do you think?"

"Not at the moment," Steve answered on behalf of Jessie. "He is not considering anything, I don't think, with the exception of a warm bed where he can bury his heart."

"Thanks for that, Steve," Jessie bit off, eyes misting over. "Jesus, this is hard." Knuckling her fingers, she swiped at a leaky tear.

Steve draped an arm around her shoulders. "You listen to me," he said earnestly. "I'm pissed at Josh for a lot of reasons, one of them being his lack of time with his kids. But I'm not going to let him go down, Jessie. None of us are. We were around to watch him sink, when you were..." He sighed. "When you were missing. So we know what demons grabbed him and pulled him under. We just need to find a way to pull him back up into the land of the living." Pausing, he asked, "What about Jacob? He sleep on the couch last night?"

Flushing instantly, Jessie half melted into the countertop in remembrance. She couldn't meet Steve's eye. "The hell he didn't. You see that guy last night, Steve?"

At that, Matt chuckled lightly. Steve frowned.

"He has always been there for me," Jessie added softly. "Always, despite knowing how I feel about my—about Josh."

Matt broke in. "I hear you will be meeting Josh face to face in Vancouver next week, Jessie."

"Yup. Glorious lawyers. Hope Josh is cleaned up by then. Sober. And that he bothers showing up."

"He'll show up. I'll drag his ass there," Steve promised, with a certainty he didn't feel.

Just then the door opened and Jacob and Charlie came in with the hot beverages, laughing about some silly thing that happened on the way home from the café. Jessie accepted one, although she still had pangs in her belly at the thought that she could no longer breastfeed her son who, at almost sixteen months, was getting past the age she planned to feed him naturally anyway.

Talk turned to her birthday, which was coming up.

"What do you want, Jessie?" This was Charlie, who had already booked her for dinner plans with himself and Jane, and a play date for Stella and Jessie's two babes while they were in Vancouver.

"I just want things to work out with the lawyers," she said, picking at her broken nail. "I want to start rebuilding my life."

Jacob glanced sideways at her while the other guys present tried hard not to look at him. She sensed him watching her, and so Jessie turned her head so she could peer into those blue eyes and offer him a silent *yes, that includes you*, because she knew he was still unsure. Like Josh, he would always be worried about an ever-present shadow.

Unable to help himself, Jacob squished a little closer to Jessie and wrapped an arm around her waist. He leaned into her and brushed his lips over the side of her temple as the guys couldn't help but watch. Steve couldn't hide a fleeting grimace. He looked over at Charlie, who frowned. Matt watched the couple carefully, stowing his thoughts on the union away somewhere deep, for later. But already his heart hurt for Jacob, who seemed to be doing so well with Rachael these last few months.

Uncomfortable with the sudden silence, Jacob took a breath and raised a question, although he left an arm around Jessie's waist as they leaned against the counter on the sink side. Steve and Charlie were now on chairs across from them, Matt standing between the men.

Morgan was off in the corner of the living room, watching TV. Jacob spoke quietly, glancing sideways at Jessie, whom he had yet to express concerns to about this particular matter.

He aimed his concern at Matt.

"So...I'm wondering about cutting Morgan back, Matt. Do you think it might be an option?"

It was a 180-degree turn in their day. Matt raised his eyebrows as Jessie responded with a quick, "What? Why?"

Jacob explained his unease over stumbling across Morgan in the kitchen the night before. He didn't mention the sex—he didn't have to, although

Jessie blushed at what was left unsaid. He finished by saying, "It's been a few months, anyway. Maybe we can back off on the security."

Studying Jessie, Matt ignored Charlie and Steve's quick rebuttals. "Jessie?" he asked.

She shrugged. "You know me, Matt. If someone wants me dead, I'm not necessarily going to spend my precious alive moments worrying every second about it."

"Mmmpphff," was Charlie's response to that. Stunned, Steve just watched her, wordless.

"How do you feel about Morgan?" Matt watched Jessie's eyes for telltale signs of anxiety.

"I'm fine with him. He's been around for what, three years now? I'm used to his hulking silences, and he's a good workout partner. But Jacob has a point. It's not necessarily comfortable having someone lurking around when you're, um, indisposed. With a guy as sexy as this one, anyway."

Without looking away from Matt, behind the kitchen island she slipped the fingers of her right hand behind Jacob's belt buckle, behind the waistband of his jeans, and down until she touched her favorite part of him. She grinned rather diabolically, blushed, and avoided the stares of Steve and Charlie as Jacob's knees buckled. Jacob placed his right hand over his crotch, stared at the countertop, quietly inhaled so she would have more room there, and pushed on her fingers. He spread his legs a little.

She continued speaking as well as probing. "I'm okay with cutting him back, or assigning him more elsewhere, I guess. I'm sure Charles has lots of places to put him."

The way Steve chewed his top lip gave away his feelings on the subject. "Where's your next gig, Jacob? Lots of concerts this summer, I'm guessing. Festivals and stuff."

"A few, yeah. Europe, all over the states, a couple in Canada." He draped an arm around Jessie's shoulders and, reddening, finally pulled her hand away from his crotch before he got too uncomfortable. "I think I'll see if this one wants to come with me."

"Thought so." Steve twisted more fully around in his chair to face Jacob straight on. "And you want to cut back on her security."

"No," Jacob said, a little hurt at what seemed like a personal attack. "No, I just don't think we need someone listening to us have sex, that's all. And he, in particular, gives me the creeps."

Jessie took advantage of Jacob's blatant discomfort by flashing a wide smile at Matt. "What about you, sexy security type? You interested in listening to me begging for mercy while this guy does his thing to me?"

"Jessie, for Christ's sake." Steve stared hard at her.

She rubbed a finger over her bottom lip before looking away from Matt's warning eyes to meet Steve's crushed ones. Swallowing, Jessie watched the hard emotions play across his face.

Steve said his piece. "Charlie and I put Josh on a plane less than two hours ago, Jessie. I don't want to rain on your parade, or yours either, Jacob, but Jesus, can we not talk about your magical fucking night while the memory of holding your husband's hair back so he could puke himself dry is still fresh? Please? Jesus. Have a little mercy."

She paled at that. *Of course Josh puked all night. Of course Steve was there for him. And I...wasn't.* Blinking, Jessie raised her chin and gripped the edge of the island's countertop.

"You suck, Steve," she whispered menacingly, firing invisible bullets across to him as he glared at her. "Might I remind you, Josh had a number of magical nights while I was locked in a basement. Oh, and after I got home, as well. Up until a few nights ago, in fact."

An uncomfortable silence greeted Jessie then, apart from the low volume on the TV where Morgan was craning an ear trying rather unsuccessfully to eavesdrop. Jessie glanced sideways at Jacob, who had turned a little green but who didn't say a word. He, too, was staring at Steve, though—confused, hurt, and afraid of what the future held in store for him as far as Jessie was concerned.

Always the wise older brother, Charlie entered the melee. "Jacob, Steve apologizes. But he's right. This is all new to us, to you and Jessie too, I gather, uh...I think...and we admit Josh is someone all of us care about. It was a rough night and it's not bound to get better anytime soon. So while you and Jessie go hopping around the world this summer, we'll be taking turns making sure her ex doesn't go do something stupid, like OD on a toxic mixture of coke and percs, and then decide to take a bath. Sorry, Jessie," he added, losing Jacob's nervous gaze and meeting Jessie's outright glare. "But it's true."

She looked back at Steve, who was angrily knifing long fingers through his hair, before she met Matt's eyes again. Telegraphing *I'm sorry* to him, because she was well aware he wanted none of the Wheeler-Sawyer drama, Jessie took Jacob's hand and lifted it onto the counter. Looking down, she ran her fingers over his.

"I'm grateful," she started slowly, "that you guys are watching out for Josh. I know it's awkward, believe me, I know. But I am going to hang out with this guy all summer because," she met Jacob's suddenly hopeful baby blues, then softened and smiled, "for one, he loves me. For two, I love him. And for three, he actually wants to be around my children, and they adore him. They need a man they can look up to. Speaking of which," she caught the other guys' gazes in turn, "I think maybe we'll take the kids with us this summer. I'm feeling better, and Charles and Dee have done their part, although, knowing Dee, she will be along anyway. And," she added unnecessarily, "I can't see Josh doing much, if anything, with the kids this summer."

Steve couldn't resist one last dig. In a stony monotone voice he jumped in with, "Sure he will. If he survives the summer."

The shock of that statement floored Jessie.

Pausing, she struggled for words with the power to appropriately mitigate the vicious comment. "Fuck you, Steve, and your goddamn guilt trip. You agreed I needed a break from the constant agony of trying to bring him back to me. So why are you on his side all of a sudden?" was what finally escaped the pretty lips. She didn't wait for an answer. "Grab your jacket, Jacob. Let's go find the others."

With his next words, Steve halted her in her tracks. He jumped off the stool to deliver them, harshly and without remorse. "I didn't think you'd abandon him altogether, Jessie. You know what's up. I know you, and I know Josh! You don't have any trouble loving him, I know how deep your feelings for him go. I was there, remember? When you met? I was his friend through that hell, and I was there when you fucked off around the world and ended up in Scotland. I held him together then, too. And I seem to recall holding you together at one time as well, although maybe it didn't rank high enough in your scale of lovers to count!"

Turning slowly, she faced him, eyes flashing and fists knuckled at her sides. "Is that what this is about? Is it even about Josh at all, Steve? I chose Jacob, so you're pissed?"

"Get over yourself, Princess! Jesus! No! Jessie, I do agree you need the break. I do. And he needed to pull away from Nadia when he was ready. I knew he would, once things settled after you were rescued. But he's not going to get through this without you. That's what I'm fucking trying to tell you! Josh is my best friend, and he's been through hell."

Steve fought to find the words to make Jessie see. Pointing a trembling finger at her, he continued. "You knew where he was, when you were locked up. But Josh didn't know where you were. His whole fucking family—gone in an instant." Making a *whooshing* sound, Steve snapped his fingers to accentuate his point. "By the time you came back, he was so far gone in terms of losing hope nobody could reach him. Nobody could even fucking talk to him! But now…now it's like the numbness is starting to wear off, you know? It's like he sees you again, and what he's lost is no longer a mirage, like it seemed it was over those first few weeks. It's like he's got to make this transition back into reality or something, I don't even fucking know. But I beg you, Jessie…" Steve looked hard at Jacob, true sorrow in his eyes. "I'm sorry, Jacob. But I beg both of you—don't do this. Don't hurt Josh this way."

Jessie was staring at him, immobile, trying to digest what Steve was telling her.

He had one last thing to say. "Jessie, do you want me to beg? Don't cut him loose, not completely. At least stay in touch, just to give Josh a reason to fight. To care. Taking something up with Jacob is going to destroy him. He didn't give a shit about Nadia. She was a drug. But he knows how you feel about this guy. He knows he could lose you forever."

She held up two quaking fingers. "First of all, Josh has two reasons to fight. Their names are Emily-Grace and David. Second of all, my capacity for hurting is done." She started out, and then pivoted back around one last time, one damp hand on the doorknob. "It's been a helluva downward spiral, Steve. I need to feel happy again. I need to feel pleasure instead of pain. I can't hold him up any longer. You know why? Because as far as how I feel about Josh is concerned? It's too fucking far to fall. And I'm already more than halfway down that goddamned ladder. Why the hell would I crawl back up it, knowing there's a good chance he'll pull it out from under me again?"

"So you just go ahead and choose a shorter ladder instead, huh Jess?" After delivering the cruel comment, Steve didn't have the guts to even consider looking at Jacob.

Behind him, Steve heard Charlie moan, "Leave the kid alone, Steve," while Matt shuffled his feet and sighed heavily.

Jessie's answer was brief and to the point. She inhaled deeply before speaking. "Steve, I love you. You are one of my best friends. I said this already, but apparently you need to hear it again. Fuck. You."

As she moved through the doorway, Jessie raised a palm to Morgan, who rose to follow them. "We're good," she said without looking at him. "Thanks anyway."

Swallowing past the sticks in his throat, Jacob let his gaze linger on Steve. When Steve finally—and rather shamefully—met the hurt eyes, Jacob said his own piece. "One day, Steve. Could you have just given me one god-damned day?"

After he swept through the door, it started to close behind him, telegraphing his thoughts as far as some kind of friendship with Steve was concerned.

Steve glanced at Matt, who shook his head. "Give her some space," he said, as the door slammed shut.

With a judgmental glance tossed in Steve's direction, Charlie raised his coffee in a half-assed toast and said, "Nice."

Groaning, Steve landed back on the stool and rotated a bit to face the deprecating stares of both Charlie and Matt. "She should not have jumped in bed with Jacob so fast. Granted, she needs space from Josh right now, I agree with that, but Jesus, she's throwing dirt on his fucking grave!"

Matt and Charlie shuddered before muttering in agreement. They sucked on their coffees and sat in stony silence until Matt pushed himself away from the counter and grabbed his leather jacket. "I'm off to get some fresh air," he announced.

"Can't leave her alone, can you Matt?" Still shaking after the heated argument, Steve slid off his stool and followed, as did Charlie.

"No, Steve, I can't," was Matt's calculated response. "Jessie might be headstrong, and she might be foolhardy with her own security, but I'm not. Over the years I learned to give her space when she needs it, but only to a point. Let's walk." He nodded at Morgan as they left. "Enjoy the peace and quiet. When the gang gets back, it'll be a madhouse in here."

Morgan acknowledged him with a casual wave. "All right, sir," he responded, settling back into the couch to watch wrestling on TV. He was relaxed and calm now that his plan was beginning to take shape. Matt had just announced to all of them that he often 'gave Jessie space' when she needed it.

Space, to Morgan, was an open window.

And that, to him, was the first seed in his plan to win back his wife.

Chapter Thirty-three

Jessie hardly spoke to Jacob for the rest of the day. She wasn't being mean, but Steve's honest words had rocked the tenuous foundation upon which she giddily thought she and Jacob had the opportunity to build. Back at the condo after their walk, she stayed close to his side, but their hard won light seemed to be dimming.

Steve felt like shit, so he tried to pour balm over at least some of the wounds he opened, for both Jessie and Jacob, but neither was receptive. Add to that the memory of Josh's agony through all those months Jessie was gone, and then last night as he drowned his sorrow in booze…well, the hard memories were just too fresh to instantly wipe away, anyway.

Late on Sunday, Jacob wasn't sure what was expected of him. Partway through the day, he messaged Rachael in a half-hearted attempt at an apology, and he considered going back to their hotel room, but wasn't sure whether she was still there or had bailed and flown back to Vancouver, so he stayed put. At any rate, he wanted to be around Jessie to see how things panned out. He *needed* to be around Jessie.

Rachael did not message him back.

That night, they took the kids back to Charles and Dee's hotel room for consistency's sake, bathed them and read to them, and tucked them in for the night before walking back to Maggie's place. Maggie was still with her boyfriend, so Jacob and Jessie found themselves alone after Matt walked the couple home, telling Jessie he was releasing Morgan for what he thought was a well-deserved month long holiday.

"I'll leave you two alone for the night, but lock the door and call me," Matt insisted before he left them, a warning light flashing in his eyes, "if anything out of the ordinary raises a single red flag."

Jessie had pocketed her hands for the twelve-block walk. Now, though, she shot a look of gratitude in Matt's direction, and watched the door close behind him. Finally, she let her gaze rest on Jacob again.

He waited, sick to his stomach at what she might have to say to him. He did not want to hear that their fairy-tale night was a singular fantasy.

Her silence was unnerving. In the end, Jacob broke it. "Do you want me to go?" Wiping sweaty hands on his black jeans, he swallowed, eyeing her from an uncertain hips-width stance. "I'll go if you want me to."

They were standing just inside the door, like last night. But both knew the illusory magic from before was no longer at play. Steve's dose of reality had quite magnificently extinguished that.

She shook her head, slowly at first, as if she wasn't sure, and then hurriedly, more definitively. "No," Jessie answered, determined. "No, I don't want you to go." She blinked uncertainly before continuing. "But Jacob... Steve's right on some level. I don't really know or understand any of this... all I know is how I feel. And if you want the truth, when I think about Josh, it hurts so much that I just push him away...I bury him. I'm sorry...he's my husband. I love him."

Her voice thickened as she tried to explain where she stood, so Jacob would know where *he* stood. "And he's hurting so bad right now. But I know...I know I can't help him. I can't. Not now, or...not yet. Steve seems to think maybe I can now, since Josh left Nadia, but...I've got nothing left in my own arsenal right now, you know? Nothing. It's black and empty. So when I think about you, I see light, pulling me out of the blackness. I see this little light that makes me want to move towards it. That makes me feel safe. But I know I'm hiding in you again." She knuckled a tear, and then swiped at the one that trickled down her cheek after it. "And I know how unfair that is to you. Don't even get me started on how shitty I feel about Rachael right now."

"I'm a big boy, Jess. I've always known where I stood with you. Last night I said to myself, if this is all I get, then that's fucking sweet. One night. A whole day to enjoy it, maybe. To enjoy her, to be hers again. But I didn't get a whole day. Steve sucked it up some old fucking vacuum! And you know what? Today

I know that what I got wasn't enough. It wasn't enough, and whatever time I get with you is not ever going to be enough. But I'm a sucker for punishment, apparently, because I want more anyway. A day, a week, a year, maybe, if you'll at least let me try with you. Right now all that's the future and so it's all in front of me, you see? Tonight, tomorrow…I have those to look forward to. If you'll let me have them. Then if it all goes to hell, it goes to hell. I might be the short ladder in this whole fucked up scenario. But that's good enough for me."

"It shouldn't be, Jacob. Rachael is head over heels in love with you."

Touching his chest, Jacob's voice broke. "But I am head over heels in love with you. And I want you, Jessie. I've wanted you from that first night in Edinburgh when you hooked up with JP. God, all those nights we snuggled up and watched classic movies in Miami…sometimes I felt you moving against me, just a little, and I thought 'she wants me too, a small part of her still wants me too.' Then last night…" He exhaled slowly. "I want more of that. Of you. I want as much as you can give. I accept that it won't be everything. I can live with that."

He had to angle his head closer to hear her next whispered words.

"Why would you want to, Jacob? Why?"

Adjusting his feet to face her more securely, Jacob shoved both hands in the back pockets of his jeans. "Because I need you in my life, Jessie. For music, for friendship, for the kids…I need you. And it's so intense now, you know, after last night?" He shook his head slowly. "I can't go back to the way things were. Not anymore. Fake loving you on *Mystic Nights*, touching you, snuggling up with you and not being able to…" He swallowed. "I need more."

Touching her chest, Jessie gave up the battle with her tears. They just kept coming, soaking her from the outside in. "There will always be Josh," she whispered. "In my heart. Despite how empty I feel right now, I will never fully give up on him. Ever."

Sickened, Jacob's knees almost gave way as her truths cornered him. "You're thinking of going back to him. Eventually."

Calming, she searched his eyes before answering. "Jacob…what if Steve's right? What if we just need some time? For both of us to heal, to get stronger? What if…what if Josh can't make it without me?"

"No, Jessie. Please. Don't consider this. Not yet."

"Don't beg, Jacob. Don't make this harder than it already is."

"You can't tell me I'm light and then…and then move back towards the darkness!"

"But…what if I'm *his* light, Jacob? What if I'm his light? Even if he and I don't get back together…what if me hooking up with you extinguishes that light?"

"He'll go back to Nadia. That's what. He won't be alone."

"She's darkness, Jacob. There's no light there. And I don't appreciate you playing dirty, by the way!"

"I'll lose you. Forever."

She pointed a finger at his nose. "You said one night was better than none."

"And then I said it wasn't enough. Having last night in my memory bank is already killing me. I need more."

"Tonight, then."

Jessie watched him process that. He blinked, and his hands came out of the back pockets. Jacob looked away, as if he was consulting some invisible soul to tell him what to do. In the end, he took what was handed to him.

"Okay, Jessie," he said, raising his chin defiantly. "And after?"

"After…I don't know, Jacob. I don't know what's going to happen. But what I do know is I don't want to live my life without you in it. Emily-Grace, too…she needs you. My daughter loves you more than she loves her own father."

"I can't do it, Jessie. I don't want just a friendship anymore. I want as much of you as you can give. With us as a couple, I mean."

Her voice was soft, scarred. "I'm scared, Jacob. For Josh."

"You're *hiding* behind Josh. He may never be any good, Jessie. He's going down a dark path."

"No." A stubborn streak darkened Jessie's baby blues. Refusing to believe that the aforementioned path was terminal, she glared.

Jacob ignored her rising ire. "Take a chance. On me." Placing a hand over his heart, he begged.

"Or what, Jacob? What will happen to us if I don't?"

Sucking in a breath, Jacob emitted a small *pfffft* sound before answering. Lowering his hand from his heart, he shook his head. "I shared you with a ghost before. I get the history, I know what I'm up against if you choose to try with me. I told you, I can live with that. What I can't live with is just being your friend again, Jessie. I can't."

Pausing, Jessie's voice cracked on her final, necessary words. "Then I guess you'll be cutting us loose once and for all. Me and the kids."

He couldn't speak, then. His hurt eyes said it all.

Then Jacob did what he did best. He moved forward and grabbed Jessie by the hand, and led her roughly down the hall, so quickly she almost had to jog to keep up. He slammed the door of the bedroom, and spun around to face her.

Brusquely brushing loose hair away from her face, he stared almost angrily into her eyes. Then he shoved her leather jacket off her shoulders, grabbed the bottom hem of her cotton top and yanked it up over her head, taking her bra with it, and dropped to his knees, unbuttoning her jeans and yanking them down at the same time. He pressed against her, ignoring her gasps as he pushed on her with the butt of his palm, and then he made an annoyed *arrhhh* sound and used both hands to pull her panties down to her ankles.

He forced her on her back on the carpeted floor, pulled off his own jacket and T-shirt, unbuttoned his fly, and shoved his jeans down to his hips. When he drove himself into her, his shoulders were shaking with anger and impending loss, but he finished strong and savored the release, even as she gasped and grabbed his fingers to help bring her to climax.

Straddled over Jessie, knees on either side, Jacob leaned on one hand and used the other to make her come, watching her with a desperation that was killing him as she wriggled and cried out underneath him; as she tensed her abs and arched her back and cried out his name.

As she reached orgasm, Jessie clutched at Jacob's hair with one hand, and shoved her other hand over his to keep him from moving it away from her body. Only when she started to come down from the surreal pleasure, twitching and still moaning, did she notice that his cheeks were moist.

He was still somewhat hard, so he eased back into her, which gave Jessie a few more lovely waves of sheer bliss as Jacob moved over her body. But soon there was nothing left, so he switched from his hands to his elbows, grasped her to him, and held tight, begging her to give him more time.

Jessie held him and soothed him as her own tears fell. She rubbed one hand over the small of his back, cherishing the feel of him in her arms.

"It's not fair," she murmured as she wept. "None of this is fair."

Jacob laid beside her then, on the floor, a leg and an arm wrapped around Jessie, until his breathing evened out and he fell mercifully asleep. After a while, after she memorized him the way she always memorized her husband when they made love, Jessie slipped out from under him and padded into the washroom. When she came back to the bedroom, her lover had moved on to the bed, still in his jeans with the fly undone. He was lying on his belly, arms wrapped around a soft pillow.

"Babe," Jessie murmured, sitting on the edge of the bed and touching his back. He turned, slightly, and she motioned for him to raise his hips so she could pull off the jeans and boxers. Then she tucked the covers up over him, and slipped, naked, in beside him.

Drawing Jessie to him, Jacob held her, but it was she who offered comfort this night.

When morning came, filling the room with a harsh, rainy grey half-light, they showered and dressed in silence before Matt was scheduled to pick up Jessie in the Lincoln. Later, when it was time to go, Jacob stood at the entrance to Maggie's building as Matt tossed Jessie's things in the back of the vehicle. As Matt pulled out from the curb and merged into traffic, Jessie watched her lover slip away.

Jessie did not wave goodbye, but she leaned her nose against the window. Like a small child, she watched Jacob until he disappeared from sight.

Chapter Thirty-four

When Jessie landed in Vancouver with the others, she checked her cell phone messages. There was one from Kayla. No message was typed in a little blue box for her to read. Instead, there was just a photograph—Josh with the two adorable children snuggled up in his arms, little David on his lap and Emily-Grace hugging his side. A picture book was open in front of David. Jessie recognized the couch as in Charles and Dee's media room.

She stared at the photograph for a long time. A certain peace was detectable in her husband's eyes. The children were in their pajamas, sleepy-eyed and sweet, totally trusting their much-absent father to carry them away, by virtue of a story about baby animals, apparently, to a fantasy world where no hurts and accompanying sadnesses prevailed.

Exhaling slowly, after exiting the jet, Jessie settled into the front seat of Matt's rented Audi. The kids travelled in the back, while Charles, Dee, Dan and Carlotta all climbed into Ulysses' SUV. They went to La Casa where, within the hour, Charles, Dee, and Jessie sat down with a lawyer to iron out details for the big meeting.

While she was in Vancouver, Jessie also kept her birthday play date with Charlie and Jane. They pigged out on birthday cake, and teased and played with the kids, although Jessie found it hard to stay focused on anything except what the next day might bring.

There was no sleep that night. No messages from Jacob, Steve or any of her other friends, no well wishes, nothing. Nobody was taking sides. And Jacob was just plain hurt, period.

Still, Jessie fared better than Josh, who got drunk at home alone and passed out in the children's playroom. A loud buzz from his cell phone jarred him awake an hour before the meeting. It was a text from Steve.

Picking u up in ten u better b ready

Shaving wasn't an option. Food less of an option. Clean clothes? Good enough for the meeting. Josh threw his green vintage jacket on over a pair of denims and a wrinkled white button down shirt. At the last second he grabbed a tie, which he half-heartedly arranged while Steve cruised down Granville Street in the silver Audi TT.

They didn't speak until Steve pulled up in front of the Robson Street Law Office of Mahoney, Gillis and Wyvill.

"Do this up right, Josh. Stand your ground. And don't fucking ask for a goddamn divorce. It's a trial separation, that's all. A temporary thing."

Instead of answering, Josh paused with one shaking hand on the car door. Then he heaved himself out of the low vehicle and strode away.

Steve's voice followed him. "Text me when you're done."

Inside, flanked by his lawyer, Josh was ushered into a glassed-in conference room. Charles, Dee, Jessie and their lawyer were already present. Josh avoided every pair of curious eyes in the space, but he could feel them on him. He was unshaven, leaching alcohol from his pores, and trembling. But he got through the meeting.

Gripping the conference table firmly with both hands in order to avoid driving the nails of one set of fingers deeply into the back of her other hand, Jessie couldn't take her eyes off him. It felt like every moment of every day was consumed by thoughts of this man—of who he was when they met, of who he became with *Drifters* and continued success, and who he was now as his losses consumed him. The sad chocolate eyes were drifting, lifeless, lost. Once again Emily-Grace's little voice jumped into Jessie's consciousness—*I lost. I hurt.*

It was enough to make Jessie force her gaze away from Josh. Otherwise, she wasn't sure she could keep herself from shoving back the heavy chair, getting up, circling the table, and climbing into his lap for a long-ached-for snuggle. Rotating her head away from the despair he rocketed towards her on some invisible air current, she lifted one hand and pinched her bottom lip, hard, so hard it almost bled—anything to divert her pain to something physical, to keep from launching herself into her husband's arms.

271

At one point the question of divorce was raised by, who else? Charles. He said, "And if Jessie decides to sue for divorce? How soon can we make that happen?"

Josh looked up then, and stared at the man, rather blankly, as the shock of the statement grabbed him by the balls. Holding his breath, he finally turned his head to meet Jessie's equally shocked eyes.

His lawyer stepped up to the plate. "To my knowledge that is not on the table at this time."

Her lawyer asked outright, "Should we be moving towards a divorce?"

At the same time, Josh and Jessie, stunned, both exclaimed, "No."

Relief washed over each like a cool rainwater mist in the dense heated jungles of the equator. Josh allowed himself time to settle his gaze on his wife, then. That simple *no* from her was unexpected. Might she want to sort things out? But…he needed to try to find a way back to himself. And… Jacob…the sight of the two of them together at the fundraiser…the tender kisses, the loving looks…

In the end, the shared custody arrangements were easy, and all parties thought they were fair. The only condition that made Josh squirm was the essential component that he check into rehab as soon as possible. He knew he had to remain sober and hangover free when around his children, that was a given. For her part, Jessie was relieved that Josh was open to her taking the kids if she had engagements across North America and around the world. His lawyer asked for substantial notice, that was all.

When the others vacated the small room, Jessie gathered her wits—and her hope—and tentatively approached Josh.

"Thanks," she said, fighting the overpowering awareness that he was still the lost man who accosted her at Saturday night's fundraiser, "for letting me take them when I have to travel."

He shrugged. "It's okay. Fair enough. I get to bring them to work too, at least for weekends or whatever…" He drifted off. Josh had no work lined up, although Hilary was negotiating a new film that would hopefully start in the fall, if he could get his shit together.

"I was thinking this might be a good time to take you up on that talk you asked for, Josh," Jessie tried, hopeful, wondering. "Can I come over?"

Regarding her carefully, he answered tentatively, "I guess."

She shifted her feet. "You don't seem all that keen."

"I don't know what's left to say, Jessie. I'm sorry about Saturday. About how stupid I was. About how it ended."

"You just caught me off guard, that's all. I should have talked to you."

He shook his head. "It went down the way it was meant to go down."

A sick feeling crashed over her. Jessie shuffled her feet again and searched his eyes. "What do you mean?"

He studied her. "Jacob." The almost mute single word was forced through bloodless lips.

"It was just a few nights. That's all."

"He's better, Jessie. For you, for the kids."

"No." She was adamant.

"You've got music, with him. He will never be the guy who has to go dry up in rehab."

"I want you." Fisting her hands, she poised for a fight. "I want my husband back. Maybe not now, but someday. After we've had some time to…to heal…"

"No," he said, bloodshot eyes tearing, backing away. "You don't. Trust me."

"You wanted me on Saturday. You came to New York for me! What, you're back with Nadia already?"

Stopping six feet away, Josh considered what to say. In the end, he wheeled cowardly towards the door and spoke with his back to her. It seemed an easy out. "Yeah. Yeah, I guess I am. Or I will be."

"What?! Why, Josh? Why? I know you want your family back. I know you."

Slowly, he licked his dry lips before turning back around and facing her, shoulders sagging. "What I want is for you to get on with your life, Jessie. I want you to be in that perfect little place where you and Jacob go when you play music together. I want you to be happy."

"I was happy with you. Every fucking goddamned second, Josh. Even when you left the stupid toilet seat up and I sat on cold porcelain at three a.m.!" She took a few tentative steps towards him. "For better or for worse, remember? We'll start with me living in my condo, we'll do this custody thing to keep Charles happy, you'll go to rehab, and we'll start spending time together again. One building block at a time. I know you want this. I know you."

He pounded in another nail. "I'm going back to Nadia, Jessie. I'm sorry."

"You fucking bastard. How can you look me straight in the eye and lie to me? I *know* you."

"You think I'm lying?"

"Yeah. I fucking do."

"Why?" He threw up his hands, exasperated. "Why would I lie?"

"Because, Josh. Because you love me, that's why. And I love you back, although at times like this you piss me off so damn much I kind of wonder why!" Jessie was shaking, a new terror streaking across her stunned face.

He cornered right, taking a new tack, but the words didn't come out the way Josh wanted them to, strong and demanding. Instead, they emerged sodden and damp in accompaniment to the wet trails on his cheeks and his trembling legs. "Leave me alone, Jessie. Just leave me the fuck alone."

"Never," she whispered, sending an eternal love over shock waves of fear. "Never, Josh. I'm only doing all this shit," she waved at the ritzy room they were standing in, "for Charles. To get him off our backs. I want my husband back. I want our family back. One day at a time if that's what it takes, from a distance if need be until both of us are strong enough to deal. I will never give up on you. Ever."

Something flickered across his eyes then. Jessie thought she may have gotten through to him, but she wasn't sure. It was impossible to tell, because Josh buried it the second it appeared as a red flush on his cheeks, and deep within his sorrowful eyes.

Holding her gaze, he watched her tremble. He knew she would crash; a major meltdown was in the works, because Josh could see that Jessie wanted something he couldn't give her—hope. For him, for them. For their children. He couldn't, not after seeing her with Jacob. Not after the realization he could never be that calm, composed man.

Still, for a moment, Josh almost caved. It was the pale eyes that almost did him in. It was the trembling girl he loved, quaking in front of him, holding out a hand now, which floated alone, adrift, desperate for his touch.

He forced himself to turn away.

"Josh! Please. Don't do this."

He stopped. Over his shoulder he said to her, to help her understand, "You know how you were always worried about fading into nothing like your mother did? If something really bad happened to you? Like, I dunno, if maybe your whole fucking family disappeared on one really bad fucking day?"

Rotating back around, Josh met his wife's eye, but his were dark again now, devoid of light. He pointed to his chest. "That's what happened to me, Jessie. I disappeared. I went somewhere safe. It feels good there, with someone I could care less if I lose, drowning myself in beer. I see why your mother stays in her secret place. Because it doesn't hurt there. It can't. Because she can't feel anything."

"She's hiding. She's a coward." Jessie spit the words at him. "And if that's what you're doing, then you're a fucking coward too! What we had was perfect, Josh! Perfect! Why would you give that up? Why would anyone give up what we had?"

Hesitating, he ached to go to her, but in his heart Josh felt he was doing the right thing. He would be no good to Jessie now. Jacob would take care of her. She was better off with her musical soul mate. Was Josh going back to Nadia? No way. Never. Did Jessie need to know that? Nah. Cut and run. Slice deep. End the bleeding once and for all.

He wasn't answering. Jessie had one last bullet in the ammo bag. "You said no. When the lawyer asked if we wanted a divorce, you said no."

His lips parted, unsure. "Let's just destroy one building block at a time," he whispered, illustrating the point with a swoosh of his hand, slicing it through the air from the top down.

Watching Jessie struggle to accept what he was throwing at her, Josh couldn't stand it. Not only was it killing him to let her go—to Jacob of all people, their grey shadow for the last few years—but also it appeared to be killing her. Jessie was crumbling. The shoulders were shaking, the fists clenched, the eyes generously afloat. Her expression was one of great regret and building anger, and she was starting to gasp for breath.

"I love you," she managed between clenched teeth, eyes firing daggers at him. "You fucking asshole."

He almost lost it then, but somehow Josh hung on, at least in part. He started to swing around again so he could leave, but one hand came up to his mouth and he scrunched the bottom lip with a thumb and forefinger before going to her and roughly pulling her close. He breathed her in—the lavender hair, the ivory soap, the agony of the memories as they all came rushing back, the good as well as the bad.

Jessie was saying something as she held on to him—but she was sobbing, hard. Josh could barely make it out.

"Don't you walk away from me. Don't you fucking walk away from me!"

She grasped him tightly, feeling the familiar body against hers, breathing in his musky Josh scent along with a good dose of stale beer. Gasping, Jessie brought a hand up to her husband's neck and pulled him closer, burying her face under his layered hair, brushing her lips against him, inhaling quickly and deeply in a desperate need to stay there, in a place that felt like home.

At first, Josh stilled, and let her essence fuel him for the difficult journey ahead. But he was a man filled with self-loathing, who thought another man was better in his place. A few great gulps escaped from between his lips as well, and he knew he needed to get the hell away from Jessie before he collapsed altogether, so he reached behind his back and grasped one wrist, and reached up to his neck for the other, and he pulled them away from his body.

Screaming now, Jessie started flailing. She punched and kicked Josh, again and again, engulfed with frustration at his refusal to admit to loving her back, at his refusal to want to try, even just a little at a time, to find his way back to her.

Although he could barely see through his own tears, Josh held her aloft until Matt and Ulysses, who were out in the adjoining hallway with Charles and Dee, came rushing in to grab Jessie. Ulysses threw his arms around her waist; Matt grabbed the swinging wrists.

Josh backed away.

When she felt him slip from her grasp, Jessie, choking on the wild emotions, opened her eyes and stopped kicking and thrashing. She forced herself to meet his gaze, which was aching and consumed by loss—by loss in the unforgiving past, by loss in the unbearable now, and by loss in the unrelenting days to come.

But there was nothing left to say. The wounds were real, and they were deep.

He broke the connection and swung around on one foot, grabbed the door handle, yanked it open, and walked away.

Inside the conference room, Jessie collapsed in Ulysses' arms, sobbing in anger and sinking to her knees. Matt bent before her as Charles and Dee quickly approached behind him. He placed his finger under her chin and spoke harshly, which did the trick and got her to focus on him.

"Jessie, you have two choices here, and in life. You lie here on the floor of this ridiculously expensive firm and crumple into a puddle, or you pick yourself up and go home to your babies, who need their mother. There's not a damn thing you can do about Josh. He's in such a bad place right now he's not capable of tying his own shoes."

She worked to control her breathing before responding to him. "I know him, Matt. I know he still loves me."

"Of course he does, Jessie. Of course he does. But that doesn't mean he's *capable* of loving you. Not the way you deserve. Not right now. And you know yourself you have nothing left to give him, either. Not right now."

"He's broken." The admission drew a new wave of sobs and tears, but Jessie sucked them back and hiccupped instead.

"Yes."

"Matt?"

"Yes, Jessie?"

"I want to go home."

Between Matt and Ulysses, with Charles somberly watching and Dee struggling to maintain her own composure in the face of Jessie's meltdown, which happened in front of a large busy office, Jessie managed to get to the elevator, sink against the back wall, and eventually climb into the SUV. Matt followed behind in his rented sedan.

On Robson, Jessie spotted Steve's street-parked Audi TT and glanced wildly around for Josh. He wasn't there, but Steve was. He was leaning with his back against the driver's door, one hand in a trouser pocket, lazily sucking on a Starbucks.

"Stop!" Jessie begged as they neared the small sports car. Startled, Ulysses slammed on the brake so that everyone pitched forward. Jessie jumped out and faced her good friend.

"I tried," she cried angrily to him, as he uncrossed his ankles and straightened. "I fucking tried, Steve. I don't know what the hell kinda miracle you were hoping for, but he wants nothing to do with me. At least he says he doesn't, and what choice do I have but to believe him, huh? So you know something? He's all yours now. He's all fucking yours. So if he takes those percs and mixes them with cocaine, and takes that bath Charlie was talking about, I hope he fucking drowns. At least then his pain will end. And mine too. Because I can't fucking stand it. I can't stand it. Good luck."

Pivoting back around, she climbed into the SUV, to the shock of everyone in the vehicle, to Steve, and to anyone in cars or on the street who happened to notice the remainder of Jessie's breakdown that day.

At La Casa, she packed up her two children since custody was now officially hers for the remainder of that week and all of the next and, without speaking to anyone except for giving orders—such as 'fuel the jet,'—Jessie left Vancouver.

She left her familiar, cozy Vancouver world behind—Charles and Dee, Carlotta, Steve, Josh and Charlie—although on the way out of La Casa, she managed to hug Deirdre to assure her she would be fine.

"Call me and we'll sort out my schedule for the summer," she said, a stoic angry strength in her pale eyes. "I'll be in New York. Oh, and Dee," she added as she paused before climbing into the SUV, where the children sat patiently waiting, "keep the lawyer on standby."

"The divorce," Dee said quietly.

Jessie paused, one leg in the vehicle and one still on the driveway. "No," she said. "Never." At Dee's raised eyebrows she added, "I'm buying a place in New York. For myself and the kids. With lots of room for all of you goofballs so you can come visit anytime. Get the paperwork in order so I can stay in the States for a while."

She set her final gaze on Matt. "I suppose you have to get back to Kelly and Michael. And Julie and Katy."

"I have some time," he answered evenly.

Matt extended a hand towards Ulysses. His rental car key dangled loosely from a finger. At the same time, he sent a final olive branch to his old boss, who was also once a good friend. Locking his eyes in Jessie's, he said simply, "That okay with you, Charles?"

Ulysses waited in silence.

Matt took Charles' low grunt as his assent. A moment passed before Ulysses grabbed Matt's key, and handed him the one to the SUV.

Jessie glanced at her children to make sure they were secure before she dropped into the front passenger seat.

Matt moved his bag from the Audi to the larger vehicle. He strolled around the side and climbed behind the wheel beside Jessie. After twisting the key in the ignition, he steered carefully down La Casa's curved driveway, and merged into traffic.

Without a wave or a backwards glance, Jessie sat in angry, voiceless, determined silence, and took her leave of the city she used to call home.

Chapter Thirty-five

Matt stayed with Jessie and the kids for a week, before he had to fly to L.A. to coordinate Kelly and Michael's security at an outdoor festival. Since Morgan was still on holiday, and Big Dan and Ulysses were taking shifts with the Keatings, Susanne flew in from Vancouver to cover for him.

When Matt showed back up in New York, he had Jacob with him.

"I found him backstage writing lovesick ballads," Matt offered by way of explanation. "I thought if I heard one more I'd smash his guitar over his head. It was either that or bring him east." Standing at the door of Jessie's new condo, Matt had one hand on the door handle. "Now, if you don't mind, I'll ask you to lock this door behind me. I'm going to my hotel. I need to call my wife, order some room service, and watch the baseball game. I'll call you tomorrow, Jessie."

It was nine o'clock at night. Jessie had fed and bathed her babies, read them a cute hopeful story about Australian wallabies, and rocked David and held Emily-Grace's hand in bed at the same time while the two children drifted off to sleep. Now, she was in black Lululemon pants, unpacking boxes in the large open concept front room. She had straightened when she saw Jacob straggle in behind Matt. Her heart leapt at the same time tears pricked the corners of her eyes.

"Hey," Jacob said now, softly, waving a hand before nervously thrusting it into his back pocket.

"Hey," Jessie replied, equally softly, a utility knife in her hand, which was poised over a taped-up box that had arrived just that day from Vancouver, courtesy of Deirdre and Carlotta.

Jacob looked around. "New digs. Looks like you're planning to stay for a while."

The place was considerably larger than Maggie's, with high ceilings, decorative moldings, and three gorgeous expansive floor-to-ceiling arched windows on the south side that, now, as the sun was going down, were opening the capacious room up to a warm, rich, golden light.

"Kids sleeping?" Jacob's gaze settled on Jessie.

"Yeah," she answered. Tipping her head and narrowing her eyes at him, she stated curiously, "I thought you weren't interested in being my friend."

Coolly, he countered with, "I thought you were staying in Vancouver. With—" Jacob bit his lip. He couldn't bring himself to say Josh's name.

In response, Jessie shook her head slowly from side to side. "He doesn't want me. Not now, not ever." She forced the terrible truth through downturned lips that startled to tremble with the admission.

"Impossible," Jacob said, letting his eyes drift over Jessie's slim body in the Lululemon pants and in one of her favorite floral backless halters. "How could anyone not want you?"

She swiped the back of the wrist holding the utility knife over her eyes, watching him as she did so.

Jacob leapt forward. "Geez, girl, watch what you're doing with that thing! You'll lose an eye!" He touched her wrist and then slid his hand outwards to grab the knife and remove it from her fingers. Bending over to set it on the box she was about to slice open, Jacob laid it down, then stood tall again. He was close enough now to catch a whiff of the lavender in her hair, and he almost closed his eyes as the best of all possible memories overpowered his senses.

Jessie caught the look. "Jacob…what are you doing here? You and me… it's too fucking complicated."

"Actually," he started slowly. "It's real simple, Jessie."

Swallowing, he reached out a hand and grabbed her wrist again. Pulling her towards him, Jacob slipped his other arm around the familiar waist. "Josh fucked up. He put you back on the market. And," he slipped his other hand up her arm, dropped it around her waist with the first, and pushed gently on her lower back so she could feel him against her, "despite your feelings for him, which I respect, I'm here to repeat the offer I made a few weeks ago."

"I'm still a mess, Jacob. I'm dealing with shit. I'm trying to move on, but it's so hard."

"Matt says it's likely over." Jacob was blunt, but damn it, maybe this girl just needed a push.

She inhaled to a count of six, closing her eyes as she did so. *I could lose him forever...* "The truth is, Jacob..." She opened her eyes. "As far as Josh is concerned...it will never be over."

His eyes flecked dimly before a new light took hold, a strong, steady light that burned beneath the surface of Jacob's intense, passionate baby blues. His voice was husky, the words spoken with awareness and conviction. "Then I guess I was right, Jessie. I'm a glutton for punishment. And why would I want this? You, I mean, like this? It's like I told you before. One night—or ten, or twenty—is worth the risk of losing you forever." Pressing one strong hand up her back, he felt her body quiver and tense.

"I'm not worth it," she whispered, resting her hands on his biceps. "I'm all drama these days."

A wide smile settled across Jacob's lips. "I'm counting on that, baby girl. Never a dull day in the Jessie Wheeler camp."

She started to say *Wheeler-Sawyer,* but caught herself. Jacob took her moan to mean she was responding to his touch across her shoulder blades, now, and not for the pain of loss and separation that haunted her every damn second of every damn day.

He lifted his right palm to her cheek and bent forward to run his tongue across her top and then her bottom lip. "Show me this drama of which you speak, Mizzz Wheeler, before I change my mind and seduce the actress across the hall."

"There's an actress living across the hall?"

"Mm-hmmm. I met her in the lobby. This is New York. There's an actress living in every second condo. And they're all stunning, by the way."

She laughed. "Oh, fuck off."

He was grazing his lips across her neck now. Jessie could feel Jacob's warm breath on her skin, which made her knees melt. Then he was playing at her mouth, probing, wanting, needing. And so, as his breath intermingled with hers, Jessie let her arms rise to encircle him completely, so she could bring him inside her body where he could love and soothe and heal all the broken parts.

～ ～

In Vancouver, Josh sat on the floor of his children's empty playroom, against the wall, knees raised, a beer in one hand and Emily-Grace's old Diana-dowwy in the other. The soft doll had a few singed parts from that long-ago Langley fire; his daughter had long ago discarded her in favor of singer-dowwy, which Jacob had bought her, and which reminded the child of her mother.

Josh sank lower against the wall, arched his neck backwards so his gaze was towards the ceiling, closed his eyes, and swallowed bitterly.

His cell bleeped. He didn't bother looking at it. Josh knew who it was— Nadia. He flipped the phone off, tossed it into a toy box, and sucked hard on the beer, draining it.

Then he lay down on the floor, curled his knees up into his chest, hugged the doll, and almost immediately drifted off into a miserable alcohol-fueled world of distorted dreams.

When he awoke at three a.m., nauseous and shivering, Josh's last dream was uppermost in his mind—he was standing alone at the edge of a golden field, watching as Jessie wandered thigh deep through waves of barley with Emily-Grace behind her, and David in her arms. Just before the dream faded, he waved to Jessie, and she turned towards him but didn't see him. Instead she spotted someone else, who caught up to her, and who scooped up Emily-Grace, who was laughing happily. The man bent forward and kissed Jessie with an intense passion that had her quivering as he wrapped an arm around her shoulders. They moved forward through the field then, as Josh watched, helpless and frantic, desperate to get her attention.

The dream ended with Jacob holding Jessie the way he had at the New York fundraiser, intensely searching her eyes while she melted inside his.

The song *Fields of Gold* was running through Josh's mind when he awoke. Hugging the doll tighter, he turned his face into the floor.

Outside, a harsh early summer rain started to fall, attempting to cleanse the world of its sins.

～ ～

In New York, the golden evening light was richer now, as it glowed resplendently into the elegant arched windows of Jessie's new home. Backlit by its glory, Jessie drew Jacob to her, opening her soul to a man who loved her, who through his music and his gentle touch, had the power to heal. At the same time, she closed it to a man who let her go, whose lingering torment and pain had no healing power, and who was so broken he couldn't see past the next bottle of Granville Island Pale Ale.

In Toronto, Morgan found Nadia in the bar outside which he and she first launched their diabolical plan to break that now broken man in the first place. One look at her glowing skin and curvaceous body, and Morgan was willing to do whatever it took to get his wife back.

Later, at home, just before Nadia knelt before him and unzipped his jeans, she smiled wickedly and said, "I knew you'd see the light, Morgan." At his nervous half-lipped smile, she added in a sensuous whisper, "Game on. Phase Two."

Behind them, as the couple reconnected to celebrate their plan to destroy Jessie Wheeler, a child's bedroom door was half open. Inside, a five-year-old's toys, layered in dust, were scattered over the floor. On the unmade bed were action figures—some of the Teenage Mutant Ninja Turtles collection, to be precise, but only the dregs. The main four dudes were long buried, in a small white coffin in a treed cemetery two miles away.

In New York, Jessie and Josh's children slept peacefully, dreaming of rainbows and unicorns. Emily-Grace had her singer-dowwy secure in the crook of one arm, her bawwet-dowwy snuggled next to it, and David was clinging to a stuffed Dalmatian puppet he called Chippie. A layer of blonde hair fell over his ear as he breathed easily.

Across the hall, after four *fuuucckkss* and seven *Oh Gods*, their mother cradled herself in Jacob's loving arms, rested her fingers in the hollow of his hip, and drifted off to sleep only to dream of a lonely man she left behind. An anguished ghost in a Vancouver storm, his restless haunt left her shaken.

His name was Josh. And he was her husband.

Always and forever, Jessie whispered silently into Jacob's peacefully slumbering form as she trembled. Closing her eyes, she sent Josh a prayer so heartfelt her toes ached.

She closed her eyes, and slept.

⁓ ⁓

Opening his eyes, Josh saw one of Emily-Grace's sunshiny-rainbow pictures from *before* on the playroom wall. Lit only by the dim fading daylight of a rainy grey day, he had to squint to make it out.

At first it hurt to see, but then somehow it calmed Josh.

In crayon on the bottom of the drawing, in Jessie's distinctive handwriting, was a phrase, scrawled in red crayon—*always and forever.*

He inhaled its promise.

Then he closed his eyes again, and slept.

⁓ ⁓

The End.

⁓ ⁓

Hello!

Like what you read? I hope you are enjoying the Drifters series as much as I am enjoying writing it. I am hopelessly in love with Josh, Jessie, Jacob, and the rest of the gang. If you have a moment, please go to Amazon or Goodreads and leave a rating and/or review. Us Indie authors depend on those for our survival in the eBook world.

Thank you!
Happy reading!

Susan

www.susanrodgersauthor.com

Facebook: search **Susan Rodgers, Writer**

Twitter: **@srbluemountain**

www.bublish.com

email: **fatcat@pei.sympatico.ca**

About the Author

Susan Rodgers' first novel *A Certain Kind of Freedom* was a Finalist in the Writers' Federation of Nova Scotia Atlantic Writing Awards for unpublished manuscripts. Her short story from the novel of the same name, published in two anthologies, has received rave reviews, as have the Drifters novels, Susan's all-time favourite books to write.

Owner/Operator of Bluemountain Entertainment, Susan is a 'Diploma With Honours' graduate of Vancouver Film School. She produces mostly documentary style client films and short dramas with plans to one day shoot a Feature Drama based on the novel Atlantic Blue.

Formerly a Museum Curator, in winter Susan lives with her partner Steve and her striped cat Oliver (Lucy Maud Montgomery once said the only good cat is a striped cat) in Summerside, Prince Edward Island, Canada. In summer, she hides in a small trailer in Darnley, P.E.I., where she writes novels, paddles kayaks, and crafts sandcastles on the beach. She makes frequent trips to Vancouver to visit her son Christopher, where she enjoys life in the hippie city while listening to great music and sipping on good espresso.

Books by Susan Rodgers

Drifters series:
A Song For Josh
Promises
No Greater Love
Riptide
Whispers of Home
And Then There Was Silence
Let the Music Cry
If I Could Sing You Home

Other:
A Certain Kind of Freedom
Seasmoke
Atlantic Blue

Feature Screenplays:
The Story of Jack & Emma
Atlantic Blue
Beautiful Jane
They Were Dreamers (adapted)

Short Stories:
S12
A Certain Kind of Freedom
A Gentle Peace

www.ingramcontent.com/pod-product-compliance
Lightning Source LLC
Chambersburg PA
CBHW060604030726
47498CB00005B/1530